Anne Droyd
and Century Lodge

Will Hadcroft

Jessica Kingsley Publishers
London and Philadelphia

Visit the Anne Droyd website: www.annedroyd.com

First published in 2002 by CK Publishing Ltd

This edition first published in 2005
by Jessica Kingsley Publishers
116 Pentonville Road
London N1 9JB, UK
and
400 Market Street, Suite 400
Philadelphia, PA 19106, USA

www.jkp.com

Copyright © Will Hadcroft 2005

Library of Congress Cataloging in Publication Data
A CIP catalog record for this book is available from the Library of Congress

British Library Cataloguing in Publication Data
A CIP catalogue record for this book is available from the British Library

ISBN-13: 978 1 84310 282 3
ISBN-10: 1 84310 282 X

Printed and Bound in Great Britain by
Athenaeum Press, Gateshead, Tyne and Wear

To Grandma,
for always believing I could do it

Acknowledgements

I thank the following for their help and encouragement:

Mum for teaching me to think. Dad for showing me how to dream. Stan, who always said, 'It's only money,' and was generous with his.

My lovely wife Carol for her total belief in me. My family: Jonathan. Matthew and Louise (not forgetting baby Dominic). Our Paul. Marie and Dan. For love and friendship.

Me old mate (and closet Time Lord) Anthony, for tea, *Time Out*, and endurance.

'Big Ken' and William Murray, who were there when the spark ignited. Calum Kerr and Nigel Bent, who nurtured the flame. Stella Morris and *Sweetens of Bolton* for zealous support.

A big thank you to those who publicly said nice things: Karl Cartlidge, Robert Dunlop, James Dunlop, Bob Furnell, Matthew Kopelke, Ian Laurenson, Gareth Preston, Witold Tietze, Stuart Wyss.

Craig Hill, who bid a large sum for a copy of the first edition on Key 103's radio auction in aid of the charity Manchester Kids. His prize, apart from the book itself, was to have the name of his then nine-month-old daughter Jodie written into the sequel. I wrote her into Chapter 1 of this edition instead!

The first of Anne Droyd's young fans who went out of their way to tell me how much they love her: Joanna Bent, Lily-Anne Bury, Abigail Edwards, Ashley Girdles, Sara and Rebecca Hawes, Lewis Jones, Robin and Peter Kenny, James Murray, Sally Naylor, Joe Whitehead, Kerry Shields, Karina, Christopher, and Philip Wolfendale.

Little baskets of flowers to those lovely girls at JKP – Lyndsey, Sophie, Alex and Sandra. A sterling job by one and all. Not forgetting CP Ranger for designing that great cover.

Finally, a big bouquet to my editor and publisher, Jessica, who loved the character of Anne Droyd so much she introduced her to the world.

Contents

On the Run

S witch on.
It is dark. Adjust eye lenses. It is still dark. Switch to infra-red. I can see wood, wood all around. I can feel it. Deduction: I am in a box.

The box is moving. I believe I am on some kind of trailer.

A voice. Elderly. Data banks identify: My father. 'Are you all right, Anne?'

Activate speech circuits. Reply: 'Yes, Father, I am all right.'

'I do not think that our team leader was very impressed with you.'

'Why not, Father?'

'You remind her of someone she wants to destroy.'

'Who is that, Father?'

An alarm bell has started ringing. I can hear footsteps, lots of them. My father is not speaking. I am hearing another voice. It sounds as though it is coming from loudspeakers in the ceiling. Data banks identify: A woman's voice. It is the team leader. 'Alert! Alert! The Professor has not returned to his laboratory with the project. Security cameras show him on level one heading to the lift. He must not reach the surface. I repeat, he must not reach the surface.'

My father: 'Oh no, Anne. They have discovered that we are missing. They are coming after us.'

The leader's voice: 'The Professor has the project with him in a tall wooden box. Get it from him. Do whatever it takes. But do not kill him. I repeat, do not kill him. We still need his knowledge and expertise.'

The alarm bell is still ringing. The running feet are closer. I can hear voices, many voices. 'This way! They're down here!'

I hear electronic doors sliding open. I feel the box bumping against something. 'Father, are you all right?'

'Yes, child. I am just getting you into the lift.'

'You must release me, Father. I am stronger than them. I can protect you.'

'No, Anne. You need to stay hidden for when we get on to the surface. I have transport waiting.'

The running feet are loud now. There are many voices. I can hear guns being readied. The running has stopped. I can hear my father's heart beating fast. He is very frightened. One voice is shouting now. 'Halt! Stay where you are, Professor, or we will shoot.'

I can hear the lift doors closing. The voice is angry. 'Fire, men, fire! Stop the lift!' There is heavy gunfire. I can hear bullets hitting metal, I can hear them. My father has cried out.

'Father, are you all right?'

'Yes, child. I am not hurt. I was just a little scared.'

The floor is shaking faintly. The lift is rising. The voices and feet and alarm bells are far away now. We are going up to the surface.

'Anne.'

'Yes, Father?'

'You must switch off, now. You must deactivate yourself.'

'They will be coming after us. How will we survive?'

'Let me worry about that. You need to save your energy cells. Deactivate. Switch off. I will bring you back online once it is safe.'

'I will switch off now, then. Deactivating in two seconds. Two... One...'

1

School's Out!

Gezz collected up her dolls and put them into her satchel. The bag dangled limply from the back of her hard wooden chair. 'Come on, it's nearly home time,' Mr Davies announced as he picked up a board duster and began wiping the blackboard with large swipes of his arm. Gezz watched as the white blocky writing vanished in zigzag arcs across the cloudy board with patches of black poking through.

'Where's Sindy?' she shouted, a little panicked. 'Who's got Sindy?' Her voice carried across the hustle and bustle of the classroom, only to be left unanswered. The girl's eyes scanned the sea of heads. They were all sorts of colours and shapes and sizes. Some blond, some brown, some ginger, some short, some long, some with ponytails, some without. Gezz didn't like ponytails because boys had a tendency to pull at them. Jane Middleton, a quiet, shy girl with gorgeous long brown hair tied in a single tail, had hers pulled all the time. The lads called her 'Jane the Chain' and pulled her tail whenever they went by. Gezz couldn't understand why the girl didn't change her hairstyle. All she ever did was burst into tears.

Short hair with a hairband, now that was sensible. Not one boy had thought of a single name for her hairband. They just called her 'Gezz', which was short for Geraldine. Mr Davies, having wiped the board clean, turned to face the class. He smiled in that gentle way he always did and urged the reluctant mob, 'Come on, hurry up! Normally you can't wait to get out.'

Gezz smiled back. It was true, they did normally pack their things away very quickly. But today was different. Today was not just the end of term. Today was not just that great last day when you brought in toys instead of doing lessons. Today was the last day of primary school – the last day *ever*. They would have six long weeks of freedom, and then it would be back to school – but not back to this school, no. Not back to 'Christ the King – Church of England School for Juniors', no. It would be a new school, a different school, a school where each lesson was taught by a different teacher and not just the same one for everything like Mr Davies. Crompton Green High School was where most of them would be going.

Gezz shuddered. *I hope it's not going to be like* Grange Hill, she thought. *Horrible kids swarming the corridors and teachers struggling to keep them under control.* Suddenly her trance was broken. The sea of faces blurred as she homed in on one ginger-freckled girl on the opposite side of the classroom. The girl's back met a row of bookcases as she swiftly snatched something long and plastic with tiny clothes and long blond hair from inside her desk into her satchel.

'Emma Bingham!' Gezz screeched across the room. 'Give me back my Sindy doll, right now!' All heads turned as Emma quickly dropped into her chair and rested her chin on the palm of her hand. 'Give it back now!' shouted Gezz, making her way through the maze of tables and chairs. She came to a halt beside the obstinate ginger head.

'Are you talking to me, Gezz?' asked Emma with an air of surprise.

'You know I am,' said Gezz, sternly.

Mr Davies huffed to himself, as if wishing he didn't have to deal with this sort of thing so close to home time. He towered above the two girls, folding his arms and scratching the side of his nose. He broke into another kindly smile and Gezz softened a little. 'Now, what's going on over here?' he said.

Gezz looked up into his friendly brown eyes. 'It's Emma, Sir. She's got my Sindy doll.'

Emma made a show of looking shocked. 'I have not!'

Mr Davies looked down at Emma and sighed. He had had a lot of trouble with this one all year, and even now, on the eve of starting a new school, she was still a handful. 'Come on, Emma, give Geraldine her doll back.'

'But I haven't got her doll,' said Emma.

'All right,' Mr Davies said. 'Turn out your bag.'

Immediately Emma began protesting. 'But, Sir. She's making it up. I haven't got her doll, honest.'

'Turn out your bag.' Mr Davies was clearly not impressed now. He folded his arms even tighter and his face lost its smile. Emma reluctantly complied. She lifted her satchel and began placing objects on her desk. A pencil case, her old exercise books full of writing which the teacher had let her keep, some artwork which had been taken down off the wall earlier in the day (complete with BluTack in the corners) and an empty sandwich box. The girl next to her, Jodie Hill, the prettiest girl in the class, retracted her arms to make room for all of Emma's things.

'That's it,' the ginger head offered.

'Tip the bag up,' said Mr Davies.

'There's nothing else in it,' Emma protested.

Mr Davies did not argue and pulled the bag from her. He reached in through the floppy opening and took out the Sindy doll. 'Here you are, Geraldine,' he said, handing the doll to a relieved Gezz.

'Thank you, Sir,' she said with sudden contentment.

Davies turned to the troublemaker as she started to pack her bag again. 'It's a good job this is the end of term, Emma.' Emma closed up her satchel, folded her arms, and said nothing in reply. The teacher returned to his desk.

As Gezz sat down at hers, she caught sight of Emma through the corner of her eye, glaring. The troublesome girl muttered something, but Gezz didn't catch it. Immediately, the girl sitting next to Emma piped up, 'Aw! You *swore*. I'm going to tell Mr Davies of you.' The girl simultaneously raised her hand and voice. 'Sir, Emma Bingham swore.'

The teacher closed his eyes and pinched the bridge of his nose. 'All right,' he said. After a few seconds he opened them and looked at his watch. Then he raised his head and smiled at the class. 'In just under a minute it will be home time and time for us to say goodbye.'

A fair-haired boy at the front of the class burst into tears, catching everyone by surprise. Mr Davies turned, 'What's the matter, Justin?'

'I don't want to say goodbye, Mr Davies.'

The teacher smiled softly. 'I know you don't, Justin,' he said, and then addressed the class. 'But in a few weeks I'll be teaching a new class and you will be going to the big school. You will all enjoy it and you will be glad you're there.'

Gezz wasn't sure about that last bit. The only thing that comforted her was the fact that Luke, her next-door neighbour and best friend, would be there with her. She liked Luke very much.

Suddenly the bell sounded in the corridor. This was it. The end of her primary school life.

The roar of screeching chairs filled the room as children got to their feet and made for the door. Gezz joined one or two at the front who wanted to say a proper goodbye to Mr Davies. He patted her on the head and winked that wink which always made her feel good inside. It was the last time she would see him do that as well.

After that she walked down the corridor, took one last sneaky look at the hall with its plastic chairs piled up in the corner against the folded dinner tables, and the big box made of long segments which they used in PE, and then joined the crowd at the main door.

The traffic was heavy and made a din, and Gezz could taste petrol fumes in the air. It was hard to see anyone through the mass of boys and girls and mums. Not to mention the odd dad. She patiently pushed her way through until she came to the railings at the edge of the pavement. Her eyes scanned the car park on the other side of the busy road.

The car park sat at the end of a row of shops and terraced houses and had clearly been left over from some past time. Gezz could tell by the way the road leading to its entrance wound round and round the newer houses further back. She wondered momentarily what it might have been part of. Another school perhaps? An old church or chapel? Or part of an old playground with swings and a see-saw and a round-about? She'd heard Grandma talk in a hushed voice about when she was a girl and how different everything was. She always sounded excited and sad at the same time. Excited by the memories, and sad that now that's all they were.

Gezz wished she could go back in time like the man on the old show she'd seen on her Auntie Beryl's cable TV, *Quantum Leap*, and witness the old times for herself. She imagined herself glowing with blue electric light, shimmering and warping as the road in front of her changed. The cars would disappear and be replaced with old-fashioned ones. They would go a lot slower and everything would be quieter because only rich people could afford to drive them so there wouldn't be so many. The car park would become an old Victorian school with a church-type roof and long narrow windows. Children would play simple games like skipping and hopscotch, because games with batteries and computers wouldn't have been invented. And everyone would say please and thank you and kids wouldn't swear. Gezz wanted to live in her Grandma's old world. She wanted to talk like them and be like them, like the kids in the *Famous Five* books. She loved the *Famous Five* books.

'Yoo-hoo! Gezz, darling!' The voice was faint, in the distance. Suddenly the traffic was loud again and Gezz could taste petrol heavy in the air. A nearby mother was ranting at her son, waving a finger in front of his scowling face. The boy glared back in defiance. Gezz knew what word was coming. The mother looked shocked and cracked the boy sharply across the head. Then she grabbed him tightly by the arm and dragged him through the swarming crowd. The voice called again. 'Gezz, love, I'm here!' Gezz looked across the road and saw her mother standing at the railings waving. Their red Nissan car was parked at the far end.

She smiled and joined the large queue gathering around the lollipop man. He stood at the curb in the gap where the railings broke and a zebra crossing stretched black and white across to the other side. The man looked both ways and then plonked his lollipop sign into the road. Cars on either side slowed down immediately, their drivers taking note of the 'Stop! Children' command written on the disc. The whole road became piled with still vehicles, lorries, buses, cars and a lone motor bike. Their drivers tried not to look annoyed and tapped their steering wheels impatiently as the white-coated man stalked out over the black and white stripes and smacked his staff down in the centre.

The assortment of mothers, children and prams heaved forward as the lollipop man waved them over. Gezz couldn't help thinking of Moses in that cartoon film *The Prince of Egypt*, when he put his rod in the sea and the waters parted high up into two massive walls leaving a corridor of dry land for the Prince's people to walk through, escaping from the angry Pharaoh and his army. She stepped out on to the zebra and pretended that the cars were the sea held back by the power of God. She passed Moses and he smiled, his hat strap stretching over his baggy chin.

When she reached the other side, she looked back at her old school. She thought of Mr Davies packing his books up and going to his car. *I wonder what he'll be doing in the six-week holidays*, she thought. *He'll probably be glad of the peace and quiet. Maybe he and Mrs Davies will be going on a proper holiday, to Butlin's or somewhere like that.* In just over a month, Mr Davies would be teaching a whole new class of ten- and eleven-year-olds all over again. It will be their last class at junior school then. It seemed strange to think of it like that. But it was true.

Moses strolled back to the pavement and gave a nod of thanks to the drivers. No sooner had he left the road than the cars and buses and lorries began to move again, like the sea crashing in on the Pharaoh's soldiers. The din gave Gezz a headache. She was glad to reach the car park.

'Well,' said her mum with a smile on her face. 'How was your last day?'

Gezz reflected for a moment. 'It was OK.' They walked together, mother and daughter, through the maze of cars. They were all different shapes and sizes, some old, like their Nissan, some quite new like Gary Innes' car. All new and shiny. Some children's parents didn't have a car at all, of course, and had to walk home or catch a bus. 'We played with our toys all day,' Gezz enthused. 'And we swapped them as well. But Emma Bingham had to spoil it as usual. She took my Sindy doll.'

'I hope you got it back,' said her mum, a little worried.

'Oh yes, I got it back,' Gezz confirmed. 'Justin cried as well.'

'Did he?'

'Yes. He was sad because it's our last day.'

'And how do you feel about it?'

Gezz turned to face her mother, whose hair was long and brown and fell over cardiganned shoulders. At this moment her eyebrows were raised, anticipating the answer to her question. Gezz pondered. 'I was sad for a bit,' she said. 'But now I'm all right.' She grinned, unable to contain her excitement as her mother pulled open the passenger door of their red Nissan. 'It's the six-week holidays!'

Gezz tossed her satchel from off her shoulder and gave it to her mum, who put it in the boot of the car. Then she slipped on to the seat, found the catch underneath, lifted it, and slid her chair forward until her knees stopped just short of the glove compartment. Then, after shutting the door, she reeled her seatbelt round and buckled it into its holster. Her mum slipped into the driving seat and shut her door. In no time, she too was belted up. The car engine burst into life and after a few neat turns was suddenly on the road trudging along with the rest of the traffic.

Gezz took one last look at her school as they drove over the zebra crossing and down into town. She watched the shops and old buildings whizz by. Farnton Common was like that, new mixed with old. Bolton was even better, though, with more of Grandma's time shining through.

A sudden sharp turn brought them to Century Lodge, a long stretch of houses semicircling an old patch of wild grass dominated by a dirty pond. Lone fishermen sat dotted about its banks daydreaming and drinking from flasks of coffee. Sometimes, at weekends, Gezz would stroll through the long grass and go and stand on the raised slopes of the water's edge. It was relaxing just staring into it and watching the ripples spreading across as birds attempted to land on bits of old tyre dotted about in the middle.

Immediately facing the housing estate, on the opposite side, was Century Mill, a large disused factory. Grandma told her it used to be an old cotton mill and just about everyone worked at it in the olden days. The pond had served as a kind of reservoir for the mill, and people in the North of Britain sometimes called these stretches of water 'lodges'. Bolton and Manchester were famous for their mills and factories at that time. But now the factory was dead, with all its windows and doors boarded up, left abandoned, standing in the distance like a ghost haunting the lodge.

The place had been there for over a hundred years, and now this was all that was left. When the council built the new houses they called the estate Century Lodge as a memorial to the old times. Gezz knew from her history lessons that a century is one hundred years, and that was why they called the factory Century Mill and the pond Century Lodge.

Their car pulled into the drive. Gezz quickly noted the open front door and the tricycle left abandoned on the lawn. That meant that her father had got back from picking up Ross from nursery. As her mum yanked the hand brake and switched off the engine, Gezz hurriedly unbuckled her seatbelt, flung open the door and rushed into the house to greet her father.

He was busy uncoupling the harness on baby Ross's buggy. He turned at the sound of her running footsteps, his back still arched. 'Daddy, I'm home!' said Gezz excitedly. She reached out her arms and the man hugged her softly, crouching down to her level.

'How was your last day, love?'

'OK,' she said. 'I'm glad it's the holidays though.'

'You can say that again,' puffed her mum as she followed her in. 'I've heard nothing but how glad she is to be on holiday all the way home.' She held Gezz's satchel in one hand and the car keys in the other.

Her dad reacted to her voice with a smile and walked over to kiss his wife gently on the lips. 'Hello, darling,' he said. 'How was the traffic?'

'Murder as usual,' she replied. 'I'm glad we don't have to do it again for another six weeks.' The couple embraced and smiled at one another. As an afterthought, she added, 'Even if it does mean having to put up with these two.' They laughed, rubbed noses a couple of times, and then released each other.

The sound of another car rumbling close by caught Gezz's attention. She raced to the window and watched the snazzy sports car zooming into next door's driveway. Gezz jumped up and down in excitement. 'Luke's home!' She turned to her mum. 'Can I play out?'

Her mum was walking to the open front door. 'Not yet, love. Not until we've had tea.' She stepped into the garden and picked up the trike.

'Aw, *please?*' Gezz begged.

'No!' came the emphatic reply. 'There'll be plenty of time after tea.' She carried the trike into the hallway and, after giving a quick wave to the new arrivals, shut the front door. Baby Ross interrupted the moment with a few warning moans to let his parents know about his little problem.

'The baby's nappy needs changing,' said Gezz's mum irritably. She held the palm of her hand to her head. 'I've got a thousand and one things to do as usual.'

'Don't worry about that, love,' said Gezz's dad. 'I'll see to it. You get tea started.'

Looking relieved, she said thanks and headed for the kitchen, as he began unsticking Ross's nappy and carefully rolling it back. His face said it all and he screwed up his eyes as the whiff hit his nostrils. 'We've got that charity do at the chapel tomorrow, Ness. Don't forget.'

Gezz's mum had not even heard him above the clatter of plates and pans in the kitchen. 'What was that, John?'

'I said we've got that charity do at the chapel tomorrow. For Barnardo's. So, don't forget.'

'Oh, yes,' came the reply after a couple of minutes. 'I *had* forgotten about it. It's a good job you said.'

Gezz was bored already. The conversation continued as her dad put the finishing touches to Ross's new nappy. She shrugged off her coat and hung it with her satchel on one of the hangers in the hall and then made for the kitchen.

Her mum was busy filling a large pan of vegetables up with water. Empty packets of frozen carrots and green beans lay strewn on the work surface. Gezz coughed nervously, knowing she was pushing it now. 'Mum?' she quizzed in a sickly nice voice. Her mum put the pan down on a gas ring and turned a knob. 'What?' she said absent-mindedly. The sound of gas hissed out of the cooker's ring and she pressed a small button on the front. With a few clicks and an electric spark, the invisible gas had burst into a short blue flame. She slammed a lid on to the pan.

Gezz faltered a little, causing her mother to become impatient. 'What?' she said again. 'What is it?'

'Can I not just go and see Luke until dinner's ready?'

Her mum put a hand on her hip and sighed. Then looking at her watch she nodded. 'Yes. All right. Half an hour.'

'Great,' said Gezz with a grin.

'But I do want you back in half an hour,' her mother insisted. 'No later, because your father can't say grace until you're here.'

Gezz was already skipping through the living room to the front door. 'Thanks, Mum,' she breezed. 'I won't be late, I promise.'

★ ★ ★

Luke had always been Gezz's best friend, for as long as she could remember. He and his family moved into next door when she was about two years old. But unlike her parents, who had to pay rent to the council, Luke's mum and dad had bought their house and had gradually done it up over the years.

Gezz stepped over the little white fence which separated her garden from theirs, skirted round the neatly cut grass border and approached the door to the porch. The porch was a white plastic affair with windows round the top half. Baskets of flowers hung on chains from the sloping roof and more plants lined the window sills. She turned the door handle, opened the plastic door inwards, and stepped up to the proper front door, which was made from varnished wood. She knocked hard and waited.

Within seconds the door had flung open and there was Luke grinning. His navy-blue school uniform fitted him perfectly. Not a crease or a line could be seen. His tie draped from his neck in a perfect line and his fine blond hair hung over dreamy blue eyes.

'Hi, Gezz,' said Luke enthusiastically. 'I knew it was you. Come in.'

She stepped into the hall and heard the unmistakable sound of laser guns and music coming from upstairs. 'It's Dad,' Luke said, opening the living-room door. 'He's got a new computer game. Says he wants to test it before he lets me loose on it.'

Gezz grinned. 'Oh, *right*.' As she entered the living room she found the television playing away to itself as usual. Luke liked to watch all the children's programmes while he ate his tea. And to be truthful, Gezz liked to watch them too. Her parents got rid of their telly a couple of years ago when they started going to chapel. They said it brainwashed kids into accepting swearing and violence as normal. With some of the programmes she could see what they meant, but others seemed harmless enough to her.

She sat down in the chair near the hall door and became absorbed in the latest episode of *Grange Hill*. It fascinated her. Was secondary school really going to be like this? She had mixed feelings about it. Some of it seemed cool and exciting, while other parts of it seemed a bit scary. All those different teachers and all those corridors!

Luke sat silently, picking his plate of salad off the floor and placing it on his knee. He tucked in, stopping only to take a sip of *Vimto* now and then.

Their concentration was broken by the sound of the microwave buzzing into life in the kitchen. A tall woman with long, wavy brown hair and bright lipstick could be seen through a crack in the door stuffing a thin cardboard box into a pedal bin. She was wearing maroon leather pants and a navy-blue sleeveless jacket. A nylon headscarf hung from her neck in a loose bow. The microwave let off a loud ding and then a click could be heard as Luke's mother opened the door and lifted her meal out. She took sharp breaths through her teeth. 'Ow,' she moaned loudly. 'God, it's hot.'

'What's she having?' asked Gezz, her eyes not leaving the TV screen.

'Pizza,' said Luke, equally transfixed. 'She's had hers though. Now she's doing Dad's.'

Luke's mother popped her head round the door. 'Luke, sweetheart, tell your dad his tea's ready.' She smiled at Gezz. 'Hi, Gezz.'

'Hi.'

The boy reluctantly got out of his chair and went into the hall. 'Daaaad!' he screamed, 'Tea's ready!' A muffled voice drifted down the stairs. 'Right.' Luke returned to his chair and tuned back into *Grange Hill*. Without looking at his mother he muttered, 'He said "right".'

Luke's mum, Paula, watched the closing moments of the school soap, going into a trance over the theme music. It was only when the presenter came on at the end that she snapped out of it. In a huff, she strode through the living room to the foot of the stairs. 'Terry! If you don't get down these stairs, I'll cut the plug off that computer!'

Gezz and Luke exchanged glances as Terry began banging about in a temper. Gezz cringed inside as she heard him say 'Jesus' as a swearword. 'It's only pizza,' said Terry's voice as he stomped down stairs. 'Anyone would think it's...' He cut himself off as he caught sight of Gezz. He coughed. 'Oh, hi, Gezz. You OK?'

'Yeah.'

The man straightened his T-shirt and went to the kitchen. Paula just stayed by the door. Terry turned. 'Not eating with me, love?' Luke's mum kept her eyes fixed on the television. 'I've had mine.' After a couple of silent seconds, she reached down to a leather bag leaning by the settee. She opened its flap and pulled out a packet of cigarettes and a lighter. Gezz watched with one eye as Luke's mum placed the cigarette in her mouth and lit it with her lighter. The woman sucked on it and the end burned an orange-red. Then she blew smoke out of her mouth and sat down.

The song to *Neighbours* suddenly blurted from the television, signalling home time for Gezz. 'I'll have to go for my tea now, Luke.'

'OK,' said Luke. 'See you in a bit.'

Gezz stood at the door. 'Fancy going to the den?'

'Yeah, OK.'

'See you.' She turned to Luke's mum. 'See you.'

'Yeah, see you, darling,' she said. Then she turned her head and shouted, 'Terry! Gezz is going!'

Terry's voice rang in from the kitchen. 'Right, see you, Gezz.'

Gezz smiled and went home.

2

Three Get·Together

'For what we are about to receive, may the Lord make us truly thankful.' Gezz's dad stood at the foot of the table with his head bowed and eyes shut. Gezz and her mum sat in the same pose. Baby Ross just watched from his high chair. 'Amen,' said Gezz and her mother together. Her dad sat at the table and began tucking in.

'I was thinking of taking some of my old shirts to the chapel jumble sale,' he was saying.

Gezz's mum scooped some carrots from a bowl in the middle of the table. 'Let me sort them out first,' she said. 'We don't want you selling anything valuable!' She cut a slice from her meat pie and put it in her mouth. Then she turned to the baby, scooped up some of his Heinz goo with a plastic teaspoon and slipped it into his mouth. The tot responded with a serious look as he tasted the mixture and swallowed. 'What about you, Gezz, love? What are you going to take?'

Gezz shrugged her shoulders and munched on her green beans. 'Dunno.'

'What about that red dress,' said her mum. 'You never wear that.'

'I do,' insisted Gezz. 'I wear it all the time. You're not throwing that out. I don't care how poor people are.'

'You're just a hoarder,' mocked her dad as he cut into his meat pie. Gravy trickled down the crack in the pastry as his knife broke into it.

Her mum sat back, pondering on something. 'I wonder if Malcolm's home OK.'

Stopping cutting his pastry, her dad leant forward. Gezz could see he didn't fancy what was coming next. 'Should we encourage him, love?' he said. 'I mean, his parents will never feed him if they know that we will.'

Rising from her chair, her mum said, 'Remember what our Lord said, John, "Do to others as you would have them do to you."'

'I know,' grumbled her dad to himself. Gezz was pleased that her mum invited Malcolm over for tea. It was exciting, and it made her feel good, because Malcolm's mum and dad drank beer a lot and were never home.

Gezz's mum stood at the living-room window and looked up the road to where the houses bent round to the shape of the lodge. And sure enough, there was Malcolm sitting on his doorstep in his school uniform waiting for someone to come home, let him in and give him his tea. She marched to the front door straight away, opened it and shouted up the road. 'Malcolm!!'

The boy looked round, saw who was calling, and needed no further invitation. He ran and he ran, his mass of brown curls bobbing up and down over his cheap wiry glasses. Slightly chubby, he paused for breath at the gate.

'Would you like some tea with us?' asked Gezz's mum politely. The boy, catching his breath, nodded gratefully and went inside.

'Hello, Malcolm,' said Gezz's dad cheerfully as the scruffy schoolboy dumped his bag and coat on the kitchen floor. Her mum reached down instinctively and took them to the hall. 'Hello, Mr Atkinson,' replied Malcolm, still out of breath. He pulled out a chair and plonked his rounded backside down on it.

Gezz got up and took a plate from one of the wall cupboards and placed it before him.

On her return Gezz's mum cut some pieces of meat pie from each of their dinners and put them on Malcolm's plate. 'Help yourself to vegetables, Malcolm,' she said.

Her dad watched as the boy eagerly tucked in. 'Your mother and father not home again?' he queried, but his wife shot him a quick glance which told him not to push it.

'No,' Malcolm said innocently. 'I keep asking them for a key, but they never get me one.'

To change the subject, Gezz's mum said, 'What are you doing after tea, dear?'

'We're going to the den,' Gezz enthused, her food tumbling around her mouth like clothes inside a washing machine.

'Don't speak with your mouth full.'

Gezz swallowed and tried again. 'We're going to our den.'

'Great!' said Malcolm with a grin.

Gezz's dad cut another piece of pie and pushed some carrots and beans on the end of it. 'What, that old air-raid shelter? It's a bit dangerous, isn't it?'

'Don't spoil their fun, John. It's only a den. We used to make them when we were young,' said her mum in a matter-of-fact way.

'Not buried at the rear of someone else's garden, we didn't.'

'Mm, that was great,' interrupted Malcolm, who had just polished off the last of his dinner. 'Cheers, Mrs Atkinson. That was lovely.'

Malcolm's appetite made Gezz speed up. The fact that they were having jelly and custard for afters helped too. That was her favourite.

Her mum took a seat in the living room and picked up a novel and began reading. Gezz had shed her school uniform and was now wearing jeans, trainers, a white T-shirt and a slightly faded blue denim jacket. Malcolm, of course, remained in his grey and black school uniform, with the maroon tie pulled tight in a knot and the top shirt button unfastened. 'We're going out now, Mum,' said Gezz.

'All right, love,' said her mother without looking up from her book. 'I want you in by nine.'

'OK, see you.' And with that they were gone.

* * *

'Is Luke coming out?' said Gezz, as Mrs Davidson opened the door. The woman sucked hard on her cigarette and threw her brown hair back across her shoulders. Then, after taking the cigarette from her mouth, she blew smoke just above Gezz and Malcolm's head. 'Hang on,' she said. 'I'll see.'

She disappeared inside and shouted, 'Luuuke! Gezz is here!'

Straight away there was a thunder of footsteps and the blond-haired boy was skipping down the stairs. Gone was his pristine uniform in favour of a very neat black tracksuit with spotless white trainers and T-shirt. 'Going to the den?' he said casually.

'Yeah,' said Malcolm.

'OK.'

Paula Davidson never returned to the door to say goodbye or tell them what time they should be back. Luke just took the door by its golden knocker and slammed it shut. With that, the three of them set off up the road taking in the early evening sunshine.

3

Coal Mountain

The den was situated alongside an old disused railway embankment. The two high walls of grass met at the bottom and a gravel path levelled out as the children approached a long steel bridge carrying a modern railway line overhead. Wooden fences cordoned off a row of back gardens and the den lay just at the foot of the one that looked least cared for.

Luke stared over the old weather-beaten fence at the mass of brambles and excuse for a shed. His mother wouldn't have been impressed at all, but for the children, the situation was ideal, because it meant no one in the house could see what lay just beyond their land. The boy stood perched on the edge of a dug-out channel and looked about suspiciously. No one but his friends could be seen. He smiled and signalled the OK.

Gezz and Malcolm ran across the gravel to the peak of the dugout. 'Come on,' gestured Luke, already pedalling his feet down the side of the small trench. He crouched down, now totally out of sight from any would-be passer-by on ground level, and leaned on the wild plant life which just failed to conceal the silver corrugated metal poking through the wall of earth. In the centre of the metal there stood a narrow green bramble-covered wooden door. Luke reached inside the neck hole of his T-shirt and pulled out a gold chain necklace threading a Yale front-door key. Then, with his other hand, he ran his fingers down the right side of the door. He stopped, smiling to himself, as the tips of his fingers traced the raised surface of the lock. He slotted the key into the door, turned it, and pushed the wood inwards.

'I said "come on",' Luke repeated, and the others wasted no time in skidding down the trench and through the door. Luke watched as Malcolm struggled to squeeze his bulky frame through the tight opening, his silhouette momentarily blocking out the sunlight. 'Come on, Malc,' hissed Luke impatiently. 'Someone's going to see you.'

'I can't help it,' chided the boy, his school uniform scraping along the hard metal.

Gezz sat on an upturned plastic bucket, her eyes squinting as she adjusted to the darkness. The air was damp and musky. 'You need to go on a diet,' she said.

Malcolm let out a yelp as he yanked himself through the door. 'I don't eat very much, as you know,' he whined. 'I only get what your mum gives me, and at school it's cheapo free dinners.'

Gezz flinched as a shaft of daylight fell across her face. 'Oh,' she gasped. 'Close the door, Malc.'

Before the great lump could move, Luke crouched forward and slammed the wooden door shut. He grinned with satisfaction as he heard the Yale lock give a firm click. He knew that without a copy of the key, no one, even if they found the den, would be able to get in.

After a little fumbling, the den was lit with artificial light. Luke watched as Gezz's hand steadied the long torch dangling from the ceiling. The girl smiled as his eyes caught hers.

Malcolm fell back against the hard corrugated metal. 'It's not my fault I'm poor,' he said.

Luke glanced across, his smile fading. 'What?' he puzzled. 'What are you talking about now?'

'It's not my fault I'm poor.'

Luke scrunched his nose. 'Who said anything about you being poor?'

'You said I was fat.'

Now it was Gezz's turn to frown. 'What's that got to do with anything?'

Malcolm adjusted his glasses. 'When you are poor, you can't afford to eat healthy food.' He pushed his mass of curls back as best he could. 'That's what my mum says anyway.'

'Huh!' Luke scoffed, pressing another upturned bucket against the metal and perching himself on top. 'My mum says the only reason your mum can't afford to feed you is because she's never out of the pub.'

Malcolm froze, apparently not sure how to answer that one. Gezz leaned forward and touched Luke's arm softly. 'Just leave it, eh, Luke?' The boy looked at her for a second, regretting what he had just said, and then turned back to Malcolm smiling. 'I'm sorry, Malc,' he said. 'Your mum's not always in the pub.'

Luke straightened his black tracksuit and sensed Gezz letting out an almost silent sigh of relief. He caught her eye and she grinned, and suddenly he felt warm inside.

Malcolm tried to return the sentiment. 'And your mum doesn't smoke like a chimney.'

'What?'

Gezz stopped grinning.

'I said your mum doesn't smoke like a chimney,' repeated Malcolm chattily. 'Because that's what my mum says about your mum.'

'Does she?' Luke grimaced.

'Yes,' replied Malcolm, excited now. 'She says it's a wonder your mum doesn't die of a terrible disease.'

'Oh, does she?'

'Yes, and that she wears far too much make-up.'

The little shelter suddenly felt unbearably airless. Gezz coughed nervously. 'Er, don't you think we should go out for a walk before it starts going dark? I mean, I have to be home by nine.'

Luke paused, still looking at Malcolm. He could see that his friend was as eager to get out of this conversation as much as he was. They turned to face the girl. 'Yes,' they both answered hurriedly, and before they knew it, all three of them were clambering for the door.

'Shush!' whispered Gezz, her finger pressed hard against her lips. 'We wouldn't want anyone to hear us, would we?'

Luke pulled at the door and the children turned their faces as daylight flooded in once more. Malcolm turned sideways this time in an attempt to leave the den more quickly than his entry. Gezz reached up for the torch, and after switching it off, left it dangling from the ceiling. Both she and her best friend crawled out and crouched in the trench outside. Luke yanked the door shut with some of the bramble leaves. 'We really ought to get a handle put on this, you know,' he said, rubbing his hands and reflecting on what might have happened if he'd caught some of the spiky prickles. 'How's it looking out there?'

Gezz slowly stood up, her eyes falling just level with the ground. 'Can't see anyone.'

'Right,' Luke enthused. 'Let's get out quick.' And get out quick they did. Both he and Gezz leapt up on to ground level. Malcolm, however, needed a bit of help. The two friends reached down and took him by each hand. They tried not to make too much noise heaving him out of the trench, not only because they didn't want anyone to hear them, but also because they didn't want to hurt his feelings.

As Malcolm straightened his school uniform, Gezz turned to Luke. 'You know, I bet when I look to see if someone's coming, the top of my head shows. I mean, if anybody was spying on us, they would see me for sure.'

Luke nodded and cast his eyes to the floor feeling quite serious. 'Yes, we need a way of seeing them without them seeing us.'

'I know what we could have,' chirped Malcolm. Luke didn't believe he knew at all, but he let him have his say.

'We could make one of those peri-scone things.'

Luke's nose scrunched again. 'What?'

'A *peri-scone*,' buzzed Malcolm. 'You know, one of those tubes with mirrors in it. I saw them make one on *Blue Peter*.'

'You're mad, you are,' said Luke, dismissing the idea.

'No, he's not,' said Gezz, suddenly grinning all over her face. 'He means a periscope.'

'A periscope?'

'Yes, it's a tube with mirrors at both ends. You hold it up and look through the bottom mirror.'

Malcolm finished her sentence off for her. 'And the top mirror shows you what's going on above you!'

'Exactly!' Gezz triumphed. Luke scowled a little. He didn't like Malc having the bright ideas. That was his job. He cleared his throat. 'Right. Let's go down the slacks and see if that old tin bath is still there.'

He watched memories of the old tin bath and the island wash over Gezz and Malcolm, and they didn't need telling a second time. Luke was pleased to have excited them again. Now things were back how they should be. 'Come on,' he beckoned, and the trio headed off along the gravel path towards the big railway bridge.

The bridge was long and heavy and quite low. Luke wondered how steam trains would have managed getting under the iron structure as they thundered along the track that, at one time, stretched over the ground where they were now walking.

As the children walked beneath the girders, with the giant nuts and bolts just visible overhead, a shadow was cast upon them and suddenly it was dark. Dark except for the light of day beyond the cold metal frame. The sound of an engine could be heard in the distance. Was it a bus or a lorry? The slight clatter of rails told Luke it was a train about to come rattling overhead. A look of innate joy spread across his lips. The noise got louder and louder. Luke laughed wickedly as Gezz clasped both her ears tight and Malcolm began running to the other side of the bridge in a panic.

The racket was deafening when the train finally thundered across. The sound of creaking metal as the long vehicle passed overhead sent a thrill of excitement through Luke's body. He clutched his fists and cried out, 'Yeah!', as the bridge creaked and vibrated.

Gezz looked up, still clasping her ears in fright, as if expecting the structure to come crashing down at any moment. The silhouette of Malcolm could be seen in the daylight in the distance burying himself behind a mound of earth. 'It's only a train, you mard!' teased Luke, but his voice was lost in the roar of the carriages up above.

And then, as suddenly as it had arrived, it was gone. The clatter of train track faded into silence and the two children continued under the bridge, catching up with their terror-stricken comrade on the other side.

'Why did you run and leave me?' Gezz scolded when she finally reached Malcolm.

'Because he's a mard,' teased Luke, his face grinning with obvious delight.

Malcolm looked at the ground and sulked. 'No, I'm not,' he said. 'I just don't like that bridge. It freaks me out.'

'Well, I'm scared too,' said Gezz reprovingly. 'But you could have told me you were going to run for it.'

Malcolm glanced up sheepishly. 'Sorry, Gezz.'

'I don't know what all the fuss is about,' said Luke, arms folded and still half-laughing. 'It's only a blummin' train.'

Gezz ignored the comment and adjusted her hairband. 'Anyway,' she announced, 'let's get to that pond before it starts going dark.' As though the bridge incident had been wiped from their minds, all three nodded in agreement and set off once more across the gravel path.

Once the trio were clear of the bridge, their path became narrow and banked up, with fields on either side. A main road with terraced houses meandered off in the distance, stopping only to allow another smaller railway bridge to stretch across. Directly ahead of them lay a giant mound of black mud. It stood above the trees and shrubbery like a big ugly monster waiting to roll over the houses and eat everything in sight. Luke knew this to be the leftover raw material from the old coal-mining days. Gezz's dad had told him the rail line that is now the gravel path used to lead directly into the mine.

The children walked for about half a mile, the big black mountain stretching up higher and higher before them, blocking out the sun, much as the bridge had done earlier. Luke watched Gezz shiver a little and fasten up her jacket. 'You're not cold, are you?' he mocked. Gezz didn't answer.

Just ahead of them was a long steel fence, and beyond that: nothing. Just a big drop leading to a road made of bricks and slutchy mud. Clearly, at one time, it had all been bricks, but now it was just a churned-up mess. After the drop the path continued with another steel fence on the other side.

Gezz's dad had told Luke that there used to be a bridge here with a big hole in it. Then one day a young girl came riding along the path on a horse, and without realizing, galloped over the hole. The horse's legs went straight through and the poor animal got stuck in the wood and metal. Luke remembered seeing a picture of the bridge and its hole in the free newspaper. Gezz's dad had showed it to him. The girl got out all right, but the horse was so hurt afterwards that they called the vet out and he shot it. Gezz's dad said it was better off in Horse Heaven where it would not be suffering. But his own dad said there is no Heaven, it's just made up.

Shortly after the newspaper article, the council had the bridge pulled down and these long metal fences put up to stop people and horses walking off the edge.

The children began to descend the high slope of the embankment, Luke first, watching carefully where he was putting his feet, then Gezz, holding his hand and putting her feet into his prints, as he had always told her, so she wouldn't slip, and finally Malcolm, who always took ages and never failed to get mud on his clothes.

They walked carefully up the muddy path and arrived at the foot of the coal mountain. All around were shrubs and brambles and trees. In the distance beyond the fields was the railway line and the row of terraced houses lining the main road. The children walked around the base of the hill to where a stretch of water like a small lake sat lifeless, stagnant.

Luke knew Gezz always loved coming here because it was the type of place adventures happened in the books she had been reading at school. He liked it because it reminded him of desolate alien worlds where war and destruction had ruined everything, making the people hide from strangers or live in underground rooms.

The centre of the lake was dominated by a raised mound, which to the children seemed like an island. They had been trying to get on to it for weeks without success. And now someone had conveniently dumped an old tin bath nearby, which might serve as a boat.

Luke dragged it across the coal-mud to the edge of the water. Malcolm stood back a little, fearful of his friend's latest venture. 'How do you know it won't sink?'

The boy didn't bother to look round. He just wagged his head from side to side, mimicking his friend in a goony voice. 'How do you know it won't sink?' he said. Then he began pushing the tin bath further into the water, his spotless white trainers getting speckled with mud in the process. 'You always have to think the worst, don't you?' Now his voice was hard and loud.

'Just a minute,' Gezz queried, folding her arms. 'How *do* you know it won't sink?'

Luke climbed into his little boat. 'Oh, not you as well,' he chided. 'Someone get me a pole or something, so I can push myself across.'

The children glanced about for a pole of some sort. It was Malcolm who saw it first, an old washing-line prop discarded round the other side of the lake. 'Here,' he ventured. 'Will this do?'

Luke rubbed his hands. 'Excellent!' He took the wooden pole from Malcolm and started to press the weight of his body against it. As he did so, the tin bath boat began to shift slowly across the water. 'It's working!' shouted Luke excitedly, and sure enough, he was going further and further out. It wouldn't be long before he could stand on the island and claim it as his own.

'No, it's not,' corrected Malcolm slowly, looking a bit worried.

'What?' said Luke.

Gezz laughed and pointed. 'The water's getting higher around you the deeper you go. You're not floating, you're just pushing yourself along the bottom.' Malcolm started to laugh as well. Gezz put her hands on her hips. 'If you carry on like that, you'll start filling up with water!'

Luke stopped pushing and glanced over the edge. As he did so, the tin bath wobbled. He struggled with the prop to keep his balance. They were right, too. The water was about to start spilling into his boat. It was hard not to get angry at his two friends, who were finding the whole business extremely funny indeed. 'All right, you've had your laugh,' he scowled, and started pushing himself back towards the land. The boat lurched hard at the water's edge and Luke fell forward onto the soggy black ground.

Gezz suddenly stopped laughing and pointed. 'Aw, Luke. Your mum will kill you.'

The boy got to his feet and wiped himself down with dirty hands. Then he looked with horror at the small tear that had etched itself into the right knee of his tracksuit. Gezz was right, his mother was going to kill him.

'I told you going in that thing was a bad idea,' sneered Malcolm, remaining at a distance.

Luke glared at him. 'Yes, Malc, I know you did.'

'I don't know why we keep coming down here anyway. I mean, we all know what your mum is like about getting clothes dirty.' Malcolm folded his arms and smirked. 'I mean, she even makes you keep your black tracksuit perfectly clean.'

Gezz looked at the floor; she was clearly having nothing to do with this.

Luke turned on his heels and advanced towards the boy. 'Well, at least my mum cares about the way I'm dressed,' he said, enjoying the sight of Malcolm backing away and looking worried.

Malcolm's bottom lip began to quiver and it looked like he was about to cry. This prompted Gezz to say something. 'Luke, let's leave it now.' She took his arm and stopped him. 'Leave it,' she said again. For a second Luke and Malcolm just looked into one another's eyes. Luke was angry, Malc was frightened and upset.

Suddenly the atmosphere changed. All three children turned. Something was coming, something large and heavy. The sound of the engine was rough, more powerful than a car. A jeep perhaps, or a Land Rover. 'It's coming from the road,' said Luke, his anger instantly evaporating.

Gezz let go of him and Malcolm edged forward.

All three crouched behind a tangle of bushes and prickles. A clump of nettles brushed over Malcolm's legs and he was glad that he hadn't been able to change his school trousers for his shorts. Gezz put a finger to her lips and peeped over the bushes, wishing again that they had a periscope with them.

The vehicle was an old van with a big oblong box stretched lengthways across its open back.

Luke brought his eyes up level with Gezz's and watched the van wobble and shake as it traversed the brick and mud road until it got on to the smooth coal wasteland and came to a halt in the wide open space.

Luke was fascinated. 'Where do you think he's going?'

Gezz shook her head, equally perplexed. 'I don't know,' she said. 'He can't be going to the farm or the fields, because there's no way to get to them from there. It's a dead end.'

'What's that box on the back?'

Gezz scrunched her nose. 'I dunno.'

Two of the children watched as the driver's door opened and an old man with straggles of wild grey-white hair slipped out of the van. Malcolm stayed hidden behind the brambles and did not see a thing.

'Look at his clothes,' said Gezz. 'He doesn't look like a farmer. He's wearing trousers and shoes.'

Luke nodded. 'His jacket is quite baggy too. He looks more like a headmaster, or something.'

The man made his way to the back of the van and pulled down the rear flap. Then, with a great deal of effort and struggling, he slid the oblong box out until it touched the ground. Then he pulled it upright until it nearly topped him in height. With more grunting and heaving, he dragged the box away from the van and left it there in the open. After puffing a little and wiping his brow with a handkerchief, he made his way back to the driving seat.

'What *is* he up to?' said Luke.

This was all too interesting for Malcolm, who finally overcame his fear and peeped over the top of the bushes. 'That box looks like a magician's cabinet or something.'

Gezz nodded. 'Yes, I see what you mean.'

'You think he's gonna saw someone in half, do you?' Luke offered sarcastically, not even bothering to look round. 'Get real.'

Gezz watched with the others as the old man returned from his truck with a small silver device in his hand. Luke saw that the girl's curiosity was further aroused. She was so much like him it was weird. 'What's he got there?'

Malcolm chanced another fanciful answer. 'It looks like a remote control.'

Before either Gezz or Luke could reply, the man held up the instrument and pointed it at the upturned oblong box. He said something.

'What was that?' hissed Luke.

'I don't know,' said Gezz. 'It sounded something like "activate".'

Luke was even more perplexed. 'Activate?'

The old man slipped the silvery device into one of his baggy coat pockets and started talking to the box. The children strained to listen. 'Now then, my dear,' he was saying, 'it is time for you to come out.' Just as he turned to go back to his van, the box began to rattle and shake violently. 'No, no,' the man shouted in a panic, 'not yet!' But it was too late.

Malcolm looked worried again. 'What's happening?'

Gezz remained still and kept her eyes glued to the wobbling box. 'I don't know.'

Luke was equally boggled. 'What's in that thing?'

'I don't know,' repeated Gezz, her voice low and serious.

Suddenly a large crack filled the air and the children jumped in unison. Something had just punched a hole in the front of the box. The children stared wide-eyed as they realized it was a human fist. Another thump brought a second hand smashing through the wood. Then a foot. The children gulped silently and exchanged glances.

With one final crash, the front of the box went flying. The children continued to stare in silence as the person within stepped out. Luke was the first to speak in whispered fascination. 'It's a girl!' he hissed, taking in the silvery all-in-one garment worn by the stranger. Gezz frowned. 'How is she so strong?'

'I told you it was a magic cabinet,' said Malcolm, looking rather pleased with himself. That is until Gezz shook her head. 'I don't think so, Malc,' she said. 'I think the box is just a box. She must be getting her strength from somewhere else.'

The old man waved a reproving finger at the girl, whose long blonde hair was tied up in a ponytail. Gezz groaned to herself, and Luke smiled. He knew what she thinking: hairbands are much better than ponytails. He chuckled as she adjusted her own. The man appeared irritated. 'When I said it is time for you to come out, I didn't mean smash the door to bits.'

The girl's face was blank. 'I am sorry, Father,' she said. 'I misunderstood your instruction.'

Gezz frowned again. The blonde girl's voice was expressionless. It was as though she was reading her answer out of a book. Gezz looked round to see what Luke made of it all. He said nothing, and appeared quite taken with the mystery girl in the silver outfit.

'Her clothes are weird,' offered Malcolm. 'Is it a tracksuit or something she's wearing?'

'Looks like a spacesuit,' said Luke at last.

Gezz groaned again. 'You would say that.'

The man, still oblivious to the fact that he was being watched, approached the girl who had called him father. 'Now then, Anne, I think we had better perform one or two tests to make sure you haven't been damaged in any way.'

Gezz, Luke and Malcolm all frowned and looked at one another. 'Damaged?'

'We'll test your legs first,' he continued. Then he gestured to the land about him. 'Run a few laps round this area.'

Her face still deadpan, Anne responded politely. 'Yes, Father.'

Straight away, the girl broke into a steady jog. Then, as she reached the outskirts of the clearing, she increased her pace to a sprint. Round and round she went, one lap after another, never tiring, never stopping to take a rest. Then she upped the speed again. She was running now, and quite fast too.

'Look at that,' marvelled Luke as he crouched by Gezz's side behind the prickles. 'Will you just look at that?'

Malcolm struggled to focus as the weird girl increased speed yet again. 'She's going faster. How is she doing it?'

'I don't know,' said Gezz, 'but it's not normal. No one can run as fast as this.'

The miracle girl had become a silver blur by now, streaking the edge of the clearing. The old man, still standing between the van and the open box, clapped his hands in excitement. 'Excellent!' he cried. Luke noted his accent. He wasn't British. More European. It sounded like German, the accent spoken by the student teacher who had visited his school, which was odd because the girl who called him father – Anne was it? – spoke perfect English.

'All right, Anne, my dear, you can stop running.'

Within seconds, the girl had slowed right down to a halt. It was incredible. She wasn't holding her sides like Luke did when he played football at school. She wasn't breathless at all. She just stood there waiting for the next instruction.

'Now, let's test your frame as a whole. Do a few backward somersaults, please.'

Anne turned to face her mentor. 'Yes, Father.' And with that she arched her body back. Her legs flew over her head and she turned a complete circle in the air, landing perfectly balanced on her two feet. Then she did it again. Then again and again, over and over.

'She's like a gymnast in the Olympic Games,' whispered Gezz, totally mesmerized by the show.

'All right,' commanded the man. 'Now, stop.' And the girl stopped. As with the running, there was no sign of Anne wanting a rest. She just stood there, smart and silver, awaiting the next instruction.

'Right,' breezed the old man. 'Let's test your senses. Eyes, ears, nose, taste. Eyes first.' The man looked about, trying to find something to test her with. Then he stopped and smiled, trying to focus on something in the distance. The children followed his gaze. He was looking at the town hall clock poking up above the trees on the horizon. 'What time is it according to that clock over there?'

Anne turned in the direction of her father's pointing finger. 'Quarter past seven.'

Behind the bushes, Luke checked his watch. Amazing! It *was* quarter past seven.

'Nineteen fifteen,' added the girl, 'on the twenty-four-hour clock.'

Again the old man clapped his hands with glee. 'Excellent!'

Gezz leaned to her right and nudged Malcolm, who began to wobble. 'I bet she just looked at her watch really,' she said. The clumsy clot threw an arm in Gezz's direction to steady himself. He missed her shoulder and fell forward, instinctively grabbing the nearest thing to stop himself toppling over into the mud. Luke turned his head in irritation but said nothing.

'Ow,' Malcolm hissed as his hand squeezed a clump of nettles. Luke watched as Malcolm's eyes watered and he tried to wince in silence. 'My hand,' he whispered.

Luke was not impressed. 'You stupid idiot,' he chided. 'They nearly…'

'Someone is over there, Father,' announced the girl, pointing and sounding very matter of fact. Her voice was loud and confident. The old man followed her hand. 'I do not see anyone.'

'There are three of them,' said the girl, 'hiding in the undergrowth.'

Malcolm grabbed Gezz's arm in a panic. 'They've seen us,' he spluttered, his mass of brown curls bobbing over his spectacles. 'What do we do now?' His feet gave way as he tried to get up, and he fell backwards into the mud. Gezz and Luke stared at one another, confused. 'How did she hear us?' gasped the boy.

Gezz glanced over the hedge in utter disbelief. 'She must have super hearing as well.'

The old man looked more worried than angry, though. He turned to his daughter. 'Who are they? The Foundation? The army?'

'No,' Anne replied. 'Just children. Three children. Two boys and one girl, roughly ten years of age. They pose no threat.'

The man held his forehead with the palm of his hand. 'They might do if they start telling their parents and their teachers what they have seen here. Have they gone?'

'No, they are still there. They appear to be frightened and confused.'

The man turned and began walking towards the bushes.

Malcolm clutched Gezz's arm in a fright. 'He's coming over here. What are we going to do?'

'You there!' shouted the man, his voice sharp and clipped. 'You children. I must speak with you.'

Luke stared at Gezz, his eyes almost popping out of his head with fear. 'What do we do?' he said nervously. 'What do you think he wants?'

Malcolm began to sob. 'He might take us prisoner and do experiments on us like he's done to that girl. He could take us hostage and demand thousands of pounds from our mums and dads. He might kill us and eat us for dinner.'

Ignoring Malcolm, Gezz glared at Luke, almost burning holes into his face. 'Don't talk to strangers, that's what we keep being told, isn't it?' she said calmly.

Luke nodded. 'I guess so.'

'Well, then, let's get out of here.'

The old man was nearly upon them. 'Do not be afraid,' he was saying loudly. 'My name is Professor Wol…' He didn't get the chance to finish his sentence.

'Rrrrun!' screamed Gezz, and she leapt up from the brambles, leaving the Professor in a state of confusion. The other two scrambled after her as quickly as they could.

4

The Professor

Anne joined the Professor at his side. 'Shall I go after them? I will easily catch them up.'

'No,' said the Professor. 'I don't want anyone else seeing you. I will go after them myself. Can you predict the course they will take?'

Anne followed the movement of the undergrowth with her eyes and monitored the sound of running feet with her ears. 'They are heading for the railway embankment.'

'Right,' said the Professor. 'You take the van and hide it. I'll go after them.'

'They could be dangerous,' the girl said in her flat monotone voice.

'If I need you, I'll call for you,' replied the man busily. 'Now go.'

Anne turned and walked confidently and primly towards the truck. 'Yes, Father,' she said.

★ ★ ★

'I need to rest!' cried Malcolm. 'My lungs are aching.' The other two yanked him up with both hands and he collapsed on to the gravel path of the old disused railway.

'No way!' exclaimed Luke, his blond hair all matted and his forehead trickling with sweat. 'You've seen how fast that girl can run. We keep going until we get far enough away.'

Gezz was also breathing hard. She held her hands on her hips and looked across the black landscape. 'The van has gone,' she croaked. 'Maybe they've run off.'

'I'm not chancing it,' replied Luke. 'Let's get back to the den at least.'

Gezz nodded. 'OK.'

The two children set off up the gravel path at a steady pace with Malcolm lagging behind. The big railway bridge loomed up ahead, heavy and threatening in appearance, but not as frightening as what they had just witnessed near the pond. All they had to do now was get on the other side of that bridge and they were safe.

They went at a half-jog, forever glancing about themselves in a fright. Luke was sure that the girl in the silver suit would catch them up. The speed at which she ran round that open ground, and those somersaults – that wasn't normal behaviour.

The ground panned out and became level as they approached the overhead railway bridge. This time the children did not concern themselves with its girders and shadows, nor did they worry about any trains which might possibly be coming at that moment. They just kept close together, their eyes focused on the terraced houses and their back gardens, and the trench which housed their den.

All three breathed a sigh of relief when they cleared the bridge and stopped at the foot of the ditch overlooking the half-buried air-raid shelter. They looked about themselves cautiously and checked to see if they had been followed.

There was no sign of that weird girl or her elderly dad. In fact there was no one about at all.

Luke fished out his key from round his neck and jumped into the trench, the others following suit. Even Malcolm managed to get down in one jump. Luke ran his fingers over the green-painted wood and found the Yale lock. His key went in easily and suddenly the door was open. The three children tried to scramble inside all at the same time. Eventually Gezz pulled the two boys back and crawled in herself. Luke and Malcolm calmed down a little and followed her, Malcolm slamming the door shut behind him.

Gezz reached up to the torch hanging from the steel ceiling and clicked it on. The three of them let out a big sigh of relief. 'I can't believe we've made it,' said Gezz.

'They must have scarpered,' breathed Malcolm, 'when they realized we'd seen them.'

Luke fell quiet for a moment; he was not sure what to think. 'I wonder what they were up to?' he said finally. 'I mean, how did she do those things? What is she?'

'Maybe she's bionic?' Gezz offered. 'You know, like on that old TV programme. A real girl, but with, like, robot legs.'

Malcolm's eyes dazzled at the suggestion, his imagination working overtime again. 'Or maybe she's an alien with special powers?' he enthused.

Luke just looked at him reprovingly and said nothing. Then, 'Why does she call the man "Father" when he's old enough to be her granddad?'

Gezz shrugged. 'There was a girl at school whose dad looked old enough to be her granddad. I think she was the youngest of several children. Maybe this Anne is his youngest daughter?'

'And how come he's so fit and healthy for an old man?' Luke continued, his eyes narrow and pondering. 'How did he lift that box off the van without any help?'

'And what was the girl doing in the box in the first place?' added Malcolm.

Luke nodded. 'Yeah,' he said, and Malcolm looked pleased that he had finally said something the others could take seriously.

There was a sharp rat-a-tat-tat on the steel frame around the door. The children froze, their eyes bulging with fear. They waited. Then a second rap sounded on the wooden door. Gezz quickly huddled up to Luke and buried her head in his shoulder. Malcolm pressed his back against the hard metal wall. Then came the voice, polite and kindly, the German accent making the children gulp with dread.

'Children,' said the voice. The foreign accent made it sound like, 'Chealdren,' Luke noted. There was another knock, then the voice continued. 'I know you are in there. Do not be afraid. I only want to talk with you.' The children did not speak or move. They just stared at the door of the den and hoped the man would get fed up and go.

'I know you saw my daughter, Anne,' he carried on, 'and the amazing things she can do.'

It was Malcolm who broke the silence, with the other two shaking their heads in terror. 'We won't tell anybody about what we saw, mister. Honest.'

'I want to tell you who I am and what we are doing. You need to know how serious this is. Please let me in.'

Now it was Gezz's turn to speak. 'No!' she said loud and emphatic.

Silence fell over the den again. Had the man given up, had he gone? Luke wished they had that spy contraption Malc had been talking about earlier. Then the silence was shattered again. The children pressed themselves against the back wall as a high-pitched whining could be heard coming from the lock. *It sounds like a dentist's drill*, thought Luke, and then wished he hadn't remembered the dentist. He had an appointment with him at the end of the month.

Malcolm was the first to notice it. 'Look!' he gasped. 'The lock! It's turning!' And sure enough it was. This was becoming unbearable. Each of the children held their breath in anticipation as the lock clicked back and the door was pushed open. Luke shielded his eyes from the evening summer sunlight as the old man crawled in and leaned back on the closed door.

Luke's eyes adjusted to the dim light of the torch and he stared at the smiling man with his baggy tweed jacket and scraggy white hair. The man pressed a button on the silver remote in his hand and the high-pitched noise ceased. Then he slipped the device into his coat pocket.

'Do not be afraid,' said the man as calmly as he could. 'My name is Professor Wolfgang Droyd.'

Luke, Gezz and Malcolm all exchanged glances with one another and then looked straight at the Professor. There was nothing they could do. They were trapped.

5

My Daughter Anne

The old man crouched, resting his back on the closed door of the hideout. It seemed to Malcolm that the Professor, while trying to keep calm, was just as frightened as they were. He found himself trying to lighten the atmosphere. 'My name is Malcolm,' he said. 'This is Luke, and this is Geraldine, Gezz for short.' The children stared at him, horrified.

He had seen films on television where this sort of thing happened. There were usually only two ways it would go. The man would either turn out to be a crazy lunatic who has escaped from a hospital for the mentally ill, or he would turn out to be a gentle old man needing their help. The boy hoped it was the latter.

No one had spoken since the Professor introduced himself to them. The atmosphere was terrible. Malcolm swallowed hard and endured the tingling sensation in his legs. The den was cramped at the best of times, and now, with a grown-up inside with them, it was positively chock-a-block. That was an expression his granddad always used when there was no room to move, 'positively chock-a-block', and he liked it. Malcolm shifted his legs from side to side, trying to ease the pins and needles. The only good side to sitting down at the moment was it kept him from wanting to go to the toilet.

The man had said not to be afraid, and so far he had done nothing but smile. Yet Malcolm knew that mentally ill people could be very nice and then suddenly turn nasty. He hoped this man wasn't one of those.

'Wolfgang.' It was Gezz who had spoken. All eyes turned to her. Malcolm was not sure whether this was a good idea, talking to the man, and he could tell that Luke was equally worried, it was written all over his face. The Professor raised his eyebrows and hunched forward. Gezz continued, 'That's a German name, isn't it?'

The man nodded excitedly, his wild grey hair wafting about. 'Yes, yes,' he said.

'I know that because I saw a programme at my Auntie Beryl's about a family who were in a war camp. They were part of a religion that was not allowed, and the dad of the family was called Wolfgang.'

The Professor stared with serious intensity as he pondered on the family in the programme and the horrible things that happened to them during the war. 'Mm,' he said, pressing a finger hard against his lips. 'That was during the Second World War when Adolf Hitler was the ruler of Germany. He hated everyone who believed something different to him. He was very cruel. Many people were killed.'

Luke looked horrified by the Professor's story. 'Why?'

'Hitler wanted to make a perfect race, all looking the same. He wanted them to be big and strong and have blond hair and blue eyes.'

Luke perked up on that last bit. 'Oh,' he chirped. 'I've got blond hair and blue eyes.'

Gezz kept her eyes firmly fixed on the Professor, clearly not impressed with her friend's observation. Malcolm was sickened by it too. 'That doesn't mean you're perfect.'

The smile was wiped from Luke's face. 'I *know*,' he said sarcastically.

'That was over fifty years ago now,' said Professor Droyd, his eyes narrow and staring into the back of the Anderson shelter. Silence fell over the huddled group again.

'But Germany's not like that now, is it?' quizzed Gezz.

Professor Droyd broke back into a hearty smile, and Malcolm noticed that the old man's skin was not even as wrinkled and lined as his own grandfather's even though he seemed at least as old. 'Oh, no, no, no,' said the Professor, wagging his finger. 'It's not like that now. But at the time it was unbearable, so my daughter and I escaped to Britain and we have been living here ever since.'

It was quiet again. The children looked at one another. The Professor had mentioned his daughter. Questions burned in their minds. It was Gezz who finally plucked up the courage. 'Professor?'

'Yes.'

'You said that you and your daughter escaped to Britain.'

'Yes.'

'And that was over fifty years ago?'

'That's right.'

Gezz put a fist to her mouth and coughed nervously. 'Well,' she said. 'That girl who was with you on the slacks, she couldn't have been born fifty years ago. She only looks about our age, about ten or something.'

The Professor started chuckling to himself. This is it, thought Malcolm, this where he starts going crazy. The laughter will get louder and louder and the Professor's eyes will go really mad looking and he will turn nasty on them all. Malc could feel his throat tightening up again.

Thankfully he didn't. 'That is not my daughter,' mused the Professor to himself. 'No.'

Malc frowned. 'Then, where is your daughter?'

Gezz turned her head and tutted. 'Well, she's not going to be living with him now, is she? She will have got married and had children or something.'

'I was only asking,' Malcolm protested.

'No,' said the Professor seriously. 'My daughter is not living with me now, and she has not got married either.' Now it was his turn to look awkward and tense.

Malcolm felt sorry for him, he looked so sad. 'Where is she?'

The Professor glared at the floor, his eyes wide and brown. 'She is dead.'

More silence. Malcolm was never sure what to do or say when grown-ups got like this. He decided the best thing to do was stay quiet. The others had obviously drawn the same conclusion. Then, 'Did Hitler find her?' It was Gezz again.

The Professor nodded and said nothing.

Malcolm tried to remember how to react when people started talking about members of their family dying. He couldn't. Thankfully Gezz could. She touched the Professor's arm tenderly and said, 'I'm sorry.'

Professor Droyd smiled. 'No, no,' he said, his German accent muffled slightly as he cleared his throat. 'It is OK. It was a long time ago.'

Luke had said nothing the whole period. He seemed to be preoccupied with something else. Then he said it. Malcolm and Gezz looked at one another, not sure how the Professor was going to react. 'Professor, if the girl who was with you on the slacks isn't your daughter, who is she? And how can she run so fast and be so strong?'

The Professor stared at Luke and gritted his teeth. Was he angry? Had Luke pushed him too far? Was this the point where the Professor would turn on them? Or was he just collecting his thoughts to tell them a long story? Malcolm felt a cool trickle of water meander from his left armpit and down his side, and his throat had dried up again.

'I am a scientist,' Professor Droyd began, slowly and deliberately. Malcolm still couldn't tell if the Professor was angry. The old man's accent was strong again as he split up the word scientist into 'sci-en-tist'. 'A professor of robotics to be exact.'

'Robotics?' Luke enthused. 'She's a robot?' A smug grin fell across his handsome features. 'I knew it,' he said, so obviously feeling very pleased with himself.

The Professor gave a mysterious half-smile and shook his head. 'Not quite.'

Luke's face fell into a pit of disappointment. 'Oh.'

'Have you heard of something called bioengineering?'

Malcolm frowned, pinched his bottom lip with his forefinger and thumb and pondered on the word. 'Bi-o-engin-eer-ing,' he said thoughtfully. 'Isn't that something to do with washing powder?'

Suddenly a loud cackle filled the stifled air, making the three children jump. It was Professor Droyd. He laughed and he laughed, shaking his head and repeating Malcolm's question. '"Isn't that something to do with washing powder", oh dear, oh dear.' He coughed and swallowed, and then dabbed his watering eyes with a hanky which he had pulled from his shirt sleeve. 'Oh my…washing powder,' he said again.

Malcolm didn't know whether to smile or sulk. Why did people always have to laugh when he got things wrong?

'I'm sorry,' said the Professor finally, his voice still trembling a little as he tried to stave off another fit of hysterics. 'You are thinking of "biological". Biological washing powder.'

'Oh, yes,' said Malcolm, feeling very silly indeed.

'No, I mean bioengineering. It's a way of...' He considered a simplified account. 'It's a way of growing a machine using human cells.'

'Oh, I've heard of this on *Star Trek*,' offered Luke excitedly. 'She's a cyborg. The machine part is cybernetic and the skin part is organic. Cyb-org. Cyborg.' Malcolm hadn't understood a word of that. He liked *Star Trek* very much when they showed it on telly, but the science bits were hard to follow sometimes.

The Professor was extremely pleased with Luke, if not a little amazed. 'Well done,' he enthused, shaking Luke by the hand. 'Most of her is mechanical. Her body frame is made from a very strong metal. Strong but light and agile. Her skin is made from human tissue, but it can re-form itself into different colours called pigments.'

Luke was impressed. 'So she can disguise herself as different kinds of people?'

'That's right,' said the Professor. 'And her eyes are real eyeballs with tiny cameras inside, so she can zoom into things that are far away.'

'What about her brain?' asked Gezz suddenly and seriously. 'Is that real or is it a computer?'

Again the Professor was surprised. 'It's mainly a computer,' he said, 'with an organic component. I was hoping she would start to develop emotions with these, you see, but so far she has remained purely mechanical in nature.'

'Like an android?' offered Luke.

'Yes,' the Professor nodded. 'Maybe she's more of an android than a cyborg.'

Malcolm was able to join in the nodding here. He knew that an android was a robot that looked like a person. Mister Data in *Star Trek* was an android, though his skin had a strange colour and you could tell his hair was not real. The Professor's android was better than Data because it looked like a real girl with real skin and real hair and eyes. Malcolm thought long and hard for a good question to ask. Finally he said, 'What's her name?'

The Professor raised his eyebrows as if taken by surprise. 'Her name?' he said. 'Her name is Anne.'

Gezz smiled. 'That's a nice name.'

'Yes, I named her after my real daughter, Annie. She is exactly like the way my Annie looked when she was ten years old.' The Professor smiled a fond smile and the children grinned too.

Then Malcolm realized something and let out a raucous laugh. 'Haaa! Anne Droyd!'

Gezz and Luke stared at him, puzzled once more by his innocent delight. 'What?' they said in unison.

'Anne Droyd!' Malcolm repeated. 'Get it?'

'No.'

'Anne Droyd, android.'

The children were still none the wiser.

'Anne – Droyd,' Malcolm emphasized. 'And an-droid. Get it? She's Anne Droyd the android!'

The Professor nodded and looked a bit embarrassed. 'Yes, yes,' he said sheepishly. 'An unfortunate play on words.'

'So,' Gezz began, trying to change the subject.

Malcolm felt silly again. Why did he always say these stupid things? The trouble was, they didn't always seem stupid to him. He was just making a simple point, that's all. But on reflection, he could have thought that last comment through before opening his mouth. 'Think before you speak,' as Gezz's dad always told him.

Gezz at this moment seemed as though she was trying very hard to think of something to say, but nothing was coming out. Luke came to her rescue. 'Professor, you say you were in the war fifty years ago and that your real daughter died. So how old are you?'

The Professor rocked back on his haunches and looked up at the low metal ceiling. 'Er,' he said. 'Well, let me see. I was born in 1918 just after the First World War, so that makes me...' He broke off to consider. Then he shrugged nonchalantly. 'Eighty something? I don't know.'

The three children boggled. 'Eighty something!'

The Professor was very matter of fact. 'Yes. I fled Germany in 1938 when I was twenty, just before Hitler triggered World War Two. Then Annie...' he tailed off for a moment as if remembering his lost daughter. He started again. 'Annie died about twenty years later.'

'But how come you look younger?' quizzed Luke. 'You look just a bit older than Gezz's dad. And how come you are so strong? You lifted that box off your van with your bare hands.'

As the children looked on, the Professor began rolling up his jacket sleeve. 'Ah well,' he began, undoing his shirt cuff. 'I damaged my left arm a few years ago during an experiment, and I applied a bit of bioengineering to myself.'

Malcolm's eyes bulged as the Professor dug the nails of his right hand into his bare left arm. The skin tore and stretched like rubber but no blood could be seen. 'Look at this,' said the Professor triumphantly. The skin peeled back to reveal a thick silver metal shaft and a mass of circuits and wires.

Luke attempted to speak. 'You're, you're, you're,' then finally he got it out. 'You're one of them,' he said, his voice all shaky and terror stricken. 'You're an android. You're here to trap us.' Malcolm's legs went weak at the knees. Oh no, this was it.

The Professor chuckled and pressed his rubbery skin back over his robot arm. 'No, I'm not,' he said. 'And don't worry about the arm. It's real skin. And the machine part of the arm will heal it up very quickly.'

Luke launched forward, taking everyone by surprise. He grabbed the Professor by the arm and yanked him across the small space and pushed him against the back wall. Malcolm and Gezz shuffled round to join Luke by the door. 'We're getting out of here.'

A look of horror shot over the already shaken Professor. 'No,' he spluttered, 'I haven't finished telling you.'

Luke fumbled at the Yale lock. Malcolm was terrified and started to blub. *Trapped in our own den with a nutter for company,* he thought. He glanced round at the angry Professor Droyd. The old-young man had slipped his left hand into his pocket. What was he going to do? Maybe he was going to pull out that weird remote control? Perhaps it was a laser gun as well as a key? Malcolm's legs were giving way and he desperately needed the toilet.

With his free arm, the Professor tried to pull the children from the door. 'No!' he bellowed. 'I have not finished telling you. You do not understand. I need your help. We both do.'

Luke turned the lock and started to pull the door inwards, but it was hard because Malc and Gezz were in the way. Then suddenly he froze. There was someone outside. 'Father?' The voice was cold, flat, emotionless, *robotic*. 'Oh my God!' screamed Luke. 'It's the android!' He slammed the door shut again and clicked the safety catch on the lock to stop it turning.

'Anne,' called the Professor, 'I need you quickly.'

The voice remained emotionless and monotone. 'You are being held captive?'

'Just get the door open.'

'Activating morph key,' announced the voice.

Malcolm trembled as he heard the sound of a serrated piece of metal inserting into the lock. He felt the colour drain from his face as he looked at the other two. 'She's got a special key like his,' he croaked, pointing to Professor Droyd while at the same time trying not to look at him.

Luke managed a half-smile. 'I've put the safety on,' he whispered. 'She'll not be able to turn the lock.'

Malcolm looked at Gezz, and her face reflected the relief he was suddenly feeling in himself. Mind you, they still had the problem of the Professor on the inside and the android on the outside. They were still trapped. *Trust me to think of that*, thought Malcolm.

'Lock not responding,' the robot girl declared. The children breathed a sigh of relief as they heard the key being removed from the lock. Then the android spoke again. 'I shall break down the door. Stand back, Father.'

Before the children could respond there was a sharp crack and a fist punched its way through the door, just stopping short of Luke's head. 'Oh – my – God,' he shuddered, giving hard emphasis to the words.

'I wish you would stop saying that,' Gezz reproved. 'How do you think God feels?'

'I know how *I* feel,' said Malcolm.

The Professor was calm and serious now. 'I think you had better stand back.'

The children did not need to hear the suggestion a second time. They huddled together next to the Professor as a leg came crashing through the wooden door, then a second fist and a head.

The newcomer ducked down and crouched in the doorway, blocking out the evening sun. Her hair hung over her sparkling blue eyes in a neat blonde fringe, with the rest falling back into a ponytail tied with what looked like a ribbon. Silver dungarees covered a white T-shirt and perfectly clean skin. Her face was pretty and round. She seemed quite ordinary in fact. 'Father,' announced the girl in that near-schoolteacher fashion. 'You require assistance?'

The Professor sat on the bucket that had been Luke's at the back of the air-raid shelter and rested his arms upon his knees. 'Children,' he declared, waving his hands forward and smiling. 'Allow me to introduce my daughter, Anne.'

6

The Story So Far

The children had frozen. No one spoke or moved; they just glared at the android girl with fearful intensity. The Professor gestured for his robot daughter to enter, and she responded accordingly, making the shelter well and truly overcrowded. The old man smiled, eager to demonstrate that he and his progeny meant no harm. 'Forgive me,' he said. 'But you were getting somewhat hysterical.'

'Do you blame us?' said Gezz, breaking the tension by having the courage to speak up. 'Your daughter is a robot.'

'Er, android,' corrected Luke.

Gezz closed her eyes for a second or two and stifled her aggravation. 'Your daughter is an android,' she began again, 'and you are half-machine yourself.'

Luke leant forward. 'Cyborg,' he said.

'Yes, thank you, Luke,' Gezz reproved sarcastically, 'for that bit of information. I don't know how I would have explained myself without you.'

The boy laughed. 'Blummin' 'eck, Gezz. I'm only trying to help.'

'Well, don't.'

Malcolm had been sitting quietly in the corner observing their new mechanical companion and the gaping hole that had once been a door. He could see the sky outside which had now acquired a beautiful orange-red hue. The sun was going down and it was beginning to go dark. The Professor silently studied the boy while the other two squabbled. Though Malcolm's observations on life were often ridiculed, the Professor could see a good heart in action. The boy was clearly a thinker, but found it difficult getting his ideas across. He reminded the Professor of what he himself had been like at that age. Asking lots of questions and no one taking him seriously.

'Your friend has ruined the door,' said Malcolm almost to himself. Gezz and Luke turned to see the splinters of wood fractured and broken, with the Yale lock hanging limply from a disjointed section.

Luke's face screwed up in anger. 'We'll never fix this!' he ranted. 'Every kid in the neighbourhood will find the den now.'

The Professor watched the reaction of the other two. He was silent but concerned. He saw their faces were full of worry. 'Do not be so alarmed,' said the Professor in a calm, reassuring voice. 'Anne will be able to reassemble the door and make it as good as new.'

The three children turned to the blank-faced automaton, anticipating a reaction or some sort of verbal confirmation. None came. The girl just sat there on her haunches staring straight ahead at the opposite wall. 'In fact,' added the Professor, 'she will make it *better* than new.'

The old man watched the children carefully. A smile came to Luke's lips. He clearly liked the idea of the door being made better than new. Gezz looked at the android thoughtfully, perhaps wondering how she could possibly do it, while Malcolm stared straight at the Professor, his mind a surge of unasked questions.

The Professor turned to his creation. 'Anne, dear,' he said. 'Repair the entrance and make it secure.'

'Yes, Father,' came the cold reply, and with that the girl got to work, swiftly and efficiently assembling the fragments of wood into some kind of order. The robot's eyes scanned every splinter and edge to see how the wood fitted together, and with her bare hands began pushing and compressing the various parts. The children looked on in amazement and the Professor smiled with affection.

'Now,' he said. 'While Anne is repairing the door, I want you to sit and listen to our story. I want you to stay quiet and hear me out to the end. And when I have finished you can ask me some questions. Agreed?'

The children exchanged glances, eager to hear the old man's tale, and said in unison, 'Agreed.'

Professor Wolfgang Droyd then set himself right on the upturned bucket, made himself comfortable, and in a hushed voice commenced his story. 'It all began twenty years ago when I was excelling in the science of robotics. My work progressed in leaps and bounds, and I was achieving breakthroughs in my own private laboratories that even the government people had not managed to reach.'

Malcolm's eyes dazzled and he rested his elbows on his knees in a similar fashion to the Professor. 'Is that when you made Anne?'

The other two turned at the same time, putting their forefingers to their lips. 'Sshh!'

Malcolm gave a woeful look of apology. 'Sorry,' he said.

Droyd smiled again, taken by the boy's enthusiasm. 'Word got out, though, that I had succeeded in building a human-shaped robot. It was nothing special, really, not compared to what I have done since, but it was the most advanced machine of its kind.'

The children were totally enthralled now, each hanging on to every word. The Professor continued: 'It could walk and pick things up and perform simple tasks. Then, when I started to develop a talking model, I found that pieces of technology were missing. Someone was stealing my ideas. So in the end I had to shut everything down and move my equipment and research to safer quarters.' He paused and gestured about him with his hands. 'I moved up here, to Bolton, and got a position teaching at a nearby university. Once I was in there, I made use of their technology to further my work.'

The sound of creaking wood caused the Professor to cease talking. The shallow sunlight from outside the den was fading and the torch dangling from the roof became the main source of light once more. The Professor and his young students watched Anne pressing the door into its position in the frame. The Yale lock now slotted back into its latch, and Anne was holding the hinges of the top right-hand bracket over the frame. Quickly and systematically she balanced all the screws in place.

The Professor chuckled. 'Watch this, now,' he said in keen delight.

As the children looked on, Anne extended her middle finger and said, 'Activating screwdriver'. Within seconds, the pink varnished nail of her finger had elongated itself into a narrow hard blade. The Professor continued to chuckle as Gezz, Luke and Malcolm watched boggle-eyed as the blade at the end of Anne's finger spun round very fast, screwing the hinges into the wooden frame and making the door secure and solid.

The wood cracked and whined as the robot's fingernail twisted in the screws one by one. 'Door repaired,' announced the automaton, retracting its pink nail to normal length. 'Integrity one hundred per cent.' Anne crouched back on her haunches and stared at the far wall with big glassy blue eyes just as before.

Luke was impressed. 'Cool,' he whispered.

Gezz ignored him and turned to the Professor. 'So, you started working at the university?' she urged.

'Yes,' said Professor Droyd, collecting his thoughts once more. 'I was able to use the university's facilities to further my experiments with human skin. I was trying to find a way of growing a skin for my robot, you see.'

'To make it more human?' offered Malcolm.

'Precisely,' said the Professor. 'And it was when I finally achieved it that I was approached by a businessman who had been sent by someone else.'

'Who?' said Malcolm.

The Professor sighed. 'I thought we were saving the questions till later.'

'Sorry.'

'So,' the Professor began again. 'The man explained that his mysterious employer, who wanted to stay unknown, was very interested in the study of robotics and that they had made a lot of progress themselves and they wanted to compare notes. Well, I had to make it clear that my project was a personal one and I did not want to share it with anyone.

'Anyway, the man kept coming back and saying that, together, we could change the world. He said we could help people with our robots. We could make the lives of ordinary people a lot easier with our machines. Robots could do all the housework and cleaning. They could do all the hard and boring jobs in factories and shops.'

Malcolm was getting excited again. 'They could tidy our bedrooms up so we don't have to do it.' Gezz and Luke shot him another reproving look.

'Precisely,' said the Professor. 'But I wasn't persuaded by any of this.'

'You weren't?' spluttered Malcolm. 'But why?'

'Because using robots for all those things would just make people lazy. If you had a robot to do all the work, you would sit around all day doing nothing or maybe not even get out of bed. I saw this as a bad thing.' He paused, reflecting on the seriousness of his own observation. 'But then, one day, the man came to me and said his boss wanted to use robotics to help poor people and disabled people and people worse off than ourselves, and I started to think about this.'

He concentrated. 'I had spent years trying to use my talent and intelligence to help people less fortunate than myself. With robot eyes, I could make blind people be able to see for the first time. With robot legs, people stuck in wheelchairs would be able to get up and walk. Imagine a disabled person going ten-pin bowling for the first time or maybe going for a swim. People who find it difficult talking could be given robot voice boxes. And with my new research on human skin I would be able to grow noses and ears and lips and tongues.'

The children were speechless. They had never thought of such things. The Professor watched them reflecting on his ideas. He was pleased to have won them over. He hoped that they could see he was a good man with good ideas; that he was a man who really cared for people and wanted to help them.

'It was then that I agreed to meet this man's boss,' he said. 'I went to a small wine bar and met a lady. She was tall and elegant and very polite. I felt happy and sad at the same time because she looked a little bit like my wife who had stayed behind in Germany and died there.'

The Professor noticed Gezz swallowing hard. She was obviously thinking about the television programme she had seen at her auntie's, and the terrible things Hitler and the Nazis had done in the war all those years ago. *Even at such a young age, this Geraldine is a caring person like me,* he thought.

He continued. 'The woman introduced herself as Angela and explained that she had been conducting similar experiments and was very keen to team up with me. She said she was very close to creating a robot that could think for itself. She had mixed flesh and blood with machine parts and had built a robot that could grow and develop like a real person. But she needed my expertise and my research on human skin to make the robot look completely human.'

He raised his eyebrows. 'Well, I thought about all this and it sounded incredible. So I asked if I could see her laboratory and her robot. But she said her laboratory and her work were so secret that I would have to agree to be blindfolded before I could go.'

Raised eyebrows fell into a frown. 'My immediate response was to say no, but I kept thinking on it. I kept thinking about all the good we could do and how much progress we could make working together. With my knowledge of computers and robotics and her understanding of bioengineering we would be a real force for good.' He paused to reflect again. Then he took a deep breath and added, 'I finally said yes.'

Luke gawped in awe. 'You let them blindfold you and take you to their laboratory?'

'Yes,' replied the Professor. 'I remember being bundled into a car and going for a relatively short distance. It was about twenty minutes' drive. Then we went into an old building, I remember tripping over some loose bricks, and then into an elevator which took me down into an underground base.'

Now it was Gezz's turn to look astounded. 'Hey,' she whispered, barely able to contain her delight. 'An underground base. It's like something the *Famous Five* would find.'

'Quite,' said the Professor. 'And it was impressive too. I don't think the team leader or her followers had actually built the place. No, I think it had been around for a while and they just took it over. But it was ideal for secret research. I recall wishing I had a secret bunker of my own!'

Luke leant forward, eager to hear more about the Professor's discovery. 'So did you see the woman's robot?'

'Yes, I did,' the Professor enthused. 'And it was very impressive.' He broke off and stared momentarily into the distance. It *was* impressive. *What a brilliant mind that woman had*, he thought. A big grin etched itself across his face. 'She had mastered the basic idea of bioengineering, but the mechanical side of things left a lot to be desired. The situation was not as advanced as she had claimed. She needed me to provide the computer programming that would enable the robot to think for itself.'

He paused again and marvelled at the amazing things they had been doing. No one on earth had got as far as that. His voice then fell into a hush of a whisper. 'And then she came up with the best idea yet. A bioengineered brain. Half computer, half flesh and blood. A brain that would be far superior to any human brain. A brain that could work out sums and ideas very quickly. The computer part would be able to do that, you see. But with its flesh part it would be a brain that could also think up new ideas and feel emotions like we do. It would feel happy and joyful and sad and angry.' He stopped again, his enthusiastic smile fading. 'Like we do.'

The Professor was feeling quite low now, because he knew what was coming next. He knew the awful truth. 'I agreed to work with Angela and her team of scientists so long as we were not trying to create the perfect race. I had enough of that when Hitler ruled Germany. There is no such thing as a perfect race, as far as I'm concerned, not created by men anyway. There was always the possibility that a race of robots could turn on their human creators and I did not fancy that.'

He pressed his lips again. 'We agreed that we were design-ing the perfect teachers. Intelligent, thinking, feeling machine-creatures who would look and sound like people but would in fact be robot instructors. As I explained earlier, the technology could also be developed to help the poor, the disabled, even the mentally ill. With a bit of additional bio-technology, real humans could be cured of mental illnesses. Criminals could be kept under better control.' The Professor grinned and tapped his robot-flesh arm. 'Why, even old people could be kept healthy and strong.'

Malcolm rested his elbows on his knees and propped his head up on clasped hands. His brow was hard and serious, his eyes intense and sharp. 'The things you could do to help others. It's amazing.' He looked Professor Droyd right in the eye. 'So what went wrong?'

Professor Droyd took another deep breath. 'Well,' he puffed. 'We finalized the design of the android and the scientists got to work on it. And then one day, when I was finding my work on the brain especially tiresome, I decided to take a walk around the base, you know, to clear my mind. And it was then that I came across the main computer room. I took a peep through the little round window in the door, and to my surprise, there was the team leader, Angela, looking over reports coming in on a computer screen. The report closed, and as the writing faded off the screen I saw, to my horror, the Nazi swastika symbol zoom up in its place.'

He held his forehead in the palm of his hand, recalling how his stomach curdled and a shiver rushed down his spine. This Angela woman was not interested in building the perfect teacher at all, and the poor and afflicted were the last thing on her mind. 'She was up to something despicable,' he said. 'Something awful. Something…,' he broke off and glared at the children who were, once more, hanging on to every word. 'Something evil.'

He continued. 'Just as I turned to go back to my work, my mind a jumble of worry and confusion, a security guard spotted me, and before I knew it I was being dragged before the team leader. She was angry, but tried as best she could to hide it. She glared at me with hard black eyes. "What have you seen?" she asked. I shook my head and stuttered a pathetic reply, "Nothing," I said. "Really." Then she pointed to the monitor and the Nazi symbol. "And what do you think of this?"'

'Well, my anger blazed. I told her that all that the image meant to me was hatred, prejudice and everything that is evil.

They had murdered my wife, for heaven's sake. And the woman stood very close to me, threatening me in a way, and said very slowly, "These people are one of several groups who are very interested in what we are doing here". I said, "What? They are interested in the perfect teacher?" And she threw back her head and laughed. "The perfect teacher?" she screamed. "No! The perfect *soldier*!"'

Malcolm looked at Anne, who remained entirely still, frozen in her concertinaed position and staring at the far wall. She'd been like that for the last ten minutes and had shown no signs of getting cramp or wanting to get up and have a stretch. The Professor smiled again as he watched the expressions on the children's faces. 'So that's why the woman had taken you to her base?' said Malcolm, not taking his eyes off Anne. 'To build an android soldier?'

'That's right,' the Professor confirmed. 'Think of it. A robot warrior programmed to fight until it cannot fight any more. A machine that will kill and keep on killing until it itself is destroyed. A soldier who can scale the walls of castles and fortresses, who can resist bullets and does not fear death. A soldier with zoom lenses in its eyes and hearing which can tap into radio and television messages. Imagine what an army of such androids could do for a country or even a small group of terrorists.'

'Yeah,' acknowledged Luke to himself, almost smiling, his eyes dazzling at the very concept. 'No one could stop an army like that,' he said. 'We would be invincible. Nothing could stop us.'

The Professor found Luke's reverie quite disturbing. It was that kind of thinking which had given rise to Adolf Hitler and the Nazis in the Second World War. It was the sort of idea that made men seek power, and with such power bully other men and women into doing whatever they wanted. It was wrong. It was not what he had been trying to bring about and if he had known what Angela was trying to do he would certainly not have agreed to help. But of course, that was precisely why she didn't tell him. She could not kidnap him, in case people started to look for him. So she had to get him to work for her willingly. And she had.

Gezz was desperate to hear the rest of the story. 'So what did you do? Did you build the perfect soldier?'

Professor Droyd leaned back on the hard corrugated metal wall, his back feeling cramped now. 'At first, I refused to do anything, and they threw me into a prison cell and told me I was going to die. I stayed there for quite some time thinking about the mess I was in and how awful Angela was, and how similar she looked to my wife, who had died. If I had a daughter, I thought to myself, she would look like you.'

Malcolm frowned. 'I thought you said you did have a daughter and that she died?'

The Professor raised his eyebrows. 'So I did,' he said. Then after a pause he flopped back into resting his elbows on his knees. 'Well, I decided to cooperate. I gave them a list of all the things I needed and then got to work. They gave me a huge laboratory full of the most amazing equipment. Angela wanted to be present at all times, but I told her I needed to work alone, and I set up a little sonic device around the security cameras to stop her spying on me.'

'And you built them a robot soldier?' pushed Luke.

The Professor leaned back again and shook his head. 'No,' he said. 'I built Anne instead.'

He watched and smiled as the children turned their heads in unison, eager to get a good look at the Professor's handi-work. It was Gezz who plucked up the courage to say what the two lads were thinking. 'It's,' she broke off to correct herself. '*She's* amazing. I can't believe that you made her.'

'That's what the team leader said,' Droyd mused with a smirk. 'Well, sort of,' he added. 'I was hoping that the sight of Anne, a robot child, completely innocent and guileless in every way, would soften the mad witch, but instead she just went crazy.'

He stopped to take in the sight of his robot daughter for himself. 'Everything that is good in a child. Innocent and well meaning, like the daughter I lost.'

Droyd could see that the children didn't know where to look. They had concluded that the floor was probably the best place. He felt guilty that his last comment had embarrassed his new friends. 'I'm sorry,' he said. 'The team leader made me deactivate Anne and box her up to be put in storage. This time the leader was going to supervise me personally and see to it that I delivered the goods. Anyway, I decided that this was make-it-or-break-it time, so I monitored the comings and the goings of the security guards and those that went to the surface and managed to time the arrivals and departures of their single piece of transport.'

'The van,' Luke guessed.

'Yes. And when the time was right, I got Anne out of storage and made it to the lift.' The Professor sighed noisily, unable to believe how lucky he had been. 'And we only just got away unscathed.'

7

The Fugitives

The children sat silently for a second or two, taking in the incredible story. It was Gezz who spoke first. 'So, you're on the run?'

'Yes,' confirmed Droyd. 'The Foundation needs me to complete my work on their robot soldier. Without me they will never be able to present it to the groups who are pledging to buy it.'

Luke was intrigued by this. 'Are all the different army groups going to get one?'

The Professor shook his head. 'I was told that they were going to sell it to the highest bidder.'

'What does that mean?' quizzed Malcolm.

'It means whoever pays the most gets the robot, dumb, dumb,' Luke sneered with contempt.

Gezz groaned. 'Don't call him dumb, he's not dumb.'

'Woo,' smirked Luke. 'Sorry.'

Professor Droyd leaned backwards on to the hard metal. 'Now there's a thought I had not considered.'

'What?' the children said together.

'That witch might build several robots and sell them to all the armies throughout the whole world.'

Luke could not contain his enthusiasm. 'Wow! Imagine what it would be like if every army in the world had robot soldiers. They would be fighting one another!'

'Precisely,' said the Professor. He was sad and heartbroken looking at his creation, who was still sitting on her haunches, staring at the wall.

Gezz checked her watch, something she did instinctively, the Professor observed. Her jaw dropped in utter surprise. 'Aw, Luke!' she cried. 'It's quarter to nine. I'm going to have to get going. I have to be home in fifteen minutes.' She started to get up and reach for the door.

Luke responded automatically and joined her. 'Me too,' he said. 'I could do with a walk anyway. My legs are killing me. I think I've got cramp.' He turned the door knob and pulled the hatch open. Orange-red light spilled into the den and the Professor was glad for that moment to see the natural world outside. The birds sang and people's footsteps could be heard on the gravel up above.

'Be careful, Gezz,' Luke advised. 'We don't want anyone to see us.'

Malcolm, who was still sitting on his upturned bucket, was appalled. 'Hang on a minute,' he hissed.

Luke glanced over his shoulder as he got ready to bob out into the trench. 'What?'

'What about Professor Droyd and Anne?'

The blond lad took a second to consider. Then he said casually. 'Oh, they can stay here if they like. No one will find them. We can come back tomorrow with food and water.'

The Professor attempted to stand up, but the low ceiling would not allow him. 'Oh, thank you,' he said gratefully.

Luke reached inside the neck of his T-shirt and pulled out his key necklace. 'Here, take this,' he said.

The Professor was most impressed. 'Are you sure?'

'Yeah,' said Luke casually. 'You might want to go for a walk and stretch your legs in the night.'

Malcolm wrinkled his nose the way he did when he thought he had seen something the others had overlooked. 'He doesn't need a key. He's got that special one that can open any door.'

Droyd bent down and touched Malcolm's shoulder. 'The device needs recharging,' he smiled. 'I will need a key for the moment. Come on now, it is time you were going home too. Your parents will be worried.'

Malcolm stood up and headed for the door, and the Professor noted the solemn look on his face. Clearly the boy's parents were not quite so worried as he had assumed. Then he thought of something. 'Hang on a minute.'

The children passed through the narrow door and kept their heads down in the trench. 'Anne,' said the Professor. 'Go outside and use your fibre-optic lens to check the ground level for human activity.'

Anne responded immediately, got to her feet and crept silently into the trench. Then she knelt down with the rest of the children and held out in front of herself her little finger. Gezz, Luke and Malcolm watched quietly, trying to anticipate what she would do next. 'Activate fibre-optic lens,' said Anne in her flat monotone voice.

As the others looked on, the pink nail on her little finger folded back. The Professor watched from the door of the den and delighted in seeing the astounded expressions on his friends' young faces as they beheld a thin wire flex rising up out of the android's little finger. The fibre rose just above the edge of the trench and began twitching to and fro like a tiny eye.

A broad smile filled Malcolm's face. 'Of course,' he beamed. 'It's a periscope.'

'That's right,' whispered Wolfgang Droyd. 'It's a science called fibre-optics. There is a tiny camera at the end of the wire. Hospitals use them for looking inside patients' stomachs.'

'Cool,' said Luke. Gezz said nothing and looked at her watch again.

'Optical sensors detect no human creatures in the immediate vicinity,' announced the robot.

'Right,' hissed the Professor. 'Go! Go now and don't look back. We will talk some more tomorrow.'

The three children did not need telling twice and scrambled up the side of the trench. Gezz and Luke jumped up in one stride, and then reached down to help Malcolm on to ground level. They walked on side by side up the gravel path and did not dare look back for fear that someone might see where they had come from, or worse still, that the mysterious Angela and her Foundation people might discover the Professor and his remarkable creation.

'Anne, retract the fibre-optic and come inside,' called the old man's voice from the interior of the air-raid shelter.

'Yes, Father,' the automaton replied in her cold blank voice. The lens flex dropped effortlessly down into her little finger and the pink varnished nail closed to seal the digit.

With that, the android entered the den, where Professor Wolfgang Droyd had already stretched himself out on the floor. He was glad of the room to move. 'Close the door, Anne,' he instructed.

'Closing the door,' replied Anne, and promptly secured the entrance.

The Professor reached up for the torch on the ceiling and switched it off. He welcomed the darkness, which seemed pitch black at first until his eyes adjusted, and then he could make out a line of faint light round the edge of the door. 'De-activate yourself, Anne. Conserve your energy.'

The emotionless childlike voice sailed over from by the door. 'Yes, Father,' it said. 'Deactivating in two seconds. Two… One…' And with that the android fell silent.

Professor Droyd curled up on the floor as best he could. *What an exhausting day it has been*, he thought, *but it has turned out all right in the end.* He smiled as images of his three new young friends drifted before his closed eyes. *They are good kids*, he thought. *They will help as best they can. And if they can't help me, they will be good for Anne.*

And with that, he fell into a deep, deep sleep.

8

Back to Normal

It was only when the children reached the safety and the ordinariness of their semicircular housing estate that anyone felt like speaking. For the whole ten-minute walk all three of them had remained in rapt silence, dwelling on the serious nature of the information entrusted to them.

'How do we know he's telling the truth?' said Luke, gazing across the road to watch the two fishermen sitting on opposite sides of the lodge. 'I mean, how do we know he isn't a criminal and this Foundation are really the good guys?'

'Oh, come on, Luke,' Gezz replied, walking at a pace in order to meet her deadline. 'You saw the Professor's arm and you saw what the android can do. Of course he isn't a criminal.'

Malcolm took the pair of them by surprise. 'Luke has a point here, Gezz,' he said. 'We don't really know if he told us all that stuff just to get in with us.'

Gezz shook her head defiantly. 'No. He was telling the truth. I can tell. And he needs our help.'

The children fell silent again until they reached Malcolm's house. The last of the evening sun cast shadows over the wild unkempt grass of the tiny garden and a dim light could be seen in the corner of the living-room window. 'What time shall I call for you tomorrow?' asked Malcolm.

Gezz turned to Luke. 'About ten?'

The boy nodded his agreement.

Malcolm gave a brief but worried smile before turning to approach his front door. He knocked hard on the battered, paint-chipped wood. A few seconds later the door opened inwards and the scruffy child slipped into the darkness beyond. A single sleeveless arm was holding the door ajar as Malcolm vanished inside. There were muffled voices for a second or two before the door slammed shut.

Gezz checked her watch again. It was now three minutes past nine. She set off again at a brisk pace. 'I'm late.' Luke just sunk his hands into his black tracksuit jacket pockets and shrugged. 'It's only by a couple of minutes though.'

The two children stopped outside their respective gardens. The Nissan and the sports car sat side by side with the little white fence positioned in between. Luke pushed open the white plastic porch door to his house and fished out his front-door key from one of his trouser pockets. 'Do you think your mum and dad will let me sleep over tonight?'

Gezz produced her own front-door key and let herself in. 'Probably,' she said. 'Just hang on.'

She went inside and into the living room to where her mother and father were playing draughts. The black and white checkers-board lay on a varnished coffee table and the two adults sat opposite one another. Gezz's stomach turned as she entered the room.

'What time do you call this?' her mum asked, staring at the black discs scattered about the board, not really too bothered. 'We said nine o'clock.'

'It's only five past,' said Gezz innocently.

Her dad kept his eyes firmly fixed on the game as well. 'Go and get washed and cleaned up. We'll be having supper in a minute.' Before Gezz could reply, he let out a sneaky laugh and picked up one of his black discs, pacing it across the gaps and over three of the red ones on her mum's side. 'Sorry, Vanessa, love,' he teased, and she held her forehead, laughing and scowling at the same time. 'Oh John! I hadn't seen that.'

Gezz stood at the hall door waiting for the banter to calm down. 'Is it all right if Luke stays over tonight?'

'Yes,' said her dad, still not looking up as he collected his wife's three discs. 'But make sure it's OK with Terry and Paula first.'

'Great!' said Gezz with a skip in her step, knowing full well that it would be OK with Luke's mum and dad.

★ ★ ★

The sound of dramatic music and heavy gunfire greeted Luke as he pushed open the door bridging the hall and the living room. The smell of cigarette smoke hit him in the face with full force and as he entered he could see it hanging around the ceiling like a disenchanted spirit. It was mostly visible above the tall lampstand in the corner where it floated, swirling and blue.

Luke's dad was sitting by the lamp in one of the leather armchairs, entirely captivated by the movie playing away on the television in the opposite corner. He rested his right elbow next to a glass ashtray on the arm of the chair, his ciga-rette pinched between his fingers in an upright position, a twisting line of smoke hovering up to the main cloud around the lampshade.

His mum was sprawled across the settee, her maroon leather trousers rubbing with the leather of the couch. She was reaching down into her handbag which sat in its usual place at the side. The noisy machine gun continued to blast its victims dead, the man wielding it being of gruesome ilk, greasy, short-haired and wearing combat clothes. He was shouting a lot, and most of his sentences contained obscene words. *No wonder Mr and Mrs Atkinson prefer me to stay at their place rather than Gezz coming here*, he thought.

His mother straightened up with a packet of cigarettes and a lighter in her hand. She flipped back the lid and slid one out. Then she popped the cigarette into her mouth and as she looked up to light the end she caught sight of her son. She snatched the cigarette from her mouth and held it lengthways in a clenched but gentle fist, careful not to crush it. 'God!' she exclaimed in a start.

Luke's dad reacted with a similar jolt, bit his lip and stifled a swear word. With his free hand he scrambled to pick up the remote control, which was lying at his feet.

'Hit it, Terry,' said Luke's mum in a panic. Then she turned to Luke. 'God, you made me jump.'

'What's the film?' asked the boy as his father pressed the 'stop' button on the video remote control, causing the picture to flicker and roll. Within seconds the violent movie had been replaced by a suited man seated behind a desk, and shuffling papers. *The boring old News*, Luke scoffed to himself.

'It's not for you, this one, son,' said his dad hurriedly. Little did he know that Luke had already seen the film when he stayed the night at his cousin John's. Uncle Darren did not mind what they watched. In fact, he didn't care at all.

His mum now sat upright in one corner of her sofa. Her face was indignant. 'What the hell are you doing creeping about anyway? We're over half-way through this.'

Luke shrugged. 'I wasn't creeping about. I just wanted to know if it's all right to stop over at Gezz's tonight.'

Her face immediately broke into a loving smile. She glanced across to her husband, who was also grinning. He put his cigarette between his lips and drew on it hard, his eyebrows raised, as if saying, 'Great!' 'Of course you can, darling,' she said in a sickly sweet tone.

She uncupped her hand and slipped the unlit cigarette into her mouth. With a flick of her thumb her lighter burst into life and she touched the neatly rolled tobacco with its flame. Then she sucked hard and her cigarette end burned an orange-red. As she removed it from her mouth, the smoke hung for a second outside her open lips before it shot down her throat as she inhaled. 'Well, go on then!' she urged, the blue mist trickling from her mouth and nose as she spoke. Then she blew the rest up into the cloud hanging in the air.

That is another reason Mr and Mrs Atkinson preferred Gezz not to stay at my house, thought Luke. *They didn't want her coming home stinking of smoke.* And this time he could see exactly what they meant. He turned to face the hall door, and as soon as he had opened it, the news reader's serious tones were exchanged for dramatic music, loud swearing and the rattle of machine guns.

★ ★ ★

'I will have to nip up into the loft to get the camp bed,' said Gezz's father as he got to his feet.

Her mum started collecting draughts together and folded the board. 'And I'll get some bedding from the airing cupboard.'

Gezz walked straight in with a skip in her step, but Luke hovered, unsure in the hall doorway. 'You don't have to stop playing your game for me, Mrs Atkinson.'

'No, it's all right, Luke,' breathed Gezz's mum as she slid the board into a narrow oblong cardboard box. 'I was getting thrashed anyway.' She jumped to her feet and dropped the game on top of a pile of others resting on a cabinet. They were all there, *Ludo*, *Monopoly*, the lot.

Gezz's dad had just reached the bottom of the stairs when the low rumble of an explosion could be heard from the chimney breast in the living room. It was heavy and deep, and the man was compelled to return to the main room. He paused at the hall door and looked at his wife with a quizzical half-smile. 'Good grief,' he said. 'What was that?'

Gezz shot a glance at Luke, who was obviously feeling a tad embarrassed. 'It's my mum and dad,' he offered apologetically. 'They're watching *Full Metal Jacket* on video.'

'Oh,' Gezz's dad replied, clearly not sure how to react. 'Sounds ominous.'

'They must have turned the sound up.'

Gezz's mum shrugged and smiled. 'So what is *Full Metal Jacket* about, then? Is it about a magic harness with special powers, or something?' Gezz cringed at her mother's lack of understanding. She was so out of touch.

'No,' Luke said sheepishly. 'It's a war film about soldiers in Vietnam. You wouldn't like it.'

Gezz quickly changed the subject. 'Do you want a hand with the bedding, Mum?'

'Oh, yes,' replied her mother, the noise next door immediately forgotten. 'But we'll have to be careful not to wake Ross. We only got him off an hour ago.'

The four of them, Mum, Dad, Gezz and Luke, made for the stairs. Her dad went first, stopping at the top to pick up his long rod with the hook in the end. The others passed him on to the landing. 'Will you steady the ladder as it comes down, Luke?' he asked.

Luke nodded enthusiastically. He rarely got to help his own parents do anything.

Gezz's dad reached up with the rod to where a square panel sat in the ceiling. He hooked the pole into a small metal loop in the door and pulled at it. After a couple of yanks the panel dropped down and a pair of silver aluminium ladders shot out automatically. 'Catch them, Luke!' he called as softly as he could, so as not to wake baby Ross, and the boy did so, cupping his hands to receive the ladder. He caught the bottom rung in his right hand and lowered it on to the carpeted floor.

Her father climbed up into the hole overhead, and a couple of seconds after he had disappeared through the blackness, a light came on. The ceiling resounded with the noise of footsteps on a hardboard floor. 'Ah, here we are,' came her dad's voice, and he re-emerged carrying a folded metal contraption in his left hand. He knelt on the inside of the hole and lowered it down to where Luke took it in both hands.

Her mum lifted sheets from the lowest shelf of the airing cupboard, which hung sturdily over the jacketed copper water tank. It always looked like an alien to Gezz, and the truth be told, she was a little scared of it. Even now, after witnessing the cyborg Professor and his android daughter, she was apprehensive about the water tank and was glad she hadn't been sent to get the bedding on her own.

She picked up one of the thicker blankets and a blue pillow case and followed her mother into the box room, where her dad and Luke were already unfolding the metal frame of the camp bed.

The main base clicked back and the steel legs fastened into place. Then her mum dropped a thin plastic mattress on top and began applying sheets and covers.

She couldn't wait for bedtime so that she and Luke could get together in here and talk over the day's bizarre events before she went to her own bed.

After her dad had put away the loft ladders and sealed the opening back up, all four of them trooped downstairs for supper. Gezz knew that Luke always looked forward to the sandwiches and hot cocoa her mother prepared because his own parents never did it.

'Right,' said Gezz's mum, clasping her hands together eagerly as Luke drank the last of his cocoa. 'It's ten o'clock and time you two were upstairs.'

Luke pulled a face and rested his chin on the palms of his hands with his elbows plonked firmly on the edge of the kitchen table. 'My mum always lets me stay up till eleven o'clock on school holidays.'

'Well, I'm not your mum,' replied Gezz's mother while collecting the plates and mugs from the table and Gezz grinned, thinking, *so there.* 'Come on now, go and have a wash and brush your teeth, the pair of you. And don't forget to be quiet.'

'I know,' groaned Gezz. She knew the speech off by heart. 'Because we don't want Ross waking up.'

Her mother did not appreciate having her sentence finished off for her. 'Less of your lip, young lady,' she chastised.

Her father decided to add a few words of correction of his own. 'Now get up those stairs,' he commanded sternly.

Without further ado, Gezz got up from the table. But before Luke could leave the room, Gezz's dad let out an exaggerated cough. 'Hang on a minute, Luke,' he said. 'Did you bring any pyjamas with you tonight?'

Luke's head fell forward in an embarrassed sulk. 'No, Mr Atkinson,' he said. 'I told you last time, I don't have any. I just sleep in my underpants.'

Gezz's mother and father exchanged glances for a second, and then Gezz's dad got to his feet. 'As we thought,' he said, suddenly smiling. 'Well, when you go up to bed you will find a surprise waiting for you.'

Gezz turned at the door and watched Luke jump to his feet in grateful excitement. 'Thanks, Mr Atkinson.' He nodded to her mother as well. 'Mrs Atkinson.' The boy joined Gezz at the door leading to the living room and left Vanessa and John Atkinson looking very pleased with themselves.

The two children passed through the living room to the hall and climbed the stairs. After washing their hands and faces and cleaning their teeth, they headed for the box room.

In the box room, Luke stood at the foot of his bed and stared at the cellophane wrapped pyjamas placed neatly on top of the blankets.

'Go on,' Gezz enthused. 'Open it.'

Luke did open it. Soon there was plastic wrapping all over the floor.

Then, while the lad changed from his tracksuit, still covered with specks of dry mud from the tin bath escapade, to his new dark-blue pyjamas, in her own room Gezz shrugged off her clothes and slipped into her nightie.

Luke came through into her room and sat on the edge of the bed.

'Are you settled in?' It was Gezz's dad at the top of the stairs.

'Yes,' whispered Gezz.

The door was pushed open slightly and her dad sat himself on a chair near to his daughter's bed. 'Are you ready for the prayer, then?'

The two children nodded, but before he could get underway, Gezz thought of something. 'Will you ask God to look after the people who are lonely and have nowhere to live?'

Her father smiled, taken by his daughter's thoughtfulness. 'Yes, of course I will.'

'And all the children who have no real family. And all the little girls and boys who aren't like normal girls and boys.'

He paused for a moment, clearly wondering what it was all about. Then, 'Yes, of course I will,' he said again. He bowed his head and closed his eyes and the children closed theirs too. 'Our Heavenly Father,' he began in a mild respectful voice. 'We come before You now to thank You for the good things You give us in life and to ask that You forgive us for the things we do wrong.' He paused again for a second, and then continued in a slightly higher tone. 'Please watch over all of us, Father, and take care of us, Geraldine, Ross, Luke, Vanessa and myself, and Mr and Mrs Davidson next door too.' His voice then went a bit stronger. 'And look after all those who are lonely and have nowhere to live, please, Father, and all the children who have no real family, and all the special boys and girls who have problems we might find hard to understand. We ask these things, Father, in the name of your son, Jesus. Amen.'

'Amen,' repeated the children.

Gezz's dad then got up from the bed and looked to Luke. 'Don't spend all night chatting. Five minutes, then I think you should go to your room.' Luke nodded.

'Night, night,' said both Gezz and Luke. Gezz's dad wished them a goodnight and stepped on to the landing, leaving the door open.

After a few moments' silence, Gezz said, 'Luke.'

The boy looked already half-asleep. 'Mm?'

'Do you think the Professor and Anne will be all right in our den?'

'Mm,' came the reply.

Grown-ups tended to worry a lot about serious things like this, but Gezz knew the old man and his daughter would be all right in the den. In fact she felt relieved on their behalf.

The girl looked across at her best friend. She had been hoping for a really long chat like they always had when he stayed over. Not this time, however. No, this time Luke wished her goodnight and wandered off to his own room, leaving her door slightly ajar. He seemed completely exhausted by their exciting day. And so, with images of her teacher Mr Davies, the pond with the island, Malcolm, the den and Professor Droyd with his robot creation Anne swimming before her in a jumbled unrelated mess, Gezz closed her eyes and fell into a deep and somewhat troubled sleep.

9

Do Humans Dream of Electric Friends?

The sound of wooden drawers sliding open in the adjacent bedroom greeted Luke as he started to come round. For a few seconds he could not remember where he was. The bed was hard and he could feel springs and wires beneath the mattress warping and wrenching as he shuffled on his side. Of course! He had stayed over at Gezz's. He flicked his eyes open wide, threw back his blanket and made for the bathroom. He slipped out on to the landing, only to bump into Mrs Atkinson coming up the stairs. 'Oh, hello, Luke,' she said in her permanently cheerful way. 'We thought we would let you two have a lie in this morning, seeing as you had such a late night.'

The boy smiled to himself. He knew it was only nine o'clock and that his own parents considered nine o'clock as rather early. To them half-past eleven or twelve o'clock was a proper lie in. He watched as Gezz's mum went into the front bedroom. She was wearing old jeans which had gone white around the knees and a light-pink polo-necked jumper. The sound of rustling bin liners joined the sliding drawers. The

Atkinsons were sorting out clothes for their church jumble sale.

Unable to hold on any longer, Luke tiptoed bare footed into the bathroom and relieved himself. After pulling the chain, he put the plug in the sink and began having a wash. It was when his face was covered in soapy water that he remembered the old man with the grey-white hair and his strange daughter Anne Droyd. He paused and looked in the mirror. A blond-headed lad with a foam-covered face stared back. Had the Professor and the android been real or had he dreamt it?

He got his answer from the landing. 'I wonder how Professor Droyd slept last night. Do you think those Foundation people discovered where he is hiding?' It was Gezz, half-asleep in her pink nightie, waiting to use the toilet. Luke swished water over his soapy face and then emptied the sink. 'I don't think so,' he said, drying himself on a bath towel. 'If he and Anne have laid low, no one will have found them.'

He passed Gezz and went back into the box room to get dressed. 'I only hope Malcolm has had the sense to keep quiet about it with his mum and dad.' There was no reply from the bathroom. Gezz was clearly having a good think about it all.

Breakfast was great. They had a choice of three cereals, *Weetabix*, porridge or *Frosties*. Luke went for his usual *Weetabix*. He loved stirring it up into a mushy brown goo. It seemed to taste better that way somehow. Gezz went for the *Frosties*. They were a bit too sweet for Luke, very sickly, but it was clear from Gezz's expression that she loved them.

Mrs Atkinson spoon-fed baby Ross some *Farley's Rusks* as he sat in his high chair, while Mr Atkinson busily cooked sausages and bacon in a big frying pan. Five eggs sat on the work surface, one each for Mrs Atkinson, Gezz and Luke, and two for Mr Atkinson. He always had two. Luke loved having breakfast here, because at his own house he always had to get his own, and that meant just bunging a bowl of cereal into the microwave and having a glass of milk.

The bacon and sausages sizzled as Mr Atkinson scooped them up on to the plates which sat evenly spaced on the worktop. He then cracked a couple of eggs and spilled their contents into the pan. 'Now don't forget, Gezz,' Mr Atkinson reminded his daughter while spooning fat onto the two frying eggs in his pan. 'We have our jumble sale for Barnardo's today. So if there is anything you want to get rid of, put it out on your bed.'

Luke watched Gezz munching on her *Frosties*. She seemed to have something on her mind. 'Do I really have to go to the jumble sale today?'

It was Gezz's mother who answered, her pretty features acquiring a look of surprise. 'Of course you will have to come,' she said, a teaspoon full of mushed *Rusks* hanging limply in her hand. 'The sale is to raise money for poor children.'

'But it's just that I agreed to meet a friend,' said Gezz as sorrowfully as she could. Luke raised an eyebrow. He knew that last bit was a lie.

Mrs Atkinson continued feeding her baby boy. 'Well, you'll just have to unagree it, won't you?'

Gezz scowled at the sarcastic remark. Luke just kept staring at his *Weetabix* and said nothing. *I thought religious people weren't supposed to be sarcastic,* he mused to himself.

Mrs Atkinson glanced up and caught sight of Gezz's sulking features. 'Put your face straight,' she commanded in a stern voice, and then almost immediately, as if correcting herself, softened and said, 'Who is your friend, anyway?'

'She's called Anne,' offered Gezz, and Luke smiled to himself. *So she wasn't really lying after all.*

Mrs Atkinson picked up the baby's breakfast bowl and dropped it into the sink. 'Oh?' she asked quizzically. 'Anne who? Do I know her?'

'Anne Droyd,' Gezz replied. 'We met her last night.'

Gezz's father let out a good-natured laugh as he dropped the last fried egg on to his plate. '*Anne Droyd*?' he smirked. 'It sounds like something out of an Isaac Asimov novel.'

Luke's curiosity was suddenly aroused. 'Who's Isaac Asimov?' He noticed Mrs Atkinson close her eyes and groan as her husband launched into an excitable display of zeal.

'Well,' he beamed, almost as though he had been turned into a ten-year-old boy and then asked about his favourite comic, 'Isaac Asimov was the first science fiction writer to use the word android. In fact he invented it. An android is a…'

Luke cut in, very matter of fact, 'A robot that looks like a real person,' he said. 'We know.'

Mr and Mrs Atkinson exchanged glances briefly, clearly not used to being interrupted by a child. 'Quite,' said Gezz's father as he placed the cooked breakfasts on to the table. 'You should read *I, Robot*. It's brilliant.'

'No, John,' reproved Mrs Atkinson with irritation. 'He's far too young to be reading Asimov. Anyway, why do you want to fill his head with rubbish like that? It's all pie-in-the sky nonsense.'

Mr. Atkinson looked a bit hurt by his wife's casual dismissal. Luke felt sorry for him. 'I once saw the film *Blade Runner* on video when my uncle rented it out,' he offered. 'That had androids in it.'

Mr. Atkinson sat at the table and stared into nothingness. 'Oh, yes,' he breathed in an almost sacred whisper. 'Classic, that. Based on the Philip K. Dick novel *Do Androids Dream of Electric Sheep?* That's another one you should read. It's miles better than the film.'

Mrs Atkinson was getting tired of this now. 'Your parents let you watch films like *Blade Runner*?' she cut in. 'That's rated 18, isn't it?'

'I don't know,' Luke shrugged. 'Anyway, it's not my mum and dad who let me watch it. It was my Uncle Darren.'

Gezz's mother tucked into her bacon, sausage and egg. 'We got rid of our television when we started attending chapel,' she said airily. Gezz shot Luke a kind of smile-frown, as if to say sorry for her mum's preaching.

'Why not bring this Anne to chapel with you, dear?' said Mrs Atkinson.

'I don't think she's very religious,' replied Gezz. Then she considered. 'In fact, I don't think she's very anything.'

'Well, that doesn't matter,' said the girl's mother. 'Your father and I weren't religious at all until we had our eyes opened.'

Gezz's dad leant forward with a kindly grin. 'So, if you've got any clothes you can part with, put them on your bed before you go out to play.' His daughter shot him a knowing smile, feeling only a little guilty over wriggling out of the chapel jumble sale. 'OK,' she said, and the family finished their breakfast in silence.

* * *

Mr and Mrs Atkinson stood at the boot of their Nissan car, stuffing it with bloated bin liners full of old clothes. Luke and Gezz watched as they tried to cram as much in as possible. Baby Ross was already harnessed into the back seat of the car and giggled and waved in his usual happy way.

Luke turned as his own front door opened inwards slowly. Embarrassment overwhelmed him as his mother appeared dressed in a white dressing gown plastered around the hem with big red love hearts. Her tangle of brown hair was tied up with an elastic band and her eye-liner from the day before was smudged down the sides of her cheeks. A line of blue smoke trickled from the freshly lit cigarette she held in her right hand as she opened the plastic porch door. 'Hiya, Lukey,' she said. 'Did ya have a good night, love?'

'Yes, Mum,' said the boy. He felt his cheeks turn a shade of crimson as the woman slipped her cigarette into her mouth so she could bend down to pick up the two bottles of milk waiting beside the step.

Mr Atkinson, whose head had been buried in the back of his car, straightened up and waved briefly. 'Good morning, Paula,' he said. 'Looking forward to six weeks of school holidays?'

The young boy's mother laughed, her cigarette bobbing up and down in her mouth as she spoke. 'Oh aye, John. Like a pain in the...' She cut herself off and grinned wickedly. 'Bum.'

Mrs Atkinson trudged out of her house with another hefty bin bag. 'Do you think you could get one more in, John?'

Before her husband could answer, Luke's mum said, 'You've got a lot of clothes there, Ness. I'll be surprised if you've got any left.'

Luke watched Mrs Atkinson struggle to control her patience. 'Did you manage to have a root round yourself?'

'Nah,' came the dismissive reply. 'We're not into church or owt like that, are we, Lukey?'

Luke glared at the floor and said nothing.

'But, surely you are interested in orphaned children, Paula?' pressed Gezz's mother. Luke noticed Mr Atkinson send his wife a reproving glance, which he imagined meant 'leave it'. And it worked too, as Vanessa Atkinson forced a smile and got into the passenger side of the car.

Mr Atkinson slammed down the boot and then headed for the front door. 'Now then, Gezz,' he said as he took the door knocker in his hand. 'You have got your key, haven't you?' Luke watched as Gezz checked her jeans pocket. 'Yep,' she said. Luke knew she always kept her house key in her jeans so as not to get it tangled with her den key hanging round her neck.

'Good,' said Mr Atkinson and slammed the front door shut. 'We are likely to be out most of the morning, until about one. So if you want lunch, you will have to make yourself a jam sandwich or something.'

'OK.'

Mr Atkinson opened the driver's door of the car. 'We'll probably be having lunch for proper at half-past one.' He paused and waved at Luke's mum who was still standing in her porch holding the two bottles of milk in her arm. 'Enjoy the rest of the day, Paula,' he said.

Luke's mum drew hard on her cigarette, which had burned down to about half-way now, and inhaled the smoke. Her eyes seemed to water a little and Luke guessed that she might have breathed quite a lot in this time. 'You too, kiddo,' she said to Luke before closing the porch door. She blew her smoke back out, leaving it swirling around in the porch, stepped through the second door and shut it behind her. *I wish she didn't smoke*, Luke considered for a second. *It can't be doing her any good.*

Mr Atkinson had climbed into the car and belted up. He turned the engine over and reversed the vehicle backwards slowly on to the road, leaving a patch of dried black oil on the parking place. Then, after a 'pip' of the horn he and Mrs Atkinson gave a quick wave and sped off to deliver the bin liners full of clothes to the chapel.

Luke huffed to himself and then gazed along the crescent of houses. 'Well,' he announced. 'I suppose we had better see if Malc's ready.' Gezz grinned and he smiled too. He knew what she was thinking. Will the Professor and Anne still be there? It was always like that these days. They knew one another so well, they could almost read each other's minds. Luke enjoyed having a friend like that. It was special.

★ ★ ★

It seemed to be taking ages for anyone to answer the door. But then it always did at Malcolm's. The closed curtains twitched as their friend peeped out to see who it was, the darkness behind him engulfing the living room like a heavy cloud about to release its downpour. Malcolm was wearing a black and white Bolton Wanderers football T-shirt which had seen better days and a pair of old jeans. With his spectacles in one hand and a chocolate biscuit in the other, he raced to the front door to greet Luke and Gezz.

'Are you ready?' asked Luke impatiently.

'Yeah,' said Malcolm. 'What's the weather like?'

'It's warm, like yesterday.'

'Oh good, that means I won't need my coat.' The chubby boy stuffed the biscuit in his mouth whole, slipped on his glasses and shut the front door. 'Do you fin the profeffer will thtill be in thedden?' he asked, crushed fragments of biscuit churning round in his mouth like the contents of a cement mixer.

'What?' asked Luke irritably.

Malcolm paused and swallowed hard. 'I said,' he replied, wiping chocolate from his lips with a bare hand and sounding much clearer now, 'Do you think the Professor will still be in the den?'

They set off walking. Gezz had a spring in her step, clearly eager to get to the embankment. 'If he's got any sense he'll stay out of sight. He won't be able to risk being seen.'

They passed a small girl on a tricycle. 'I think I'll go on my bike later.'

'You'll have to get the chain fixed first,' Luke reminded her.

'I know,' groaned Gezz adjusting her hairband slightly. 'My dad still hasn't got round to it.'

'You'll have to bring it to my house. My dad's good at that sort of thing.'

'OK, I will.'

* * *

The children arrived at the road which led to the disused railway embankment. There were houses stretching down the road, quite posh ones too, and then there was a railing for a few metres, after which the houses continued. The children understood that where the railing was now, a bridge used to be when their grandparents were young. Steam trains once ran on the embankment and went under the road to the other side. But now the whole thing had been filled in and there were just slopes of grass on either side.

A gravel path lay where the track used to be. On the right-hand side, the path went all the way up to Bolton, while on the left it passed the swimming baths and stretched up into Worsley and then Monton. Before it got to the swimming baths, though, it forked off into two lines, and it was the second line which arched round to meet the back gardens of terraced houses and the trench that hid the den.

Malcolm froze as he caught sight of the low heavy railway bridge in the distance, threatening the horizon with its over-bearing presence. Luke tutted, irritated by his friend.

'It's only a bridge,' he grumbled.

Gezz walked on, her thumbs resting on the ridges of her jeans pockets. 'Come on,' she breezed. 'Let's see if they're still there.'

Cautiously, the three children hovered near the dugout containing their headquarters. Gezz looked about suspiciously. 'Can't see anyone.'

'Right,' said Luke authoritatively. 'Let's go for it.' And within seconds both he and his best friend had jumped into the groove. Luke looked up and tutted again. 'Hurry up, Malc,' he hissed. 'Someone will see you.'

Malcolm negotiated the steep narrow ridge and landed on his knees with a bump. 'Sorry,' he muttered, wiping himself down.

Luke leaned on the prickly door of the air-raid shelter. There was no sign of movement whatsoever. *They can't still be asleep*, he thought. He put his mouth as close to the door as he could without being stung by nettles and whispered, 'Professor Droyd? Anne?' But all that greeted him was silence. He turned to the others. 'No answer.'

Malcolm went into a panic straight away. 'Oh,' he mumbled pathetically. 'The Foundation must have caught them. They will have taken them away for questioning. If they torture the Professor, he might tell them about us. Or they might download Anne's memory banks and get the information from her. They will be straight round to our houses to get us.'

Luke did not even answer. Malcolm always got in a panic like this. He was no help. Luke put his hand inside the neck of his T-shirt, but something was wrong. No key. Then he gave a relieved smile as he remembered. 'Of course. I gave my key to the Professor.'

'Here, take mine,' offered Gezz and reached for the chain hanging about her neck. Luke took it and inserted it into the Yale lock. 'Professor, Anne,' he whispered to the door. 'Stand back. We're coming in.' And with that he turned the key and pushed open the door.

All three children looked on in stunned silence. Apart from three upturned buckets and a torch dangling from the ceiling, the shelter was empty.

10

Two Minutes to Surrender

Gezz frowned and turned to Luke. 'They've gone,' she said.

'So I see,' said Luke.

Malcolm began to panic again. 'See,' he moaned. 'I told you they would be. The Foundation has got them.'

'Shush!' hissed Gezz authoritatively. 'Someone's coming.' The three children threw themselves against the wall of the trench.

Luke held his breath as best he could, letting it in and out a little at a time. He glanced at Malcolm, who was gritting his teeth and screwing up his eyes. *Stupid mard,* he thought. *As if that's going to make any difference.* He saw Gezz looking at the door of the den, which was wide open and revealing its secrets to the world. He tried to move in an attempt to close it, but it was no use. Any movement at all would alert the unknown passers-by.

Suddenly there was a voice from up above, right over their heads. To Luke's relief it was flat and emotionless, a little girl's voice. 'Optical scan reveals no humanoids for half a mile, Father.'

'Excellent!' came the reply, the second voice elderly and yet youthful at the same time.

The Professor leapt down into the trench, followed by his android daughter, neither of them exhibiting signs of fatigue. The children exhaled noisily and entered the den. The Professor and Anne followed, closing the door behind them.

It seemed strange to Luke as they all took their positions and the den became tight and overcrowded once more. It confirmed in all the youngsters' minds that the events of the previous day had been very real indeed. No one spoke for a minute or two, until Luke finally plucked up the courage. 'So,' he said. 'What were you doing outside? I mean, weren't you risking it a bit?'

The Professor smiled that gentle smile as all eyes fell on him. All except Anne's eyes, that is, who remained in her usual trance staring at the opposite wall. 'It's good to have a brisk walk early in the morning,' the Professor said. 'And when your neighbours get up as early as the birds do, you have little choice but to wake up yourself.'

The children smiled, each imagining how hard it must be to stay asleep through the dawn chorus. 'We also needed to hide our van properly,' added the old man.

Malcolm's face had adopted that serious glare again. 'Are there any signs of the Foundation?'

The Professor leaned back on the corrugated metal wall. 'Oh yes,' he sighed. 'They were out in force this morning.'

Luke was appalled by the statement. 'They were?' he wondered. 'We haven't seen anyone.'

'They are posing as plain-clothes police officers,' said the Professor with a wry grin, as if admiring their guile. 'They are knocking on people's doors and asking them if they have seen an old man with a young blonde child.' He turned to his creation. 'Is that not so, Anne?'

The automaton remained expressionless, her eyes fixed on the wall in front of her. 'Yes, Father,' she said.

'They won't stop until they have caught us,' sighed the Professor, almost to himself.

'No, Father, they won't,' responded Anne.

Gezz had been very quiet, quite absorbed with the seriousness of it all. She adjusted her hairband. 'So, what are you going to do?'

'Well, I cannot stay here forever, can I?' laughed the man. But Luke recognized the laugh as a worried one, the type of laugh you do when you have no way out. 'Once they have knocked on all the houses they will rethink their operation. And when they check Anne's blueprint documents and study them closely, they will discover that she has a homing beacon.' He paused, his eyes grey and sad. 'And that will be that.'

'Can't you turn her homing beacon off?' suggested Malcolm.

The Professor shook his head. 'I need it at the ready in case I get parted from her myself.'

Luke felt a surge of hope and leaned forward to pat Professor Droyd on the knee. 'Well, so long as you're with us, you'll never lose her.'

'It is not as simple as that,' smiled the Professor weakly. 'We need provisions if we are to live as fugitives. We cannot stay here. If we do, it will mean that you are involved and then the Foundation will come after you.'

Luke shrugged. 'It's all right. We don't mind.'

'Speak for yourself,' muttered Malcolm.

'No, no,' Droyd shook his head. 'It is not all right. I am grateful, really I am. Geraldine, Luke and Malcolm, really I am. My true friends in my hour of need.' He stroked the side of his nose. 'But I am hungry and thirsty. And Anne needs a place to recharge her power source. She has conserved it as best as she can. But she cannot recharge herself here.'

Luke shot a glance at Gezz. 'What about your place?'

Gezz looked horrified. 'Eh?' she gulped.

'Your mum and dad are out till lunchtime.'

'So?'

'Well, the Professor and Anne could rest up there.'

Gezz was shaking her head the way people do when they really don't like the sound of something. 'Oh I dunno, Luke. What if those Foundation people find us all together?'

'They won't,' Luke insisted. 'We'll take the Professor and Anne back for a bite to eat and to recharge her batteries.' He shrugged confidently. 'Your mum and dad won't even know they've been there.'

This time the Professor said nothing. Luke could tell that, really, he desperately needed food and drink and that the robot would soon run out of power if she wasn't recharged. The Professor had turned down their offer of help out of politeness and concern for their welfare, but really he needed them. Luke recognized that Gezz had noticed it too. She wasn't thick. She knew that if she didn't agree, it would be the end for Wolfgang and Anne Droyd.

Gezz nodded slowly, still looking worried and unsure. 'All right,' she said. 'But we'll have to be quick. If my mum and dad find you, there'll be lots of questions. They might even call the police.'

Malcolm suddenly got to his feet in a flurry of uncharacteristic determination. 'Well, let's get to it,' he said. 'The sooner we get them there, the sooner we get them away.'

Gezz nodded again and stood up. As she did so, the Professor launched forward and hugged her affectionately. Luke could see she was overwhelmed and he had to stifle a laugh. The Professor's wild hair brushed against the girl's face. 'Oh, thank you, my dear,' he was saying. 'A thousand times, thank you. You are a very brave little girl.' Then he stood as best he could with his back to the door and faced Luke and Malcolm, his complexion red with emotion, his eyes glassy and tearful. 'You are all brave. And kind. You have good hearts.'

Luke gestured at the door, the tenseness of the situation getting to him now. Professor Droyd responded accordingly and opened the door an inch at a time, all the while checking for unknowing passers-by.

The coast was clear. The four humans filed out into the trench and ducked down below ground level. The Professor called in a whisper to his android creation, who was still sitting on her haunches and staring at the far wall inside the air-raid shelter. 'Anne, dear,' he croaked. 'Come out here and use your fibre-optic lens to check for humans on ground level. Make sure that you are not seen.'

As the robot girl confirmed the order and came into the trench, Droyd smiled and whispered to his friends. 'You have to make the instructions as precise as possible, you see. Her brain, at the moment, is more of a computer than a mind. So she will interpret your wishes literally. She can only do that.'

The children watched, mesmerized, as Anne held up her little finger as she had done the night before, and extended her wire-thin camera lens just above the ridge of the dugout. The fibre swivelled, taking in the view up above.

'Back at the base,' the Professor began in a whispered grin while awaiting the verdict, 'I had this very basic room built into the corner of the main laboratory. It had a bunk and a table for reading and studying, one door and a little window with a pair of small curtains. Anyway, one evening while Anne was still activated I said, "Anne, child, draw the curtains for me please", meaning close the curtains. And before I knew what was happening she picked up a biro and one of my notepads and drew a sketch of the curtains!' The old gent chuckled as quietly as he could. 'It was a real work of art too, but you can see what I mean about being very literal with your instructions.'

The children's stifled laughter was halted abruptly by the authoritative voice of the automaton. 'There are no human creatures in the immediate vicinity.'

Professor Droyd reacted with sharp instinct. He yanked the door of the den shut and began scrambling up the trench on to the wild grass surrounding the gravel path. The children followed suit, Luke and Gezz first, with Malcolm taking a little longer as usual. Anne retracted the fibre-optic lens into her little finger and then positioned herself in a crouch.

Luke watched in fascination. *She's not going to jump it, is she?* he thought to himself. Then he got his answer as Anne arched her arms back and leapt in the air. Her mechanical legs catapulted her up above ground level. Then, in an instant, she thrust her right leg forward and landed before them, her blond ponytail swishing from side to side with the G force, but her face as undisturbed and deadpan as ever.

'Wow,' whispered the children in unison. Luke was especially impressed. It felt different, more personal somehow, seeing Anne use her superhuman strength right in front of them. He looked at her pretty face and stared deep into her crystal-blue eyes. She was amazing.

'Come on,' said Gezz, breaking his trance. 'We had better go.'

As the entourage moved on up the path toward the main road, the Professor turned to his daughter, who was still standing rigid by the edge of the trench. 'Follow us, Anne.'

'Yes, Father,' replied the girl, before setting off behind them at a rhythmic pace.

Gezz led the group, her mind clearly taken up with the seriousness of what they were doing. Luke hovered at the back, trying to get a better look at his wonder girl, while Malcolm walked at the Professor's side. Big scruff and little scruff, like father and son. 'Professor,' the boy inquired. 'Why does Anne only speak when you ask her a question or give her a command?'

The group headed up the gravel slope to where the railed main road stretched across. 'Because,' Professor Droyd answered, all the time glancing about for unusual activity and strangers, 'she is just a walking computer at the moment, as I said before. I haven't activated her learning circuits yet.'

Malcolm was getting out of breath now, the steep climb a little too much for him.

'Come on, mardy,' Luke teased from behind. 'Get some of that weight off you.'

Malcolm ignored the slight and continued quizzing the Professor. 'So when you activate her learning circuits, will that change the way she acts?'

'Not at first,' said Droyd. 'At first she will be very much as she is now. But her brain will start to question things, and as her data banks store more and more information, in time she will become like a real person.'

'So, how will she learn?'

'The same way we learn,' said the Professor simply. 'She will ask questions and process the answers. And if she receives more than one answer, or conflicting answers, I am hoping she will be able to reason them out.'

Luke was intrigued by this. 'So will she be able to feel emotions like we do, Professor?'

'Ah, well,' Droyd replied, somewhat out of puff himself now. 'That all depends on the biological part of her brain, the flesh and blood part. It's only small, and protected by the machine part, but I hope she will develop feelings like a normal person.' He stopped walking to catch his breath. 'Only time will tell.'

Luke watched as the old man bent down to rub his legs. 'I thought your legs are part machine.'

'They are,' breathed the Professor.

'Then why are you getting tired?'

'The power in the battery cells is getting low. I am having to rely more on my eighty-year-old bones.' The Professor stood upright, his face etched in pain. 'Ooh,' he moaned. 'It's no use, I am getting old.'

Anne stopped abruptly behind her aged creator. 'Father, are you all right?'

The Professor nodded, the colour coming back into his lined cheeks. 'Yes, dear,' he puffed. 'I am all right. Follow us.' At the command the robot immediately resumed its rhythmic walking.

Gezz was standing on the pavement by the railing. She turned to face Luke and the others. 'There's a man coming,' she hissed. The two boys looked to the Professor for instructions. 'Is he on his own?' he asked.

'No,' said Gezz. 'He's got a dog with him.'

The Professor smiled. 'Right,' he announced. 'Everyone stay together. Pretend we are a family. I am your granddad taking you out on a walk. You are my grandchildren.'

The children nodded their agreement and the motley crew caught up with Gezz on the pavement. And sure enough, there was a middle-aged man wearing a maroon V-necked pullover and tweed trousers walking up the grass slope on the other side of the road. He held an extendible lead in his hand.

The cable flexed and retracted as his black spaniel at the other end mooched about in the undergrowth. The man nodded and smiled at the Professor and his children. 'Hello there.'

The Professor grinned back and waved. 'Ah, good morning, sir.' His German accent changed the word 'morning' into 'morninck', and it seemed to Luke that the man had recognized this. He could tell by the subtle change in the man's smile. The boy felt worried now. Had the man heard about the German Professor and his android daughter? Had those people from the Foundation been to the man's house posing as concerned police officers, as the Professor had seen earlier in the morning?

'All right, children,' said the Professor, standing at the edge of the curb and taking Gezz and Luke by the hand on either side. 'Wait until the road is clear and then cross.' Luke flinched again. 'Children' sounded like 'chealdren' and 'wait' like 'vait'. It was a stupid plan. It was obvious to all and sundry that they were not his children.

A car trundled by at reasonable speed, and then the old man urged his group to cross the road. As he reached the other side, Luke chanced a quick sneak at the man and his dog. To the boy's horror, the man had now crossed the road himself and was glancing over his shoulder back at Anne, who was trailing the group at the rear, still walking in that funny rigid robotic way. When the man's eyes met with Luke's, he turned quickly and hurried down the gravel path.

★ ★ ★

'So this is where you live?' exclaimed the Professor with great enthusiasm as the children led him to the opening of Century Lodge. The old man grinned and took in the environment. The lodge itself dominated the landscape with two or three fishermen dotted about its banks casting lines and drinking coffee. To the left stood the gritty mill, its bricks dirty and old, its windows long and black, and an extremely long chimney stretched up like a giant cigar. The building haunted the place like an old ghost refusing to budge, desperate to remind the people of a bygone age.

To the right of the lodge was an area of wild grass, a single tarmac road and a semicircle of new-looking houses, very new compared to the mill. The housing estate directly faced the old factory, as though challenging it. To Luke, it seemed like the houses were saying, 'This is our land now. Push off, you've had your time,' and Century Mill was saying, 'No. I was here first. I've been here for a hundred years. I've seen two world wars. I have more right to be here than you.'

'That's where I live,' said Malcolm excitedly. He pointed to the house with the battered front door and dark living-room windows. The Professor looked at the dwelling momentarily and gave a polite smile. It was obvious to everyone that Malcolm's mum and dad were still in bed. The closed upstairs curtains were a dead giveaway. Luke had heard adults mutter and point as they walked by this house. They would snigger and scowl and say things like, 'They'll be sleeping it off again. That poor lad. I feel sorry for him.' Luke kept one eye on Malcolm as they continued on up the pavement. At times he felt sorry for him too.

An expression of relief fell upon Gezz's face as she saw the empty drive in front of her house. The Nissan was nowhere to be seen. An oval black mark graced the area where the car normally stood. There had been an oil leak last summer and Mr Atkinson spent a whole afternoon trying to repair it. Mrs Atkinson tried her best to shift the stain, but to little avail. Luke didn't know what the fuss was about. No one ever noticed it normally.

Gezz's eyes scanned the next-door garden. The Davidsons' sports car was still parked in front of their pristine white plastic porch door. 'Your mum and dad are still in, Luke.'

The boy shrugged nonchalantly. 'Oh, that doesn't mean anything,' he said. 'If anyone has knocked on our door, they wouldn't have got very far. My mum and dad don't like talking to people at the door. Sometimes, if they know who it is and don't want to be bothered, they don't even answer it.'

The group fell silent as they approached Gezz's house. The girl adjusted her hairband nervously and reached into her jeans pocket for her front-door key. She struggled and fumbled and her eyes began to water. 'I can't get my key out, I'm so nervous.'

Luke's heart went out to her. He tried always to protect her when she got like this. But this time there was little he could do. He looked to the Professor, who in turn addressed Anne. 'Anne,' he said, choosing his words carefully. 'Scan the lock of this house and select the appropriate key shape. Then unlock the door.'

'Yes, Father,' replied the robot blonde, and immediately set about running her outstretched right palm over the varnished wood. She brought it to a halt over the golden handle and key hole. 'Lock identified,' she announced out loud. Then she inserted the tip of her forefinger into the lock. 'Selecting,' she said, her voice as blank as ever. Luke stepped closer to watch the wonder girl in action. His eyes bulged as the girl's finger was morphing and changing shape. It was going narrow and curved to match the shape of the lock as it pushed its way in.

Once the android's finger was in as far as it could go, her eyes wobbled slightly, as if her computer brain was acknowledging a job well done. 'Key shape selected,' she said. 'Unlocking door.' And with a turn of the finger, the lock rattled and rolled back.

'Incredible,' said Malcolm in a whisper. 'It's just incredible.' All three children watched in amazement as the robot removed her finger from the door, its tip moulded perfectly into the shape of Gezz's key, while still having all the features of a human finger. It had skin and tiny hairs and a varnished pink nail covering the key-shaped end. In seconds the nail had changed from its jagged form back into a regular little girl's forefinger.

Gezz stepped forward and tried the door to her house. It clicked open with ease and a broad grin replaced her worried look. 'Cool,' she enthused and beckoned the others inside.

The Professor surveyed the neat and tidy living room with interest. A bookcase stood where a television would normally be and the old man was impelled to take a look. He scanned the middle shelf and stopped at a large family Bible. 'Ah,' he beamed approvingly. 'I see your mother and father cling to old-fashioned principles.'

Gezz blushed a little and sat in her favourite armchair. 'They say the principles are timeless and that if everyone lived by them there would be no wars in the world.'

The Professor slid the book back on to the shelf. 'Love, joy, peace, kindness, self-control,' he said loudly. 'Mutual respect and common decency.' He seemed to be talking to himself rather than to the children. 'Yes, these are the things which make a better world.'

Luke flopped on to the settee. 'My dad says religion causes all the wars in the world,' he scoffed. 'If there was no religion, people would have nothing to fight about.'

'Oh,' said the Professor, waggling a bony finger at the young sceptic, but still smiling all the same. 'People will always have something to fight about whether religion exists or not. They don't seem to be able to help it.'

Malcolm looked quite stirred by that last observation. 'That's why the Foundation want to turn Anne into the perfect soldier and sell her to the world's armies.' The Professor put his arm around the boy's shoulders in a fatherly way. 'That is correct,' he said proudly. 'Some people will do anything for money. Anything, even kill.'

Luke pulled his face, not at all impressed by the old man's speech. 'My dad says there's nothing wrong with money. If people are lucky enough to make it they should have nice things. What's wrong with having nice things?'

'It depends what they do to get them,' said the Professor, staring down his nose at the boy.

'My dad says it's only people who have no money that complain about it,' Luke continued. 'They're jealous.'

'Really,' said the Professor with an exaggerated nod. 'And what does your mother have to say about money?'

Luke shrugged. 'Nothing,' he said. 'She just spends it.'

The reaction was instantaneous. The whole group burst into laughter. The Professor first, then Gezz and Malcolm, and finally Luke, who had to admit it did sound pretty funny. Only Anne stayed silent, her face smooth and unmoved. She wasn't refusing to laugh, Luke knew that, nor was she trying to make a point like grown-ups sometimes do. She just didn't understand what 'funny' was, the same way that vacuum cleaners and CD players don't understand. She was just a machine like them. Who ever heard of a washing machine having a laugh? It simply did not happen.

And yet in other ways Anne was more than just a computer. What computer could talk and run? What machine had the ability to morph a finger into a key and unlock a door? Even Luke's computer in his bedroom couldn't do that.

'I don't mean to be rude,' piped Gezz, making everyone calm down. 'But if you want to eat, and recharge Anne before my parents get back, you had better do it now.'

The Professor nodded seriously. 'Of course, you are right.' His eyes darted about the room searching for something. 'Do you have an ordinary 240 volt socket in here?'

Gezz clearly had no idea what a 240 volt socket was. 'Eh?' she frowned.

'A p-l-u-g s-o-c-k-e-t,' said Luke, almost spelling it out.

'Oh, yes,' replied Gezz. 'Behind the bookcase.'

Professor Droyd rubbed his hands eagerly. 'Excellent,' he said, and turned to the android. 'Anne,' he directed. 'Connect yourself to the power supply behind the bookcase and charge yourself to maximum power.'

The robot gave a slight nod and strolled over to the bookcase. 'Yes, Father,' she said politely.

The automaton sat herself down and leaned against the radiator on the wall beneath the main window. Then she unbuttoned her silver dungarees on the left side and rolled up her white cotton T-shirt.

Luke strained himself to watch as a small bump pushed itself up in the girl's side just below her rib cage. 'Extending power connector to mains supply,' she announced. The bump grew and narrowed until it thinned out into a skin-coated flex. The end of the wire hovered over the electric plug hole for a moment, swishing to and fro. Anne's eyes moved slightly as her computer brain processed some information. 'Connector type identified,' she said.

Suddenly the long wire grew itself a standard three-pin electric plug, skin coloured, of course, and slotted itself into the socket. Anne's eyes closed as she absorbed the energy from the wall. Luke stared in silent fascination.

'Oh,' Professor Droyd exclaimed, wiping his brow with the back of his hand. 'I could do with regenerating myself.'

Malcolm was shocked. 'You're not going to plug yourself in as well, are you?'

The Professor let out a hearty laugh. 'No, no, no, child. I mean I could do with some food. I have a built-in mechanism that will convert the body's energies into electrical power for my robot limbs.'

'Will ham sandwiches do?' asked Gezz, already heading for the kitchen. The Professor and Malcolm followed.

Luke was now aware that the others had gone for a bite to eat. He sat alone with the 'sleeping' android. He couldn't resist touching her left hand with the tips of his fingers. His face screwed as he felt the skin, cold and peach-like with steel bones running underneath.

He jumped as the machine's eyes flicked open, blue and dazzling. 'Please do not touch this unit while regeneration is in process,' it said. And it was then that Luke realized 'she' really was only an 'it', a machine, a tool, nothing more.

'Mm,' said a voice at the door bridging the living room and the kitchen. It was the Professor, munching on a ham sandwich. 'This is delicious,' he beamed. He stared at Luke for a moment in his weird absent-minded way and then at Anne, who had closed her eyes again, almost drinking in the electricity. Then he snapped his fingers and burst into excited life again. 'Do you have any clothes that would fit Anne?' he said to an unseen person on the other side of the door.

'I might have,' said Gezz's voice. 'In fact, my parents have been sorting out clothes for a jumble sale and they couldn't fit all the bags in the car.'

The Professor clapped his hands. 'Excellent!'

Gezz emerged from the kitchen and passed Luke, who was still kneeling by the radiator, to trot upstairs to her parents' room.

'Power cells fully recharged,' announced Anne, taking everyone by surprise. Luke watched as she unplugged herself and began retracting the flesh-covered wire until it was just a bump under her rib cage. Then the bump smoothed itself out and was gone. Anne rolled down her T-shirt and fastened her silver dungarees, before getting to her feet. She stared, unblinking, at the far wall, awaiting her next instruction.

Suddenly there was a knock at the front door. Everyone froze. Even the movement upstairs as Gezz searched for old jeans and tops ceased. Luke turned very slowly and peeped through the corner of the living-room window. His eyes bulged. 'There's a police car outside,' he hissed. 'There's a bloke stood at the front door in a suit and an overcoat.'

Professor Droyd looked terrified. 'Is there anyone with him?'

'There are two uniformed policemen stood behind him.'

'Anyone else?'

Luke strained at the car in the road. There were shadows in the back seat. Two men. He struggled to control himself as he recognized one of them. 'There's a chap in the police car,' he whispered. 'I think it's the man who we saw walking his dog earlier. He must have grassed us up.'

'They probably contacted him this morning,' said the Professor hurriedly. 'He must have recognized the description of Anne and myself when he saw us on the road.'

There was a further rap of knuckles on the door. Everyone stayed silent and did not move. Luke could hear his own heart thumping through his chest. He tried to control his breathing, keeping it as slow and deliberate as he could. His heart felt as though it was going to burst through his ribs. Almost unbelievably, Anne did not react at all.

'Open up,' commanded a gruff voice. 'This is the police. We know you are in there, Droyd. You have two minutes to surrender. After that, we are coming in.'

11

'We'll Look after Her'

Malcolm could be seen peeping round the kitchen door, a half-eaten ham sandwich hanging from his mouth. 'What are we gonna do?' he whined, his voice muffled by bread and thinly cut meat. He was unable to mask his fear though.

The man's voice continued. 'Any other people in there, you are harbouring a dangerous criminal. He has abducted a young girl from her parents and has stolen government property.'

All eyes were on the Professor now, who shook his head violently and mouthed, 'He's lying,' silently.

'If you release him to us,' said the voice, 'your part in this will not be documented.'

By now, Gezz had managed to creep to the bottom of the stairs, clinging to a polythene bag full of clothes. She entered the living room and, like the other children, awaited the Professor's next instruction.

The old man glared back, his eyes alight with anxiety. 'All right,' he finally said. 'There's only one way to deal with this.' He turned to face the open door of the hallway and raised his voice. 'Very well,' he shouted. 'I will give myself up. Please give me a minute to bid my young friends farewell.'

The children looked at one another. They did not know what to do. Gezz burst into tears, unable to handle the tension any longer. Luke put his arm around her and gave her a loving cuddle. The voice outside responded, 'No tricks, Droyd. We're ready for you now.'

Malcolm plucked up the courage to enter the living room and stand by his friends, while the Professor knelt before them. 'Now,' said Wolfgang Droyd. 'You have been very brave, all of you. But I have yet one more favour to ask before I go.'

'We'll do anything for you, Professor,' said Malcolm valiantly and the others nodded their agreement.

'Good,' smiled the Professor gently. The children were not ready for what he had to say next. 'Will you take care of Anne for me while I'm away? Will you teach her the ways of humanity?' He looked Gezz right in the eyes. 'Will you teach her to be a girl like you?'

Gezz wiped her eyes. 'You're not taking her with you back to the Foundation?'

'Not if I can help it,' said Droyd defiantly, and the children smiled. 'If you take care of her and treat her as your friend, she should be able to assimilate herself into your society.'

Luke knew the word 'assimilate' from *Star Trek*. The evil robot people called the Borg assimilated humans into their world and turned them into beings like themselves. But here, Anne was going to do something different. She was going to assimilate *herself* into the human community. 'Don't worry, Professor,' said the boy. 'We'll look after her.'

The old man stood. 'Yes, you will,' he said. Then he shot a glance across to his robot creation, who was still staring at the wall, unaffected, unemotional. 'Anne,' said the Professor. 'Activate your learning circuits.'

'Learning circuits activated,' said Anne.

'Activate organic brain component.'

Anne turned to face her creator, as if seeing him for the first time. 'Organic brain component activated, Father.'

'Good,' said the Professor. 'Now, Anne, I have to go away for a while. You must stay here with your new friends, Geraldine, Luke and Malcolm. You will obey their instructions unless they conflict with your prime directives. Do you understand?'

The android stepped forward and scanned the young faces with her sparkling blue eyes. 'I will obey my new friends.' Her eyes focused on each child as she spoke their names out loud. 'Geraldine, Luke and Malcolm.'

'Learn all you can from their experiences as well as your own.'

'I will.'

Professor Droyd tried hard to hold back his tears. 'Goodbye, Anne,' he said, his voice trembling.

'Goodbye, Father,' replied the robot, her tones flat and devoid of feeling.

The man outside had now reached the end of his tether. 'Droyd!' he screamed. 'Your time's up. We're coming in.'

The old man leapt to the front door and flung it open. He beckoned with his left hand for the children to get out of sight. They responded quickly and hid in the kitchen. Luke strained to hear the conversation. 'Well, well,' the Professor was saying. 'Inspector Bullimore. So the Foundation finally persuaded you to use the police force for your own means. How much are they paying you? Does your superior know about this?'

'Watch your tongue, Wolfgang,' the gruff voice replied. 'Now, where's the android?'

'Where you will never find her,' bluffed the Professor.

'Right,' commanded the voice. 'Search the house.'

'No!' the Professor shouted. 'It is me you have sought, and now you have found me.' His voice softened. 'I know our illustrious leader is trying to crack the code for the homing beacon. They will find the robot soon enough. Leave these small children alone. Do you really want to be seen manhandling three eleven-year-olds?'

There was a long pause. Then, 'All right. Take him away.' And with that the front door was slammed shut. The children jumped as the thud resounded through the house, as if punctuating the fact that the Professor had gone. Luke felt all mixed up. He was happy that the ordeal was finally over and that the police had left them alone, but he was deeply troubled too, for the old man had been taken away and who knows what they might do to him? On top of that was the android. She stood there with no sign of concern on her face. What had they let themselves in for?

12

Just Testing

The children sighed loudly. They were not sure whether to be upset or relieved. The sound of rattling keys in the front door renewed the air of tension. Gezz looked at Luke, while he raised his eyebrows at Malcolm. Their new friend said what they were all thinking. 'Someone is entering the house. Have the police returned?'

Gezz peeped round the kitchen door and caught sight of the red Nissan sitting on the drive through the living-room window. Every bone and muscle relaxed and a sense of well-being flooded over her. 'It's my mum and dad,' she breathed with a large grin. 'They've come back from chapel.'

'Great!' Malcolm punched the air. 'We'll be getting some lunch.'

Gezz grimaced at the comment. It irritated her sometimes the way Malcolm simply expected feeding, but she was patient because she knew his own parents did not look after him properly. She remembered how he had devoured his ham sandwich earlier. *He clearly hasn't had any breakfast this morning*, she told herself.

★ ★ ★

'What the heck has been going on in here?' asked Gezz's dad as he stood in the middle of the living room. He picked up the polythene bag containing Gezz's old clothes. Her mum shut the front door and joined him with baby Ross in her arms. 'Was that a police car I saw going up the road?'

'Yes,' her husband said absent-mindedly.

Gezz's mum's eyes homed in on the bag. 'What have they been up to with these old clothes?'

Gezz decided to come clean. 'Oh, hi Mum,' she breezed as she walked into the living room with Luke and Malcolm in tow. 'I was just sorting out some old clothes for Anne. I think they might fit her.'

Her mum frowned. 'Who's Anne?'

'Remember, that new friend I was telling you about?'

'Oh, yes.'

Gezz looked round, only to find that Anne had not joined them from the kitchen. *She must still be in there*, thought the girl, and she recalled what the Professor had told them. The robot should be given very specific instructions at first. 'Anne,' she called. 'Come in here.' Then as an afterthought she added, 'Don't be shy.'

The robot blonde walked into the living room in her rhythmic way and stared at Gezz's parents as though in a trance. They smiled, expecting a few words of greeting. None came. Gezz could feel her face going warm as she blushed with embarrassment. 'Er, this is Anne,' she said.

'Hello, Anne,' offered Gezz's mum meekly.

'Hello, Mum,' replied the automaton.

Luke put his hand to his mouth and tried to halt the fit of giggles taking him over. Gezz's mother gave a very surprised look and turned to her daughter for clarification. Then Gezz realized. She had referred to her mother as 'Mum', and so to all intents and purposes, Anne would call her 'Mum' as her actual name.

Gezz cleared her throat. 'Er, this is my mother, Mrs Atkinson.' Then she pointed to her dad. 'And this is my father, Mr Atkinson.'

'Mrs Atkinson and Mr Atkinson,' repeated Anne.

'That's right,' said Gezz.

'Not Mum and Dad.'

Luke pinched his nose and screwed up his features, trying to hold back his laughter. Tears streamed down his rosy cheeks. Malcolm too attempted to resist the smirk pushing itself about his chops, but it was no use. He turned to face the other way, yet Gezz could still see his shoulders bobbing up and down. 'No,' she explained patiently. 'The words mum and dad are short for mother and father. So I call them Mum and Dad, but you call them Mrs Atkinson and Mr Atkinson.'

'Very well,' said Anne.

Gezz's dad had a go at engaging her in conversation. *This is typical of him*, thought Gezz, *he always thinks he will be able to do it when Mum can't*. 'So then, Anne,' he began. 'Where do you live?'

'I have no fixed abode,' the android stated simply.

'She means,' Gezz cut in quickly, noting more raised eyebrows from her parents, 'that she's an orphan. She lives in a special home up the road.'

'Oh,' said her mum and dad together. Then her mum cleared her throat and started to busy herself about the house. 'Well, it's time I started getting lunch ready.' She turned to the children. 'Do you want some? It's oxtail soup. Luke?'

Luke wiped his eyes with the sleeve of his shirt and nodded. 'Yes, please, Mrs Atkinson.'

'Malcolm?'

Malcolm turned, having got himself under control. 'Yes, Mrs Atkinson, that would be lovely.'

Gezz's mother reluctantly addressed the newcomer. 'Anne?'

Anne glared at her with that blank expression. 'Yes, Mrs Atkinson?'

'Do you like oxtail soup?'

'I do not know,' came the honest reply. 'What is oxtail soup?'

'Oh,' said Gezz's mum with an awkward half-smile. 'Well…it's nice. You can give it a try, can't you? You never know, you might like it.'

'Yes,' said Anne. 'I can give it a try and I might like it.'

'Quite.' And with that Gezz's mother made for the kitchen as quickly as she could. Gezz bent down to her dad's level as he lay Ross on the floor to change his nappy. 'Anne's OK, you know, Dad,' she whispered. 'It's just that she has…' she tried to think hard and remember what her old teacher Mr Davies would have called it. Then finally, '…learning difficulties,' she said. 'But she's nice really.'

Her dad just smiled and carried on undoing Ross's nappy, not entirely convinced.

The children took their places at the kitchen table as Gezz's mum served up piping hot oxtail soup from a pan. She poured the brown liquid into each bowl and put a small plate of buttered bread at the centre of the table. Gezz sat herself next to Anne in case she needed to whisper more instructions. Then a thought occurred to her. Do robots eat food and drink water? She supposed that Anne would have refused lunch if it was going to do her any harm. After all, the flesh part of her still needed feeding.

Gezz's mum sat in her usual place and her dad carried Ross into the kitchen and slid him into the high chair at the end of the table next to his mother. Then he stood at the back of his own chair, bowed his head, closed his eyes and said grace. Everyone except for Anne, who just stared straight ahead at the opposite wall, bowed their heads respectfully. 'For what we are about to receive may the Lord make us truly thankful,' said Gezz's dad in a quiet dignified tone. 'Amen.'

Each in turn repeated, 'Amen,' and then looked gleefully at the steaming bowls of oxtail soup before them.

Anne turned to face Gezz's dad, and Gezz held her breath in anticipation. 'Who were you talking to?' inquired the robot innocently.

Her dad frowned, picked up a piece of bread and began rolling it into a cylinder shape. 'When?'

'When you said, "For what we are about to receive may the Lord make us truly thankful. Amen".'

He just stared at her, his roll of bread gripped horizontally in his hand. His wife shot him a look that might have meant 'be easy on her'. He coughed and gathered his thoughts. 'Well,' he said. 'I was saying a prayer. I was thanking God for the good food He has blessed us with.'

'Where is He?'

'He's in Heaven,' he said slowly, and Gezz could tell he was trying to see whether or not Anne was making fun of him.

'And He can hear you from there?'

'Yes,' he continued, still unsure. 'He is the Almighty, the Creator. He can see everything and hear everything. He can even read your mind.'

'I would like to meet God the next time He comes with good food for us,' said Anne, 'and thank Him myself.'

Gezz's dad dipped the bread roll into his soup. 'Well, you can do it now if you like.'

'I will,' said Anne in her monotone voice, and with that she bowed her head and closed her eyes. 'Thank You, God, for bringing us good food. I would like to meet You the next time You come.'

Gezz watched her parents' reactions. Her dad simply refused to look up from his soup. He carried on dipping his bread and eating its soggy ends. But her mum broke into a smile. 'What a charming innocent you are, dear.' She looked at the android with a warm grin and beckoned. 'Tuck in. Your soup will be getting cold.'

Gezz turned to Anne and tapped her on the arm. The ponytail swished from side to side as the pretty blonde head smoothly rotated to face her. 'Watch me,' Gezz whispered. 'Watch the way I eat my soup, and copy the actions.'

She picked up her spoon and dipped it into the oxtail. Anne did the same. Then Gezz brought the spoon to her lips and took a sip. She flinched, the hot liquid burning her mouth. The soup hadn't gone cold at all. 'Ow,' she hissed through gritted teeth and covered her mouth. 'It's hot.'

Anne copied the movements exactly. She brought the spoon to her lips, hesitated, took a sip, swallowed the juice and flinched. Except the flinch was not exactly natural. It was flat and monotone, the most rehearsed, robotic flinch Gezz had ever witnessed. 'Ow,' Anne repeated, expressionless. 'It's hot.'

Luke started to giggle again, which in turn set Malcolm off. This assimilating lark was not going to be easy.

After lunch Gezz took Anne up to her bedroom with the bag of clothes and untied it. Inside were a pair of old dark green cords, a white blouse that was frayed around the collar, several pairs of darned socks and an old pair of trainers, size four. The girl tipped everything out on to her bed and tutted. 'It's no wonder they wanted to give this stuff away,' she said to herself. 'It's rubbish.'

The android stood by the bed, her crystal-like eyes fixed on the assortment of jumble. 'Rubbish,' she repeated, her voice deadpan and unconcerned. 'These items of clothing are to be discarded?'

Gezz turned sheepishly and forced a weak smile. 'They were,' she said. 'But you can have them now.' She watched, expecting some sort of reaction, offence at least, but none came. This was fine by Gezz, who was only doing her a favour anyway. She stopped feeling guilty and helped Anne change from her space-age dungarees into the old blouse and cords.

'There you are,' Gezz said, feeling rather pleased with her job well done. 'Very fetching.'

She turned Anne round so she could face the dressing-table mirror. The automaton seemed to look at her reflection but said nothing. If she was impressed, it didn't show.

★ ★ ★

The following morning the children rose early and went to collect Anne from the den, where she had spent the night. They had the time of their lives introducing their new friend to the ways of the average eleven-year-old. Naturally, the two boys had to present the automaton with test after test in order to marvel at the miracles she could perform.

'See that old iron bar,' said Luke, pointing to a long brown rusty exhaust pipe.

Anne focused on the piece of metal, strewn carelessly on the overgrown grass surrounding the lodge. 'Yes,' she announced. 'I can see the old iron bar.'

'Can you bend it in half?'

'Yes,' Anne replied.

Gezz groaned inwardly. This had been all very interesting to her at first, but now she was actually tiring of it. The boys, of course, rarely grew weary of such things. 'Go and do it then,' commanded Luke, and the automaton immediately stepped over to the exhaust pipe and picked it up.

The length of rusty metal was plucked off the ground effortlessly, leaving a yellowed patch of flattened grass in its wake. The girl held it at both ends and began to push them together. Gezz sighed quietly as Malcolm and Luke gawped at the feat of strength with bulging eyes and broad toothy grins. Anne's face showed absolutely no sign of strain whatsoever. It remained calm and static as the metal pipe buckled and creaked until it was bent round as easily as Gezz might bend a cardboard kitchen tube, like the ones with cling film or tin foil on. The android dropped the loop of iron in its place on the grass once the task was accomplished.

'Wow,' said the two boys in mutual fascination.

'Anne,' Malcolm then started, and Gezz rolled her eyes, letting the lads know openly that she was sick of all this. 'You are a computer, aren't you?'

'Yes,' said Anne primly. 'My brain is a computer.'

Malcolm folded his arms and tried to look serious. 'What is twenty thousand and three times five hundred?'

The robot looked to Gezz for clarification, and, rather annoyingly, the girl found herself rephrasing the question. 'He's asking you to multiply twenty thousand and three by five hundred.'

Anne turned back to face Malcolm. 'Twenty thousand and three multiplied by five hundred?' she began.

The boy adjusted his glasses and rubbed his hands together, barely able to contain his excitement. 'Yes?'

The robot's blue eyes blinked once, very deliberately, as if to show that her brain was busy computing the answer. Then. 'Twenty thousand and three multiplied by five hundred is ten million, one thousand, five hundred.'

Malcolm's eyes widened and he grinned. 'You're going to come in very handy at school, Anne.'

Anne turned to face him. 'What is school?'

'It's where we learn things.' It was Gezz who was speaking. Anne turned back to face her. 'It's where we absorb data.'

'Define "come in very handy".'

Gezz smiled. 'He means you will be useful to us.'

'Yes,' agreed the automaton. 'I will be useful to us.' Then she paused, as if considering something. 'I will…come in very handy.'

The three children smiled and exchanged glances. They were happy, because Anne had shown the first signs of development. She had learned something. A voice in the distance shattered the moment of warm contentment. 'Yoo-hoo! Gezz!' It was her mum, standing by their car. The red rear lights were on and smoke was pumping out of the exhaust. Gezz's mother and father were setting off for chapel.

Thankfully, they had agreed to let her stay home just this once. Not that Gezz didn't like chapel. It was just that she had become so excited with her new-found friend and was eager to spend time with her. She had also worried about what antics the boys might have got up to without her supervision. They needed someone to keep things sensible.

Gezz lifted her right arm high up and waved back to the house. 'See you later, Mum!'

Her mum gave a final wave and got in the car. Seconds later, white reverse lights blinked on to join the larger red ones, and the car backed slowly off the drive. Gezz heard the gears crunch as her dad forced the vehicle into first. They'd had a lot of trouble with the gears a couple of months back, and now they seemed to be playing up again. The car revved up and then sped off up to the main road.

Gezz looked at her house for a moment, with its varnished door and oil-stained drive. Then she glanced across at Luke's next door, and typically the place seemed dead, with curtains upstairs and down pulled resolutely shut. *They won't be up till midday,* she told herself.

13

Calling for Anne

The holiday period seemed to go by very quickly. The children had spent the whole of August playing out with Anne, and now, before the children knew where they were, it was the first Wednesday of September and time to start at the new school. Gezz stood at the hall doorway in her burgundy V-necked pullover and tie and felt only one emotion: fear. Well, fear and nervousness, and butterflies in the tummy. She adjusted her new purple hairband as her mum strolled in from the kitchen with Gezz's brand new rucksack and handed it to her. 'Don't look so down,' she said softly. 'When you come home at three thirty, you'll be wondering what all the fuss was about.'

Gezz had been hoping for a lift, but her new school was nearer than her old one and her parents felt it was time she was given a little more independence. She gave a weak and pathetic smile and hugged her mother before leaving the house. Pulling the front door shut behind her, she strode over the little white fence parting her garden from Luke's. She tapped on his plastic porch door and waited, still feeling awful.

The boy emerged from the inner door in good spirits, clouds of blue smoke floating above his head as his dressing-gown-clad mother, cigarette in hand, bent down to give him a kiss on the cheek. 'Have a good day, sweetheart,' Gezz heard her say. Luke's mum disappeared inside as he stepped from the outer door.

Closing the porch behind him, he beamed, 'Hi, Gezz. All set for Crompton Green High?'

'Not really,' the girl mumbled, holding the straps on her shoulders with both hands.

Going to school with Luke was a good idea. He was so looking forward to secondary school and it helped her stay calm. Gezz asked, 'Are we calling for Malc?'

Luke nodded without enthusiasm. 'I suppose we'll have to.'

They set off up the semicircle of houses, the sky clear and blue and the warmth of the summer sun touching their faces. The downstairs curtains of Malcolm's dark and gloomy house twitched as the boy and girl approached. Then the door flung open and he appeared. Even his brand-new burgundy uniform managed to look wrinkled and worn.

'How are you feeling?' he asked as he joined the others, holding an old crumpled Tesco bag full of bits and pieces over his shoulder.

'Awful,' said Gezz, feeling quite sickly now.

'Me too,' Malcolm nodded. He looked it too, his face as white as a sheet. He looked ill.

Luke gave a gentle laugh and shook his head. 'I don't know what's wrong with you both. I can't wait to get in there.'

Gezz ignored him. 'Have we got enough time to get Anne?' she said.

Luke's face suddenly went very serious. He nodded. 'Should have.'

★ ★ ★

Gezz dropped into the trench and ducked down out of sight. It was agreed that Malcolm and Luke should stay back at a distance and wait for her to retrieve Anne. She tapped on the door of the den and whispered, 'Anne, it's me, Gezz.'

The bramble-covered door opened immediately and the robot emerged, donned in full school uniform. Gezz recalled how she had taken Anne to see Grandma Atkinson and her sewing machine. In no time at all, the robot had picked up techniques Grandma had taken a lifetime to refine. Within minutes, Anne had run up a grey knee-length skirt and a white blouse. The burgundy tie and white socks took a little longer. But the most amazing thing was watching Anne knit. The android observed the basic principles of knit one, pearl one, and then processed the code of the knitting pattern. Gezz smiled as she remembered how quickly Anne knitted the burgundy V-necked jumper, and how the boys thought she had nicked it from a clothes shop, the quality of it was so good. Thankfully, Anne had run up the whole uniform in under twenty minutes while Grandma cooked dinner, and so a lot of awkward questions were avoided.

Very precisely and with gentle care, Anne closed the door of the den. Gezz smiled as she took in the sight. 'Very smart,' she said.

The android nodded her agreement. 'I am very smart.'

'I mean smart as in bright and fresh in appearance,' Gezz corrected.

'I am smart as in bright and fresh in appearance,' repeated Anne.

'Very good,' said Gezz, crouching down by the edge of the dugout. 'Now, extend your fibre-optic as usual and tell me if there's anyone there.'

Anne obeyed the command and held up her little finger. The thin wiry camera extended and the android's eyes wobbled ever so slightly, processing the images filtering into her head. 'There are no humans nearby,' she announced, 'except for Luke and Malcolm hiding in the undergrowth exactly one hundred metres right of this location.'

'That's OK,' said Gezz. 'Let's get going.' She scrambled up to ground level and waited for her friend to jump out of the ditch and join her, which she promptly did in one breath-taking leap. Then they walked on across the gravel path to where Malcolm and Luke were hiding. After that they headed up the grass slope to the main road.

Gezz felt her stomach turn as she and her friends joined the swarm of children and teenagers trudging up the main road to school. They were all different shapes and sizes. Some tall and thin, some big and heavy. Some going for the first time like her, others, clearly older and a lot more confident, beginning what would be their final year.

They marched on, the boxy shape of their new school looming up on the horizon. Even Luke had fallen into a subdued silence, anticipating what the day might hold in this much larger set of classrooms. Cars heaved up the road, each one carrying serious-looking children to their destination.

A rowdy laugh hit the air as two or three big lads pushed a young black boy from one to the other. 'Stop it, stop it,' he kept saying. And the more he said it, the more they laughed. Gezz was disgusted with them.

She turned to Anne, who was watching a couple of girls further up on the opposite side of the road as she walked. *No, 'watching' is the wrong word*, thought Gezz. *'Preoccupied' is more like it. Yes, she is preoccupied with them.*

Both seemed about thirteen. One was a brunette with long shoulder-length hair, her complexion a mixture of make-up and spots. The other was fairly tall and blonde. Her hair was long too and tied up in a ponytail. A modest fringe fell just short of big blue eyes. She was very pretty, and looked a bit like Anne. *Maybe that's why Anne is studying her*, Gezz reasoned, *she's noticed the likeness in their physical appearances.*

The two girls who had caught Anne's attention slowed down their pace and glanced about nervously, giggling in a cheeky fashion. They stopped where an overgrown tree arched its branches over a tall brick wall, partially covering them. Then the pretty blonde one reached carefully into her left pullover sleeve and slid out a cigarette and a couple of matches. The pair of them stared at the cigarette with glee, and Gezz scowled in anger. The blonde had obviously stolen the dodgy items from her parents.

Anne kept her eyes fixed on the pair while at the same time continuing to walk alongside Gezz. The blonde slipped the filter end of the cigarette into her mouth and struck one of the matches on the mossy brick wall behind them. The match snapped in half and the two girls swore in their frustration. Gezz, who was glancing up as often as possible, while still trying to keep an eye on where she was going, chuckled to herself, glad that their mischief had failed.

The blonde held her last match carefully and paused for a second, trying to steady her nerves. Then she struck it against the wall and this time the end sparked into a flaring yellow flame. She touched the end of the cigarette and sucked at the filter. The end burned an orange-red and the girl could barely contain her delight as blue smoke puffed from her mouth. She cast the match to the ground and the pair of them set off again looking very pleased with themselves.

Gezz continued to watch as the blonde drew on the cigarette again, kept the smoke in her mouth for a second, blew it out, and then handed the cigarette over to her spotty friend. The brunette took it confidently between her fingers and sucked on it hard, the way Luke's mum did, and inhaled deeply. The girl was trying to hide the strain she felt as the smoke entered her lungs, but her furrowed brow and watering eyes rather gave the game away. The brunette blew the smoke out and took on a cocky air, holding her head up high. Gezz so wanted to cross the road and tell her that if she thought she was grown-up because she was smoking, then she wasn't, she was just stupid.

Anne finally turned round, still walking ahead, and asked Gezz the question she had been expecting. 'What is that girl doing over there?'

Gezz kept her eyes on the path in front of her. 'She's smoking.'

'You are mistaken,' Anne said. 'The girl is not smoking. She is not on fire. It is the paper tube that is alight. Your optical lenses may be malfunctioning.'

Gezz shook her head and smiled. 'No,' she said. 'My optical lenses, my eyes, are fine.' She emphasized the word 'eyes' to make sure Anne understood their proper name. 'The paper tube in the girl's mouth is full of tobacco, which is a plant they grow in another country. The tobacco is crushed and rolled up in the paper. The girl has lit one end with fire and is sucking the fumes up from the other end into her lungs. We call that process smoking.'

'What is the purpose of smoking?' asked Anne innocently.

Gezz sighed noisily. 'I don't know,' she conceded. 'Mrs Davidson, that's Luke's mum. She says it calms her nerves. But my mum says that is an excuse because smoking actually damages the nerves. And if she tries to stop or cut down a bit, her nerves will be bad because of the withdrawal symptoms.'

'Define "withdrawal symptoms",' said Anne.

'Well,' Gezz replied, trying to recall the explanation her mother gave her and to find the right words. 'The tobacco has a drug in it called nicotine, and when the smoke is breathed into the lungs, the drug is carried into the veins, into the blood. The body adjusts to it and mixes it in with its own natural chemicals. But when the nicotine levels in the blood start to drop, the body demands that they be brought back up.' Gezz shrugged, having delivered the best explanation she could think of. 'And then the person starts feeling nervous and jumpy and bad tempered.'

Anne gave a simple nod. 'And these feelings are withdrawal symptoms,' she concluded. 'The individual then inhales more smoke to feel normal again.'

'That's right,' said Gezz with a smile.

'Why do they wish to practice something that will make them feel withdrawal symptoms?'

'You mean, why do they want to get *addicted?*' corrected Gezz, emphasizing 'addicted'.

'Yes.'

'I don't know,' said the girl honestly. 'I mean, I don't smoke, and neither does Luke or Malcolm. Some children see others doing it and they think it will make them more acceptable to their friends. They also see lots of adults doing it who have become addicted like Mrs Davidson. Some children smoke because they think it will make them look more like adults.' She laughed to herself. 'The funny thing is, most adults are trying hard to stop.'

'They can stop being addicted?'

'Yes.'

'How?'

'Well, by not smoking for a long time, I suppose,' shrugged Gezz. 'When the body realizes it won't be getting any more nicotine it sort of starts to accept it and the withdrawals stop.'

'How is this a source of amusement?'

Gezz frowned. 'What?'

'You said, "The funny thing is, most adults are trying hard to stop".'

Gezz frowned and adjusted her hairband. 'Well,' she began. The English language is so weird at times. It was hard to phrase things exactly. 'Oh, forget that bit,' she said dismissively.

Anne turned her head forward and blinked her eyes. 'Erasing the sentence, "The funny thing is, most adults are trying hard to stop" from memory banks.' She paused, and then turned back to face Gezz. 'Memory erased.'

The children arrived at the main gate of the school. The building loomed in front of them, its odd blocky shape casting a shadow on to the playing fields by its side. Swallowing their fear, the three eleven-year-olds joined the mass of burgundy uniforms trudging up the narrow road to the main door with their android schoolmate in tow.

14

Back to School

The corridors were exactly like the ones in *Grange Hill*, full of noisy kids making their way to the hall. Two year elevens, a girl and a boy dressed in black pullovers and wearing prefect badges, wore pleasant smiles and directed the children along the nearest corridor. 'Straight down there to the hall,' they were shouting above the din. 'Keep to the left.'

Gezz caught sight of a teacher leaving what she guessed was an office. He was tall and old, and wore a tweed jacket like the one Professor Droyd had. For a second a troubled feeling swept over her inducing nausea. It was an odd kind of feeling, as she remembered the old man being whisked off by bogus policemen from outside her house. She hoped he was all right – wherever he was.

The children filed into the hall, which opened before them like a cathedral, and they took their seats. The four of them sat on plastic moulded chairs at the edge of a row near the back. Gezz made sure Anne sat next to her so she could keep an eye on her. Luke and Malcolm sat to her other side. Gezz scanned the audience for children she knew. She saw the boy who was being pushed about earlier. He was smiling now. And the two smokers were there as well. They were sitting further up near the front. Then Gezz groaned to herself as she recognized Emma Bingham arguing with another girl. One of the teachers lining the wall went over to sort it out. *Typical*, she thought.

Suddenly the peal of the school bell rang out across the building and a more settled atmosphere fell over them. The main door was closed by a female teacher, middle-aged, wearing glasses with her hair up in a bun. Gezz was not sure what to make of it. Even she had to concede that a ponytail was better than a bun.

A male teacher went up on to the stage which dominated the front wall and stood before an eagle-shaped lectern. 'Children,' he announced, clapping his hands. 'Settle down, please.' And with that the hustle and bustle of excited voices fell to a hush.

Gezz thought of something and tapped Anne on the arm. 'Anne,' she hissed. 'If you have anything to say or any questions to ask, save them to the end.'

Anne replied in her ordinary monotone voice. 'Please clarify the instruction.' Gezz cringed as the automaton's speech echoed across the hall. 'Don't talk again until I give you permission,' she hissed.

'Very well,' said Anne, her voice seeming quite loud against the lull of the other children. 'Deactivating speech circuits until further notice.'

The lady with the bun hairdo stepped over and glared a meaningful stare, putting a finger to her lips. 'Be quiet, girl,' she whispered. Gezz felt her face glow a warm crimson. *Thanks, Anne*, she thought.

The man on the stage gestured with his hands outstretched. 'Everybody rise,' he said, and in unison, everybody did, not daring to speak. 'Mr Turnbull, the headmaster, will now address you.' The teacher left the stage and Mr Turnbull entered the hall through a second door further up that side aisle. He strolled on to the platform, his ceremonial black gown flapping about. He adjusted his black squared-off cap, his short grey hair poking through, before grasping the lectern. 'Thank you, Mr Ford,' he said, his voice surprisingly resonant for an old man.

The headmaster coughed and then forced a smile. 'You may be seated,' he said, and straight away the mass of bodies sunk back into their plastic seats. 'My name is Mr Turnbull, and I am the headmaster of Crompton Green High.'

Gezz found it difficult to listen, because Anne was distracting her by scanning the audience and carefully examining every nook and cranny of the hall, including each person present in the room. Gezz caught something from the headmaster about the great inventors who were once taught in Bolton and how this school had been named after one of them, and that the school was like a bank, you only get out of it what you put in, but that was it.

'And now I will hand you back over to Mr Ford, who will assign you to your classes.' The headmaster smiled and stalked from the platform to the applause of the teachers. Unsure of what to do, the children clapped as well. Gezz peeped round at Anne and chuckled. *I bet she's dying to ask me what clapping is*, she thought, and leaned back in her chair folding her arms and grinning.

Mr Ford held in his hand a big navy-blue register. 'Will the following children please come out to me,' he said, and then began announcing names. Gezz watched as the black boy she had seen earlier joined the little group forming at the front.

'Malcolm Hardy,' said Mr Ford. Gezz looked down her row and signalled her friend. He looked visibly shocked, and she realized he had been hoping they would all be in the same class together. The boy adjusted his glasses and got to his feet, his wild curls bobbing about as he walked timidly to the front.

'Ronald Higgingbottom,' Mr Ford continued. There were a few titters in the audience until, that is, a huge meaty boy got up, his eyes all mean and narrow, his cropped hair almost standing on end due to its extreme shortness. The boy barged his way to the front and Gezz gulped in awe.

Several other names were called and then Mr Ford addressed his group. 'OK, then, children,' he announced.

'Follow me.' The entourage of boys and girls filed out through the top door and were led off to their classroom, or 'form room', as they called it.

Then it was Bun Hairdo Teacher's turn. 'I am Mrs Croake,' she said with a slightly bossy air. Someone sniggered on the front row and she shot them that stony-faced hard stare which had given Gezz a fright minutes before, and silenced them. 'Will the following children please come to the front. Geraldine Atkinson.'

A shiver ran down Gezz's spine. She tapped Anne on the arm again. 'Remain seated here until Mrs Croake leads us to our class,' she commanded. 'Then join the group as quick as you can.' She didn't wait for a facial response, she just got up, slung her rucksack over her shoulder and skipped to the front.

Then Mrs Croake said the name Gezz had been dreading. 'Emma Bingham.' She cringed inside as the ginger trouble-maker headed out towards her. Another name, though, made her tummy flutter.

'Luke Davidson,' continued Mrs Croake, and Gezz watched with keen delight as her next-door neighbour and best friend strolled confidently to the front.

The selection process continued until there was a group of about thirty children. Mrs Croake snapped her register shut. 'Well,' she said to herself, but loud enough for everyone to hear. 'That's my lot.' She turned to the exit and waved the children on. 'Follow me, please.'

As soon as the class began to move, a white and burgundy streak of light shot across from the back of the aisle lining the wall. Teachers and pupils frowned for a moment, unsure of what they had just witnessed. Gezz turned to see what the fuss was about, only to find Anne standing calmly by her side, not out of breath and not a hair out of place. 'Wow,' she whispered.

* * *

The form were led along three brightly lit corridors to their new room. Mrs Croake marched up to her desk and dropped her open register on to it. 'Now,' she clapped her hands. 'I think we had better go over the register again, just to make sure everyone's here.'

Gezz took her seat and gestured for Anne to come and sit next to her, which she promptly did. Luke sat at the desk in front. He turned, looking extremely worried. 'What are we going to do about Anne?' he said, his eyes bulging and tense. 'She's not on the register.'

Gezz sensed all the colour leaving her cheeks. 'I hadn't thought of that,' she said slowly. Then she turned to her robot friend, tapping her on the arm. 'Anne.' The android looked round, but did not answer. Then Gezz remembered. 'Activate speech circuits,' she commanded.

Anne gave a single blink of her clear blue eyes. 'Speech circuits activated,' she said. 'I have many questions.'

'No, not now,' Gezz shook her head. 'Listen, can you add your name to the register in the style of Mrs Croake's hand-writing?'

Anne nodded, her eyes empty and blank. 'Yes, Gezz. I can do that.'

Mrs Croake had become engrossed in a conversation with another teacher at the door. The other children were preoccupied with getting to know one another. Luke shot a glance over his shoulder. 'It's either now or never.'

Gezz agreed. 'Anne,' she commanded authoritatively. 'Join us at the teacher's desk.'

The sound of scraping chairs was barely heard above the hustle and bustle of the chatty form. Anne quickly and precisely rose from her seat and joined the two friends at the front. Luke shot another look at the classroom door. Mrs Croake was still busy sorting out whatever needed sorting with the other teacher.

'It's written in red ink,' said Gezz, surveying the register's graph-like white pages. The names of each and every class member were written down the left-hand side of the page, with a column down the right for ticking or crossing, depending on whether or not each child was present. Gezz turned to Luke, who was frowning hard. 'It's in alphabetical order too,' he was saying.

Gezz was getting worried now. She glanced at Mrs Croake, and thankfully the form tutor was still busily in discussion. 'So, in order to put this right,' she began, 'we can't just write her name in at the bottom?'

'No,' said Luke. 'The whole page will have to be rewritten in Mrs Croake's handwriting, and Anne's surname put in the right place.'

'Where?'

Luke scanned the surnames. 'Collins, Dagnall, Davidson, Farrell.' He broke off and stabbed the book urgently with his forefinger. 'There,' he said. 'There, between my surname and Farrell. That's where her name needs to go.'

Gezz looked into Anne's blank features. 'Can you do it?'

Anne replied gently and with great calm, which gave Gezz a feeling of reassurance. She didn't know why, because Anne always spoke like that. 'Rewrite the whole page with red ink in the style of Mrs Croake's handwriting,' she said, 'inserting my surname between Davidson and Farrell. Yes, I can do it.'

Luke needed no more convincing. He took a ruler from a plastic beaker on the teacher's desk containing many such things, placed it carefully down the left-hand side of the book, pressed hard, and with his other hand tore out the page. Gezz felt tremors of nerves running through her legs. They turned to jelly and she was sure her knees would give out. She felt as though she were going deaf at the same time, the children in the class seeming like they were in slow motion or under water, muffled and distant. Her throat dried up too and she kept one eye on Mrs Croake, who was bound to turn round any minute now and catch them rewriting her register.

Anne held the torn page in her hand momentarily, studied it, and then quickly snatched up the red ink pen, which had rolled off the book of names on to the desk. She began scribbling.

'What on earth are you three doing here?' The bossy voice of Mrs Croake sent further shivers through Gezz's body. She looked down, a bit ashamed of herself, and watched the register slip from Anne's hand and drop on to the table. Had the android reacted on impulse? Had she jumped nervously at the sound of the teacher's reprimand? No, that could not be it. Anne had no feelings, she was a machine. Unless, of course, the flesh and blood part of her computer brain had started to develop emotions?

Gezz stared at the register. It was exactly as before, a list of names on the left and a red vertical line down the right. She cast her eye across the page. Collins, Dagnall, Davidson, Droyd, Farrell. Then she stopped, jolted, and went back a couple of names. Davidson, Droyd. An overwhelming sense of euphoria swept over the girl. She had done it! Anne had added her name to the register!

'We were just looking, Miss,' Gezz piped suddenly, the noise of the class becoming ever present again.

Luke stepped back and tossed the original page, which he had rapidly screwed up into a ball, into the waste-paper basket by Mrs Croake's desk and made his way back to his own. Gezz retreated to her table as well, and Anne followed, not before placing the red pen back on top of the open register.

Mrs Croake clapped her hands and cleared her throat. 'Right,' she shouted. 'Settle down. We have got a lot to get through.' The class settled, half-nervous and half-excited, and Gezz just knew secondary school was going to be great.

15

Systematic Instruction of Subject

Gezz found moving through the cramped corridors a bit of an ordeal the first time, as the children left their various registration classes to start their first lesson. This was it now, thought Gezz, *Grange Hill* all the way. She took note of how each lesson was taught by a different teacher and how members from other forms were sometimes present. That shy boy from Malcolm's form was there for History, and thankfully, Emma Bingham was in a different set for Maths. But sadly, neither Luke nor Gezz had caught sight of Malcolm all morning. She hoped he was all right.

Things became easier for Anne as the day unfolded. She learned quickly by observing the way teachers addressed the class and asked questions and the way kids put up their hands to answer. The first lesson was Religious Education, and Gezz dreaded what comments Anne might have to offer. But strangely she just sat and listened. The teacher went on about how different cultures interpreted God in their own way, and that in almost every instance they recognized Him as the creator of heaven and earth.

The only time Anne really embarrassed Gezz was when the teacher mentioned prayer and Anne put up her hand to comment. The teacher, Mrs Virgil, smiled and nodded. 'Yes, er, Anne, isn't it?' she said. 'You have something to tell us?'

'Yes,' replied Anne curtly. 'I have something to tell you. I have told God in a prayer that when He next goes to Geraldine's house with good food I want to speak to Him.'

Mrs Virgil grinned, clearly charmed by the robot's innocence. 'Really,' she enthused. Then she turned to Gezz, who was hiding crimson cheeks behind the palms of her hands.

'God comes to your house quite regularly, does He, Geraldine?'

Gezz went even darker in shade, turning a deep purple as everyone laughed. Everyone except Anne, of course.

The next lesson was English. Mr Ford, whom Gezz had seen earlier in the hall, took this lesson. He began by issuing copies of the *Oxford English Dictionary* to each class member and spoke of the importance of enlarging one's vocabulary, that is one's knowledge of different words.

Anne spent about ten minutes absorbing the words in the dictionary and all their definitions. Again it was slightly embarrassing for Gezz, as the android turned each page very quickly and, unfortunately, with rather a lot of noise too. By the time Mr Ford had run out of patience, Anne had read the entire book. 'Er, excuse me, Miss er,' he paused, trying to wrack his brains.

'Droyd,' offered Luke, enjoying the fun.

'Er, Miss Droyd,' said Mr Ford. 'Thank you, Luke.' He beamed at the expressionless automaton and folded his arms. 'Are you going to spend the whole of the lesson reading that, or are you going to listen to me?'

Anne blinked a couple of times in that very deliberate way. 'Lesson,' she announced flatly.

Mr Ford frowned. 'What?'

'Lesson,' said Anne again. 'Noun. Spell of teaching. Systematic instruction of subject. Thing learnt by pupil. Experience that serves to warn or encourage. For example, "let that be a lesson to you". Passage from Bible read aloud through church service.'

Mr Ford coughed loudly, annoyed by the girl's string of definitions. 'Yes, thank you, Miss Droyd,' he rapped. 'I do know what a lesson is, thank you very much.' He turned his back to the girl and headed to the front of the class. 'If you are trying to be funny,' he continued, 'you had better stop now. I am not one to be mocked.' He faced the class, arms still folded. 'That goes for all of you.'

'Funny,' said Anne, her face blank and devoid of emotion.

'What?!' Mr Ford spat, unable to believe his ears.

'Amusing, comical. Strange, hard to account for. Slightly unwell, eccentric, etcetera.'

Mr Ford was fuming now and Gezz sensed the other children fighting off fits of hysteria as best they could. She thought she had better put her hand up and try to save the day.

'Miss Atkinson,' bellowed the teacher.

'I must apologize for my friend's behaviour, Sir,' she fumbled. 'Anne is an orphan and has learning difficulties. She doesn't realize what she is doing.'

Mr Ford narrowed his eyes and stared straight into Anne's. Blank, emotionless blue crystals shone back and the teacher seemed to soften, perhaps recognizing that there was indeed something quite odd about this outspoken pupil.

'All right,' said Mr Ford at last. 'But Anne, please don't keep shouting out definitions. Your enthusiasm for the English language is encouraging, but to speak when the teacher is talking is very rude.'

'Rude,' said Anne, and Gezz held her breath, hoping Mr Ford's lecture had sunk in. 'I will not shout out any more definitions.' She paused, and then added, 'Sir.'

For the first time Mr Ford smiled briefly, before continuing his lesson.

★ ★ ★

The peal of the bell rang out across the school, signalling morning break. Gezz could not believe how quickly the first hour and a half had gone. Chairs screeched as children went eagerly for the door. Gezz got to her feet and made for her best friend, only to find that Luke had gone off with a couple of new friends he had made. It was up to her now to supervise Anne through break-time.

The two girls walked slowly through the maze of corridors, pushed and shoved by the mass of bodies behind and ahead of them. Gezz could not wait to get out into the playgrounds and take a breath of fresh air. She checked up on Anne, who now had her eyes fixed firmly ahead. What could she see? Gezz wondered.

Near the end of the corridor two year nine girls stood chatting and smiling. One was tall and blonde like Anne, the other more chubby with greasy brown hair and a spotty complexion. It was those girls again, the smokers. They were excited about something. Gezz watched as the blonde tugged the sleeve of the other and they both went off in a tizz.

Then Gezz stopped in her tracks by an adjacent exit. The open passage led to a locker area and then a big wooden door leading to the playground. A number of children filed through it while others carried on ahead.

The locker area was quite spacious with tall thin metal boxes lining the walls and coat hangers dominating an iron frame. Four first year boys stood in a circle and tossed an old Tesco bag full of books to one another, laughing and jeering all the while. She recognized one of them immediately. It was that huge boy with the skinhead who was in Malcolm's class. He was clearly goading the others on. A voice was shouting and whining, 'Stop it, oh please stop it, I need those books for my next lesson,' and the more he whined, the more they laughed.

Gezz looked closer and saw a pair of arms waving about in a panic, trying to catch the bag. Then her face dropped and her heart sank as she caught sight of a lot of brown curly hair springing about. It was Malcolm who was in the middle getting bullied. She could see he was close to tears.

'Anne,' she said, not taking her eyes off the heartless mob. 'Push that big oaf aside and rescue Malc. If anyone tries to stop you, knock them to the floor, but leave them unharmed.'

She waited for confirmation, but none came. The girl looked round, and then ran back into the corridor. 'Anne?' she called. 'Anne!' But Anne had gone.

16

How to Be a Human

Gezz had to make a decision, stand up for Malcolm or search for Anne. Regretfully, no matter what fondness she had for Malc, she knew she had to find the android. The Professor had entrusted Anne to her and her friends and she could not allow Anne to fall into the hands of that police inspector Bullman, or whatever he was called.

Reluctantly, she left Malcolm to the taunts of Fatty Skinhead and his cronies and pushed her way up the corridor to where the two smokers had been standing. When she got to the T-junction at the end, she looked both ways, up and down, but the automaton was nowhere to be seen.

A beam of light shone in half-way up the right-hand corridor. Gezz guessed this to be another exit leading to the playground. *Anne must have gone out to play,* she concluded. Again that didn't feel right. Did robots play and enjoy themselves? One thing was sure, though, Anne had started to develop a level of curiosity. She had gone off to investigate something.

* * *

Hidden at the back of the far wing of the building was the gym used for indoor PE. Beyond that was the boiler room, outside which were two large industrial bins and some rickety looking brick shelters with worn corrugated-iron roofing showing signs of neglect. Gezz searched high and low across the playground, only to be disappointed. This was the last possible place the robot might be. If she wasn't here, the only other explanation was that she had left the school premises entirely. But why would anyone want to hang about these old bike sheds away from the other children? Maybe that was it. Maybe Anne didn't like the crowds.

Gezz soon had to revise her ideas, though, as she got nearer the row of shelters. A pall of blue mist hung conspicuously over the shelter at the far end. Gezz groaned with disgust. It was the smokers. *What do they see in it*, she wondered momentarily. Oh well, she would still have to go and ask them if they had seen Anne, just in case.

As she got closer, she recognized the two girls from the corridor puffing away, the tall blonde taking short drags, clearly not used to the practice, and the bigger girl breathing in great lungfuls, trying desperately to look as if she had become hardened to it. The fact that her eyes watered and her face went as white as a sheet every time she took a drag betrayed the truth of the matter.

Two boys were also present. They looked like they might be year sevens, but Gezz did not recognize them. As with the girls, they shared a cigarette between the pair of them. Then Gezz got the shock of her life. Standing in the far corner, watching with interest, was Anne. She just stood there, all calm and reserved, taking in the cigarette-smoking procedure. Gezz marched over to the bike sheds, totally infuriated.

'Anne!' she screeched. 'What are you doing here? I've been looking all over for you.'

One of the boys held his cigarette between finger and thumb and turned to the silent observer. 'Hey up,' he smirked. 'Looks like your mother's here.'

'You are mistaken,' replied Anne, very matter of fact. 'Geraldine is not my mother, she is my guardian.'

The boy's smirk became a half-snigger, as he did not seem sure whether Anne was joking or really meant it. 'Yeah,' he said. 'That's a good one.'

Gezz ignored the playful banter and scowled at Anne. 'What are you doing here? Don't you know it's not allowed? This area is off-limits.'

'I am observing at close range the act of smoking,' said Anne innocently. 'I wish to become better acquainted with the practice.'

Gezz's anger now lessened to an emotion closer to frustration. 'But it's bad for you,' she protested. 'It will give you cancer and you will die.'

'I am an android,' Anne stated, again very matter of fact. 'I cannot contract such diseases.'

'I thought part of you was flesh and blood,' said Gezz, exasperated. 'You don't want to damage that.' Then she thought of something. 'You don't want to damage the part of your computer brain which could develop emotions and make you more human.'

The statement seemed to have an effect on the android. Her eyes blinked as she considered the truthfulness in Gezz's logic. The other children continued to draw on their cigarettes, apparently unaware of Anne's claims to be less than human.

'Oh, stop going on,' dismissed the big greasy girl with the brown hair. 'My granddad has smoked all his life and he hasn't got cancer, and he's seventy. Don't knock it until you've tried it, that's what I say.'

'Yeah!' chimed in the others automatically. The boy held out his right hand, cupping back his fingers so that the tip end faced Gezz. 'Go on,' he said. 'Take a drag. It won't kill you.'

'No,' Gezz replied hesitantly. 'I don't want to.' Her eyes widened and she stared at the white tube of tobacco with its fluffy filter wrapped in an orange-brown colour infested with yellow speckles. She remained silent as it was presented to her.

The fact was she had often wondered what it was like to smoke and had fancied trying it on many occasions. When Luke's mum drew hard on hers, for instance, she always looked like she was really enjoying it.

The tall blonde put on a pleasant smile and gently urged, 'Go on, you might like it.'

Feeling very nervous and awkward, Gezz took the cigarette from the boy. It felt warm, partly because of it having been in the boy's hand and partly because the other end of it was alight. Blue smoke meandered up into her face and her eyes began to smart. The four children watched in full expectation. Anne just continued with her usual zombie manner as Gezz put the cigarette between her lips and sucked.

The end burned a wild orange-red and Gezz couldn't take her eyes off it. She was going cross-eyed staring at the glowing tuft of ash, almost unable to believe it was her doing it. Keeping her mouth closed, as she had seen the adults do, she plucked the filter from her lips and kept the smoke inside her mouth. The taste was vile, like a mixture of strong black coffee and that stuff they make roads out of, yes that was it, strong black coffee and tarmac. She blew it out slowly, sensing the after-taste on her tongue.

Greasy Brown Head was not impressed. 'You didn't inhale it,' she complained. 'You've got to breathe it into your lungs. Take it into your mouth, hold it like you did, and then breathe in deep.'

Gezz had been hoping no one would notice that she had not inhaled it. All eyes were on her again, she could not back out of it now. She took another drag, held it in her mouth, and then after plucking up some courage, closed her eyes tight and breathed in. The smoke hit the back of her throat hard and she felt a sharp rush as it shot down her windpipe and into her lungs. Her eyes watered with the strain and a sort of dizziness overcame her, her legs wobbling slightly at the knees. She knew, from what her mother had told her, that the dizziness was caused by the drug nicotine entering her blood and rushing to her brain. It took just seven seconds for the effect to reach her head and she did not like it one bit.

The foursome burst into hysterical laughter as Gezz coughed and spluttered the smoke back up into her mouth and out. The taste of black coffee and tarmac was much stronger this time. She quickly handed the cigarette back to the boy, who was still laughing. As she did so, she hoped she wouldn't have yellow-brown nicotine stains on her finger and thumb.

'You have to keep doing it,' said the tall blonde, again with an affectionate smile. 'Then you will get used to it and you won't even notice the taste. You don't get dizzy or anything after a while.'

Gezz shook her head. 'I don't want to get used to it,' she said determinedly. 'I don't see how it can do you any good.' She turned to her friend. 'Come on, Anne.'

But Anne was not budging. 'I wish to experience the practice.'

Gezz looked on, appalled, as the boy held out his cigarette a second time. By now it had burned down to about a third of its original length. Without any hesitation, Anne took the cigarette between her finger and thumb and then placed it in her lips. She drew hard, very hard, harder than Gezz or the other children had ever seen anyone draw before. The tip glowed hot and the paper tube burned, the ash on the end getting longer. Or was it the cigarette getting shorter?

The children watched, transfixed, as Anne continued to suck more smoke into her mouth. The cigarette burned and burned until there was nothing but a filter and a line of ash. The remains of the cigarette collapsed and fell from the girl's fingers on to the floor. Then she took a deep breath, inhaling the blue mist into whatever she had for lungs. Her eyes blinked, but not because she was struggling to breathe or because she thought it tasted horrible. No. Gezz realized what the android was doing. It was testing the contents of the smoke.

'Analyzing,' announced the little blonde, her ponytail swishing as she cocked her head ever so slightly. 'This smoke contains up to seven hundred different chemical additives including heavy metals, pesticides, and insecticides.' The blue mist puffed itself out of her mouth and nostrils as she spoke. 'Toxic ingredients include about four thousand substances, such as arsenic, carbon monoxide and cyanide.'

Gezz had just taken a lungful of that poison too. She felt sick. 'And how would all that affect a person's chances of getting cancer?'

Anne cocked her head again. 'Cancer,' she stated very simply. 'Malignant tumour in the body. Mouth cancer, throat cancer, lung cancer, bowel cancer. No known cure. Causes death to humans.' She reached out her hand to the big greasy girl, who, despite the facts and figures, had lit herself a fresh cigarette. *Probably on purpose*, thought Gezz.

'Further analysis required,' said Anne, and the girl reluctantly handed over her fag. This time Anne just sniffed the smoke as it rose from the end. 'Your lungs and those of people nearby are exposed to at least forty-three known cancer-causing agents every time you do this,' she concluded.

Then to everyone's surprise, she turned the long white paper tube in on her palm, and with the end still burning vibrantly, she crushed the cigarette in her fist. 'This is an illogical pastime,' she said, and Gezz was unsure if Anne might be displaying anger. It did seem like anger, although the voice was just as flat as ever, and the face showed no signs of emotion at all. 'The chances of getting cancer are very high,' she continued. 'The chemicals in the smoke are slowly rotting your mouths and tongues away. Your lungs are also being affected. You run the risk of heart disease later on in your lives if you do not stop. The nicotine drug in your blood is damaging your brains.'

The two boys and the blonde girl looked crestfallen and sad. Anne had spoiled their fun. But they were not daft, Gezz observed. Each of them in turn dropped their cigarettes on to the ground and stamped them out with the soles of their shoes. Only the big girl continued. She yanked the sports bag from the boy who had said smoking wouldn't kill you earlier on, and in a display of rebellion, unzipped the bag and pulled out a packet of ten and a lighter. 'You won't be needing these any more then, will you?' she sneered.

Disgusted, the others watched as the girl lit up a fresh cigarette. Anne stared at her. 'Why are you doing this?' she asked. 'Why do you want to destroy yourself?'

Gezz tugged the automaton by the sleeve. 'Come on,' she said. 'Let's get back to the main playground. The bell will be ringing in a minute.' The other children nodded their full agreement and set off for the playgrounds, leaving the stubborn lone smoker to puff on her cancer stick.

★ ★ ★

It seemed strange on the main playground, watching the different shapes and sizes at play. Some of the younger ones of about Gezz's age ran about and played games like Tig, much as they had probably done at primary school. Others, older and bigger, just stood in groups talking.

As Gezz walked at a pace across the hard ground to one of the entrances, the summer air breezed about her and she could smell that horrible coffee-tarmac odour wafting off her clothes. The taste hung in the back of her throat too, and she imagined all the chemicals working their evil and rotting the skin in her mouth, throat and lungs. She vowed to herself never to touch another cigarette again.

A bellow of group laughter broke her concentration. It was coming from a group of year sevens hovering round a low rail which accompanied the concrete path leading to the main door. As the school bell rang and the crowd dispersed to start their next lesson, Gezz's heart sank. For there, arched over forwards, his pullover dishevelled and his glasses lying on a patch of grass, was Malcolm. He was crying silently to himself and trying to unfasten his necktie, which had been wrapped tightly round the metal rail. He knelt down in an attempt to loosen the knot, but it was no good.

Gezz knelt beside him and tugged at the boy's tie. As she did so, it just got tighter and tighter around his throat. More laughter could be heard from various open windows as most of the schoolchildren had made their way to class. 'Who has done this, Malc?'

The boy tried to wipe his eyes. 'Oh, Gezz,' he blubbed. 'Thank goodness it's you. I've lost my glasses. My mum'll kill me.'

'It's all right,' Gezz said gently, feeling very motherly towards him all of a sudden. 'I have your glasses here.' She picked the spectacles up from the grass and slotted them over Malcolm's ears. 'There.'

Anne, who had been standing at Gezz's side, walked round to the other side of Malcolm and without warning started to work on the crazy knot of his tie. Her hands moved like lightning, like a speeded-up film of someone working. In no time, the tie was undone and Malcolm was free.

'Thank you,' he said very sincerely, much calmer now. 'Both of you.'

The android returned to its usual pose, its task complete, but Gezz did not stand up. Instead she stayed crouched at Malcolm's side and put a friendly hand on his back. 'Who did it, Malc?'

The boy started filling up again, his eyes streaming with tears, his speech full of crackles and catarrh. 'That big lad in my form,' he spluttered. 'Ronald Higgingbottom. They call him the Fist.'

Gezz helped him up. 'The Fist, eh?' She was indignant. The cretin had probably called *himself* that and his followers just liked the sound of it. 'What's your next lesson, Malcolm?'

'Art,' Malcolm replied.

'Same here. Who have you got?'

'Mr Brahm.'

Gezz tapped her bottom lip and frowned, much the way the Professor used to do. She wondered for a second how he might be going on. 'You're in a different set to me,' she said. 'I've got Mrs Spencer.' She looked and smiled. 'Tell you what. Meet me in the dining hall at dinnertime. I'll save a seat for you and you can stay with us. The Fist won't try anything while we're about.'

Malcolm stopped crying and wiped his tears. 'Oh, thanks, Gezz.'

'Now, go on. We're both going to get done for being late for our lessons.'

The trio set off through the main door, skipped up a flight of stairs and walked along a brightly lit corridor. This was the art corridor, Gezz told herself. She *hoped* it was the art corridor, anyway. Malcolm entered the door at the end and Gezz could hear a faint 'Sorry I'm late, Sir' before the door closed behind him. She and Anne paused outside the middle room. She could still smell the foul odour of stale smoke on her clothes and could taste it on her lips and on her tongue. As she tried the door she hoped her classmates, or worse still, the teacher would not be able to smell it.

★ ★ ★

'And where have you two young ladies been?' boomed a middle-aged woman by the name of Mrs Spencer. 'The lesson started ten minutes ago.'

Gezz homed in on Luke, who sat alone on a stool at a large table near a window that overlooked the spot where Malcolm had been tied up. She headed for it, all the time dragging Anne by the edge of her sleeve. 'Sit next to me,' she commanded the automaton, and the pair of them took stools and sat opposite the boy. 'Sorry, Miss,' Gezz called. 'We got a bit lost.'

The room was spacious with lots of paintings and sketches lining the walls. A big kiln dominated the far end with lots of clay sculptures filling an old workbench by its side. The centre of the room was taken up by a big round table full of junk. Bits of car engine, a milk bottle, a clump of different coloured wires, among other things.

Gezz noticed that Luke had brought a glass with one of those inbuilt twisting spiral straws to their table and a fairly big piece of paper. 'We've got to choose something and draw it,' he said.

'Right,' said Gezz. She turned to address her robot companion. 'You wait here and I'll bring you something to draw.'

The android did as she was told and Gezz got up. As she walked past Luke and made her way to the pile of rubbish, the boy sniffed, frowned and wrinkled his nose. When his friend passed him again with an old shoe and a car radiator fan in one arm and two sheets of paper and some pencils in the other hand, he frowned again. 'Gezz,' he said curiously.

'Yes?' replied Gezz, absent-mindedly climbing on to her stool.

'I don't want to be funny or anything,' continued the perfectly turned-out boy. 'But have you been smoking?'

Gezz stopped dead and blushed. She felt ashamed and embarrassed all at the same time. She could not look her friend in the eye. He started to giggle to himself. If it was possible to whisper a laugh, then he was doing it. 'I can't believe it,' he croaked to himself with a huge grin. 'Squeaky clean, chapel-going Gezz, smoking.'

The girl finally looked up, but she was not laughing. 'I don't recommend it,' she said. 'It's horrible.' Then she turned to their robot friend. 'Anyway, it was her fault. She was desperate to try it.'

Luke cackled even more, all the time trying not to attract the attention of Mrs Spencer. 'Anne's been smoking? What will Professor Droyd say?'

It was the android who answered, surprising them both. 'My father will no doubt agree with my conclusions. Cigarette smoking is highly dangerous to human health and people who persist in engaging in it lack intelligence.'

The statement wiped the grin from Luke's face in one swoop. He scowled at the mechanical girl. 'My mum and dad smoke.'

'Their chances of contracting a life-threatening disease are high,' said Anne. 'I do not understand how they can enjoy something that is slowly killing them.'

The scowl intensified. 'Just draw your stupid fan, OK?'

'The fan does not have the capacity for being stupid. It has no mental awareness at all.'

'Well, it's like you, then, isn't it?'

Before Anne could reply, the sound of Mrs Spencer carried across the room. 'Er, we're not interested in your private life, Mr Davidson,' she grumbled. 'Just get on with it.'

The trio fell silent and began sketching their pieces of bric-a-brac. Anne watched the two children, and then seemed to realize what they were doing. She too picked up a pencil and started to draw the curved lines of her car radiator fan. In seconds the drawing was complete and she put the pencil down and sat silently upright, unblinking, as she always did when not engaged in conversation, staring at the kiln on the far wall.

Mrs Spencer scanned the class as their heads were down working away and the noise of light scribble filled the room. She stopped as her eyes fell upon Anne, who sat bolt upright in her weird trance. The teacher pointed a bony finger. 'You girl!'

Anne's head turned slowly and rhythmically. 'Are you addressing me, Miss?'

Luke and Gezz buried their heads further into their work as the teacher burst into a rage.

'Yes, I am addressing you!' Her voice was coarse and her words spat themselves out very deliberately. 'What is your name?'

'Anne Droyd, Miss.'

Rage turned to a kind of bemusement. '*Anne Droyd?*'

'It's true, Miss,' piped up one of the other children. 'That is her name. Her father was German, or something.'

'Well then, Miss Droyd,' boomed Mrs Spencer sarcastically. 'Can you tell us why you have stopped sketching your piece?'

'Yes, Miss,' Anne replied innocently.

'Well?'

'Well what, Miss?'

Mrs Spencer gritted her teeth. 'Don't well-what-miss me,' she spat. 'Get on with your work before I send you to Mr Turnbull.'

Anne, entirely unflustered by the teacher's tone and manner, said simply, 'I have finished the task, Miss.'

That was the final straw for Mrs Spencer. She marched across the room to the table near the window, her fists clenching and unclenching. Gezz shivered and prayed to God that the teacher wouldn't smell the smoke on her clothes. 'How dare you talk to me like that, you insolent…' Mrs Spencer broke off as she caught sight of Anne's paper.

Gezz glanced up and watched Mrs Spencer staring, mouth agape, at the drawing in her hand. The sketch was perfect, the perspective and shading exactly right. In fact it looked almost like a black and white photograph of a car radiator cooling fan. A real work of art. Gezz and Luke joined the teacher in gawping, awe struck, at the masterpiece.

'You insolent what, Miss?' asked the automaton blankly. 'You did not complete your sentence.'

Not even hearing the statement, Mrs Spencer broke into a broad smile. 'Why, child,' she said softly and with sudden affection. 'What remarkable talent you have. This is amazing, truly amazing.' She swiped the paper from the table and held it up to the rest of the class. 'Look, everyone. Look what Anne has done.'

A low mumble of group admiration and wonder filled the room and Gezz was proud that her friend Anne had provoked such a response. Mrs Spencer patted the automaton on the head. 'Well done, dear. I will enter this into the Young Artist of the Year competition.' Her voice grew loud enough for all the class to hear. 'And I shall assign you a merit mark.'

The teacher went to her desk, flipped a square yellow card from one of the drawers and began scribbling something on it with an old-fashioned fountain pen. Then she presented it to the robot.

Anne read the card out aloud. 'This merit is awarded to Anne Droyd for excelling in her age group at natural artistic talent.' A hush fell over the class and Mrs Spencer smiled. Then Anne turned to face her friends. 'This is to signify that Mrs Spencer is pleased with my work?'

'Yes,' said Gezz with a smile.

Luke nodded. '*Very* pleased.'

Anne turned her head rhythmically back to the teacher. 'Your pleasure in my work has been noted, Mrs Spencer,' she announced seriously. For a second everyone paused, not knowing how they should react for the best. Even Mrs Spencer was taken aback. Then, with a shake of the head and a laugh that could almost have shattered the windows, Mrs Spencer returned to her desk. And then, with some relief, everyone else laughed too.

17

Recharge

Lunchtime was quite hectic as, once again, the corridors heaved with bodies, all surging in one general direction. The unmistakable smell of chips and pies greeted Gezz's nostrils and her stomach juices reacted with accorded enthusiasm. She was starving.

Luke walked with her, and she just knew he would be smelling the stale smoke as it oozed from her, advertising to anyone who came into close contact with her the dirty deed she had been engaged in during morning break. The taste of black coffee and tarmac, although not as strong now, was still lingering on her tongue and in her throat. She could not wait to eat and drink and wash away this awful reminder of what she had done. It staggered her to contemplate that most adults who smoked always had a cigarette *after* a meal. Why on earth would they want to do that? Gezz was as baffled by this particular human practice as her android friend had been.

'I can't see Malc anywhere,' said Luke, breaking the girl's trance. 'I thought you said he was meeting us in the dining hall.'

'He is.'

'Optical sensors indicate that Malcolm is standing in the queue ahead,' piped the robot suddenly.

Luke groaned. 'Don't talk like that in here,' he chided. 'Don't say "optical sensors indicate". Say "I can see Malcolm standing in the queue".'

'I can see Malcolm standing in the queue,' Anne repeated.

Luke and Gezz smiled together. It was always good to see the android making progress. 'That's more like it,' said the boy.

Malcolm was indeed standing in a queue. It stretched in a long line to a single table stationed at the entrance to the dining hall. Behind it sat a white-haired woman from the school's reception office. She was ticking names off in a register before handing out to each pupil a small green ticket. Gezz realized what was going on. 'Free dinners,' she said absent-mindedly.

'What?' frowned Luke.

'Free dinners. All the kids whose parents can't afford to give them dinner money are entitled to free dinners.'

Luke raised his eyebrows. 'The lucky bandits.'

'Not really,' Gezz said, making sure her friend got the message. *There's nothing lucky about having no money for food*, she thought. As the children passed Malcolm in the queue, Gezz waved. 'Malc!' The boy looked round, somewhat dazed. He caught sight of his friends and grinned, waving back. 'We'll save you a seat inside!' Malcolm nodded and put up a thumb to indicate his approval.

Secondary school dinners are great, Gezz told herself once they had got inside the hall. Much better than the primary school ones, which just arrived already made in big tins. The dinners here were clearly cooked on the premises. Gezz's stomach juices were really going now, as she saw her favourite chippy dinner – meat and potato pie, chips and gravy – on the menu. Her mouth glands were also keenly anticipating the nosh-up, but all she could taste was nicotine.

She got a tray and worked her way along the serving hatches, picking up her chips and gravy, and that custard thing people called 'Manchester Tart' for afters. A mug of tea always tasted good after a big greasy meal, so she ordered one of those too.

Then came the problem. She could see all the prices on the board, but because she had only been given a couple of pounds, she could not be sure she had enough money to cover it. She tried to reckon up the price in her head, but the more she tried, the more she failed to see the numbers in her mind's eye, and the more she panicked. Gezz was starting to feel very unsure of herself now. At any minute, the lady on the till would ask for the money, and she might have to start putting things back and look silly in front of everyone.

'What's the matter, Gezz?' asked Luke, his voice breaking through the confusion of panic in her mind.

'Eh?'

'What's the matter?' the boy repeated. 'You look like you're going to start crying. You're not worried about Malc, are you?'

'No,' said Gezz sheepishly. 'I don't know if I've got enough money for all this.'

Luke cast his eyes to the menu board on the wall and scanned very business-like across it. Then he looked at the coins in Gezz's hand. 'You've got enough,' he said simply, and Gezz felt that warm glow inside her again. What would she do without him?

The boy presented his plate of salad before the till lady. It was typical of him, always thinking of his slim figure. That was his mother coming out in him. She didn't mind smoking like a chimney, but she did have a thing about being over-weight. She said it was bad for the heart!

The threesome found an empty table near the wall and sat at it. Luke slid his plate off his tray on to the table and Gezz did the same with her assortment of delicacies. Only then did she realize that Anne had nothing to eat. 'Not having anything, Anne?'

'No,' replied Anne blankly. 'It is not necessary for me to ingest food. However, I am quite low on electrical power. It might be necessary to shut down and conserve energy.'

Luke shook his head slowly, a mouthful of lettuce tumbling as he spoke. 'No,' he said. 'You can't do that. You can't leave the building until home time.'

Then Gezz thought of something. She looked over her shoulders at the painted wall behind her, knife and fork still clutched firmly in her hands, and homed in on a wall socket. 'How about plugging herself in here?'

Luke darted his eyes to where Gezz was pointing. The socket was not too far away. 'She might get away with it,' he said.

Gezz stood up. 'Anne,' she said. 'Change places with me.'

Anne obeyed the instruction, and once the pair of them were reseated, the android lifted the side of her jumper. Underneath, sewn into the white cotton blouse, was a small square panel sealed by a lone press stud. She reached round with her left hand and flicked it open to reveal smooth white skin. Then, swiftly and precisely, a bump emerged and grew into a narrow flesh-covered wire and snaked itself over to the electric socket. In seconds a three-pin plug had formed and slotted itself into the wall. Anne closed her eyes and absorbed the power.

By this time, Malcolm had found his way into the hall and had begun surveying the price list. Gezz watched him looking at his dinner ticket and then at the menu board, and then back at his ticket again. She nudged her friend with her elbow. 'Luke,' she whispered. 'Malcolm is having trouble pricing his dinner. It's his ticket, you see. It's only worth so much. Go and help him.'

Luke watched Malcolm for a minute and then slammed down his knife and fork. 'God,' he said in a huff. 'I'm never going to get my dinner eaten at this rate.' The boy stood up, his chair screeching and whining as it scraped back across the floor, and he walked over to poor old Malcolm, who, like Gezz had done earlier, was getting flustered over his poor mental arithmetic skills.

Gezz started on her Manchester Tart. She loved the way the thin layer of milk skin on top broke as it hit the roof of her mouth and the thick congealed custard spread itself out over her tongue. The meat and potato pie, chips and gravy had completely annihilated the cigarette taste, and now she was able to enjoy her sweet all the more. She took a sip of her tea and watched Malcolm approach with his dinner.

The tray was crammed with food. Fish, chips and peas lay neatly arranged on the plate smothered with gravy. The boy picked up the salt and vinegar pots, one in each hand, and tossed their contents generously over his meal. Two buttered barm cakes sat aside the plate, and a can of *Coca Cola* fought for supremacy with a bowl of jelly and blancmange. Luke stared at the tray in disgust. 'How can you stomach all that?'

Malcolm, who had already begun to fill his face with chips, paused and gave a show of looking offended, his mouth hanging open with its contents visible to all. 'What?' he said.

Even Gezz had to concede that gluttony on this scale did indeed look revolting, but Malcolm just ignored them and carried on feeding his face. Then he noticed the android sitting with her eyes closed. 'What's with her?'

'She's recharging herself,' said Luke.

Malcolm swallowed his food in one go, and Gezz could see he was wishing he hadn't. She imagined the huge lump of fish and chips slowly working its way down his neck, wrenching every muscle and stretching the walls of his throat along the way. He stood up and bent over his dinner to see the skin-coloured cable leading from Anne's back to the plug socket in the wall. 'You're risking it a bit in here, aren't you?'

'She's got to recharge herself somewhere,' Gezz reproved. 'Why not here?'

Malcolm looked about nervously, sitting himself down again. 'Because anyone might see her,' he hissed. 'I mean, teachers come in and have their dinner with the kids at secondary school, you know.'

Anne's eyes flicked open. 'Power cells recharged,' she announced. The children looked on, forgetting their lunches momentarily, and watched the skin wire shoot up into Anne's back like a length of spaghetti being sucked into someone's mouth. The android closed the panel on her blouse and straightened her pullover.

Gezz, having finished her dinner, reached into her rucksack and produced a piece of paper with a black grid printed on to it. In each of the squares was blue biro writing. She traced her finger to Wednesday and found the last two squares. 'I wonder what we've got this afternoon.' She glanced at the timetable and felt an overwhelming sense of dread wash over her as the single five-letter word greeted her eyes. 'Oh my God,' she said slowly. 'We've got double maths. That's maths *all afternoon*. Two hours of it.'

'Aw,' Luke teased with a wicked grin. 'You said "oh my God". I thought that phrase offended you.'

'It does,' said Gezz sheepishly. 'It just slipped out.'

Anne leaned forward slightly, as if her next sentence might somehow arouse suspicion. 'Why is the phrase "oh my God" offensive to Gezz, but not to Luke?'

Gezz, Luke and Malcolm paused each in turn, exchanged glances and then looked straight at the android. 'Oh shut up,' they said simultaneously.

Anne leaned back and blinked. 'Shut up,' she said, analysing the phrase. 'According to the *Oxford English Dictionary*, that phrase means to stop talking.' She gave a single nod of the head. 'Very well. This unit will cease to speak until invited to do so.' And with that, the children enjoyed the remainder of their lunch hour in peace.

* * *

Maths was the subject Gezz hated the most. Fortunately, Malcolm and the other two had been assigned to the same class for this. It was what they called 'mixed ability' and the class was designed to find out who was good at it and who was not. Gezz thought that this was a waste of time. She could have told the teacher she was rubbish at the start and have done with it.

This particular teacher was quite old and had a bald head. He was called Mr Shawcross and was extremely boring. *This is great,* thought Gezz, *I'm in the most mind-numbing and difficult lesson there is, and when I could really do with a funny and lively teacher what do I get? A boring, serious one.*

Once again the children sat as close together as they could, with Gezz and Anne sitting at the same table. Gezz noticed that the black boy from her registration class was here for this one too.

I wonder what it's like being black, thought Gezz. The boy, Daley was it? He probably wondered exactly the same thing about being white. Then she looked at her friend Anne and tried to imagine what it was like to be made out of metal and have no emotions. Anne was the only person on earth who knew what that felt like. *I wonder if she gets lonely, being the only one*, Gezz thought again. *Probably not*, she concluded. *If you have no emotions, you can't feel lonely.*

'Now,' said Mr Shawcross in his low, sleep-inducing voice. 'We are going to cut different shapes out of card and make a collage.' He paused and glared slowly at individual members of the class, almost staring them out in certain cases. 'Now, who knows what a collage is?'

Malcolm shot his hand up. Shawcross nodded. 'Yes, boy?'

'It's a big school like a university,' grinned Malcolm.

'No,' said Shawcross simply and continued to glare with old brown eyes. *He is almost as emotionless as the android*, thought Gezz. Luke leaned across his desk and sneered, 'That's a *college*, dumb, dumb.'

Malcolm scowled. 'I've told you, Luke. Don't call me "dumb, dumb".'

Anne put up her hand and the teacher responded coldly, his face straight and expressionless. 'Yes – you!' he said, pointing to Anne.

'Collage,' announced the robot. 'Form or work of art in which various materials are arranged and glued to a backing.'

Mr Shawcross nodded. He did not smile or show any sign of being pleased. He simply stood at his desk and acknowledged, 'That is correct.'

Anne leaned toward Gezz and whispered into her ear. Yes, she actually whispered, having observed other children talking to one another during their various classes. 'Mr Shawcross displays no human emotional characteristics at all,' she said. 'I am suspecting he is an android.' She paused, as if to consider her own theory. 'Yes,' she concluded. 'It may have been manufactured by the Foundation to seek us out.'

Gezz doubled up immediately, holding her tummy as it wrenched. She felt her face go blood red and tears streamed down her cheeks. Anne almost frowned. 'I have caused you distress?' she said. 'Do not worry, I shall protect you.'

'She's not crying, tin girl,' jeered Luke, as quietly as he could. 'She's laughing.' He looked at his friend, who was still wiping tears from her eyes and mimed with his mouth, 'What did she say?'

Gezz cleared her throat and got her breath back. 'Oh,' she sighed. 'I'll tell you later.'

The Maths lesson was actually quite enjoyable, because they were not doing the sums the children had expected. They spent the whole afternoon measuring out different shapes using rulers and compasses, cutting them out and gluing them on to a large sheet of paper.

Naturally Anne did several before anyone else had even got started. Then she wowed the class by making a three-dimensional dodecahedron. That is a solid shape with twelve sides! Mr Shawcross was so impressed he put the shape on his desk next to his pot of pencils and pens.

Then he wrote a yellow merit card out and gave it to Anne. Two in one day! Her very first day at school – ever – had not gone badly, at all.

18

Integrate

Gezz skipped into her house, where her parents already were, having picked up Ross from nursery. 'Well?' said Gezz's mum, with some apprehension. 'How was your day?'

'It was great!' enthused Gezz. 'Anne was brilliant. When we were in English, she read the whole dictionary from cover to cover and knew lots of long words. Then in Art, she drew a really amazing picture of a fan. You know, a fan that goes in a car engine? And she had it put in a competition, and she got a merit card too. Then she found out what was in cigarettes and put some kids off smoking for life.'

'Good heavens,' said her dad, standing patiently with his hands in his trouser pockets. 'They start smoking at eleven?'

'Sometimes younger,' nodded her mum thoughtfully. 'It's a sign of the times, John.'

Her dad nodded with a glum expression. Gezz continued her exciting account. 'Then after dinner, we had Maths all afternoon and made shapes for a collage, and Anne made this weird box with, like, twelve sides called a dodecahedron and got another merit card.'

'Well,' said her dad, folding his arms. 'It sounds like Anne had a great day. The question is, did you?'

Gezz grinned and nodded. 'I just told you I did.'

Her mum grinned back and held out her arms. She walked towards her daughter, oozing with pride and love. 'Aw, my baby girl. Come here.'

Gezz almost stepped forward to receive the hug when she caught a whiff of something. A smell that floated about her and hit her in the face whenever she moved at speed. A smell that was something like black coffee and tarmac all mixed up.

She instinctively backed off, her face probably saying it all. 'Not now, Mum,' she said, trying to swallow a stammer. 'I want to get out of this uniform. I'm feeling a bit sweaty, you know.'

She trotted upstairs to her bedroom to get changed and could just make out the whispers at the foot of the stairs. 'What was all that about, John?'

'Oh, it's big school now, Ness. Just wait until she hits thirteen. Then it will be rock music, make-up and boys.'

The girl smiled to herself as she finally wriggled out of her stinking clothes. She would bung them in the washer when her mother was not looking and have done with it. What a day!

★   ★   ★

The remainder of the week seemed to fly by. Thursday brought a second English lesson where they had to write an essay about their happiest day. Anne spent a whole half-hour staring at a blank piece of paper, and then when Gezz asked her what was wrong, she said that because she was devoid of emotions, she had never had a happy day.

Gezz had to rephrase the instruction from 'happiest' to 'most fortuitous'. Then Anne spent a couple of minutes writing twenty-five pages about the day she met the children. The spelling was faultless, but there were no full stops and commas in the piece, and it was hard to tell where one sentence finished and another began. Then when Mr Ford wanted to know why Anne had finished so early, he read the piece and said at the top of his voice, 'This is a wonderful story, Anne. But really you should have written about something that has really happened to you.'

Gezz loved it when Anne didn't get embarrassed. However, she did have to prevent her from answering the teacher's snide remark.

The best lesson of the week, though, was Games. The boys had to go and play football with the sour-faced Mr Shawcross out in the rain and mud, but the girls had the use of the gym. It was warm inside, almost cosy in fact, and their teacher, Miss Cole, was a lovely bubbly type, eager to reward effort, so she loved Anne. The wall bars posed no problem, Anne just went up them, like Spider Man scaling the walls of a skyscraper, right to the top in seconds. Then she climbed down halfway, took one of the ropes dangling from a frame connected to a shaft in the ceiling, and swung like a monkey right across the room to the bars lining the opposite wall. Gezz just hoped she wasn't going to demonstrate any of those backward somersaults she saw her doing when the children first discovered her.

News of Anne's acrobatic talents soon spread throughout year seven.

Everyone kept pointing her out, teachers and pupils alike, and whispered to one another in hushed voices whenever she went by. She was becoming the most popular girl in school, and in just two days too! Teachers asked what her opinions were on different subjects and her answers always provoked food for thought and, more often than not, well-meaning laughter. Children adored her and she was often surrounded by a sizeable crowd at break-times.

Gezz didn't really mind Anne getting all the attention because it made life easier on her. It also helped Gezz, Luke and Malcolm fulfil their role as guardians to the robot. The Professor wanted Anne to integrate herself into human society and become more like a real girl. Her popularity among the children especially helped in this regard.

The only thing that had bothered Gezz in all of this was that Luke had started showing more and more interest in the automaton. Rather than feeling embarrassed by her and going off with his new pals as he had done in the first couple of days, he now tended to hover around Anne and answer questions in her behalf. On a couple of occasions, Gezz had spotted him gawping at Anne in that dreamy way people do when they fall in love.

Gezz hated it.

19

Everybody's Friend

Thank goodness it's Friday, thought Malcolm to himself as he parted his bedroom curtains. The sky was clear and the sun gave a warm hue to the morning which was at odds with the way he was feeling. Gezz and Luke seemed to be enjoying every minute of their new school life, but then they would. They were in the same form, in virtually every other class together, and they had Anne with them pretty much all the time.

He turned from the window and tried to guess what time it was. It felt about the right time to go downstairs. His mum and dad had little need for an alarm clock, so he had to rely on his built-in 'timer' to wake him. He changed out of his pyjamas into his school uniform and headed for the hall landing, leaving his bed covers ruffled and unmade.

The landing was like the rest of the house – dark. Even with all the curtains opened, it still managed to look grey and gloomy. He walked past his parents' bedroom door. A floor-board creaked, but it didn't bother him. He knew they wouldn't hear it. They would be out for the count for several more hours yet.

Malcolm entered the bathroom and pulled the cord that switched on the light. The bulb was unshaded and gave off a pitiful amount of light. The bathroom seemed eerie, swathed in shadows. He ran the hot water tap for a few seconds, but the water stayed cold. *They must have forgotten to put the immersion on last night*, he told himself. *Too out-of-it as usual.*

He cupped his hands under the tap and threw the frigid water onto his face. He blinked as the fluid washed over his tired eyes and then reached for the old damp towel left strewn across the edge of the bath. Once he had finished with the toilet, he flushed it and went back to his bedroom to get his glasses.

★ ★ ★

'We've run out again!' said Malcolm aloud to himself as he emptied the remains of an old box of cornflakes into a bowl. The bowl was barely half-full but it would have to do. He went to the fridge and opened the door. A weak interior light revealed a plate of butter all alone on the middle shelf and a single tomato immediately above it. A half-pint of milk was slotted inside the door. Malcolm lifted the lid and sniffed the contents. It was starting to go off, but it would do. It would have to.

His parents did not eat much cereal, nor did they drink much milk. They didn't even drink tea and coffee like other mums and dads. When they eventually did get up, they tended to have a glass of lemonade or some such fizzy drink. Then, in the early afternoon, they had a pint of beer each before setting off out for the day. If he was lucky they would be back in time for a chip-shop supper. Then they would go out again after *EastEnders* (his mum loved that programme) and Malcolm would be in bed by the time they got back.

As he scraped up the last of his cornflakes and shovelled them into his mouth, there was a sharp knock on the door. Was it that time already? He dropped his bowl into the sink full of grey water and tried to push it down along with the several plates, mugs and pint glasses that had been accumulating since the start of the week. Then he dried his hands on the hem of his pullover and rushed to the living-room curtains.

He peeled back the edge of the far right curtain as his mother had taught him to do and then smiled as he saw his two friends standing on his doorstep looking vibrant and smart. He went into the hall and picked up his Tesco bag full of books, tossed it over his shoulder and opened the front door.

* * *

'Hi,' said Gezz with a grin. Malcolm felt a tingle of warmth inside his tummy as he took in Gezz's pretty features.

'Hi,' Malcolm replied and closed the rickety door behind him.

'All set for the last day of your first week?'

'Well, I'm certainly set for the end of it,' said Malcolm. 'Roll on half-past three.'

Luke put his left hand in his pocket and steadied his sports bag with his right and set off up the semicircular road, taking the lead as usual. 'You can't spend your whole life at Crompton Green waiting for half-past three,' he said. 'You've got five years to do at this place, you know.'

Gezz giggled. 'You make it sound like a prison sentence.'

Malcolm adopted a serious frown as he trailed behind. 'Malcolm Hardy,' he bellowed, trying to sound as adult and important as he could. 'You have been found guilty of being a miserable old boot.' He glared at his friends over the rim of his glasses. Gezz and Luke started to laugh. 'And,' he continued, enjoying the positive reaction of the others, 'I sentence you to five years' imprisonment at Crompton Green High School.'

The three of them laughed heartily, and Malcolm was pleased to have said something the other two found funny. It rarely happened, so he appreciated it when it did.

They hit the main road and that awful swarm of cars and kids trudging up to the school. The building loomed menacingly on the horizon like a death camp. Malcolm remembered the television programme Gezz had seen about those camps. School was one of them as far as he was concerned.

'Right,' said Luke, rubbing his hands together. 'I'll go and get Anne. See you in class.'

Gezz seemed troubled by Luke's out-of-character act of self-sacrifice. 'What? Wait a minute. On your own?'

'Well,' breezed Luke with an almost nervous smile. 'We don't all have to go, do we?' He appeared to Malcolm to be quite edgy, which was unusual for him. 'I mean, it only takes one to get her from the den. You go on and I'll meet you in reg.'

Reg was short for registration, but Malcolm personally liked to use the whole word. 'Seems like a good idea to me,' he said.

'No,' Gezz replied adamantly. Her anger took Malcolm by surprise. 'Anne is the responsibility of us all, and we will all go and meet her.'

Luke was not going to push it, which again was out of character for him, although he did look disappointed. 'OK,' he said, shrugging carelessly. 'Keep your hair on.'

And so the three of them went about their morning ritual. He and Luke hid in the undergrowth near the den while Gezz went to get Anne. The automaton emerged from the old air-raid shelter in her immaculate uniform, carrying a rucksack full of homework that would have taken her no time to write, and performed the fibre-optic lens routine before leaping up, *Bionic Woman* style, out of the trench and on to the gravel path.

'Good morning, Malcolm,' said the robot, her face as deadpan as ever. 'How are you today?'

Malcolm was impressed. 'I'm very well, thank you,' he said, eager to play a part in her development. 'And how are you?'

Anne blinked that blink which told the children she was processing information. 'All systems functioning perfectly.'

Gezz coughed in that way people did when they meant to say 'I beg your pardon' and the android corrected herself. 'I mean I am very well, thank you, Malcolm.' The children smiled as they led the robot up the steep path to the main road which would take them to school. Anne was coming on nicely.

No sooner had they got on to the pavement than shouts and whistles carried through the air from all directions. Malcolm watched his two friends become subdued. They knew the cries of appreciative fandom were not for them. And Malcolm knew only too well that they were definitely not for him. Anne's popularity worried them all a bit, because the more loved by others she became, the harder it would be for her guardians to keeps tabs on her all the while and fulfil their promise to the Professor.

Two year ten boys suddenly appeared out of nowhere on flashy looking mountain bikes. Mind you, all mountain bikes looked flashy to Malcolm. They rode alongside the three friends. 'Oi, Anne,' one of them called. 'Fancy coming ice skating with us this weekend?'

Malcolm knew what they were up to. They wanted to show Anne's ice-skating talents off to their pals, which undoubtedly would be better than the skills possessed by any professional ice skater on the planet.

Anne's head turned and she gave her pre-instructed response. 'No, thank you. I will be staying with my cousins this weekend.'

'Well, they can come too,' enthused the boy. 'There will be a few of us going.'

Suddenly Luke turned, catching them all by surprise, and pointed an accusing finger. 'Look,' he scowled. 'She said she's staying with her cousins for the weekend. OK?'

'Yeah, yeah,' said the boy, trying to shrug his shoulders and ride his bike at the same time. He turned to the other boy, who had stayed silent the whole time. 'Come on.' Both of them smiled at Anne and said, 'Bye, Anne. See you later,' before riding off up the road to school.

'Goodbye,' said Anne in her monotone voice, and turned her head to face forward.

Gezz prodded Luke in the shoulder with her finger. 'What's up with you, all of a sudden?'

Luke gave a show of looking bemused. 'What?'

'You know what.'

'I don't.'

'Getting all upset because they asked Anne to go ice skating with them.'

Luke tried to laugh it off. 'Well,' he said. 'She can't go, can she? How are we going to look out for her if she goes off with other kids?'

'We could have gone with her,' said Gezz, scrunching up her nose and staring with blood-shot eyes. Malcolm had never seen her so angry before. 'We could have kept an eye on her and gone with them.' She looked like she was going to cry. Why was everyone acting so weird today? Must be the hot weather they had been having recently, Malcolm concluded.

'Oh yeah,' Luke jeered. 'So when did you get into ice skating, then?'

A call from across the road interrupted the argument, and Malcolm was grateful for the distraction. 'Hey!' said a girl's voice. Malcolm looked round. It was those two year nine girls who liked to smoke on the way to school. But this time they were without a cigarette. 'Anne!' they shouted again. The android turned her head. 'Look!' called the duo, both waving their hands in the air. 'We've given up!'

Gezz broke into a pleasant smile. She looked so pretty when she smiled. 'What? Both of you?' she called.

The spotty one with the brown hair nodded and grinned. 'I'm still dying for a ciggy,' she said, 'but I think I've cracked it.'

'You hear that, Anne?' said Gezz enthusiastically. 'They've stopped smoking.' She slipped an arm around the girl's shoulders and gave the automaton a warm hug, and then released herself quickly, the hard metal of the robot skeleton putting her off. Malcolm sensed Gezz's uneasiness. Anne might look like a real girl, with skin, hair, eyes and a voice, but really she was a machine, just a clever machine. Yet he found himself joining his friend in praising her. 'It's all down to you, Anne. Well done.'

★ ★ ★

The time soon arrived for Malcolm to part company from the others. He stood in the playground with them and shivered as the bell rang its peal. 'Well,' he said. 'I'll see you all at break-time then.' He gave a brief wave and then set off for his registration form, all the while his stomach churning with foreboding and anticipation.

20

The Humiliation

Malcolm held his breath before turning the door handle and entering the room. His eyes darted about the class. His form tutor, Mr Ford, was nowhere to be seen. Tremors ran through his knees and his stomach churned all the more. With Mr Ford about he felt safe, but now he would have to suffer the taunts of the Fist until the teacher returned to take charge of this unruly mob.

Most of the class sat quite normally, talking and laughing with one another, but all Malcolm could see was the rotund backside of the Fist staring him in the face. The boy was leaning across his usual table and engaged in an arm wrestle with some fool who had decided he could take him on. The contestant was thin and weedy and was at that moment going blood red, his eyes watering, his brow running with sweat, as all his strength ebbed away. With a loud thud the boy's arm buckled and crashed on to the desk. The Fist roared with glee and the small group of boys surrounding the table joined him in his moment of glory.

Malcolm watched the big bottom flop back on to its seat, its crack showing ever so slightly over the waistband. The monster flexed his fingers and stretched his arms. 'Is there anyone else daft enough to take on the Fist?' he bellowed, his teeth square and stained, pale blue eyes bulging with manic delight. The Fist's followers all shook their heads and giggled. But their laughs were a combination of admiration and wonder mingled with fear, Malcolm noted. They were more frightened of the Fist than they were amused by him. Children who were weak in character, who perhaps wished they could be like him, who wished they could command an audience and be popular, they were the ones he tended to attract.

One of the boys, eager to change the subject and take the Fist's attention off him, pointed over the skinhead's shoulder. The potato-shaped head turned, and immediately on catching sight of Malcolm, roared its horrible laugh. 'Well!' he sneered. 'If it's not speccy four eyes!'

The Fist's disciples fell about in hysterics and Malcolm resisted the temptation to burst into tears. It was hard, though, as his eyes started to fill and his bottom lip quivered. The bulky lad waded through tables and chairs and bore down upon him, slipping a chunky right arm about his shoulders. 'So then, fat-so,' he beamed, the other boys holding their mouths and noses in mock hysteria. 'What's it like being the ugliest lad in Crompton Green?'

Malcolm avoided eye contact and stared at the floor. The Fist tightened his grip. 'I hope you're not ignoring me, Hardy,' he said. 'Because that would be very rude. Now.' He raised his voice and spun Malcolm round to face the rest of the class. All of them, boys and girls, some cheerful, some worried, some strong, some shy, some Malcolm had spoken to, and some he had not – all of them turned to face him and the Fist, an acute hush falling over the class. 'Now,' said the bully. 'I'll ask you again. Who is the ugliest lad in Crompton Green?'

There were a number of possible replies to this. Malcolm thought of what others might say. 'You should know' was a favourite. That one seemed to work a lot. It usually turned the class on the bully himself, but Malcolm knew he dare not try it. It would probably backfire and make everything worse, knowing him. Another option was turning the jibe over to someone else, singling out another boy and saying something like, 'I don't know, why don't you ask him?' But Malcolm couldn't do that. He could not put another person through the feelings he was experiencing right now. It would be cruel.

There was an additional problem, though, a deeper one. Malcolm looked sheepishly at different members of the class. Many of the girls were very pretty, and even the plain ones, even though being quite plain, were not so plain as to be classed as ugly. The boys of the class were appealing in their way. Some were what a girl might call handsome, others had dreamy eyes and nice smiles. Why, even the Fist himself, despite being a fat bulk of a lad, despite his skinhead haircut and mad staring eyes, managed to be popular, and among his little group of followers he was *adored*.

No one adored Malcolm. In fact, most of the class barely spoke to him at all. His hair was long and scraggy, his uniform was an untidy mess, he was overweight, his breath stank, and worst of all, he wore glasses. No one thought he was clever and the only times he ever made people laugh was by accident or when being ridiculed, like now. Truth be told, Malcolm believed he really was the ugliest boy in Crompton Green. 'I am,' he croaked, his throat dry and tense.

Some of the girls adopted that motherly look that Gezz's mum sometimes had, which suggested, 'Aw, poor thing'. But none of them spoke. Not one person was going to come to his aid. No one ever did. A couple of boys, not with the Fist faithful, tried to subdue their fit of giggles, gritting their teeth and closing tear-filled eyes tightly. But their bobbing shoulders gave their true feelings away. Malcolm sensed the Fist grin with delight as he stood behind him. 'Say it again!' he sneered.

'I am,' Malcolm stammered.

'Louder,' commanded the Fist. 'We can't hear you.'

'I am,' said Malcolm, quite clear now.

'We still can't hear you,' the Fist laughed. 'Who is the ugliest boy in Crompton Green?'

With a clear, definite cry, Malcolm spat the words out. 'I am.' He was close to breaking point now.

A sudden waft of air swept over the class. Chairs screeched and children busied themselves as though nothing had occurred. The Fist leapt back to his table leaving Malcolm standing in the middle of the room. He removed his glasses and wiped his eyes with the sleeve of his pullover.

'What's going on?' said Mr Ford, standing by the open door.

Malcolm glanced round and slipped his spectacles on. 'Nothing, Sir,' he stammered. 'I just had something in my eye, that's all.'

'Well, sit down then,' said the teacher and closed the door. He marched to the front of the class and picked up the register from his desk. Malcolm could not wait to get out of the form room and move to his first class, Woodwork, which thankfully had Ronald Higgingbottom placed in a different set.

He took his seat at the back of the class and waited for his name to be called, all the time scowling at the chunky head of the one they called the Fist. Burning hatred welled up inside him and he imagined himself changing into the Incredible Hulk. A high-pitched sound accompanied glowing white eyes and his skin adopted a greenish tinge. His shirt and pullover burst at the seams and his shoes and socks peeled off large green feet. He imagined his eyebrows thickening and his already wild hair turning into something not unlike a dark-green frizzy wig.

With a roar of anger he stood and flexed his muscles, and then in slow motion, he picked up his desk and threw it against the blackboard. It sailed through the air and girls screamed as it shattered against the wall. He dreamt of over-turning a couple of other tables until he had reached his imagined cowering adversary. The fat skinhead scrambled back in terror, only to hit the window. Malcolm as the Hulk picked him up by the scruff of the neck and sent him flying into Mr Ford's desk, which collapsed under the weight of the cruel oaf.

The fantasy went some small way to making Malcolm feel a little bit better about things.

★ ★ ★

Woodwork went OK. The teacher had them making dovetails with a view to constructing an oblong box for pencils and pens. Malcolm worked alone, his box not quite fitting together, but glad of the peace and the confidence given him by the elderly instructor. The lesson was over all too quickly. The bell rang and pupils got their things together, welcoming the chance for fresh air and a break.

The teacher dismissed them and they filed out into the corridor. Malcolm passed a notice board exhibiting various little posters advertising extra-curricular activities. Some of them had taken place during break and dinnertimes, like the Gardening Club for example. Malcolm was not particularly interested in gardening, but if it got him away from the bullies, it was worth a try.

He stepped through one of the exits and into the play-ground. The central swarm of kids grew and spread as they poured out from the different exits. Then they broke up into their usual groups. Malcolm struggled with feelings of deep anger and hatred. He knew he shouldn't hate them, but his emotions were running strong. No one had given him a chance. No one had allowed him time to prove what he was really about. The popular ones banded together quickly within hours of meeting on the big first day, and people like him were just left to wander about aimlessly. Even the teachers, like Mr Ford, should have detected that something was wrong by now. When Ford had walked into his form to take the register earlier on, he *must* have known something had happened. He *must* have seen it a thousand times before with other children.

The boy set off to the sparsely populated part of the school grounds where few children ever went, to the far side at the back of the gym, where only the smokers congregated by the boiler house and the bike sheds. He eased up, feeling free again as the main body of children became a blur of burgundy, black and grey in the distance.

A blue tangled mist hung about the old brick shelters as two or three older kids puffed away on their cigarettes. It was tempting to go and join them, for they would surely accept him if he shared in their secret ritual. But Anne's analysis had put paid to his even trying it. He didn't fancy getting heart disease or lung cancer when he grew up.

He watched them from the shadow of the gym, wishing he could just ignore the truth about smoking and go and take a drag. As he was dreaming of how it might be, something heavy and meaty landed on his left shoulder. He winced in pain and turned on his heels, his stomach churning and his hips loosening as he took in the nightmarish sight. It was the Fist.

'So,' snarled the hideous creature, his eyes wild and mad. 'This is where you hide away at break-times.'

Malcolm said nothing. The Fist grabbed him by the shoulder of his pullover and slammed him hard against the cold brick of the gym wall. The boy spluttered as the air was knocked from him. The grotesque stepped forward and brought his awful insane-looking expression very close to Malcolm. 'You've got a face like the back end of a bus,' he spat, his eyes raw and burning. Then he grinned, his yellow-stained teeth spreading across his mush like dirty tombstones. The Fist's voice fell into a whisper. 'Say it.'

At first, Malcolm just looked at him, afraid to speak. The Fist took the boy's arm and twisted it back with his free hand and squeezed tightly. 'Say it.'

'No,' breathed Malcolm weakly, his eyes starting to fill. Another twist of the arm sent pain darting down his back and he winced. 'I have a face like the back end of a bus,' he said tearfully.

The Fist threw back his head and let out a manic roar of laughter. 'Excellent!' he shouted. He snatched Malcolm forward, keeping one hand on the scruff of his jumper and the other on his twisted arm, spun him round and half-dragged him across the playground to a group of year ten lads. 'Oi! Bradley!' shouted the Fist.

Bradley, the obvious leader of the little group, looked over and smiled. As he did so, the Fist wrenched Malcolm's arm further back. The boy's eyes glazed with restrained tears and he reluctantly delivered his line. 'I have got a face like the back end of a bus.'

Bradley and his friends collapsed into manic laughter straight away, each of them holding their tummies and wiping their eyes. Delighted by the reaction, the Fist dragged Malcolm over to his next venue.

Three year seven boys stood in a huddled group by the railings. They were exchanging trading cards with one another. 'Oi, Hawsy!' called the bully. Malcolm recognized the lad who had absent-mindedly glanced up from his cards. He was from his Woodwork class. 'You wanna hear something funny?'

Hawsy was only half-interested as Malcolm was put on display, tripping over his own feet as he was positioned into place. 'What?' said the lad.

'I have a face like the back end of a bus,' said Malcolm on cue, feeling the Fist's hand twisting his arm back even further and giving him a Chinese burn in the process.

Hawsy did not really react, being too engrossed in his trading cards. But the other two boys did. They cackled away, nearly dropping their packs. 'Nice one, Fist,' said the one on the left, and Malcolm struggled to keep his bottom lip from quivering. He felt terrible. His eyes were burning, his head ached, his legs were like jelly and his heart felt close to exploding. He tripped and wobbled as the Fist tugged at his jumper, moving him on to the next performance.

His heart did not explode. Rather, it sank into his tummy and then fell into his shoes. The next little group to receive his confession were his dearest friends. They stood quietly chatting in the shadow of a large tree where the main school building backed on to the playing fields. Gezz and Luke tried not to look horrified as the big bully dragged their comrade in front of them. Anne followed their gaze, her face totally unresponsive.

It was all too much for Malcolm. He finally broke down, taking his glasses off with his free hand and dabbing his eyes with his sleeve. The Fist grinned his sickening grin. 'Your friend has something to tell you.'

Malcolm yelped as pain darted down his spine again, his arm almost disconnecting from its socket. He could see through his tears the distorted images of Gezz and Luke waiting to hear his admission. 'I,' he said, and started crying again. More pain made him finish his sentence. 'I have a face like the back end of a bus,' he said limply.

21

Wound for Wound

Luke tried to conceal his reaction as best he could and turned to face the other way, his wobbling shoulders betraying him. Malcolm dabbed his eyes and slipped his glasses back on. Gezz looked visibly pained, a tear of empathy trickling down her blushing red cheeks.

Unexpectedly, Anne piped up, 'Bus: Large passenger vehicle, especially one serving the public on a fixed route.'

The Fist released Malcolm and was seized by a fit of uncontrollable hysteria. He doubled over and held his stomach, his breath faltering as he laughed all the air from his lungs. The android turned to Gezz for confirmation. 'I have said something amusing?'

'No,' said Gezz, her voice trembling with anger. 'This boy who calls himself the Fist is really a vicious bully called Ronald Higgingbottom.'

'Ronald Higgingbottom,' repeated Anne studiously.

Gezz gave a sarcastic smile to the Fist as he straightened himself up, clearly annoyed by the girl's use of his real name. 'Er, it's the Fist to you, sweetheart.'

'I'm not your sweetheart,' Gezz asserted. She looked Anne directly in the face. 'What is your definition of a bully?'

The answer was straightforward and concise. 'Bully,' stated the automaton. 'Person using strength and power to coerce others by fear. To persecute or oppress by force or threats.'

Other children joined themselves to the group, interested in what Anne was getting up to. They were always interested in the things Anne got up to. Some of them were children who had witnessed Malcolm's humiliation only minutes before.

Even Luke, now intrigued, had managed to calm himself and face the growing crowd.

The assembling mass seemed to grow for absolutely ages, with smaller children standing on tiptoes in order to get a good view. The crowd pressed in, leaving room only for the Fist and Anne, who were now standing face to face at the centre. Gezz stood on the inner circle, goading the android on. 'What do you recommend should be done with bullies, Anne?'

The robot's eyes blinked as she searched her data banks. 'My understanding of the issue is limited,' she announced. 'But data extracted from the religious text known as the Bible suggests that a balance of justice must be carried out.'

'Define a balance of justice,' teased Gezz.

'Biblical definition of justice in the so-called Old Testament,' Anne replied, 'is eye for eye, tooth for tooth, hand for hand, foot for foot, burn for burn, wound for wound, bruise for bruise.'

Gezz touched Malcolm gently on the arm, her voice soft and soothing like a bandage to his soul. 'Malc,' she said. 'Where did the Fist hurt you?'

'My arm, mainly,' stammered the boy. 'He twisted my arm round my back. He pulled it so hard, I thought it was going to come out.'

'Right,' Gezz smiled wickedly. She addressed the crowd as best she could. 'Who of us here thinks they can single-handedly give the Fist what he deserves?' A muffled buzz came from the mob, who were exchanging glances and shaking their heads.

'I could,' announced Anne simply.

The Fist belted out an exaggerated cackle. 'You?!' he sneered. 'I'd like to see you try.'

'Very well,' said Anne. 'I shall administer justice to you.' Immediately the robot blonde advanced upon the bully. He stood there grinning and sniggering. But the blocky grin was soon wiped off his face as the little girl with the ponytail gripped his right arm firmly and twisted it right round behind his back.

He yelped in pain, his eyes watering and his yellow teeth grinding together. The crowd looked on, amazed by the show of strength. Two or three older lads wolf-whistled their approval and the tall blonde ex-smoker from year nine shouted, 'Go for it, Anne!'

The Fist was trying very hard to contain his shock, the pain visibly bothering him. Anne continued pulling the thick meaty arm back, twisting the skin all the while. The bully started to gasp. Anne peeped over his broad shoulders. 'Are you hurting, Ronald?' she asked.

Some of the children started laughing silently. Anne wasn't being sarcastic, of course, she was just asking a simple question. But the way she said it, in her no-nonsense emotionless tone, made it sound as if she was being sarcastic, especially when she called him Ronald.

'Yes,' hissed Ronald, taking in short breaths.

Gezz grinned again. 'What was that, Ronny?'

'Yes!' screamed the Fist. 'Please,' he begged. 'Please let me go.'

'Not yet,' teased the girl. 'We still have the question of humiliation. What is the definition of humiliation, Anne?'

Anne continued to stand behind the Fist, slowly wrenching his arm back. He leaned backwards a little and bent his knees, trying to ease the pain. But the more he did it, the more Anne compensated for it. 'Humiliation,' announced the girl. 'To harm the dignity or self-respect of a person.'

'This is what Ronald was doing when he forced Malcolm to make an insulting statement about himself,' explained Gezz.

'I understand,' said Anne's voice from behind the buckled hulk. 'I shall administer the just amount of humiliation.' She said flatly: 'Ronald. You are by far the most hideous, contemptible being in this school. Say, "I am fat, ugly, smelly and have intelligence just marginally greater than that of a chimpanzee".'

Luke held his nose, trying again without much success to stifle his laughter. The Fist held his breath and said nothing, that is, until Anne twisted his arm even further. 'Say it,' she said.

Ronald Higgingbottom's eyes streamed as he recited the sentence in a pitiful mumbling voice. 'I am fat, ugly, smelly,' he began, to the titters of the whole playground audience. 'And have intelligence just margarine-ally...'

Anne cut him off. 'Correction,' she said. 'Not *margarine-ally*, but marginally. You have intelligence just *marginally* greater than that of a chimpanzee.'

Ronald struggled to complete the sentence. 'I have intelligence just marginally greater than that of a chimpanzee.'

Well, everyone fell about, holding their tummies and leaning on one another, trying to stay on their feet. Gezz and Luke collapsed in a giddy fit. Only Malcolm seemed to feel sorry for the oaf as Anne released him from his torment.

Suddenly the laughter ceased and a shocked silence fell over the crowd, as in a fit of rage, the red-faced bully pulled himself together, clenched his fist and swung his best punch at Anne's face. 'Take that, you stupid cow,' he snarled and everyone gasped as the girl fell backwards and landed on her bottom hard.

One of the lads who usually sided with Higgingbottom called out from the mob in disgust. 'You hit a girl, Ron. Only mards hit girls.'

The crowd suddenly turned angry. 'Yeah,' they kept saying to one another, nodding and frowning.

Anne got to her feet, her face undamaged by the punch. She walked over casually to the big lump, stopped just short of his face, and launched an unexpected knuckle sandwich which sent him flying on to his back. The crowd laughed and cheered as the Fist staggered to his feet, clearly stunned by the power in the little girl's arm.

As he stood up, dabbing his bleeding nose, Anne advanced again. The Fist backed off, blubbing something about mercy, but the android applied both hands this time, lifted him off the ground and hung him up in the branches of the nearby tree. Again everyone jeered and applauded.

Ronald Higgingbottom could take no more. He burst into tears, and the more he cried the more everybody laughed. Everybody, that is, except for Malcolm, who was grateful for the sound of the bell.

The crowd dispersed quickly and everyone headed for the open entrances and their next class. Anne left Higgingbottom dangling in his tree and joined Gezz, Luke and Malcolm as they walked towards the door.

Gezz gave Malcolm an affectionate hug. 'I think you will have seen the last of him, Malc,' she said. The boy managed a weak smile, still feeling awkward about the android's piece of retribution exacted on his behalf. *Three more lessons to go*, he thought, *and then it's the weekend.* He couldn't wait.

22

A Bit Different

'Hello and welcome to a brand new series…!' shouted a rather energetic young man above the climax to the opening theme music. Luke sat, half-dressed on the settee, his eyes still partly welded together with sleep. *How do they do this show so wide awake*, he puzzled to himself. *They look like they have been up for hours.* Lots of shouting and cheering accompanied a tall slim girl, a pleasant smile gracing her attractive face. The racket came from lots of kids sitting in and around the television studio. *They must have been up for hours too. How on earth did they do it?*

The hall door creaked open and Luke's mother slowly popped her head round. 'Keep it down, love,' she said, her face a ghostly mixture of white make-up, smudged black eye-liner and cracked lipstick. 'Your dad and me are trying to sleep.'

'OK,' said Luke reluctantly and hit the remote control as his mother shuffled back through the hall door and climbed back upstairs.

Suddenly the doorbell rang. Luke jumped off the settee. 'It's all right,' he shouted as he reached the foot of the stairs. 'I'll get it.' He knew it would be Gezz coming round to watch telly with him. And he was right.

By eleven o'clock, Luke's dad had finally decided to get out of bed and come downstairs. He entered the living room wearing an old pair of jeans and a crumpled T-shirt. His hair was a mess, his face was unshaven and he had nothing on his feet. He wandered into the kitchen half-asleep.

Luke and Gezz sat side by side on the couch, glued to the Saturday morning entertainment. An assortment of pop stars and actors were sitting on a panel as judges, watching the latest music videos. They gave their opinions and marks out of ten. One of the actors, a middle-aged man that Luke had seen in a comedy series, pulled his face and shook his head, not impressed by the last song. He turned his thumbs down and the presenters and audience laughed with him. Luke was appalled. 'What's he going on about?' he said, half-talking to Gezz and half-shouting at the telly. 'It was good, that. I was thinking of buying it at *Jackie's Spin-a-Disc* with my pocket money this afternoon.'

Gezz gave a look of absolute disgust. 'You're not going to get *that*, are you?' Luke didn't feel too thrilled about the way she said 'that', as though it was a disease or something. But then, all her parents ever listened to was classical music and Jesus songs, so her reaction didn't surprise him much.

The television presenters enjoyed a bit of silly banter with one another and then introduced the cartoon series which had become all the rage a few months ago. Luke and Gezz tried as best they could to listen, but it was hard because Luke's dad was banging about in the kitchen. 'Where's the *Fruit and* flippin' *Fibre* gone?' he was shouting.

Luke's mum appeared at the hall door wearing tight navy-blue jeans and a denim jacket. A purple T-shirt bore the Yves Saint Laurent logo emblazoned across its chest in white. Her hair was tied up in a shaggy ponytail, her eyes perfectly enhanced with mascara and shadow, her lips gleaming with red lipstick. She held in her nail-vanished fingers her cigarettes and lighter and stood silently watching the animation playing away on television. 'Is this that thing they're all going crazy about at school?'

'Yeah,' said Luke and Gezz simultaneously.

'Don't know what all the fuss is about,' came the voice from over their heads.

'Well, don't watch it then,' said Luke, his eyes not leaving the screen.

This feeble excuse for conversation was interrupted with more banging and slamming from the kitchen. Luke's mum exhaled noisily through gritted teeth. 'What's wrong with him, now?'

'He can't find the *Fruit and Fibre*,' said Luke.

She marched into the kitchen, cigarettes and lighter clutched tightly in her right hand. 'What is wrong with you this morning?' she hissed as she disappeared round the door.

'We've run out of *Fruit and Fibre*,' Luke's dad was whispering in a rage, putting a lot of emphasis on each 'f' as he repeated the sentence. He didn't say 'flipping' this time, he said something else, and Luke sensed another row kicking off.

'You ate the last of the *Fruit and Fibre* last night, remember?' said his mum irritably. 'You'll have to have *Coco Pops* or something instead.'

'But I don't like *Coco Pops*,' came the reply in a pathetic sulky childlike voice.

More whispered cursing followed, this time from his mum, who had run out of patience. 'Look, just have your breakfast and get dressed. I don't want to miss Donna at the Trafford Centre,' she said. The door flung open and she came back into the living room. 'God,' she exclaimed, preparing to light up.

A knock at the door made her pause, cigarette in her mouth and lighter at the ready. 'Who can this be?' she groaned. She walked over to the arm of her husband's chair and frowned. Then she glanced about the room, mentally overturning every item. 'Where have I put the ashtray?' Then, still thinking aloud, she continued, 'Oh, yeah, it's in the bedroom. God, I'd forget my head if it wasn't fastened on.'

She trotted up the stairs to retrieve her crucial piece of equipment. 'Luke, sweetheart, get the door, will you?'

Luke huffed and puffed, annoyed by the distractions, and rose to answer the door, all the time keeping one eye on the cartoon. He clicked back the safety lock and unbolted the four catches, two at the top and two at the bottom, before pulling open the front door.

Luke just stared at the little blonde girl who stood facing him from outside the porch. She was wearing brand-new jeans and a smart navy-blue blouse. Clearly she and Gezz had been busy on the sewing machine again. Her crystal eyes met his, blank and vacant as ever, and butterflies fluttered in his tummy. His mind raced with questions. 'What are you doing here?' he whispered to himself.

Anne began to speak while Luke inserted the key to the porch and turned the lock. 'I decided to call for you,' she said. Luke pulled open the door. The fresh morning air hit him in the face and he smiled vaguely, taking in yet another cloudless deep-blue sky. He loved summer.

'What?' Luke said absently.

'I was answering your question,' said Anne.

'What question?'

'The question: "What are you doing here?".'

'Oh, yes, I forgot,' said Luke. 'You have super hearing.'

'And,' replied the robot. 'I have mastered the art of lip-reading.'

'Great,' said Luke. He was feeling quite ill now, his stomach churning, his knees going numb. He stared at the blonde, her fringe highlighting her pretty features and her ponytail swishing gently as she spoke. He loved the way it did that.

Gezz joined him at the door. 'Anne?' she mused. 'I thought it was you. What are you doing here? Is everything all right?'

'Yes,' acknowledged Anne. 'Everything is all right. I decided to call for you.'

Gezz raised her eyebrows, quite taken by the display of initiative. 'You decided to call for us?'

'Yes,' said Anne. 'I heard different children making arrangements with one another yesterday at school. So I decided I had better engage in the practice with you.'

'Right.' It was Luke who was speaking now, taken aback by the explanation. 'Well, you'd better come in then.'

Luke's mother had returned to the foot of the stairs with an ashtray in one hand, cigarettes and lighter in the other and a freshly lit cigarette in her mouth. She squinted a little as the smoke drifted up into her eyes. 'Who's this, then, love?'

'This is Anne,' said Luke with an element of pride in his voice. 'She's my new friend.'

Gezz tried to hide her look of annoyance. '*Our* new friend,' she corrected, and Luke just smiled.

Luke's mum led the way into the living room, dropping her smoking tackle into her leather bag by the settee and sitting on her husband's chair, with the ashtray back in its rightful place on the arm. She drew hard on her cigarette and inhaled as the trio entered the room. He whispered into Anne's ear. 'Don't say anything about smoking to my mum.'

'Very well,' whispered the automaton in return.

Luke's father suddenly pushed open the kitchen door. He stood in his scruffy attire with a bowl of cereal in his hands. A spoon full of milky something had just been shovelled into his mouth. 'Who's this?' he slurped.

'This is Luke's new friend,' said Luke's mum with a wicked grin. 'She's called Anne.'

The lad caught sight of Gezz rolling her eyes. He knew that she understood what his mother was suggesting, and that she didn't like it one bit. Before his dad could answer, Anne turned her head to face the cartoon playing away to itself. 'What are you watching on the television set?'

'It's that cartoon programme everyone was talking about yesterday,' piped up Luke, warm affection oozing from him. He pointed out the different characters on the screen as they appeared, the way a father might do to a toddler. 'See, these are the characters from the cards you saw people swapping.'

The automaton nodded and absorbed the animation.

Luke's mum waggled a finger at Gezz, indicating 'come over here'. Gezz obeyed, leaning over the arm of her chair. She coughed as blue smoke drifted under her nose, and the woman slipped the cigarette into her other hand, holding it away. 'Sorry, babe,' she said and then whispered, 'Is this Anne a bit backward or summat?'

'Backward?' Gezz frowned.

'Yeah, you know, retarded or something like that.'

Luke spun round on his heels, furious. 'No, she isn't!' he shouted.

His dad waved a reproving spoon from the kitchen doorway. 'Show more respect for your mother.'

The boy scowled and marched into the hall in a tantrum. 'You make me sick, you two do,' he said, before disappearing up the stairs with stomping footsteps, each punctuating his anger.

*　*　*

'Now look what you've done,' said his mum, turning to the kitchen door. 'You've embarrassed him.'

Luke's father screwed up his unshaven features and mouthed another swear word before stepping out of sight to drop his breakfast bowl in the sink.

Paula took another drag of her half-burned cigarette and hit the remote control. The television went dead immediately and an awkward silence prevailed for a second or two. Gezz and Anne stood side by side awaiting an instruction as blue smoke trailed gently from the woman's nose. 'Go upstairs and see what's up with him,' she said finally, and Gezz gladly obeyed, tugging Anne by the sleeve of her navy-blue blouse.

*　*　*

Luke's room was exactly the same size and shape as Gezz's, only his was decorated with wallpaper sporting pictures of racing cars. Fitted wardrobes lined one wall and a computer sat on a desk by his bed. A small compact disc player rested on the window sill alongside a hideous grey model alien creature.

Luke lay sprawled across his puffed quilt and stared angrily at the ceiling. He was disturbed by a knock at his door. 'What?' he said sharply.

'Luke,' came a meek voice from the other side. 'It's me, Gezz. Can we come in?'

On principle he just carried on staring at the ceiling for another second. Then he sat up and swung his legs round to the floor. 'Yes,' he called, and the two girls entered. Gezz sat on the edge of his bed with him, while Anne remained standing. 'I'm sorry about that,' he apologized. 'It's just that I get sick of people talking about Anne like she's some sort of weirdo.'

'Weirdo,' repeated the android. 'Derived from weird.'

'You can't blame them,' Gezz offered, ignoring the walking dictionary. 'People are going to say things if they notice she's a bit different. I mean they do it to anyone who is a bit different, don't they?'

Luke said nothing, he just glared across at her very seriously, so she continued. 'I mean, they say it to Daley because he's the only coloured lad in our form. And if you were the only white boy in a class full of coloured people, they would do it to you too.' She paused to collect her thoughts. 'They single out anyone who doesn't follow the crowd, anyone who has the courage to stand up for what they believe in. They did it to me in RE when they found out I sometimes go to chapel. They do it to that boy who blushes a lot, and call him gay.'

'They don't pick on me like that,' Luke retorted with a scowl. 'They wouldn't dare.'

'Well,' Gezz shrugged. 'That's because you join in with them. There's nothing about you that causes them to think you are different. When they swear, you swear. When they tell rude jokes, you laugh along with the others, even when sometimes you don't agree with them. The only reason you haven't tried smoking is because Anne put you off.'

Luke sat up. 'You really think I'm that scared of them?' he said dejected. 'That I just join in for the sake of it? That I have no principles?' He shook his head in dismay. 'You've been thinking all that while you've been watching me having a laugh with the lads at school?'

'No, I hadn't even noticed,' said Gezz, concerned by Luke's realization. 'It was your precious girlfriend who pointed it out.'

The boy looked up into the android's sparkling eyes. Was that all he was to her, just something else to study and analyse? Was that all anybody was to her?

Without warning, the noise of loud rock music thundered in from the hall landing. The children could feel the vibrations coming through the wall and floor. The music was up-beat and lively. A man's vocals joined the tune, cheerful and positive. 'Oh God,' muttered Luke, his frown still intact. 'He's listening to George Michael while he gets dressed.'

To the boy's utter dismay Gezz began patting her knee. 'Oh, this is Wham! I like this one,' she said.

Then another voice joined itself to the tones of the lead singer. 'Wake me up before you go-go,' screeched the voice. It was awful, totally off-key. Gezz stopped her knee-patting and cringed with a half-smile. 'Goodness,' she said.

Luke grimaced. 'He always has to sing along. I've told him he can't sing to save his life, but he just carries on.'

Anne stepped over to the wall and felt the vibrations with her fingertips. Her eyes blinked that very deliberate blink several times. It was as though she was enjoying it. Luke went over to her and touched her arm gently. 'You like it, don't you?' he whispered.

'The sound is repetitive,' she announced, not taking her eyes off the wall. 'This is the concept known as rhythm.'

Luke grinned and turned to Gezz excitedly. 'She understands!' he exclaimed, raising his voice to compensate for the racket. Gezz joined him at the android's other side.

'The words rhyme at the end of each statement,' Anne continued. 'The lyrics are structured into verses and a chorus. This is a conventional style of song.'

Luke touched her arm again, at the risk of winding Gezz up that bit further. His eyes were burning with intensity. 'How does the song make you feel, Anne?' he pressed, his voice strong and insistent. 'How does it make you *feel*?'

The robot turned her head and stared him out. 'I am an android,' she stated simply. 'I am incapable of displaying emotions.'

'No,' Luke shook his head fervently. 'You are not just an android,' he said. 'You are not just a machine. You are a cyborg. Cybernetic-organic. Part of your brain is human. You can develop feelings, I know you can.'

'The organic part of my matrix serves an experimental purpose,' said Anne. 'My father was not sure if the emotional responses would ever develop. Evidence accumulated so far indicates that they will not.'

The announcement had a depressing effect on Luke. His eyes dropped and he adopted a sullen cast. The android turned her whole body to face him, inadvertently turning her back to Gezz. 'I wish to examine the music more closely.'

Luke shrugged. 'Sure,' he said and led his friends to his parents' bedroom.

23

Made in the UK

Terry stood in front of a long mirror which was built into the fitted wardrobe dominating the far wall. A knock at the door interrupted his zealous sing-a-long. 'Come in!' he shouted, and the three children presented themselves at the entrance. Luke's dad grinned, straightened his black *Boddington's Beer* T-shirt over his jeans and turned down the hi-fi system tucked into a little cubby hole beside the mirror. An open compact disc case declared *Wham!'s Greatest Hits*, and the man flopped the plastic container shut, making sure it landed on its back.

'What can I do for you, kids?' said Luke's dad as he combed his hair with a pocket comb.

'Anne wants to have a look at your digital sound set-up,' breezed the man's son. 'As well as the George Michael CD. God knows why.'

His face lit up. 'Does she?' He smiled at Anne. 'You like 80s music, do you, love?'

Before Anne could query the expression, Gezz interrupted. 'Eighties is short for 1980s. This recording was produced during Mr Davidson's teenage years which were in the 1980s.'

'Yes,' replied Anne politely. 'I do like 80s music.'

Luke's dad seemed quite thrilled with the idea and handed her the CD packaging. She slid out the sleeve notes and flicked through them very quickly. Then she handed the flimsy plastic box back to him. 'Thank you,' she said. 'It was most interesting.'

Luke was kneeling down by the collection of compact discs lining the bottom shelf of the hi-fi. He glanced up at his dad's bemused face. 'Got that ELO album *Time* in here?'

'No,' shrugged his dad. 'Lent it out. Why?'

'It's all about androids and aliens and the future, innit?'

'Yeah,' his dad nodded. '*Pleasure Principle*'s a bit like that and all, if you wanna try that one.'

'*Pleasure Principle*?' frowned Luke.

'Yeah,' said his dad with a smile. '*The Pleasure Principle* by Gary Numan. He was one of the great electro pioneers.' His smile evolved into a full-blown grin as a thought occurred to him. 'I know,' he beamed. 'How about Positronique?'

Luke's face wrenched at the very idea. 'God, not that weirdo.' He found the CD and pulled a disagreeable face at the cover. It sported a picture of a young woman with short bleached spiky hair who was wearing what appeared to be a bin liner sprayed silver. Her face was plastered with white make-up and her eyes glared an eerie pinky-white. Contact lenses, obviously. 'She always sounds like she's singing in the bath.'

Gezz giggled and covered her mouth with her hand as Luke's dad scowled and cracked his son across the back of the head. Then he removed the Wham! disc from the player and replaced it with the Positronique one. 'Which track do you want?'

'Any that talk about androids and stuff like that,' said Luke.

Luke's father picked up the sleeve notes and studied the inside cover. 'Well the two main ones are *Made in the UK* and *A.I.*, which stands for "artificial intelligence" by the way.'

'Put *Made in the UK* on then,' said Luke, and without any further prompting, his dad selected the track and hit the play button.

The music began with a rhythmic electronic buzz, urging Gezz to tap her forefinger against the top of her leg. Then a pathetic-sounding drum machine beat its way into the rhythm, followed by something that was supposed to be bass guitar. The track now sounded a little bit more like a conventional song, decided Luke, though still feeling distinctly cold and detached.

Anne tilted her head slightly, as if noting the difference between this track and the Wham! one. 'How is this music produced?' she asked.

Luke smiled, glad to have provoked a response. 'The main rhythm is electronic, it's produced on an instrument called a synthesizer.'

'It's music by machine, effectively,' added Luke's father, also pleased that the little girl seemed to be enjoying it.

The main vocal began, the woman's voice whining and screeching like a cat getting set upon, and yet somehow still managing to sing in tune. 'You say you love me, but what does that mean?' burbled the peculiar voice. 'I only know require-ment and need.' Her vocals scratched on, struggling to hold the key, as she added, 'I do not laugh and I do not cry/When I'm sleep I am devoid of dreams.'

Luke's father was completely wrapped up in it now. 'There's one song where something malfunctions while she is recharging and fragmental memory images filter into her mind,' he enthused. 'And she's, like, wondering if she's dreaming.'

'Really,' said Luke, sarcastically.

Gezz folded her arms. 'You're right,' she said with a knowing smile. 'She does sound like she's singing it in the bath.'

Luke started to snigger, taking in his father's enraged expression, but he soon stopped when Anne asked, 'Is Positronique an android?'

This time it was Terry's turn to laugh, while the children adopted very serious casts. 'No,' said Luke, feeling very fatherly again. 'The lyric is a made-up story about an android noting the differences between itself and human people,' he said, talking over Positronique's next line. 'I think it's supposed to be from the android's point of view. Some of it is about a boy who falls in love with her too, but she can never love him back because she has no feelings.'

Gezz was tapping her leg harder now, absent-mindedly in time with the rhythm. Another line warbled out. 'Everyone is ahead, everyone is behind / I am like no one on earth.'

Luke's dad nodded his head to the music and joined in with the singer. 'What is my value? Why am I here? / If I'm not like you then what am I worth?' he sang. Gezz and Luke shot one another exaggerated strained facial expressions, as if to say 'Oh dear, he sounds even worse than Positronique!'

Anne shocked them all by suddenly picking up the sleeve notes. Instead of whizzing right through them in a couple of seconds, as she had done earlier, she read each line slowly and deliberately. An extra synthesizer sound added itself to the main rhythm and real drums were now pounding their way into the piece, intensifying the song as a whole. Then there was a whoosh of noise and the tempo slowed to a march. The structure of the lyrics changed at this point, becoming a series of questions. The pop artist continued: 'Do you look around you and wonder whence it all came?'

Luke and Gezz both broke into caring affectionate smiles, like parents rejoicing over their baby saying its very first word. Anne was following the printed lyrics in the sleeve notes as the performer sang them. On cue she turned to Luke's father, anticipating his accompaniment, and in perfect tune added, 'I do.' They both continued. 'Do you find their data is driving you completely insane? – I do.'

Luke could not contain his joy. He clapped his hands and gave the automaton a big hug. She just stood there, blank, and waited for him to let go. Her lack of response made him feel dejected, and yet at the same time, he had a strong feeling of pride. This was real progress.

Positronique, Luke's father, and Anne all sang the next two lines in the strangest sounding harmony the children had ever heard. 'Do you have electro-chem saline caressing your matrix? – I do/Do you have "made in the UK" on the base of your cortex? – I do.' The drums reached their crescendo and the song suddenly fell back to its original bleak, crass melody, with different lyrics. 'You say you love me, but what does that mean?/You wonder if I feel the same/I need no love, I am complete/I will never understand your pain.'

On the last word everything stopped and suddenly the room was silent. Such was 80s music.

Luke's father took the disc from the player and clicked it into its case and then slid the flat box back in with the rest of his collection. 'Now, I'm afraid kids, we'll have to leave it there,' he said. 'Paula wants me to take her to the Trafford Centre to meet her friend Donna.'

Gezz was the first to move, heading for the bedroom door. 'Thank you, Mr Davidson. It was very interesting,' said the girl. 'Though I still think Abba are better.'

Father and son exchanged glances, appalled by the very suggestion. 'Abba?!' they cried.

Paula Davidson appeared on the stairs. 'Are you ready, Terry, or what?'

'Yep,' said Luke's father, and the entourage all trotted down the stairs in single file. 'The kids just wanted to hear a bit of old Positronique.'

Luke's mother scoffed at the claim. 'Who in their right minds would ask you to put that rubbish on? She sounds bl...' Paula corrected herself. 'She sounds flippin' awful. That girl hasn't got a single tuneful bone in her body. I don't know how she has the nerve to go on stage in front of hundreds of people. I'd be flippin' embarrassed if it was me.'

'You are mistaken,' said Anne as she reached the bottom of the stairs. Luke's mother opened the front door, pausing to hear the little girl out. 'I requested the song myself,' she concluded.

Luke's mum raised her eyebrows in disbelief. 'You actually asked him to put it on?'

'Yes.'

'You want your head seeing to, girl.'

'What has my head got to do with it?'

Paula Davidson raised her hands in mock frustration. 'God help us!'

Anne turned to her friends for confirmation. 'She is praying?'

The children laughed as Luke's mother and father left the house and got in their sports car. His dad started the engine and put on his seatbelt, while his mum wound her window down a little and lit herself a cigarette. With a swift gear change, the car was reversing quickly off the drive. With another move of the hand, Luke's father clicked it into first and zoomed up the lodge to the main road.

The blond-haired boy hovered by the open front door and waved his parents off. 'What shall we do now, then?' he said dreamily.

'Call for Malc?' suggested Gezz.

Luke nodded reluctantly. 'S'pose so.'

★ ★ ★

Anne did not say a single word as they walked up the crescent of houses towards Malcolm's. Even when the chubby boy came out to play, she said nothing. It was as if she had become preoccupied, as though she had something on her mind.

'It was great to see the Fist getting his comeuppance, wasn't it?' Luke enthused, trying to provoke a response from the android. Malcolm grinned and rubbed his hands together. 'Yeah,' he said. 'And it's all thanks to Anne and Gezz.' He smiled and gave a nod of acknowledgement. 'Thanks, girls.'

Gezz blushed. 'It's OK.'

The children walked on, making their way to the den. Malcolm took in Anne's new clothes. 'Hey, she's getting a dab hand on that sewing machine, isn't she?' he said. 'You don't think she could rustle up a few shirts and pants for me, do you?'

'Oh, I don't know,' replied Gezz awkwardly. 'The material still costs money. I've been paying for it with my spends.'

Luke shot her a look. 'You daft thing,' he chastised. 'You should have said. I would have chipped some of mine in too.'

The conversation was cut short, as Anne caught them all by surprise. Luke stared at Gezz, and Gezz stared at Malcolm, and all three stopped walking and stared, mouths agape at Anne. It was incredible. She was singing. The girl was actually singing.

'Do you have electro-chem saline caressing your matrix? – I do,' sang the automaton. Her voice was angelic, nothing like the actual recording everyone but Malcolm had been listening to. 'Do you have "made in the UK" on the base of your cortex? – I do.'

'Did you hear that?' Luke laughed. 'She identifies with it. She's applying the song to herself.' He struck the air with an excited fist. 'It's an emotional reaction!'

Malcolm was not convinced. 'That's a bit over the top, isn't it?'

'No.' It was Gezz who corrected him. She spoke slowly and never took her eyes off the robot, who was still singing to herself. 'It is an emotional reaction, sort of. She associates herself with the lyrics.' The girl fell into an awe-struck whisper. 'It's incredible.'

The cyborg continued her perfect rendition of the song, like a girl performing solo before an audience of admirers. 'You say you love me, but what does that mean?/You want to know if I feel the same.' The children stood and listened with rapt attention, like people standing round a talented carol singer at Christmas time. 'I need no love, I am complete/I will never share your pain.' When the singing stopped as abruptly as had the original track, the three children exploded into zealous applause, each grinning happily and patting the robot on the back.

24

In Big Trouble

The next few weeks saw all of them settling into the pattern of secondary school life. Luke enjoyed Games and Art especially, while Gezz seemed to have a general interest in most subjects, but particularly English. The class had started to read a novel called *The Pigman* by American author Paul Zindel. It was turning out to be about a couple of children who befriend an eccentric old man. It covered themes like being different to the crowd and bullying: themes which fascinated Gezz.

Malcolm struggled with most lessons, especially Maths, and he was always the last person to be chosen for the football team. He seemed to like English best. He enjoyed writing far-fetched stories, and like Gezz, was seeing bits of his own life in the story of the lonely old man.

Of course, Anne did not appear to savour any one lesson above another. She was brilliant at all of them and wowed the teachers constantly with her efficiency, her enthusiasm (or at least what the teachers *thought* was enthusiasm) and her strange viewpoints on very ordinary situations. She had accumulated a great many friends who invited her out to every social event on the calendar, many of which had to be turned down because Gezz and Luke were not available to supervise her.

There was one lesson which everyone loved, though, and all because of Anne. That lesson was Music. The little blonde excelled at playing every instrument to hand. The class had begun with the recorder, playing simple tunes like *Three Blind Mice*, but by the time the first session was over, Anne was giving solo performances of a really tricky television theme tune, which she had picked up from an old children's programme called *Bod* she'd seen on Luke's television. As the weeks rolled by, she progressed from the recorder to piano, to synthesizer and violin.

Her singing went down a treat too. All the teacher had to do was play her a song on the piano just once, and she would repeat it perfectly. The pieces were from a number of sources and were as varied as the Spice Girls, Gary Barlow, Abba's Greatest Hits, Enya, the songs of Lennon and McCartney and bits of classic opera. The one called *Madame Butterfly* was the teacher's favourite, although Anne seemed to prefer singing the one that Luke's dad had played, *Made in the UK*, most of all.

Then one October morning, while Mrs Croake was calling out the register, there was a knock on the classroom door. Reluctantly she suspended the procedure at the name Grenville and glanced over the rim of her spectacles toward the door. 'Come in,' she called.

A very sensible-looking girl with pleasant features presented herself at the door. Her black uniform told Luke she was a year eleven, and the badge pinned to the jumper marked her as a prefect. 'Mr Turnbull wants all the year seven forms to assemble in the main hall immediately after registration, Miss,' she said.

Mrs Croake nodded. 'Right, thank you, Helen.' The prefect gave a nod of acknowledgement and swiftly disappeared into the corridor. A faint buzz of curiosity pulsed through the class as the pupils wondered what the special assembly might be about. 'All right,' commanded the form tutor. 'Settle down. Now, where was I?'

Emma Bingham swung round and shot Mrs Croake a sly grin. Then she sniggered at one of the girls sitting parallel. 'I think you were up to G-G-G-Granville, Miss.' The girl opposite adopted a thunderous expression, resenting the gag which had dogged her from her very first day at Crompton Green. Luke wasn't sure where the joke had come from but thought that it was from the chap with the stutter in an old comedy series called *Open All Hours*. Granville was his dozy nephew played by that bloke out of *Only Fools and Horses*. He'd seen both programmes with his parents, who were always watching UK Gold.

Thunder Face scowled at the ginger-haired tormentor. 'It's Gren-ville, actually.'

Mrs Croake clapped her hands impatiently. 'Girls, please,' she shouted. 'Settle down. Now. Grenville.'

'Yes, Miss,' replied Grenville, after which she turned slightly and pulled out her tongue. Bingham had not noticed, having twisted to face her friend sitting with her at her own table. Luke couldn't help smiling to himself. He appreciated how Grenville was feeling; he couldn't stand the bully himself.

After registration the bell rang, and instead of going to their first lesson of the day, History, the class filed down the corridor to the main hall where Mr Ford and his form were already waiting.

Other classes merged, arriving at the same time, and took their seats, filling at least a third of the hall in the process. Once all the year seven forms were seated, Mr Ford introduced the headmaster, Mr Turnbull.

The headmaster stalked into the room, his black gown flapping and, looking very serious indeed, stood by the lectern on the stage. 'Good morning again, boys and girls.'

The pupils responded quickly. 'Good morning, Mr Turnbull.'

'No doubt you are wondering why you have been summoned here,' he began. 'Well, believe it or not, I have, this morning, been paid a visit by a police inspector.'

Luke was dying to say, 'Why? What have you done?' but he thought better of it. He remained, like the others, in rapt silence.

Turnbull continued, red faced and intense. 'It has been brought to my attention that we have a runaway in our midst.' He paused, anticipating the hushed mutterings from his audience as they wondered who it might be. 'And apparently, this child is a girl with extraordinary gifts and talent. In fact, genius is not too exaggerated a description. She had been living with her aunt in a special home for gifted children and was making fine progress.'

The headmaster cleared his throat, somewhat uneasily, before delivering his punch line. 'It was first thought that the girl had been kidnapped from the home, but it is now believed that she absconded of her own free will and is being sheltered by someone here.'

Mr Ford and Mrs Croake stood with other form tutors along the aisle where the two main doorways opened onto the corridor. Luke, Gezz, Malc and Anne were sitting in their usual row towards the back of the assembly. Luke watched the teachers shooting one another knowing looks and frowning, and he concluded that they were sort of saying 'This is ridiculous' to each other.

Mr Turnbull cleared his throat again. 'Now, I'm going to hand you over to the inspector himself, who will give you a description. So listen carefully.' He glanced through the top open door to an unseen person waiting outside. 'Over to you, Chief Inspector,' he said, and left the stage to join Mr Ford and the others on the aisle.

The acids in Luke's stomach started to work overtime and he felt as though he was going to be sick as the grey-coated Inspector Bullimore marched in and on to the stage to take the lectern. Gezz stared, her face all white and ill-looking. 'It's Bullimore,' she whispered. The girl held her forehead in shock. 'I don't believe it. They've come for Anne.'

The stone-faced inspector scanned his audience, trying to pick out the automaton. 'It has been brought to my attention,' he began, all gruff and cold, 'that you have a star pupil here at Crompton Green High.' Luke shuddered, the voice sending him harking back to when the four of them were huddled in Gezz's kitchen, helpless and terrified as the police took the Professor back to their mysterious underground base. How had the inspector managed to trace Anne to the school? Then Luke remembered that the mother of one of the year ten boys was a policewoman. All it would have taken was an innocent remark from the boy, then a bit of gossip at the station, and Bullimore, who was actually a real inspector hired by the Foundation, would have put two and two together.

'I'm talking about a girl who can read a dictionary in under a minute, someone that can draw a sketch so brilliantly it looks more like a photograph than a picture.' The hall felt quieter than quiet could be. Absolutely everyone in that room knew who the inspector was talking about. Luke chanced a look down his aisle to see how Malcolm was coping. The boy was very troubled, his eyes strained and his brow furrowing with globules of sweat. Sitting between him and Gezz was the miracle girl herself, all prim and attentive, apparently unaffected by the stress of the situation.

Bullimore continued. 'This is a girl who has broken not only every school sports record in the history of Crompton Green High, but every sports record everywhere on the international scene.' The voice was trembling now, and the police inspector's thick black fringe was wobbling over his piercing blue eyes. Luke could tell he was trying to contain his anger as the audience remained ever silent. The only person who seemed to gel with the man was Ronald Higgingbottom, the so-called Fist. No doubt he was dying to say something, but even he wasn't that daft.

'The girl is about five feet in height,' said Bullimore. 'She has bright blue eyes and blonde hair tied in a ponytail. She was last seen wearing silver dungarees, but now wears a school uniform for obvious reasons.'

Luke felt numb all over. He glanced down his aisle to look upon his dream girl, and then numbness turned to absolute shock. Anne had disappeared. Another girl was now sitting in her place. She was a little taller, with long black shoulder-length hair and hazel eyes. Luke nudged Gezz with his elbow. 'Where's Anne?' he hissed. 'And who's that?'

Gezz turned and jumped as she took in the appearance of the stranger. 'Excuse me,' she whispered, tapping the newcomer on the shoulder. 'Where did you come from?'

The stranger turned her head slowly and both Gezz and Luke gave a quiet sigh of relief. The hair may have been long and black and the eyes might have been hazel, but the deadpan expression was unmistakable. Luke's feelings of numbness gave way to a tingling of euphoria. He stuck up an approving thumb and grinned. 'Excellent!' he said.

Bullimore was still droning on. 'Finally, if you hear of anyone talking about a Professor Wolfgang Droyd, let Mr Turnbull know immediately.' He shot a brief excuse of a smile and then nodded. 'Thank you.'

The inspector stepped from the platform and marched from the hall back into the corridor. Mr Ford walked to the front and dismissed the assembly. As the children buzzed with low-key conversation, the teachers whispered seriously among themselves. Then Mrs Croake approached Luke and company as they filed out of their row. 'Luke, Geraldine, Anne and Malcolm,' she announced. 'Would you make your way to the school library please? Mr Ford and I need to talk with you.'

Luke's stomach turned again. They were in big trouble, he knew it.

25

The Interrogation

The four children stood alone in the library, which seemed extremely quiet and foreboding. It was as though they had been selected for trial and execution. Adult footsteps clicked down the corridor outside and Luke was expecting his knees to go at any moment. The children looked at one another nervously. This was it. Croake, Ford, Turnbull and Bullimore were going to walk in at any moment.

The door swung open admitting Mrs Croake and Mr Ford. The man gently closed the door behind him. They scurried over to the foursome, glancing about with a great deal of unease. 'Quick,' said the woman suspiciously. 'Mr Turnbull is keeping the inspector occupied for a few minutes, but we haven't got long. Can you tell us what this is all about?'

Luke did not trust them one bit. For all he knew, Mr Turnbull and Bullimore were waiting outside. 'Your guess is as good as ours,' he said.

'Oh, come on,' hissed Mr Ford. 'We realized there was something special about Anne the moment we first taught her. All the teachers did. I mean, she has no parents, no address on record, and the girl's a genius.' He looked over his shoulder to make sure the door was still firmly shut, his face pained with worry. 'But when this Bullimore chap started sniffing around, we knew there was more to it. If your friend had run away from a children's home of some sort, there would have been social workers and all sorts of people here. No.' He shook his head fiercely. 'Something else is going on.'

Mrs Croake broke into an uncharacteristic warm smile. 'Look, we realize you don't want to risk telling us where she's hiding, but at least tell us what she is.'

The children fell silent, not daring to speak. Then Anne stepped forward. 'I am not hiding anywhere, Miss,' she announced flatly. 'I am here.'

The two teachers stared in utter disbelief. 'Incredible!' hissed Mr Ford. 'How have you disguised yourself so well?'

'I am an android,' stated the automaton simply.

Mr Ford glared with a fascinated sense of awe. 'Well I never,' he whispered slowly.

Luke, Gezz and Malcolm dropped their bottom jaws, completely unprepared for Anne's innocent confession. 'No,' whispered Luke. 'They'll take you away.'

Anne ignored him and addressed the teachers. 'I am the product of Professor Wolfgang Droyd and have been financed by a team of guerrilla scientists who call themselves the Foundation. The Professor was supposed to be designing the perfect soldier, but instead he produced me, a facsimile of his own real-life daughter, who died many years ago. We escaped from an underground facility and the Professor left me in the care of these children when he was apprehended by Bullimore and his policemen.'

Mrs Croake stared so hard her eyes nearly shot through her glasses. 'So,' she said slowly. 'You are a robot?'

'Of a kind,' said Anne. 'I am an android.'

Mr Ford held his chin and frowned, the way people do when they are terribly interested in something. 'So, what were these Foundation chaps going to do with their perfect android soldier?'

The automaton turned her head slightly to face the man. 'The Professor had theorized that they were going to sell it to the highest bidder on the political scene. Big government agencies and terrorist groups would find such a tool useful. They may also have been planning on building a robot army. In the wrong hands this concept would be very dangerous.'

Mrs Croake smiled at Anne. 'So the Professor made you instead?'

'Yes,' said the girl.

'How sweet.'

Malcolm swallowed his fear and joined Anne at her side. 'So what are you going to do with her?' His voice trembled, but he had courage, more courage than Luke had credited him with.

It was Mr Ford who answered his question. 'Well, first of all, we are going to put Mr Turnbull in the picture. We firmly believe all the teachers will be persuaded to stay silent if we can convince the head. Everybody loves Anne. I can't think of a single person who would turn her over.'

Mrs Croake walked over to the door and opened it slightly, letting a fraction of bright sunlight from the window adjacent beam into the room. She peeped up and down the silent corridor. 'Coast is clear,' she whispered. Mr Ford put affectionate hands on the heads of Malcolm and Gezz. 'Now, in an hour or so, Bullimore will call every year seven child in for questioning. When it's your turn, you need to be strong and calm.'

'We will also need to get Anne's name off the register,' whispered Mrs Croake.

'Do not worry,' said Anne in her robotic way. 'I can rewrite the whole register, complete with names, ticks and crosses, and omit my name.'

'Excellent,' said Mr Ford. 'Now stay here until the bell rings and then just go out into the playground and mingle with the other children.' He joined Mrs Croake at the door. 'Good luck,' he said, and the pair of them disappeared into the corridor.

Luke puffed loudly. 'Well,' he said. 'What do you make of that? Can we trust them?'

'I think so,' said Anne. All eyes were on her, and the children just hoped she was right.

★ ★ ★

The common room was a place where year tens and elevens could go and listen to CDs and tapes and play snooker at break-times. Luke wished year sevens had a place like that for them.

But break-time had been and gone. Now Luke, Gezz and Malcolm sat among the other year sevens in the seats which had been put out especially. Inspector Bullimore was sitting at a desk in a store room that had been converted into a make-shift office. A single policeman stood by the desk as, in alpha-betical order, each and every year seven pupil was called in to be interviewed.

Half-terrified, Gezz had been one of the first to go in, since her surname began with 'A'. She came out as white as a sheet and told of how the inspector had pressed her about the Professor hiding in her house. He had become quite angry at one point and had banged his fist on the desk. She'd told him she did not know that the old man was a criminal on the run from the police and that he had just knocked on the door asking for food. Bullimore had shouted some more about the dangers of letting strangers into the house, and then went all quiet and kindly on her when asking about Anne. Thankfully, Gezz said very little. She admitted that she had heard of the girl but that was all.

Luke was proud of his friend. It had taken a lot for her to lie, because she believed in always telling the truth. But Gezz had conceded that this situation required cunning. The less Bullimore found out, the better.

Luke was relieved that Mr Ford had managed to get the black-haired, hazel-eyed Anne into a special class of year eight children. He instructed her to work to the standard of the other children and she had no problem complying.

'Emma Bingham!' called Mrs Croake as the boy called Daley emerged from Bullimore's office. The ginger-freckled girl got to her feet, straightened her pullover and made for the office. She knocked on the door, waited for a second, and went inside. Gezz leaned over to Luke. 'Do you think she will tell?'

'Nah,' said Luke, scrunching his nose and shaking his head. 'She might be spiteful at times, but she's not a hateful person. Besides, Anne has been helping her with her science homework.'

'I didn't know that,' said Gezz, a little taken aback.

'There are only two people in here that worry me,' Luke continued, gazing about vaguely.

'Only two?'

Malcolm was intrigued. 'Who?'

'Well, the first one is you,' Luke admitted with a bit of a smile. 'I'm worried you might buckle under the strain of Bullimore's questioning.'

'Thanks a lot.' Malcolm was genuinely offended by the suggestion, but Luke had said it on purpose, knowing that his apparent lack of faith in the lad might spur him on that bit more.

'And the other?' queried Gezz. She need ask no further, as she followed the gaze of her best friend. His eyes fell upon the bulky oaf with the skinhead and bulldog face striding about the snooker table with a long wooden cue in his hand. 'You mean Ronald McDonald?'

'Well,' breathed Luke through gritted teeth. 'He never got over Anne showing him up in front of everybody, did he?'

Gezz bit her lip. 'I suppose not.'

The door of the makeshift office flung open and Emma strolled out, clearly glad that it was all over.

Others went in and came out until the moment when Mrs Croake checked for the next name and announced, 'Luke Davidson!'

The lad felt sick straight away. 'God, I hate this,' he said, his voice juddering as he got to his feet. He sensed the blood drain from his face and he went all light-headed, as though he was about to pass out. Gezz touched his hand gently and he straightened up. 'You'll be all right,' she offered softly.

He walked over to the door of the office, knocked hard, and heard Bullimore's gravel voice call from inside. 'Come in.' Luke held his breath, turned the door handle and entered the office.

'Ah, Mr Davidson,' said Inspector Bullimore with a phoney smile. 'Take a seat.' Luke sat down and glanced at the serious-looking policeman standing rigid by the plastic desk. *You're not a real policeman*, he thought to himself, but he dared not say it.

'I see from your records that you live on Century Lodge,' began the Inspector. 'Right next door to Miss Atkinson.'

Luke struggled to keep calm. 'Yes,' he said. 'Yes, I do.'

'That's interesting,' said the man, and he leant back in his chair, his open grey overcoat flopping behind him. 'Because a couple of months ago my men traced a known criminal back to her house.'

'Did you?' said Luke, trying to feign surprise. 'What was he like?'

'He was an old man with long, white scruffy hair,' said the inspector. 'He spoke with a German accent and had a young blonde girl with him. He abducted her from a special home for genius children, you know.'

'Wow.'

'Her guardians are worried sick.'

'Yes,' nodded Luke. 'I suppose they must be.'

Bullimore smiled. 'Do you know how we traced them back to Miss Atkinson's?'

Luke tried to convey an air of vagueness. 'No.'

'We had been doing some house-to-house inquiries, and one of the people we called on was walking his dog when he saw the old man and the girl later the same morning.'

'Right.'

'They had apparently befriended three other children. A brunette girl with a hairband and two lads, one thin and smart with fair hair, the other chubby with glasses. The man with the dog followed them to Miss Atkinson's house on Century Lodge, which is where we apprehended the criminal.'

Luke said nothing. His eyes itched, his stomach rolled and his throat completely dried up.

Bullimore leaned forward suddenly and glared right into Luke's face. 'You are playing with fire, boy,' he sneered. 'That girl you think you are helping is a danger to society.' He pressed even closer, his beetroot face nearly touching Luke's fair skin. The boy gulped, his breathing tight and strained. 'She will be a danger to you and your friends in time,' said Bullimore. 'She'll turn on you, she's loyal to no one. Save yourselves a lot of trouble and tell us where she is.'

'I thought you said she was a genius,' Luke said weakly. For a moment he thought Bullimore was going to hit him. But the man just sat back and exhaled noisily. 'Thank you, Mr Davidson,' he said with dismissive politeness. 'That will be all.'

Luke had to force his legs into action. He stood up, straightened his jumper and walked as best he could to the door. His hand was weak and limp, and he had to force it to turn the handle. He staggered out into the common room and collapsed on the nearest plastic moulded chair. Mrs Croake, trying to look as casual as she could, said, 'Loosen your tie, Luke, and undo your top button. Take deep breaths. You'll be all right in a minute.'

'Thank you, Miss,' breathed the boy and he did as he was advised.

After about half an hour, he felt as right as rain. That is until they got to Malcolm Hardy. The boy stood up shyly, adjusted his glasses and headed quite confidently, for him, to the office. He seemed to stay in there a long time and both Luke and Gezz feared the worst. Finally, he emerged, looking quite pleased with himself.

'What did you tell him?' pushed Luke.

'Nothing,' Malcolm shrugged. 'I just cracked on I was a bit thick.' He smiled as he took his seat. 'After all, it's not far from the truth.'

Gezz frowned and put an arm about the boy's shoulders. 'We don't think you're thick, do we, Luke?'

Luke took Malcolm's hand and shook it once, firm and resolute. 'No,' he said, and he really meant it too. Malcolm had been surprisingly brave. 'I don't think you are thick at all. A bit irritating at times, yes, but not thick.'

Mrs Croake called out another name. 'Ronald Higging-bottom!'

Silence fell over the common room as the Fist placed his snooker cue on the green table, and grinning that awful grin, started to walk over to the office. As he did so, children rose from their seats and surrounded him. The boy looked to Mrs

Croake for assistance, but the teacher kept her eyes on her register, pen in hand, pretending not to notice. Emma Bingham and that lad called Daley pressed in on the thick-set bully. The meathead cleared his throat. 'Er, are you gonna let me knock on the door, or what?'

'Not just yet, wobble bottom,' chided the ginger head. 'Not until we've got a few things clear.'

'Like what?' The Fist raised his eyebrows, seemingly unimpressed by the show of comradeship.

The thin-featured Daley dug a finger hard into Higgingbottom's right shoulder. 'Like, if this dude has anything to say about a certain little blonde kid with a ponytail, you know nothing.'

'Why should I take any notice of you, Blacky?' sneered Higgingbottom.

Emma shot him one of her smarmy smiles. 'Because you will have to answer to the whole of year seven and any other kids that you have managed to upset in this school, that's why.' The children pushed themselves in closer, as if to punctuate the girl's statement. Luke and his friends watched from their seats, touched by the display of loyalty to Anne.

Higgingbottom stretched out a thick hand and banged on the door. The voice of the inspector called from inside. 'Come in.'

'Remember,' said Daley. 'If they ask you about Anne, you say nothing.'

The Fist scowled at the mass of faces and then at Mrs Croake, who was still making a show of examining the register. Then very reluctantly, he said, 'Anne who?'

The children smiled with satisfaction and dispersed back to their seats. Daley patted the bully on his broad shoulder. 'That's what we like to hear.' The Fist took a breath, gritted his square yellow teeth hard, entered the office – and told the inspector and his false officer absolutely nothing.

26

Cracking the Code

Everyone breathed a sigh of relief when Bullimore and his lackey left the building. Anne was brought from her year eight class, and as soon as she was in the company of her young guardians, morphed herself back to the physical appearance everybody had grown accustomed to. The children watched in amazement as hazel eyes shone blue and long shoulder-length black hair changed to blonde and tied itself up in a ponytail.

The day went very quickly and emotions ran high. The children knew that Bullimore would be back with more authority, and that he might even put pressure on their parents if his other methods failed. What were they going to do?

Luke's final lesson was Information Technology, which he adored because he loved computers. They had already learned the basics and even how to send emails to one another. But today was going to be good, because today they were going to have a go on the Internet.

He summoned all his favourite sites, including BBC Sport and Bolton Wanderers. He agreed with Malcolm, they were the best football team, but he never told anybody that. If people asked, he would normally say Manchester United, or something like that. He even looked up the Electric Light Orchestra, Wham! and Positronique for his dad.

Gezz checked out her chapel's web page. Then she looked at those of different authors, like that woman who wrote the Harry Potter books. Meanwhile Malcolm kept typing in wrongly the addresses of different chocolate-making companies and getting 'error' on the screen.

After a while, the three children grew weary of their own computers and were grateful when Miss Sutton set them a task and then informed the group that she had to go out for a minute. As soon as the door pulled shut, the class began to talk quietly among themselves. Luke, Gezz and Malc got to their feet and sneaked a look at what Anne had typed up.

Luke frowned as he took in the image on the screen. 'What are you looking at, Anne?' The screen was full of words, lists to be exact. A red oblong sat in the left-hand corner. The boy's jaw dropped as he noted the words 'Top Secret' emblazoned on the shape in startling white.

'Anne,' he hissed. 'You can't look at things like this. It's illegal.'

The automaton appeared to ignore the protest. 'I have cracked a number of government codes,' she said. 'This is a list of known terrorist organizations.'

Gezz looked scared stiff. 'I don't like the sound of this,' she said. 'Quick, hit the delete button.'

As the girl reached out, the android gripped her arm tightly with her right hand. Anne's eyes met Gezz's and the robot spoke with a firm insistence none of the children had ever heard before. 'No,' she said. 'You will not delete.'

Gezz struggled against the metal hand, but to no avail. Her eyes watered and she winced.

'Anne,' she gasped. 'You're hurting me. Let go, please.'

Luke reached across and tried to peel back the android's fingers, but they would not budge. He gave up. 'Bullimore said you were dangerous,' scowled the boy. 'He said you'd turn on us in time.'

Anne released Gezz's arm and the girl nursed it in her other. 'Bullimore was lying,' stated the robot. 'I am no danger to humans. The very concept goes against my programming.' She looked at the three children one at a time. 'You are my friends and my guardians. I will never betray you.'

'You were instructed to follow our instructions.' It was Malcolm speaking. 'But now you are resisting our guidance.'

Anne's head turned in that smooth robotic way to face Malcolm. 'The research I am conducting here will lead to the location of my father.'

'What?' said Luke, a little stunned. 'You think you can find where they're holding him?'

'Yes,' Anne replied. Her head turned again. 'This list contains all the likely buyers of the robot soldier the Foundation are trying to build.' She manoeuvred the mouse and clicked a small grey box on the control bar at the top of the screen. Immediately a map of the local area sprang up. It showed the school, the railway networks, the old coal wastes and the housing estate where the children lived. 'My father never revealed the location of the Foundation base to me, but I calculate from the period I was deactivated in the storage box to being released on the wasteland where I met you was one hour and twenty-three minutes.'

'What does all that mean?' quizzed Malcolm.

'It means that the underground base where they are holding my father prisoner is within the radius of this map.'

Gezz stood up straight, excited now, her earlier restraint forgotten. 'It could be a part of the old coal mine. Perhaps one of the tunnels?'

'No,' said the cyborg. 'I have checked government information on the site.'

'So, where is it then?'

Anne ran her fingers over the keyboard with lightning speed. Pictures and graphs, columns of writing, signs flashing up 'prohibited' and 'access denied' all filled the screen at various intervals. Anne worked swiftly, but tirelessly, cracking every code the computer could throw at her. Finally the screen dragged up five words written in green and another two presented in a red oblong underneath. The sign read 'Her Majesty's Government Military Files: Top Secret'.

Malcolm began to stutter nervously. 'Er, I'm not sure about this, guys.'

Anne ignored him and tapped the 'enter' button. The sign was replaced by another set of lists. The automaton's fingers sprayed across the keys. 'I am attempting to retrieve information on all the underground bunkers utilized during the Cold War.'

Gezz sniggered out loud and ridiculed the idea. 'Oh, yeah,' she laughed. 'Like, there's gonna be an old underground army base round here!'

The picture on the computer changed again, back to the map of the local area. One particular part flashed virulently on and off in different colours. It was the area in which the lodge was situated.

'Why's that flashing?' asked Gezz, pointing.

Anne was as monotone as ever. 'It is flashing because there is an abandoned military underground base approximately fifty metres below the lodge.'

The children were speechless. How could this be true? A waft of warm air blew over the pupils as the door of the classroom opened and Miss Sutton returned with a few packs of computer printout paper in her arms. The class fell deadly quiet and got on with their assignment, and Anne whizzed her right hand across the console and hit the delete button. The picture flickered for a couple of seconds and then returned with a large colour photograph of pop singer Geri Halliwell and some facts and figures about her departure from the Spice Girls.

Miss Sutton dumped the packs of paper on her desk and raised her eyebrows in an exaggerated fashion, beaming at the three children huddled over Anne's shoulders. 'Er, what are you three doing over there?'

Malcolm smiled sheepishly. 'We were looking at Anne's website, Miss,' he offered.

'Well,' replied Miss Sutton. 'You won't be marked on what Anne Droyd's website is all about, will you? You will be marked on your *own* assessment of your *own* sites.'

'Yes, Miss,' mumbled Malcolm, adjusting his glasses and looking somewhat foolish.

'So get to them,' Miss Sutton ordered, a bit more harshly this time.

The children made as if they were straightening up and returning to their seats. Luke whispered into Anne's left ear. 'Can you get all that information back up if I let you have a go on my computer at home?'

'That is not necessary,' reported Anne. 'I have downloaded the data into my own brain.'

Luke was amazed. 'How have you done that?' he frowned. 'Just by looking at the screen?'

Anne turned to face him, her eyes were glowing from within. 'Yes,' she said.

'You are amazing,' whispered the lad.

'Thank you,' said Anne politely.

Luke could sense Miss Sutton standing with her arms folded and glaring. He straightened up and glanced about, only to find that Gezz and Malc had deserted him. 'Why have you downloaded the information into your brain?' mumbled Luke out the side of his mouth, slowly edging over to his seat. 'What are you going to do?'

Anne had learned another human tactic, she had realized that talking to Luke face to face would attract attention. So, she kept her eyes on the computer screen as she said, 'I am going to rescue my father from the base that is under Century Lodge and then expose it to the authorities,' she said.

The boy sat in his seat, once again overawed, and said nothing.

27

Century Lodge

'Did you know that Luke's dad likes those books you are always going on about?' said Gezz as she sucked milk from her spoon.

Her dad dug into his bowl of cornflakes and took a mouthful. He chewed and rolled his eyes, really savouring the taste. 'What books?' he quizzed as he swallowed.

'You know,' said Gezz, pressing her spoon down over mushy frosted flakes and letting it fill with more milk. 'Those android books by Philip Asimov, or whatever he's called.' She sucked the milk from her spoon again.

'Geraldine,' her mother cut in. 'Don't slurp your breakfast. Eat it properly.' Then she scooped up a teaspoon full of baby food and shovelled it into baby Ross's mouth.

'Sorry, Mum,' said Gezz, and dug into her breakfast properly.

Her dad paused and frowned, as if finding it difficult to comprehend the piece of information his daughter had just given him. 'Wait a minute,' he began. 'You mean Terry reads Isaac Asimov and Philip K. Dick novels?'

'Yes,' said Gezz.

'You don't just mean he watches the films? Like *Blade Runner?*'

'No.'

'He actually reads the books?'

Gezz laughed with her spoon still stuck in her mouth. 'Yes.' She swallowed the last of her breakfast. 'And he has records where people sing about being aliens and robots.'

Gezz's father smiled, staring into the far wall in a happy trance and shook his head, the way people do when they are thinking 'Well I never. I don't believe it!' The girl got up and dropped her bowl into the soapy mass of bubbles floating in the sink. Her father turned, still smiling. 'Well, what are you going to be doing on your first day of half-term? Penny for the guy?'

Her mum laughed out loud as she shovelled more goo into Ross's bottomless pit. 'That's a bit premature, isn't it, John? Bonfire Night is not until next month.'

'Well, what else is there at this time of the year?' shrugged her father.

'Halloween,' Gezz replied casually.

'No, Gezz,' said her mum suddenly, the teaspoon dangling between her finger and thumb. 'You know how we feel about that. Witches and wizards, goblins and elves. It's not Christian. It's one step away from the occult.'

'Dad,' Gezz started, but not just to change the subject, she had a genuine question to ask. 'Is there a secret war base buried under the lodge?'

Without giving any time for thought, her dad burst into hearty laughter. 'You what?' he jeered merrily. 'I think you've been reading too much Enid Blyton, love.'

Gezz was undeterred. 'But have you ever heard of anything like it round here?'

Her dad placed his elbows on the table and gestured with his right hand. 'Well, if there *was* a secret base in the area, it wouldn't be very secret if people like us knew about it, would it?'

Oh yeah, Gezz thought. Then, as if the issue had never been raised, she excused herself from the kitchen and went to call for Luke.

★ ★ ★

The computer screen flashed into life and the children stood bent over an empty swivel chair waiting for the Internet software to establish itself. Once the control bar had unfolded at the top of the screen, Luke gestured for his electronic girl-friend to sit down and do her stuff. Gezz marvelled as Anne's fingers got to work, racing over the keyboard in a blur as she accessed a web page that had been written by some war nut who had obviously made it his life's ambition to chronicle every single detail about conflict.

'It would seem,' said Anne, scrolling pages over by the second, 'that there were several of these underground bases across the country.'

Malcolm stared at the screen and Gezz could almost see his mind racing away. 'But what were they built for?' he quizzed.

Anne continued to scroll page after page. 'They were constructed as fail-safe bunkers in case of all-out nuclear attack.'

It was Luke's turn to look engrossed. 'What?' he whispered, clearly very impressed by the operation. Nothing about war impressed Gezz. It was just completely stupid as far as she was concerned.

'If the country had received advance notice of a nuclear attack,' Anne continued, 'all the people of society deemed important for running Britain's affairs would have been preserved alive in these bunkers placed in strategic locations about the country.'

'While all the ordinary people fried,' Gezz added in a low tone. She was disgusted.

'Yes,' replied Anne flatly. 'Once the danger had passed, the preserved humans would then venture up on to the surface and repopulate the country.'

'So,' said Malcolm with great enthusiasm. 'The bunker would have had an air supply, electric generators, food and water. As well as crude computer technology.'

Luke frowned, which pleased Gezz. It was good to have Malcolm coming up with the answers and Luke scratching his head for a change. 'And there's one of these places under the lodge?' he asked, his voice conveying utter disbelief.

As if to answer the boy's question, Anne placed her hands on to the keyboard and started to type too fast for her friends to see. The monitor seemed to flicker for a second or two, and Gezz watched in amazement as the map of her local area presented itself once more, the section of the grid containing the lodge where the fishermen sat flashed on and off every colour of the rainbow. Anne positioned the cursor over the image and gave a couple of clicks on the mouse.

'Woah,' Luke whispered in admiration as the map dismantled and redesigned itself into a flat two-dimensional plan of a building. Anne's eyes flashed as she continued to feed the computer with information. As she did so, the image on the screen unfolded and turned, becoming a three-dimensional box detailing two floors, a good number of rooms, air ducts, and a corridor with a single lift shaft at the end.

Gezz puzzled over the drawing. *Only one way out,* she told herself. She leant over Anne's left shoulder and tapped the glass screen with a finger. 'Where does this lift shaft come up?'

The automaton ran her right-hand digits over the console again and the three-dimensional picture merged into the original map. The lodge flashed away in its bright colours again, and then a second glow, a line, extended itself and formed a tiny square box at the end. The extension flashed emerald green, now part of the main highlight. Gezz frowned. 'Is this line some sort of tunnel?'

'Yes,' Anne replied.

'It stops under the old mill.'

'Yes,' said Anne again. 'The lift shaft emerges in the cellar of Century Mill.'

Luke's bedroom fell deadly quiet, with only the hum of the computer floating above what otherwise would be absolute silence. Gezz looked at her friends and wondered what they were thinking. Then she looked at Anne. The robot just sat there, staring at her monitor, still, as though dead at the desk, her shiny blonde ponytail limp and lifeless. Gezz knew what she was thinking, it consisted of just four words: *Rescue Professor Wolfgang Droyd.*

The children jumped as Anne announced her next move. 'Disconnecting floppy disc.' She withdrew her disc-hand, and in no time at all it had re-formed into a regular five digits with pink nail varnish. The girl spun to her left and faced her friend. 'I am going to infiltrate the base and rescue my father,' she said. Gezz smiled, touched by the robot's apparent concern. 'He needs me,' continued the blonde. She paused, as if considering something. Then she added: 'And I need him.'

Luke took to the swivel chair and shut down his computer. Meanwhile, Malcolm shared Gezz's unspoken curiosity. 'Why do you need him?' enquired Luke thoughtfully. 'Is it because he programmed you to rescue him?'

'No,' Anne replied, her face deadpan and emotionless.

'Is it because you love him?' pushed Gezz. Both children stood waiting in expectation.

Anne nearly gave a frown. It was clear that she was struggling to compute that last question. 'He is familiar to me,' she said.

'You have a fondness for him,' Gezz urged. 'He is your creator, your *father.*'

Anne really did look like she was frowning now. She spoke slowly, as if struggling to find the right words. 'I… I… He is…' She broke off, her eyes burning a dazzling blue. 'He is… He…' Gezz and Malcolm clenched their fists and gestured, punching the air gently and grinning, urging the cyborg to vocalize how she felt, if she felt anything at all. 'Go on,' Gezz incited. 'You can do it.'

'He… He is…' Anne forced the sentence to completion. 'He is familiar to me,' she said. 'I must rescue him.'

The children's faces dropped. Maybe the android's brain, despite being partly flesh and blood, would never really develop human feelings. It was, after all, only intended to be an experiment. Perhaps the Professor might have to go back to the drawing board on this one.

Luke jumped to his feet and clasped his hands, seemingly unaware of the wonder girl's almost-first expression of deep feeling. 'Right,' he breezed. 'The computer is off. So when do we check out this army base, then?'

'Now,' said Anne resolutely.

Gezz shrugged and smiled. They might as well try and find the entrance to this place if nothing else. 'Well,' she said. 'I suppose there's no time like the present.'

28

The Secret Door

The late morning sun beat down upon the foursome as they strolled through the uncut grass to the edge of the far side of the pond. Bits of old rusty railing lined the bank and two junior school children joined their elderly granddad in casting a fishing line. It was incredible to think a two-storey building lay beneath this stretch of water, undetected and forgotten.

A cool dark shadow threw itself upon the children. Gezz looked up in awe of the decayed dirty red and brown bricks, punctuated every so often with long white window frames displaying nothing but darkness within. The mill seemed like a terrible monster overlooking the new clean houses that bent round the lodge in a semicircle. It was as if the building, with its board-covered ground-floor windows, smothered in graffiti and big red 'Danger: No Entry' signs, was saying 'I've been here for over a hundred years, and I'm not having you new houses pushing me out. I don't care if times have moved on. I was here long before you lot came. *This is my lodge.*'

The children stopped just short of touching the mouldy walls. Gezz shivered. 'I don't like this,' she said. 'It spooks me out.'

Luke began pulling at one of the boarded-up doors and Gezz's stomach turned. 'How do we get in?' asked Luke, pulling and heaving at the nailed-down boards to little avail.

Anne raised her eyes and took in the entire building. 'Scanning,' she announced. 'The lift shaft is concealed in the cellar on the east side.' The robot girl turned on her heels and marched off to the far end of the building and disappeared round the corner. The children hurried after her, eager to keep her in their sights, and yet at the same time reluctant because of overwhelming feelings of dread.

Gezz imagined what it must have been like for her grandmother and all those like her who used to work in this blot on the landscape. Of course the air would have been filthy then and people would have walked to work because most people could not afford cars. When she had looked at her old primary school, she had imagined life a hundred years ago and yearned to go back to it, but now, looking at the disused factory, she was glad to be living in the twenty-first century.

'My sensors indicate that this is the entrance to the cellar,' announced Anne, pointing to a flight of concrete steps sinking down into the floor. They stopped at a pair of dark-green wooden double doors. A big sign, painted in red, had been screwed to the left-hand door.

'Prohibited,' Malcolm read out loud. 'Trespassers will be prosecuted.' He turned to face the other children, shrugged and began walking away. 'Oh, well,' he said. 'That's that then.'

Gezz caught him by the hand. 'No, you don't,' she said. 'You're not getting out of it that easily.'

Luke kept his eyes on the flight of steps. He looked fascinated by them. 'This must have been where the factory workers accepted their deliveries. Cotton and stuff.'

'That is correct,' said Anne. She trotted down the steps and ran her hands over the set of doors. 'Processing,' she said, testing the strength of the wood with her fingertips. 'The door is secured with two mortise locks and four bolts.' Then she held out her little finger. 'Activating fibre-optic lens.' Her fingernail flicked open and a thin skin-covered flex wove itself through one of the locks. 'It is very dark. Switching to infra-red.' The robot's eyes blinked as she accessed the information being fed to her.

Luke trotted down the steps to stand at his friend's side. 'What can you see, Anne?'

'The room is virtually empty,' the automaton reported. 'There are a few stacks of newspapers arranged as a bed and some old coats. There is the remains of a fire. Perhaps the cellar has been used by homeless people or squatters.'

'Is there any machinery or old stock?' asked Luke.

'No. It is likely that the original proprietors or government receivers took the machinery when the mill was shut down. Sensors indicate that the building is empty.'

Luke was puzzled. 'Why not just demolish it then? I mean, the place is an eyesore.'

Gezz skipped down the steps and stood just behind her friends. 'Maybe the government know about the bunker and the secret passage?'

'No,' said the android. 'The information I retrieved from the Internet leads me to believe the government are under the illusion that the base was destroyed after the Cold War.'

Luke pushed at the doors. They wouldn't budge. 'How are we going to get in?'

Anne removed her fibre-optic lens and reverted it back into a regular little finger. Then she extended her first finger and held it over one of the locks. As she did so, her finger narrowed until it could slide into the hole. Her eyes blinked as she found the correct key shape. Then she turned her finger and Gezz heard the lock fold back with a click.

When Anne removed her finger, its shape was in that of a sturdy squared-off key, not unlike the one Gezz locked her back door with. She watched as Anne slotted her key finger into the second hole and unlocked it. On retrieving her finger the second time, the robot just looked at it momentarily and the digit returned to normal. *This is good*, thought Gezz, because it meant that Anne was learning to give the commands to her body silently instead of speaking them out loud every time.

Luke rested his hands on his hips. 'Now, how do we unbolt the latches on the other side?'

'You will recall how I tore down the door of the den,' said Anne, 'and then secured it again afterwards?'

'Oh yes,' said Gezz with a smile. 'I was forgetting you could do that.'

The two of them watched in utter amazement as the little blonde girl tugged at the centre where the two doors met. Her ponytail flopped about as the sound of wrenching metal greeted their ears. The doors began to buckle as Anne relentlessly pulled at them with her fingertips. Suddenly the wood gave way with a loud crack and the doors released themselves, swinging outwards slightly on their rusty hinges. 'You've done it!' shouted Luke, unable to contain his excitement.

'I don't want to worry you guys,' said the voice of Malcolm from behind them. He stood at the top of the steps looking all frightened. 'But there's a gang of kids on their way.'

'That's all we need,' said Gezz. 'Get down here, Malc. We haven't a moment to lose. We'll have to go in the cellar and seal it up from the inside.'

Malcolm hovered at the top of the steps. 'Oh, I don't know, Gezz,' he stammered. 'I don't like the look of that place.'

'You'll be all right,' urged Gezz.

Malcolm froze. 'Those kids are coming, I can hear them.'

Gezz lost her patience. 'Get down here, Malcolm,' she shouted. 'Now!'

Very reluctantly, Malcolm obeyed and Gezz felt bad for shouting at him. But the three of them had been in this adventure with Anne from the start and she wasn't going to let Malcolm chicken out now. The four of them stepped through the buckled doors and into the blackness.

★ ★ ★

'I can't see a flipping thing,' said Luke, his voice echoing and resounding around the empty space. The air was suddenly very cool as though a cloud had just blocked out the warmth of the summer sun.

Anne was busy putting the finishing touches to the bolts on the doors. At least that was what Gezz imagined she was doing, because Luke was right, it was absolutely pitch black. It was all right for Anne, though, she had night vision which allowed her to see in the dark.

'My visual sensors indicate that there are no things flipping in this vicinity,' said the android and everyone laughed. 'You are amused?' said Anne. 'Why?'

'It doesn't matter,' said Luke's voice.

'You are correct in your assumption,' Anne replied. 'The matter is of no concern.'

Gezz could hear movement as the robot ran its fingers over the walls. 'According to the top-secret files retrieved,' the cyborg continued, 'one of these bricks serves as a trigger and opens a concealed door.'

Gezz shivered, the cold beginning to set in. Goose pimples surfaced on her sleeveless arms. Then something made her jump. She knew it was not an old soft drinks can, nor was it a pile of newspapers. It was something living – and it had just run across her toes. The girl froze, not with cold this time, but with fright. 'Anne,' she stammered. 'I think there is something down here with us.'

'Oh, don't say that.' It was Malcolm's voice. It trembled with fear.

'What do you mean there's something down here with us?' said Luke. His tone carried that usual cynical edge. 'Just because we're in a cellar and it's dark, it doesn't mean there are ghosts here.'

Gezz jumped again. Something was sniffing her ankle. She could feel its cold nose brushing her skin just above her socks. 'Arrgh!' she cried. 'What is it?' She heard a tiny squeak as she kicked the creature off.

'Do not be alarmed,' said Anne in her matter-of-fact way. 'The rodent is curious. There are many such animals living down here.'

'Rodent?' said Luke suspiciously.

'Rats,' replied Anne.

There was a lot of scuffing and hysteria as Gezz ran up and down on the spot. 'Oh my God. Oh my God,' she kept saying over and over again. 'I don't believe it! There's rats down here with us! Oh my God!'

'You are not supposed to say that,' Luke's voice teased. 'Do not take the Lord's name in vain.'

'Shut it, you,' Gezz commanded.

The children were silenced as a scraping, grating noise rumbled through the stale air and vibrated the concrete floor. They watched on in squinting astonishment as an oblong ray of light opened up before them. 'You've found it!' cheered Luke, his voice echoing about the cellar. 'You've found the secret door!'

Dim light fell upon their faces and they were glad to be able to see one another again. Anne took the lead and walked through the open slab of brick into the purple hue beyond. Another short flight of steps took the children down to a second set of doors. The automaton ran her fingers over the entrance. 'These doors are made of steel,' she said. 'They are secured with an electronic lock.'

'Oh, great,' chided Luke. 'How do we get through this one, then?'

'An electromagnetic pulse should render the device inoperable. I can also emit a high-frequency sonic sound which will disrupt any listening devices. Please cover your ears tightly.'

The three children did as they were told, each wondering what Anne was about to do. The robot girl then took a step back and pouted her lips. Gezz, Malcolm and Luke screwed up their faces and pressed hard on their ears as an almost unbearable high-pitched whistle filled the air. It was awful. Gezz was not sure whether the noise was in the cellar above them, around the steps where they stood, or in her head. It overwhelmed them. She was relieved when, just above the sonic whistle, she heard the heavy steel door click and release itself. Anne closed her mouth and the sound ceased.

Luke wiped his watering eyes. 'God,' he breathed. 'What the heck was that?'

'A high-frequency sound wave,' said Anne simply and pushed open the doors. The children flinched again as they were greeted with normal bright electric light.

'It's the corridor,' Gezz exclaimed with great zeal. 'The lift must be at the other end of here.'

The corridor stretched on for quite some way and then bent to the left a little, and sure enough, at the very end lay a pair of golden elevator doors. The android strolled determinedly towards them with the three very nervous children in tow. 'How do you know there aren't any hidden cameras around here?' mumbled Malcolm. 'They might be waiting for us down there. Have you thought of that?'

Anne pressed the button on the panel next to the lift door. It lit up, signifying that the elevator was on its way. 'I have considered every possible eventuality. My sensors detect no security devices on this level,' said Anne. 'Though there may be cameras in the actual complex. My high-frequency sound will render them useless.'

Gezz just hoped she was right. She shivered again as she heard the lift arrive and settle into place behind the doors. For all they knew, someone might be in it, coming up to the surface for some fresh air. What would they do if they found four children waiting for them? What would they do if they realized one of them was Professor Droyd's creation? Gezz was beginning to appreciate Malcolm's reservations.

The lift doors rumbled open and Anne gestured the children inside. 'We shall go to the first level and search from there,' she said, pressing the 'level one' button without any hesitation at all. Nerves were running very high now as the doors closed and the lift juddered downwards with a sinking feeling. Gezz's legs were like rubber and her stomach churned. She felt sick. The lift seemed to take a long time dropping, but then it would: the first level was fifty metres below ground – below the lodge to be exact. She thought of the old man and his grandchildren fishing up above. He had no idea what she and her friends were up to right under his feet.

The lift slowed and Anne readied herself at the doors with her lips pouted. As soon as the gold colour plates of metal rumbled back, she let out her brain-piercing whistle. The children stuck their fingers in their ears and winced again. Gezz could just make out small black lenses, like little video cameras, dotted about the corridor. Each had a little red light above it. No sooner had Anne emitted her strange sound than the little red lights went out, dead.

The noise ceased again as Anne closed her mouth. 'We haven't got much time,' she said. 'Once the guards realize the cameras are down, they will come looking for us.' Again she led the way with the children following very reluctantly.

Gezz could not get over how warm it was. The corridor was well lit and it felt a little bit like a deserted hospital. Their feet clicked on the polished floor and the girl marvelled at how this world had managed to stay secret for so long. *Just think*, she contemplated, *my house is above all this.*

Anne came to a halt by a large square grille suspended off the floor in the wall on the left. She started to pull at it with her fingernails. In no time at all the screws had come loose and the silver metal pin-pricked sheet was in her hand. 'Luke and Malcolm,' ordered the robot. 'You climb into the air ducts and find the Professor's room. They will have given him new quarters beyond the laboratory now. His request for absolute privacy will have been annulled.'

'Eh?' spluttered Malcolm.

'Alternatively, find the laboratory on the second level. All the shafts are interlinked. There are no obstacles that I can detect on the map.'

'Now hang on a minute.' Malcolm looked terrified. 'I'm not crawling through miles of tunnel. What if I get stuck?'

'You will not get stuck,' Anne replied. 'The dimensions of the ducts will accommodate you.'

'Well,' the boy was getting panicky now. 'What if they have been experimenting on mutations or something? What if there's monsters in there?'

Gezz found herself laughing. 'He's only saying that because he saw Sarah get trapped like that in *Classic Doctor Who* last Sunday on UK Gold. His granddad tapes it for him.' she said casually. 'I know. Luke and I saw that one. Didn't we, Luke?'

Luke ignored the question, probably because he did not want to admit he watched the old episodes of *Doctor Who*. He just started shoving Malcolm in the back and pushing him towards the open air duct. 'Come on, you mard, get in there.'

Malcolm bent down and climbed on to the hard silver metal of the square tunnel, nothing but blackness stretched up for who knows how far. Then he shuffled out again. 'No,' he moaned. 'You go first.' Luke huffed and rolled his eyes and then climbed into the tunnel. Malcolm followed and Anne sealed the grille over the hole.

'Do not take too long,' the android called through the slits in the metal. 'Once they know we are here, it will be harder to escape.' Gezz watched over Anne's arched back and could just make out the rounded bottom of Malcolm, waddling up the chute as the two lads crawled deeper in.

Gezz turned and pulled her T-shirt straight in a very business-like fashion. 'Now,' she said, daring to enjoy herself. 'What are we going to do?'

Anne bolted up, her face as serious as ever. 'Now we find the computer room,' she said. 'It is located at the other end of this level.'

29

To the Rescue

'Ow!' Luke hissed, catching a tiny spike of metal on his knee. 'These screw heads are everywhere.' Malcolm said nothing, so Luke carried on. 'It's cold in here, isn't it? And I can hardly see a thing. Have your eyes adjusted yet?'

'We should never have got involved in all this,' said Malcolm finally, his shoes scraping against the metal as he shuffled up behind Luke. 'It's too dangerous.'

'It'll be even more dangerous,' Luke replied, 'if these scientist guys get the Professor to build a robot soldier. You've seen what Anne can do. Imagine if they manage to create a fighter robot that has her powers. Imagine if they built an army of them. Imagine the kind of wars that would be fought.'

'Yes, all right,' moaned Malcolm. 'I get the point.'

Luke stopped crawling and he felt Malcolm's head crash into his backside. 'Sorry!'

'Why have you stopped?'

'I think I can see a beam of light up ahead. It must be another grille.'

The two boys crawled as slowly and as quietly as they could up the shaft and peeped out through the pin-pricked metal into the light. It was just another corridor like the one they had come from. It could even be the same corridor, for all they knew. Luke flinched as he heard footsteps clicking on the polished floor. As the steps got louder and closer he realized they belonged to two separate individuals. 'Are you sure?' a voice was saying. It was a man's voice. 'Yes,' said the other. 'Every single camera on this level. Might be a fault, but we'd better check it out all the same.'

Luke watched as two men wearing black uniforms strolled by, each wearing black-domed metal hats and large guns dangling from their shoulders. The boy gulped as they passed him and continued on. 'Oh no,' he breathed. 'They've got guns.'

'What?!' hissed Malcolm, backing off into the tunnel. 'I'm getting out of here.'

'And how far do you think you'll get?' Luke whispered. 'To the corridor? To the lift? And how will you get out of the cellar? Anne sealed it before we came down here remember.' Malcolm stopped shuffling backwards. 'That's it,' said Luke softly. 'We carry on.'

The children scraped and shuffled their way forward, bypassing the grille, and on into the darkness. The tunnel seemed to go on and on without a break, and the further it went, the darker it became. Finally, after a few minutes, they hit a dead end.

'It seems to stop here,' said Luke. 'I can feel metal in front of me.'

'No,' Malcolm replied. 'It can't be. I can still feel cold air brushing my face.'

Luke rested his body weight on his left hand and traced the wall ahead with his right. 'It's a corner,' he sighed. 'It's just a corner. Come on.' They shuffled on, turned the corner, and continued up the second shaft. Another beam of light hit the wall of the chute up ahead. Another grille. The boys dragged their legs and crawled on, slowing down when they thought they might be in earshot.

Luke peeped through the grille, his eyes accustoming to the light again. 'It's a room,' he hissed. 'It's quite small. It has a single bunk bed, a fold-up metal table with a mug and kettle on it and a stack of magazines.'

'Let me have a gander,' said Malcolm. His friend edged forward so that the boy could get a glimpse. 'It looks more like a prison cell,' he said. Then he caught sight of the design on the cover of the top magazine. '*New Scientist*,' he hissed excitedly. 'It's *New Scientist* magazine. This must be the Professor's room. Anne was right. They no longer allow him to stay unsupervised in the laboratory.'

'But it's empty,' said Luke. 'We'll have to carry on.'

'What?!' Malcolm complained. 'Why not wait here until they bring him back for a rest?'

'And how long do you think that will be?' said Luke authoritatively. 'No. We haven't got that much time on our hands. We'll have to try and find the laboratory.' With cramp starting to set in their arms and legs, the two boys shuffled on ever forwards into the dark of the tunnel.

★ ★ ★

Anne walked the corridors of the forbidden underground military bunker as though she did this sort of thing every day. Worse, she walked about like she owned the place. But then, that was the advantage of having a computer for a brain, Gezz told herself. You could download maps of buildings and then walk about the place as if you knew them like the back of your hand. But that was just it, Anne *did* know it that well, even though she had never seen these corridors before.

The pair of them edged slowly to the next corner. Anne's voice fell to a whisper. 'The computer room is on this next stretch. It is likely to be guarded.'

'Brilliant,' said Gezz sarcastically, her hands on her hips. 'You just take a peep and see.' She tiptoed silently to the edge of the wall, her breathing slow and hard, and waved her friend over. 'Activate your fibre-optic thingy and see what's going on.'

Anne obeyed and the thin wire extended itself from her little finger and wound itself round the corner. Her free hand morphed itself into what looked like a set of binoculars. 'You wish to see?'

Gezz nodded and peered into the skin-covered 'lenses'. A single uniformed guard stood there, his back to a standard wooden door with a little round window at the top, and staring directly at the wall in front of him. He looked extremely bored, with his black tin hat and a machine gun slung over his shoulder. Gezz boggled and pulled back. 'He's got a gun!' she hissed.

'There is only one,' said Anne. 'Good.' She deactivated her fibre-optic and lenses, her hands swiftly returning to normal. 'Put your fingers in your ears, Gezz.'

'Eh?' Gezz frowned. Then she realized. 'Oh, I see.'

Once Gezz had her fingers firmly rooted in her ears, Anne stepped into the next corridor. The guard, bored though he might have been, had lightning reflexes. He spun on his heels and levelled his gun. 'Halt, or I'll fire!' Then he paused for a brief moment, confused by the sight of the little blonde girl with the ponytail. That brief moment of hesitation was all Anne needed. As the soldier appeared to realize who the girl was, Anne pouted her lips and let out her high-pitched whistle.

The guard flexed and wrenched in pain, his gun falling from his hands. He tried to cover his ears with the palms of his hands, but it was too late. He dropped to the floor, unconscious.

Gezz joined Anne at her side. Her eyes nearly popped out of her head when she set them on the felled guard. 'Have you...killed him?'

'To kill a human is against my programming,' said Anne simply. 'The sonic frequency is more than the organic brain can bear, so it shuts itself down. I have, in effect, put him to sleep. He will recover.'

'Right,' said Gezz busily. 'Well, let's get into that computer room and do whatever we have to do.'

Anne responded immediately by inserting her already morphed forefinger into the lock of the computer room. Gezz stole a look through the little round window in the door and took in all the high-tech wizardry. It was like the bridge of the *Starship Enterprise* in there. Within seconds the android had unlocked the door and opened it. 'Hold the door open while I bring the guard inside.' Gezz did as she was told and the automaton dragged the man effortlessly into the room.

Once they were all inside and the door was shut, Anne locked it up again to give them time to think of something, should any unexpected visitors come across them. Anne sat herself at the main console and got to work.

Gezz glanced about at the walls, all lined with banks of machinery. Spools of tape wound from reel to reel and lights flashed and beeped. It was like something out of a James Bond film.

'The technology is very old,' said Anne, her fingers running a blur across the console. 'Most of this equipment was left over from when the Cold War ended. The Foundation people have adapted it and made it compatible with modern developments. They are very clever people.'

'You sound like you admire them,' said Gezz, keeping one eye on the window and the other on their unconscious friend.

'I do not have the capacity for admiration,' Anne responded. 'But I can recognize outstanding human achievements.' She broke off, nearly frowning at the monitor screen in front of her. 'As I anticipated. The program will require a password. It is a good job I downloaded that government information.'

Gezz raised an eyebrow and joined her friend at the terminal. 'A good job?' she teased. 'That sounds very human.'

Anne morphed her left hand into the shape of a computer cable and inserted it into the back of the computer. 'It stands to reason that the longer I spend time in the company of humans, the more I will sound like them.' She broke off again, images, pictures, graphs, charts and lists all flashing before her at incredible speed. Her fingers tapped code after code into the console, every possible combination, until the screen finally flashed up the sign: 'Access Granted'.

Gezz marvelled as a list of agencies and organizations flicked into place. 'Who are these people?' she whispered.

'These are the organizations who have requested demonstrations of the android soldier once it is complete.'

Gezz balked at the screen, hardly able to believe her eyes. 'But I've heard of some of these,' she said. 'Some are major world governments.'

'And a few of them are small terrorist groups,' Anne concluded.

Gezz held her brow. 'This is terrible,' she gasped. 'We've got to do something.'

The android moved the mouse to another section and clicked. A small box flitted into the centre of the screen and maximized. Anne began typing a series of numbers in its large white space. The figures grew and grew until they filled the screen. Then they moved up to make room for more. It was clear that Anne had a very definite purpose in mind, and Gezz realized that the cyborg had probably thought it up even before she had left Luke's computer an hour or so ago.

Anne clicked on a box marked 'send' and the square full of numbers vanished. A little light green arrow produced itself in the corner of the screen alongside a caption which read 'sending mail'.

'What have you done?' asked Gezz, intrigued.

'I have sent a multiple email to all the organizations on this list,' Anne replied. 'That means that each government and terrorist group will receive the equation that I have just devised.'

'And what will that do?'

'It will act in the same way germs affect the human body,' said Anne simply. 'Once it is introduced to their computer systems, it will work its way through every single computation until there is nothing left. It will be as though they had never known about the android soldier.'

Gezz grinned, impressed with the automaton's plan. Indeed, she was feeling quite proud of her. 'Is that what they call a computer virus?'

'Yes,' said Anne. 'That is the colloquial term for the procedure. Computer virus.'

Gezz folded her arms in a business-like fashion. 'So all we have to do now is find the Professor and…' She tailed off as she glanced to where the unconscious guard should have been lying. The girl gaped and her heart fluttered. The door of the computer room was open very slightly and the guard had gone.

'The guard has escaped!' said Gezz. The android closed the computer down and got to her feet. 'Time is short,' she said. 'We must get to the Professor, destroy whatever progress has been made with the new robot and flee before we are discovered.'

'You what?' said Gezz in disbelief. 'Are you mad?'

'Mad,' repeated Anne flatly. 'With disordered mind, insane. Wildly foolish; wildly excited or infatuated. Frenzied. Angry. Rabid. Wildly light-hearted.' Then she walked calmly over to the door and opened it. 'No,' she said. 'I am not mad.'

30

Mistaken Identity

The android emerged into the corridor and Gezz followed close behind, shutting the door. 'It may be possible to find the guard and render him unconscious again,' said Anne.

Gezz stood at the junction at the end of the corridor. 'The question is, which way did he go?'

Anne pointed down past the computer room. 'I shall trace him this way for eighty metres. If there is no sign of him, I shall meet you here.'

'And I suppose I will have to go eighty metres up this way, will I?' said Gezz, hands on hips and not feeling remotely impressed with her friend now. 'And what if it's me that finds him? I mean, I don't have a sonic whistle, you know.'

'Just come back here and alert me,' said Anne. And with that she set off at a good pace up the corridor.

Gezz shrugged to herself and slowly retraced the path they had originally come by. The air was warm and the walls shone a hospital green-white colour. Her shoes seemed to click louder as they touched the floor now that she was alone. She crept along with her escapee nowhere to be seen.

Gezz began to wonder how long the guard had been conscious. How much had he heard? When did he escape? How far had he got? The girl was sure she had walked more than eighty metres. She turned the bend at the half-way point and gawped in horror at the opening gold elevator doors down at the far end.

'This is exactly the sort of thing I feared would happen if I left you on guard alone, you imbecile,' a woman's voice was saying. A scared-stiff soldier replied, 'How was I supposed to know the android was going to appear out of nowhere and whistle at me?'

The woman stepped from the lift and Gezz froze in a panic. *Come on legs,* she told herself. *Come on. Move!* But her feet remained rooted to the shiny concrete floor. Gezz tried to control the tremors running up through her body and she forced her mind to stay disciplined. She took slow deep breaths. *Calm the heart down,* she told herself. *Concentrate, yes that's it.* 'Our Father,' she muttered to herself. 'Who art in heaven.' Her legs relaxed a little. 'Hallowed be Thy name.' She decided not to look at the tall woman and her escort advancing down the corridor towards her. 'Thy kingdom come.' She kept her eyes on her feet. 'Thy will be done.' Her feet began to lift. *Yes, that's it. Walk, come on, walk!*

Gezz managed to turn and take her first step. Then she froze again, instantly, as the roar of the guard's voice echoed down the corridor. She heard the rifle click and she knew it was trained on her. 'You!' screamed the guard. 'You child! Stand still or I will open fire!'

Gezz tried to control her breathing as she heard the footsteps of her captors closing in behind her. *Remain calm,* she told herself. *Remain calm and think.*

'Well, well, well,' said the woman's voice slowly from behind. It was silky in texture, purring like a cat. Gezz could tell the woman was smiling. She turned, copying the robotic movements she had seen Anne do so many times and kept her face as blank as she possibly could. The woman smiled at her and Gezz examined the sight. The woman was tall with short, cropped blonde hair. She wore earrings and a red business suit. It was difficult to tell how old she was. She looked quite young, as young as Gezz's mum perhaps, but her voice sounded older, like her Auntie Dorothy.

The guard pointed his gun at Gezz, and she tried hard not to look terrified. 'This isn't the girl I saw at the computer room,' he sneered.

'Oh, but it is,' purred the woman, waving a dismissive hand. 'The Professor had been working on a number of morphing techniques with the prototype project. Its defensive instincts would have caused it to adopt a new appearance as soon as it knew it had been discovered.'

Gezz did not like the way her new mistress kept referring to her as 'it'. But the ruse was working. The woman obviously believed that she was Anne. She cringed, but tried not to show it, as the woman ran a long painted fingernail over her cheek and spoke with mock affection. 'So,' the woman smiled. 'The progeny has returned to save its creator. How very touching.' She took Gezz by the arm and started to guide her back to the lift.

The soldier stood in the middle of the corridor shaking his head. 'It's dangerous!' he called. 'What about that whistle I was telling you about?'

The woman stopped at the lift doors and smiled at Gezz. 'What is this whistle of which he speaks?'

Gezz knew that Anne would have just answered the question truthfully as she was programmed to, but she herself had the capacity to lie. But was it OK to lie? Would she be forgiven? Would her parents be disappointed if they knew? She thought it through quickly. Giving incomplete information, or allowing someone to believe a misconception, was not the same as outright lies. Gezz's mother had told her that people did this sort of thing in a wartime situation. *Well*, thought Gezz, *what is this if it's not a wartime situation?* Lives were at stake, including hers. In any case, Gezz was not an android, so she would be telling the truth.

'I do not possess the capability of which he speaks,' she said, copying Anne's deadpan expression.

'I thought so,' replied the woman. She turned to her subordinate, who was still standing in the middle of the corridor. 'Get back to your post,' she ordered. 'And stay alert this time.'

The soldier turned, somewhat disgruntled, and marched back to his computer room.

As she and the woman entered the lift and descended to the lower level, Gezz could not help wondering where Anne had got to. And what about the two boys? Had they found the Professor, or were they still crawling through miles of tunnel? She tried to work out who of the four of them had the best deal. Then she concluded only Anne could have. She was the only one unaffected by fear, and the only one capable of dealing with these deadly grown-ups.

The lift doors parted and they disembarked. Gezz was surprised to find the lower level bustling with black-uniformed security men and white-coated scientists, all walking back and forth very busily.

After some time, they passed through a set of double doors and strolled down another corridor. Gezz remained silent, as Anne had done when the children first met her. She had spoken only when the Professor asked her a question or issued a command. So far the bluff was working.

They came to a halt outside some tall, heavy steel doors. The woman put her eyes to a narrow slit built into a panel next to the doors. A computer voice beeped from a grille underneath, 'Retina identified. State name.'

'Angela Droylsden,' said the woman clearly, and Gezz wondered who this person might really be. The name sounded strangely familiar.

'Voice pattern verified,' beeped the electronic voice. 'You have clearance, Angela Droylsden.'

With a hiss of hydraulics and a rumble of moving steel, the huge metal doors activated and opened themselves inwards. Gezz gulped as she took in the sight on the other side, while at the same time trying to look blank and indifferent. 'Remember this?' said Droylsden, gesturing grandly with her arms outstretched.

Gezz walked into the chamber, sensing the bulky doors closing behind her. 'Yes,' she said, blinking very deliberately, as if computing the answer to the question. 'I recall this room.'

'This is where you were born,' said Droylsden. She stopped, turned dramatically, and pointed a finger at Gezz. 'And where you will be reborn.' The woman broke into a broad wicked smile and purred, 'As the perfect soldier.'

Gezz tried not to be overwhelmed by the awesome room, with its huge transparent cylinder-shaped compartments lining the walls, each containing child-sized featureless mannequins. Androids. They reminded Gezz of the plastic dummies you see in shop windows displaying the latest fashions and bargains. Anne must have looked like this in the early stages, she concluded.

A white-coated scientist was busy at a workbench. He hadn't even noticed the new arrivals, he was so engrossed in his task. Gezz watched him messing with what looked like a disembodied human arm. The hand, wrist and arm looked very human with fingersnails and real-looking skin up to the elbow. After that it was plastic and metal all the way. A series of wires and circuits emerged at the shoulder where they connected to a sort of power pack, rather like one she operated her train set with.

As the man turned the dial on his console, the hand coiled itself into a fist. Then, as the scientist turned back the switch, the hand released itself. Gezz watched as the man placed a glass beaker, like the ones they used at school in Science, into the android hand. He turned the dial again and, as he did so, the hand took a firm grip of the beaker. It squeezed and it squeezed as he continued to twist the control very slowly. Gezz flinched inside, all the time trying to look unconcerned, as the beaker smashed into a thousand pieces, the hand completely unaffected and not a drop of blood in sight.

'Excellent,' smiled Droylsden. She approached the scientist and took him by the arm, to take his attention from his work more than anything else. 'Now, Richards,' she said, guiding the man to another much bigger console built into the wall. 'How is our second prototype coming along?'

Gezz could not help noticing a pile of white dinner plates stacked in the top corner of the console. What on earth could they be for? Richards pressed a button and pulled a lever. As he did so, one of the cylindrical chambers began to rise, and Gezz got her first proper look at the new android. It was like an eleven-year-old boy, but with no hair and blank eyes. Gezz shivered. No colour, no pupils in the middle, just white soulless eyes staring at her. The rest of the automaton was donned in brown, black and shades of green, the colours of army camouflage gear, right down to black boots.

'Its reflexes are near perfect,' said Richards. Gezz stayed fixed to the spot as Anne would have done, but inside every instinct was telling her to run for it. Her eyes widened and she felt extremely disturbed and sickly. The faceless android was walking out of its chamber in a rigid robotic fashion. Wires and cables trailed from its back and connected to the rear of the compartment. Richards picked up a plate from his pile and threw it in the air. 'Defend!' he shouted.

Before Gezz knew what was happening, the android had bent its knees slightly, launched its right arm out, and fired a hail of bullets. Short flames shot from the robot's hand and a rattle of loud gunfire, like that of a machine gun, filled the room. Gezz resisted her instincts again and kept her arms at her side, even though she so desperately wanted to stick her fingers in her ears.

The plate shattered before it even had time to drop, scattering fragments all over the laboratory. Richards tossed out a second and a third, and they too fell to the floor in pieces. Droylsden pulled a face as silence returned to the lab. 'No,' she groaned, like a child on a rainy day when every good idea and suggestion put to it seems rubbish. 'It's not perfect. Get the Professor to fine tune it. It must be faultless.'

Gezz was trying as best she could to stay calm, but her rib cage, which was going up and down quite quickly as she took sharp breaths, was going to give her away. She tried to breathe more slowly as Droylsden strolled confidently over to her. 'Where is Droyd, anyway?'

'Just finishing his lunch,' said Richards.

Angela Droylsden gave another wicked grin and she touched Gezz's face with her fingertips with mock fondness. 'Just wait until he sees that his little baby has come back to rescue him.' She turned, suddenly very serious. 'Perform a few tests on this unit. I want to make sure it's still fully operational.'

Gezz gulped hard, realizing that any attempts at being superhuman would blow her cover. Richards strolled over with another glass beaker in his hand. He held it out in front of the girl.

'Take it,' ordered the woman.

Gezz remained perfectly still.

'Take it!' Droylsden screamed, clearly not used to being ignored. Gezz swallowed her nerves, raised her arm at the elbow in a robotic fashion and opened her hand. Her breathing was becoming hard again and her throat had dried up. She was terrified. What if she lacked the strength to smash the glass? What if she did manage it and she winced when it broke? And what if it cut her skin and her hand bled? They would know she was not really Anne Droyd at all. Then what would they do?

Gezz took the glass from Richards and gripped it firmly between her fingers and thumb.

'Apply force gradually,' said the scientist. 'Keep going until the glass smashes. Once the task is complete, give me your assessment.'

Gezz squeezed the glass hard. Her hand started to go red as she applied more pressure. Anne's hand never did that. Even when she had bent the car exhaust pipe on the lodge, it never went blood red or anything like that. Gezz's deep colour was bound to give the game away. She wished so much that she was on the surface right now playing with Luke and Malcolm like ordinary children, skimming stones across the lake and doing what kids do.

She squeezed and squeezed at the glass, the ends of her fingers slowly going white. The beaker felt like it was about to buckle at any second, and there would be shards of glass all over the place. Her skin would be slashed and she would be bound to cry out in shock and pain. And who knows what Droylsden and her people would do then?

31

'They've Got Gezz'

Gezz could feel Droylsden's eyes burning into her face. Was the woman fascinated by the experiment? Was she keenly anticipating the shattering of the beaker? Or was she wondering why it was taking so long? Was she beginning to suspect?

Suddenly, the huge vault-like doors hissed with pressure and heaved themselves open inwards. Out the corner of her eye, Gezz could just make out a lot of grey-white hair on top of another white coat, and underneath, a pair of brown check trousers. The newcomer was elderly and yet youthful at the same time. 'What the blazes?' Gezz heard him say, his accent unmistakable. She risked turning to face him. Not her whole body, though. Just her head – the way Anne always did it.

'Father,' said Gezz, trying to conceal the relief she felt upon seeing Professor Wolfgang Droyd. 'I have found you.'

Droylsden and Richards both had their eyes fixed on the Professor. It was tempting for Gezz to drop her arm and release her grip on the beaker, but she knew that in order to keep her captors fooled, she would have to remain completely static and wait for an instruction.

Droylsden walked over to the Professor in a very confident, refined manner. 'It seems to have perfected the chameleon quality,' she smiled. 'I congratulate you. The android changed its physical appearance as soon as it realized we had discovered it.'

The Professor looked straight at Gezz, his face full of anguish and questions. She knew she dare not show any emotional response, though inside she was desperate to say 'Thank goodness I've found you'. Or was that 'Thank goodness you've found *me*'?

Like a father overcome with tears during a great family union, Wolfgang walked straight over to his young deliverer. He patted Gezz on the head and smiled. 'So the child has returned to her father.' He spoke loudly, his German accent clipping the word 'child' into 'chilt'. Gezz also realized he was speaking mainly for the benefit of the two scientists, who were now standing side by side.

Wolfgang's voice dropped to a semi-whisper. 'What are you doing here?'

Gezz kept her eyes level with his and tried to talk without moving her lips. It wasn't easy. 'It was Anne's idea. We couldn't let her try to rescue you single-handed.'

The Professor was clearly horrified, though again he was trying to convey an expression of scientific interest. 'It looks undamaged,' he said loudly for the benefit of Droylsden and Richards. 'There are no outward signs of malfunction at all.'

'It seemed hesitant to smash the beaker,' replied the woman coldly, arms folded.

'I shall have to conduct some tests on the limb,' Droyd offered.

'It's not the limb I'm worried about,' said the team leader through gritted teeth. 'The unit was apprehensive. It wouldn't go all the way.'

'That is impossible,' declared the Professor. He dropped to a whisper again and stared Gezz straight in the face. 'Where are the others?' Then he turned to Droylsden. 'Apprehension would indicate an emotional development. I must remind you, team leader, this is an android.'

As the old man finished his speech, Gezz whispered, 'Anne is on the first level and the two boys are in the air duct. They're trying to find you.'

Angela Droylsden unfolded her arms and joined the Professor at his side. She looked with contempt at Gezz. 'There must be something wrong with its command circuit, then,' she sneered. 'It's probably the influence of those interfering kids Bullimore told me about.'

Gezz shivered at the sound of that name and dropped the beaker in a panic. The glass shattered. Droylsden was not impressed. She winced suddenly and hopped about the chamber on one leg. 'Oh!' she shouted. 'A splinter of glass has gone down my shoe!' She stopped shouting and bent down to take her shoe off, scowling all the time at Gezz. 'What is wrong with the blasted thing?'

'I suggest running a full diagnostic,' said the Professor with haste. He turned to Richards. 'Open a cavity.' Richards nodded and touched a control on his console. Another hiss of pressure filled the room and one of the cylindrical compartments at the far end lifted to reveal an upright steel bed. The Professor faced Gezz, who stayed as expressionless as possible. 'Get into the cavity for assessment.'

'Yes, Father,' said Gezz without any emotion present in her voice at all. As she turned to walk over to the compartment, she heard the Professor whisper, 'You should never have come here. Now we are all in great danger.'

★ ★ ★

Luke wanted to cry, but he knew he dare not allow Malcolm to see how frustrated he was feeling. They had taken a turn about a mile back and now the tunnel just went on and on with not a beam of light to be seen anywhere. He realized what had happened. The new tunnel did not run parallel with any particular corridor. Rather, it went deeper into the wall, probably into the floor in the space between the first level and the second. His skin rippled with goose bumps as the cold air slithered around it. He tried to look ahead for a possible outlet, but all he could see was blackness. He started to sob quietly.

'Why have you stopped?' said Malcolm's voice from behind him. 'We need to keep going. If we stop, we'll freeze to death.'

'My legs are aching,' replied Luke, his teeth chattering with the cold. He lifted his right hand and dabbed the tears emerging from his eyes. Oh, how his back and his neck hurt! They had been crawling in this bent position for over an hour. 'I've got pins and needles and my arms are freezing,' he cried. 'The metal is so cold. And there's no light ahead. I can't see a single thing.' He started to cry for real, now; he just could not hold back the tears any longer.

Malcolm remained silent for a minute, gathering his thoughts. 'We have got to keep going,' he said, his voice gentle and reassuring. 'We've got to keep our hearts pumping and the blood going. Exercise does that.'

'I can't go on,' sobbed the boy. 'We're going to die in here, I know we are.'

Malcolm was having none of it. 'We are not going to die,' he stated, slowly and deliberately. 'We were sent to find Professor Droyd and rescue him. We can't let the girls down. They might need us later.'

'I'm so cold,' breathed Luke, his voice worn and fatigued.

'Well, that's great, isn't it?' Malcolm began with a touch of sarcasm. 'The great hero of the pack turns out to be a big mard.'

'Stop it,' cried Luke.

'All the times you've called me a mard and a coward,' Malcolm spat. 'And really you're no better yourself.' He paused, and Luke felt angry. The fat lump was always scared, how dare he say that he's no better. But deep down, Luke knew he was right. Malcolm continued, all self-righteous and conceited. 'And we all know you fancy that android. I mean, it used to be Gezz, but now it's a girl made of tin.'

'Shut up,' said Luke suddenly, wiping snot from his dripping nose.

'I mean, who's ever heard of a boy fancying a machine?' Malcolm continued. 'It's like falling in love with a vacuum cleaner.'

Luke banged his fist hard on the cold metal, and the sound reverberated all around. 'I said shut up!'

'Ooh,' Malcolm jeered. 'Having a tantrum now, are we? Well, if you really want to do something impressive, why not crawl along this damn tunnel and find a way out for us?'

'Right,' said Luke with renewed determination. 'I'll show you.'

With the blond taking the lead, the two boys overcame the cold and the cramp and shunted further up the passage like a two-carriage train with a whole track to itself. They covered about another half of their current distance before something very unexpected happened. The floor literally disappeared from beneath them.

The two boys yelped as they fell through pitch-black space. *This is more than I can take*, Luke thought to himself, and then hit something cold and hard at an angle. More metal. Down and down the pair slid until they landed in a heap at the bottom of the shaft. Naturally Malcolm landed straight on top of Luke. And boy, was he heavy!

'I can't breathe!' shouted Luke in a frenzied panic. He found, to his absolute horror, that he could not move either. He tried to lift himself, but his muscles were powerless. It was as though someone had just turned the gravity up and he was stuck to the floor like a magnet. Malcolm's voice filtered down from above. 'We've dropped to the second level. There should be another tunnel. Reach round with your hands.'

Luke did as he was told, and sure enough, there was another opening and a fresh tunnel stretching off into the blackness. 'Found it!' exclaimed the boy. He began pulling himself along it, and gave a sigh of relief when finally his feet broke free of Malcolm's weight.

With renewed zeal, and with Luke taking the lead again, the two boys crawled up the new tunnel. It did not go on for too long before there was another turn. Defying the cramp in his arms and legs, not to mention his neck, Luke dragged himself round the corner. He looked up to see if the next shaft held anything other than black space. His eyes nearly welled up again, but this time with nothing less than relief, as he noted a faint light ahead. 'I can see light!' he shouted. 'Malc, I can see light.'

Malcolm heaved himself round, his head stopping just short of Luke's bottom. 'I'm afraid I can't see very much from here,' he said, with that haughty casual air which always got on Luke's nerves. 'It might also be a good idea, if we are so close to a corridor, to keep your voice down.'

Luke ignored him. 'Come on,' he urged. 'Let's get to that vent.'

With more shuffling and scraping, the boys clambered up the square tunnel, the pin pricks of light getting stronger as they neared the grille. It was like running a long race, thought Luke. It was like getting very tired at the half-way mark, when your body can take no more and you feel like giving it all up, and then suddenly you see the finishing line just ahead, and somehow, somehow you find your reserve energy coming through – and you complete the race.

Luke felt like an Olympic winner when he finally reached the grille. He sat there welcoming the rays of light into his eyes, revelling in the heat of the corridor as it blew and caressed his skin. It was like playing out and getting caught in a heavy rainstorm. You get soaked to the skin, so that the rain actually goes right through your coat and all your clothes are sticking to you. Your hair is matted and the rain punches your head with freezing pellets. But when you finally get through that door and pull your clothes off, when you stand by the bathroom radiator and dry your hair with a lovely warm towel from the airing cupboard – nothing can beat that feeling. And Luke had that feeling right now.

'Is there anyone out there?' asked Malcolm.

Luke closed his eyes and smiled. 'Nope,' he said, and then opened them again. 'It's like the corridor we arrived in. It's dead. There's no one there.'

'Right,' said Malcolm resolutely. 'Let's get out of here.'

Luke didn't need telling a second time. He crawled up past the grille, and for a second gazed ahead into the blackness before him. Then he rolled, almost hovering in the air, and flipped himself on to his back. Lying on his elbows, he coiled up his legs and held his feet over the grille. Oh, it felt so good. And with one energetic blow, he kicked at the mesh with both feet.

The grille flew off the wall straight away and landed in the corridor with a loud rattle. Half-desperate to escape his prison, and half-terrified that the guards might have heard the noise, he scrambled feet first into the corridor.

The shock hit him immediately, like a great assault on his senses. The light was powerfully strong. He had to squint in order to see, although he could make out the light-green colour of the walls. It always seemed so dreadful in hospitals, but Gezz's dad had told him green was a very gentle colour on the eyes. The warm air enveloped him like a blanket and the smell of disinfectant seemed strong to the nose.

Luke heard a crash and a yelp, and guessed that Malcolm had landed, much as he had done, in a heap on the floor. 'Oh,' groaned the lump. 'I can't stand up.'

'You will,' said Luke, his own legs getting stronger. Putting his hands on the wall, he staggered to his feet and took in his surroundings. He glanced about himself quickly and frowned. 'It looks exactly like the corridor we first arrived in,' he said.

'It can't be,' complained his friend. 'We crawled for miles, and I'm sure we didn't go in a circle.' Malcolm stood up and rubbed his eyes, making sure to wipe the lenses of his spectacles in the process. 'Anyway, we're on a different floor, remember?'

The blond scanned the ceiling with a curious eye. 'The tops of the walls,' he began.

'What about them?'

'There are no security cameras.'

Malcolm nodded, a little dumbfounded. 'Oh yeah.'

Luke began to stroll along the corridor, enjoying the use of his legs. 'I wonder why they don't have cameras down here.' For once, Malcolm didn't seen to have an answer. Then Luke suddenly stopped dead in his tracks.

'What is it?' hissed Malcolm, almost cuddling up behind his friend. Luke shrugged him off and began tiptoeing towards the curiosity. 'It's a door,' he whispered. The two of them edged closer and closer to the door until Luke was able to peep through the window.

'Wow!' he whispered.

'What is it?' Malcolm repeated, and Luke could sense a level of wonder mixed with fear. 'It's a kind of posh bedroom.'

'Let me see,' urged Malcolm and pushed his way to the square panel of glass. He said nothing as he took in the amazing sight. The room was like a luxury hotel suite. It was lined with expensive wardrobes and was dominated by a four-poster bed. A long narrow curtain trailed against the far wall. 'What do you think is behind that?'

'Well, it can't be a window,' said Luke, almost to himself. 'I mean, we're right underground.' Just behind the curtain, Luke could make out what looked like metal. Gold metal, in fact.

The pair were suddenly startled by a clicking, scraping sound, coming from inside the room. Or was it coming from the wall itself? It sounded like something Luke had heard many times before. It sounded metallic, like the clanging made by an elevator when travelling down its shaft. The sound ceased with a low thud and the two boys had no idea what to expect next.

Luke glanced over his shoulder to make sure no one was coming. No one was. The place seemed as quiet as a grave. Then Malcolm gasped. 'Luke! The curtain!'

The lads watched in stunned silence as the material shifted in a slight current of air. More metal scraping came from the top-class bedroom and they now knew for sure what was being concealed by the rug-like curtains. A pair of dainty hands parted the material and a person stepped from the cubicle behind. It was a lift!

Malcolm and Luke marvelled as the little girl with the blonde ponytail scanned the room with her crystal-blue eyes. They finally fell upon the main door. 'Luke and Malcolm,' she said and made for the door. It was not an exclamation as such, nor did it brim with longing affection. But it did sound like an expression of familiarity. Almost.

'Are we glad to see you?' said Malcolm eagerly, his face beaming with a big excited grin.

The feminine voice sounded muffled as it filtered through the glass of the window. The android's eyes met those of Luke and the boy felt his heart skip a beat. 'You want me to guess whether or not you are glad?'

Luke laughed softly, shaking his head in a parental way. 'No,' he said. 'It's an exaggerated question. It means we are very glad to see you. Very glad.'

Anne puckered her lips and emitted her sonic whistle. The steel door beeped as it yielded to the high-frequency vibrations. A more conventional lock then rattled as the robot girl inserted her morphed finger just below the handle. 'This room is very secure,' she announced. 'There are two kinds of lock on the door. I speculate that this is the team leader's personal quarters.'

'Well, it's certainly got a bit more going for it than Professor Droyd's cell,' said Malcolm. Luke just glared at him and said nothing.

Anne pulled at the door. 'You have found my father?'

Luke shook his head. 'Not exactly, no.' He had no sooner finished his sentence when all hell broke loose. The main bedroom light suddenly flashed a violent red and an alarm bell rang ferociously throughout the corridor. Malcolm stepped back and clamped his hands on his ears. 'What's happening?' he shrieked.

Anne emerged from the room, seemingly unconcerned by the sounding claxon. 'I must have tripped a secondary security device when I opened the door,' she simply stated.

Luke took her hand and started trotting down the corridor. 'Let's get out of here,' he urged. 'This place is going to be flooded with security guards any second now.'

Malcolm was still pressing his ears with both hands, his brow furrowing with sweat. 'Where are we gonna go?' he cried. 'We don't even know what part of the bunker we're in.'

Luke continued jogging forward. 'Anne,' he said. 'Where does that elevator in the leader's room go to?'

'I was investigating that very question when I arrived in the room,' said Anne, still holding the boy's hand.

'Yes, but where does it go the other way?' said Luke, exasperated now.

'Since it does not appear on the old documents I downloaded from the Internet,' Anne replied, 'I can only speculate that it is a new addition. Perhaps an auxiliary shaft leading up to another exit point on the surface.'

Malcolm lowered his hands, fascinated by the concept. 'A sort of quick getaway,' he said.

The trio skidded to a halt as the corridor ended at a sudden turn. 'Anne,' commanded Luke. 'Activate your fibre-optic lens and tell us if there are any people round the next corner.'

'Especially people in black uniforms and carrying guns,' added Malcolm. 'They're called guards.'

Anne did as she was instructed and projected her wire-thin flex out from underneath her little fingernail. A fine prick of light shone from the end. Holding her finger out just short of the corridor edge where the two walls met, she extended her fibre-optic until it could turn the corner and 'look'. 'Coast is clear,' announced the girl in a whisper.

Luke tried to steady the tremors in his knees. This was scary stuff. Once Anne's finger had restored itself, the three-some turned into the empty corridor. Then, before anyone could take another step, a voice shouted, 'Halt! Halt or we will open fire!'

The children froze. The voice was coming from behind them. Luke kicked himself for not realizing. The soldiers had come down in the secondary lift. 'Turn around,' demanded the gruff voice. 'Turn around very slowly.'

The children did as they were told. Luke's tummy per-formed a perfect somersault. Though this time it was not the flutter of little butterflies, but that horrible churning sensation that made him want to go to the toilet. He heard Malcolm audibly gulp as he focused on the two rifles levelled at them. 'So,' said the guard on the left. 'You have come to rescue your little android playmate, have you? How sweet.'

Luke sensed that Malcolm was about to ask 'What do you mean? She's here' and kicked him in the ankle. The boy stifled a yelp. Luke whispered through clenched teeth. 'They've got Gezz. They think she's Anne.'

'Put your hands on your heads and follow my comrade here,' snarled the soldier. 'But no funny business. I'll be right behind you.' He broke off and took his position at the rear of the group. 'Yes,' he began again, quite airily. 'I think Miss Droylsden will be very pleased to meet you.'

32

The Twin

Professor Wolfgang Droyd pulled levers and pressed buttons and tried to look as absorbed in his console as he possibly could. Richards was busy seeing to the new android and its machine-gun hand, and Droylsden was standing, arms folded, in the centre of the laboratory. Thankfully, neither she nor her lackey could see that, as Wolfgang twiddled his switches and observed his dials, he was not really doing anything at all. Gezz, while standing inside the sealed cylinder, had not actually been connected up to the cables inside.

'Oh yes,' said Wolfgang with an air of great satisfaction. 'Very good. Very good indeed. There are hardly any repairs needed at all.' He made a show of shutting down the machinery.

'Excellent,' purred the team leader. 'Release it.'

With the flick of a switch, the cylindrical chamber lifted itself aloft, revealing a slightly tense Gezz underneath. Wolfgang could tell that the poor girl's face was beginning to ache, she had maintained the same blank facial expression for so long. 'Come forward,' he commanded, and Gezz complied.

Droylsden clasped her hands together with zeal. 'I want the android to resume its regular appearance,' she said.

Wolfgang stared at Gezz and Gezz stared back in disbelief. Then the Professor looked at the woman. 'What?' he stammered.

'Change it back into a blonde,' repeated Droylsden. 'The way it was when you first presented it to me. Ponytail, the lot.' She rubbed her hands together and began pacing about the giant room with great enthusiasm. 'You see, Droyd, I have realized there is a place for this robot child after all.'

The Professor cleared his throat nervously. 'You have?'

'Yes,' said Droylsden. 'While robot soldiers can fight the wars of the world, little innocent children make the perfect spies.' She turned on her heels and smiled an excited smile. 'Who would ever think a child could be spying on them for an army?' She broke off and clenched her fist triumphantly. 'Or a government even? Children are so uncorrupted and innocent, aren't they?'

The Professor tried to hide his sorrow, but his sunken eyes said it all. He was heartbroken. He had been heartbroken for a long, long time. The woman stalked over to him. 'So change her back to her original appearance.'

'I can't,' said Wolfgang limply.

'Why not?!' demanded the woman.

'Because...' He was about to tell her that the circuit which controlled the morphing was one of the ones that needed fixing, when the huge bulkhead doors suddenly hissed into service.

Droylsden spun on her heels to greet the black-uniformed soldier. This one was a bit different from the others, since he had no hat and was older by about ten years. His black-grey wiry hair and permanent frown were unmistakable. Chief Inspector Bullimore marched in and addressed the team leader.

'This had better be good, Bullimore,' snarled Droylsden.

'It is,' replied the corrupt police inspector. 'My guards have apprehended three children who not only have managed to get into the complex, but had even forced their way into your private quarters.'

The Professor flinched as Droylsden shuddered with rage. 'What!' she festered.

'And that's not all,' continued Bullimore with a nervous weak smile. 'One of them is a little girl with blonde hair and a ponytail. I have reason to believe it is the android, Ma'am, returning to effect the Professor's escape.' He tailed off, surveying the old man and the young brunette by his side. His eyes bulged as he realized who Gezz was. 'You!' he shouted. 'The girl from Century Lodge!'

The Professor instinctively slipped a reassuring arm about the girl's shoulders, sensing her terror. Droylsden spun to face the old man and his young friend. 'What is this?' she snarled. 'You would wilfully deceive me?' The woman was speaking slowly now, as though she could not believe her ears. Her face remained as cold and hard as ever. 'You would take such a risk, knowing what it would mean for you?'

'Nothing you could do would ever hurt me, Annie,' said the Professor softly. 'I passed that stage many years ago.'

The woman launched into a frightening fit of unbridled rage. 'Don't call me Annie!' she screamed violently, her face red as blood with fury. 'I am Angela Droylsden!' She took several deep breaths through her nose and exhaled hard through her mouth, trying to calm herself down. Then her eyes bore holes in Gezz's face. 'Who are you?' She spat out the words one by one.

'She's called Geraldine Atkinson,' said Bullimore. 'It was at her house that I apprehended Professor Droyd. When I went to the school to find the android I knew she had something to do with the cover-up. Some of the teachers were in on it too. But I couldn't find anything to nail them on.'

'So,' said Droylsden, 'children are not as innocent as they seem.' She paused, glaring at young Gezz with ferocious eyes.

'Where are these children?' she sneered menacingly. 'Where is the android?'

'I'm here,' said a voice. Now everyone turned to face the door. The Professor smiled a warm fatherly smile as his eyes greeted the sight of Anne standing at the entrance to the laboratory with Luke and Malcolm at her side and a couple of black-uniformed guards taking up the rear. Gezz instinctively left the Professor and ran to Luke, who gave her an affectionate cuddle. 'Oh, thank goodness you're all right,' she said.

'Well, well, well,' declared Droylsden, rubbing her hands. 'Isn't this a lovely reunion?' She stood a short distance from the ensemble of children, scientists and security men. 'You present me with a bit of a conundrum. Do you know what a conundrum is?'

Anne tilted her head slightly. 'Conundrum,' she said. 'Riddle or hard question. Especially one with a pun in its answer.'

Droylsden clapped her hands and smiled with delight. 'Well done, little robot. My, my, you have been busy, haven't you? I must congratulate you again, Droyd. It would appear our little automaton has swallowed a dictionary.'

'What are you going to do with us?' It was Malcolm speaking. The poor boy could not cope with the suspense any longer.

'I've been wondering that myself,' replied the woman airily. 'I cannot allow you to leave here alive, that much is certain.'

Immediately heart stopping dread enveloped the children. 'What?!' stammered Luke. 'You can't kill us.'

'Why not?' Droylsden shrugged.

'Because our parents will go out of their minds,' said Luke. The Professor watched the three children huddling up for mutual security. He felt so sorry for them. How had it all come to this?

'That is very touching,' said Droylsden, waving her hand about casually in the air. 'But I cannot allow anyone to discover this base or know about the work we are doing here. So I'm afraid, little darlings, you will have to go.' She held her chin and considered for a moment. 'A group drowning would look believable, I think,' she said. The children were horrified, their faces going sickly white as the blood drained from them. 'Yes. Kill them down here, fill their lungs with water from the lake up above and then place their bodies in the centre of the lodge. Children are always having stupid accidents near rivers and lakes.'

The room fell silent. Except for the hum of machinery, not a sound could be heard. Then, rather unexpectedly, Bullimore stepped forward. 'You're not serious?' His expression was one of abject horror. His brow wrinkled with stress. 'You can't kill these little children,' he said. 'That's murder.'

Droylsden said nothing. She just looked him right in the eye and grinned. Then she purred with delight, 'That is very astute of you, Chief Inspector. That's why I hired you, because of your attention to detail. You are absolutely right, killing is murder. But I am sure you will be able to make it look good and, what's the word? Authentic, yes, it will look authentic. That is the other reason I chose you. You are so utterly corrupt.'

The chief inspector's blood boiled. 'No,' he said with a quiet confidence. He was nervous, yes. They all were. Bullimore stood to attention and stared the team leader out. For the first time Wolfgang saw a quality in him he had never seen before: dignity.

'No, what?' Droylsden jeered. 'No, you are not astute? Or no, you are not corrupt?'

'When I joined this outfit,' seethed the inspector. 'I joined because I believed in it. I believed in what you were trying to do. To build the perfect soldier, the ultimate deterrent. Who would dare fight a machine? Who would take on a really efficient killer?' His voice fell into an emotional hush and his eyes filled with tears. 'Wars would end, crime would vanish, because of the fear of android soldiers and policemen.'

The Professor turned to address the broken man. 'You really believe she wants world peace?'

Bullimore shrugged. 'I did. My God, man, we *all* did! You did, at first.' He shook his head, holding back the tears. 'But not now. Now I see it clearly. She doesn't want peace.'

Droylsden had grown tired of the moral speeches. 'Peace?' she screamed, and jeered a violent, coarse and horrid laugh. 'There will never be peace on this globe! No. The only way to maintain order is to take total control. Crush all resistance.' She struck the air with a tight fist. 'Crush it all. Eliminate the deadwood. Exterminate the wasters.'

Gezz summoned the courage to speak up. Her voice was soft and pitiable. 'You sound like a Nazi.'

'Thank you,' said Droylsden with a smile. 'It is a shame you must die. I admire your resourcefulness. You have insight, also spirit.'

Bullimore could not contain his rage any longer. 'They are just children, for God's sake!'

Anne turned to face the inspector. 'Why are we children for God's sake?' she asked innocently. 'Does God require the company of children?'

Droylsden marched over to the two guards, who had been quietly observing the proceedings. 'I tire of this prattle,' she said. Then she clicked her fingers. 'You men, take these three children and prepare them for execution.'

Gezz, Malcolm and Luke clung to one another for dear life and the guards hesitated, wrestling with their consciences. Angered by their lack of obedience, the woman snatched one of the rifles and pointed it at the group. 'Very well, I'll finish them off myself.'

'When did you go insane, Annie?' said the Professor slowly, his voice trembling with a cocktail of emotion.

'I've told you,' spat the woman, keeping her gun level on the children. 'Don't call me Annie. My name is Angela.'

'No, it's not,' said the Professor. 'It's Annie. You are Anne Droyd, my daughter.'

'No!' Droylsden blazed. 'I am not Anne Droyd! Don't call me by that ridiculous name! Do you know how much I had to suffer with that name at school? Do you know what anguish your thoughtlessness brought me? Do you realize how long it took to be rid of that German accent?'

'I named you after your mother, child,' said the Professor. 'You must remember that.'

'My mother is dead.'

'Yes,' said the Professor. He addressed the whole group now. 'My wife refused to leave Germany with me in 1938. I had watched the rise of Hitler and his Nazi party with interest, but when he became Germany's leader in 1933, I began to realize where he was heading. My wife died at the hands of that evil regime. A regime my daughter here is determined to resurrect, it seems.'

'You should have stayed with her,' Droylsden barked, 'instead of bringing me to Britain. I suffered because of my name and I suffered because of my accent. Well, I'll show them. I'll show them all.'

Anne turned her head and blinked, responding to the last statement. 'How will you show them?'

Droylsden threw her head back and laughed. 'I might as well tell you,' she sneered, still holding her rifle level at the children. 'Soon you will all have been disposed of anyway. I have made contact with several government agencies around the world, and a handful of terrorist guerrilla groups for good luck. Each of these organizations has bid a price for the perfect soldier. When the prototype is fully tested, they will each receive a robot, thinking that they are the sole owners. Once the robots are in place I will activate a pre-programmed order and the androids will seize control on my behalf.'

'And then what?' asked the Professor, disgusted. 'You will take over the world? You will hunt down all those whom you deem unworthy of life and exterminate them?'

'Yes,' nodded the Professor's daughter with a wry smile. 'I could not have put it more succinctly myself.'

'Look at the android, my daughter,' said the Professor. 'Look at it. This is who you used to be, so innocent, so guileless. So sweet.'

Droylsden scrunched her nose up and scowled at the automaton. 'That person died decades ago. There is nothing left of her now.' The Professor felt deeply hurt by the remark, it was so cold and so ruthless. So detached.

'You are mistaken,' piped Anne suddenly. 'Your plan will not succeed.'

'Oh?' Droylsden turned and raised her eyebrows. 'And why, little robot, will my plan not succeed?'

'Because I went to the computer room and sent computer viruses to each of your clients,' the automaton answered simply. Bullimore stifled a laugh with his hand. 'Any information on robotics they might have gleaned from you has been eliminated,' Anne continued. 'A virus is also slowly working through the networks of this bunker. Very soon, all computer-controlled systems will be totally inoperable.'

Droylsden's eyes bulged as the automaton finished her report. 'Whhaaatt!' she hissed. Without warning, Anne launched herself at the team leader. Droylsden fell back, stunned by the sudden action. Anne retrieved the rifle at lightning speed and snapped it in half across her knee.

Lights flickered and the hum of the machinery wavered a little. Gezz gazed across the huge room as the failing lights cast odd shadows about the place. 'What's happening?' For the first time, her friend Luke broke into a smile. 'It's the computer virus Anne introduced into the system. It's shutting everything down.'

Chaos reigned in the corridor beyond the giant vault-like doors as black-uniformed men and white-coated scientists dashed about in a panic. The two guards standing over the children ran off, abandoning the laboratory in fear for their lives.

Droylsden got to her feet in the confusion and threw herself at the console. 'No!' she screeched. Her old-young hand pulled one of the larger levers, and the Professor stared in horror as the new featureless android, who had been deactivated in its cylinder alcove, suddenly came to life. 'Kill them!' screamed the woman at the android, banging her fists on the console, her eyes bloodshot and furious. 'Kill them all!'

The robot walked slowly forwards, the wires and cables attached to its back lifting off the floor and straightening out as the automaton went its full distance. The Professor glared as the faceless little man lifted its right arm. 'Get down!' he yelled, and everyone dropped to the floor as the android opened fire. The machine gun hammered out round after round, the noise deafening its victims. Fire blazed from its fingertips as it sprayed the whole area with bullets.

Anne's reflexes were perfect and she struck with lightning swiftness, leaping into the air. The android ceased firing for a couple of seconds, trying to get the girl in its sights. At incredible speed Anne performed three backward somersaults across the chamber, landing just in front of the robot. As it levelled its gun arm and opened fire again, Anne jumped above the spray of bullets. She landed just behind the automaton.

The robot jerked back, its gun arm flailing and ripping thousands of holes into the ceiling as Anne grabbed the cables connected to its steel spine and yanked them from the wall cubicle.

Then she stepped back as the gunfire stopped, and allowed the robot to collapse in a limp lifeless heap on the floor. She knelt beside the crumpled body and touched its face with her hand.

'Incredible,' hissed the Professor as he got to his feet, bits of plaster flaking down from the ceiling and falling in his hair. 'She has an affinity with the other android.'

'She will have,' said Gezz, joining him at his side. 'It is the only other being in existence that is like her. And she had to kill it.'

Droylsden stood back from the console and seethed with hatred. After taking a moment to regain her composure she turned on her father, arms outstretched, and gripped him firmly round the throat. His eyes fluttered in a wild panic and his face started to redden as he fought and gasped for air, the woman bringing him to his knees. He clasped his hands about those of his daughter and tried to prise them off. But it was no use, she was too strong. 'You can't stop me, Professor,' sneered the woman, speckles of plaster dropping on to her short blonde tufts. 'These cybernetic-enhanced limbs are a couple of grades higher than yours.'

Gezz ran across to Anne, who was still kneeling over her fallen brother android. 'Anne,' she tugged at the automaton's sleeve. 'You must protect your father.'

Immediately Anne stood erect, her eyes glassy and pained. Agony seemed etched in her features. Could it be that she was grieving the death of her twin? She stood quietly and opened her mouth. Instead of emitting her deafening whistle, Anne opened her jaw wide and let out the most dreadful high-pitched sonic scream she could muster.

The sound was ear splitting. The children pressed the palms of their hands against their ears, and clenched their teeth, the pain was unbearable. Droylsden reeled back, her eyes almost popping out of her head. The Professor was more preoccupied with gasping for breath as his daughter finally released him.

The noise continued relentlessly and massive cracks appeared across the ceiling. Suddenly part of the roofing caved in, dropping soil and clay on to the floor. Water began to trickle down, like a bath shower with the sprinkle nozzle blown off. More mud dropped on to the ground and then the water increased, gushing more freely from several points up above. Sparks flew and one of the huge cylinder chambers exploded, the door flying outwards onto the opposite wall.

'You fool.' Droylsden's voice could just be heard above the terrible racket. 'This whole area is riddled with underground coal mines. The ground is unstable. You'll bring the lodge down on top of us.' She turned, bent double with agony, her hands firmly over her ears, and ran into the corridor to join the others charging about in frenzied hysteria.

As soon as Droylsden had cleared the room, Anne stopped the noise and closed her mouth, her face returning to its usual serious expression. A deep rumble echoed through the complex. The Professor darted about the laboratory, trying to avoid the avalanche of water cascading around them at full force. 'We need to get out of here quickly,' he shouted. 'The whole place is about to cave in!'

'We'll never get out!' shouted Malcolm in a panic. 'Everyone will be scrambling for the lift. We don't stand a chance!'

'You are forgetting about Droylsden's elevator, Malc,' said Luke, standing at the bulkhead door. 'No one seems to be heading for that!'

Gezz frowned. 'There's another lift?'

'Yes,' said Luke, water slapping about his feet. 'We found it before. It's in Droylsden's personal quarters. Only she and a handful of guards seem to know about it.'

'Well, what are we waiting for?' called the Professor, waving his arms about in a frenzy. 'Let's get to it!'

33

'We'll Never Get Out!'

The old man and his young disciples pushed forward up the corridor in entirely the opposite direction to everyone else, who were pushing their way down. All his life the Professor had been travelling in the opposite direction to other people. The majority were so boring and predictable, so wrapped up with their own lives. They never wondered about things, never tried to ask. They dreamed of a better life, oh yes, but did little to try and realise one. The Professor had always gone against the grain and had rarely followed the crowd. Even now he was moving upstream.

At times like this though, he wondered if the ordinary closed-minded people had the best approach. As he dragged himself through the maddened tangle of scientists and security people, he thought of Luke's parents, who never did anything adventurous and cared for no one but themselves. Was that the best way to be? Then there was Gezz's mother and father, so dedicated to serving those less fortunate. So noble and selfless – so unappreciated. And Malcolm's parents, who no one ever saw because they had blotted the world out with alcohol.

Then he remembered his wife, who stayed behind in Germany, who followed the crowd and never questioned anything, the girl of his youth who chose to hang on to what made her feel secure rather than take a chance. Now she was dead. Their daughter had feared the opinions of others, and because of that fear, she had turned bitter and twisted against the world – against her father. Now she too was as good as dead.

Wolfgang was glad that he dared to be different. Yes, even now.

'Through here,' beckoned Luke, gesturing to a set of double doors. The corridor beyond was surprisingly quiet. No one ran or shouted. It was empty. 'Droylsden's room is just down here.'

They made their way at a half-jog until they arrived at the classy bedroom with its wall-to-wall wardrobes and four-poster bed. The Professor tried the door. It clicked open with ease. 'Well,' grinned the old man. 'It seems our host left in a big hurry.' A deep rumble interrupted the banter. It sounded heavy and powerful. The children looked at the ceiling, where the sound seemed to be coming from.

'What's that?' whispered Malcolm, his face saying it all.

Luke turned to the Professor for confirmation. 'The lodge?'

'Yes,' nodded the Professor. 'It will have broken right through to the laboratory by now.'

Gezz looked horrified. 'What about all the people in that part of the complex?'

The old man shrugged, making sure he did not catch her eyes. 'Who knows?' he said. 'Maybe some of them will manage to get to the surface in time.'

Ignoring the implication that some of the people might drown, Luke took the lead and went into the bedroom. He parted the curtains on the far wall and summoned the lift. 'Come on, come on,' he said to himself, impatiently tapping the gold-coloured doors.

Malcolm was the last to enter the room. A thundering noise rushed down the corridor. The boy plucked up the courage to peek out through the door. Immediately he raced back, panicking and slamming the door firmly behind him. 'It's coming!' he whimpered, almost running up and down on the spot, he fretted so much. 'It's like a tidal wave!'

Luke sighed noisily. 'Don't exaggerate,' he groaned.

Before Luke had finished his sentence, the bedroom door was blown open with gusto. The filthy pond water heaved its way into the room, covering the base of the luxury bed, turning its white satin blankets into sheets of muddy grey. A varnished coffee table plopped up and floated on the steadily rising water. Everyone in the room seemed to realize at the same moment that if they did not get out quickly they would not be getting out at all. Gezz huddled up to the Professor for comfort while Luke hammered frantically on the lift door in mortal fear. 'Come on!' he screamed.

The Professor held his breath in anticipation. He was too old for this sort of thing. Filthy water lapped around his knees while the children, Anne included, had to endure the freezing deluge as it reached their upper thighs. The lift rumbled into place and the doors slid open, polluted stinking pond water swooping into its beautiful golden interior. 'Everybody in!' Wolfgang ordered, and the children wasted no time in complying.

As the elevator doors rattled shut and the Professor pressed the button marked 'surface', the girl and two boys let out a long sigh of relief. They felt the elevator rock and clang as it hauled them out of the danger and returned them to relative normality. A final shudder brought the lift to a stop. Each of its passengers waited with bated breath for the doors to slide back and release them.

'Trees,' said Anne as the elevator doors parted. The others followed her gaze, and sure enough, they had emerged among a lot of bushes. They stepped out and pushed their way through brambles and wild plants until they found themselves on one of the banks of the lodge.

'I don't believe it,' said Gezz to herself. The Professor stared across the body of water. Immediately opposite in the distance was the semicircle of houses, the children's actual homes. To the far right, towering above all the other buildings, loomed the black square silhouette of the mill, with its long cigar-like chimney reaching up into the sky. The old man nodded and repeated the girl's exclamation. 'Well I never,' he whispered. 'We have come out right on the other side of the lodge.'

A fisherman stood on the far bank, scratching his head and staring at the waters, which had receded quite considerably. The Professor chuckled to himself and then fell sombre as he remembered why the water had gone down. Malcolm served as a distraction. 'Look!' called the boy.

The Professor and the children looked. A group of black and white figures could be seen staggering and retching on the far corner of the mill. In the seconds it took for them to emerge from the cellar, sirens and flashing lights were on the scene and the assortment of security guards and scientists were bundled into the back of some large black police vans.

'How did they know about them to arrest them?' frowned Gezz.

Anne stepped forward and stood beside the girl. The Professor smiled. It was as though the two young women were soulmates. It was all very different from the android he was used to. 'When I was in the computer room,' Anne explained, 'I took the liberty of notifying the police. I told them I had seen some very suspicious activity in the Century Mill area, and they promised they would investigate it.'

Luke joined the two girls on what had once been the water's edge, but now was just a patch of wet mud. 'Good thinking, Anne,' he said. Malcolm came up behind the trio. 'Yes,' beamed the boy, resting his arms across their collective shoulders. 'Well done.'

The Professor watched his creation turn her head and look her fair-haired friend up and down. 'Luke,' she said in her flat monotone voice. 'Yes?' replied the lad, so obviously infatuated. The android pointed down innocently to Luke's blackened, stinking jeans. 'I think your mum is going to kill you.'

Wolfgang Droyd continued to beam affectionately like a proud grandfather as each of the three children fixed their eyes on their soiled leg wear. 'And,' said the automaton, 'by "kill" I mean punish, rather than actually terminating your life.'

In an instant the young friends burst into good, honest, hearty laughter. The Professor started to chuckle as well, but realized with some sadness what he had to do.

34

Farewells and Promises

Another beautiful morning greeted Gezz as she parted the curtains to her bedroom. The sun shone over Century Lodge and the girl could not help staring for a couple of minutes at the old lake, which was now only a third of its original diameter. The rest of the water would be underground, of course, channelling corridors, rooms and the central laboratory. She hoped that everyone had managed to get out in time.

'Do you think the Professor will settle down now that his natural daughter has gone?' The voice came from behind Gezz. It was Luke, coming into her room in his smart blue pyjamas. Her mum had agreed to let him stay over again and had washed his jeans so that Mrs Davidson would not go mad. She was good like that.

Gezz tightened the bow on the front of her dressing gown and turned to face her friend. 'I don't know,' she said. 'I mean, we don't even know whether or not Droylsden got away.'

Luke grinned, nodding his head and wrinkling up his nose. 'Of course she did. She left before us. She would have been up in that lift and away before the coppers knew what was happening. She'll have surfaced right on the other side of the lodge, remember.'

Gezz turned to the window and stared out across the body of water. She could just make out the tall oblong shape of the lift entrance masquerading as an old brick shelter and con-

268

cealing itself behind branches and undergrowth. What a crazy day it had been. And who would believe them? Who would think that three kids, an eccentric professor and a robot schoolgirl had just saved the world from a new dictatorship and all-out war? No one at all, that's who.

* ★ ★

Gezz's mum busied herself in the kitchen while her dad set the table for breakfast. Gezz and Luke, now fully dressed, wandered in and took their places. The atmosphere seemed a little tense and awkward. Maybe her mum had not forgiven her dad for going round and joining Mr Davidson to watch his video of *Blade Runner* the night before. After he had come home, it was all he could talk about. He kept saying that it was 'the director's cut', which meant the film was the full unedited version as the director had originally intended it.

But her mum hated anything to do with science fiction. She always said she found Terry hard to like because he was an atheist and didn't believe in God. Gezz knew that, in this case, it was not the real reason. Her mum just hated science fiction. She called it 'pie-in-the-sky rubbish' all the time.

'So what have you got planned for today?' asked her dad cheerily. 'Not more scraping around in the mud, I hope.'

Gezz grinned at her father. 'No,' she said. 'We're going off to the den to meet Anne.'

'Again?' he said quizzically. 'Anyone would think she *lived* in that old Anderson shelter the way you talk about it.'

Luke gave a wry smile. 'She does.'

'Oh yes,' Gezz's dad laughed. 'Very funny.' He went into the living room to get Ross, who was busy making some sort of weird shape out of building blocks. Seconds later, he was back with the toddler under his arm. He seated the tot into the high chair positioned in its usual spot at the edge of the table.

Gezz's mum placed four bowls of cereal in front of their respective recipients. Gezz was having *Frosties* again, her favourite. Milk swished from the jug in her mum's hand and the girl grinned to herself with deep satisfaction. She was glad she lived here and not at Malcolm's or Luke's. It was true she was not allowed to go where she pleased and stay up all night, and if they knew where she had been yesterday, they would have gone spare. She might not have expensive toys or the best clothes, and she didn't even have a telly. But she did have parents who really cared, and no amount of money could compare with that.

After breakfast, Gezz and Luke went to call for Malcolm, who emerged from his gloomy unkempt house with a slice of toast. 'Hi,' he said, with his mouth full. 'What's with the bags?'

Gezz held up the polythene bag, which was almost tearing under the strain of an old blue anorak which she had stuffed inside. 'It's my dad's,' she said. 'He thinks it's for a Guy Fawkes I told him we were making. The Professor will need something to wear other than that stupid white coat, so I brought this.'

'And the pump bag?'

Gezz swung the old woolly pump bag from off her shoulder. It was all blocky and bulky. She would not be using it for secondary school, so what the heck? 'Food,' she said simply.

Appearing a tad embarrassed that he had not brought anything for the Professor, Malcolm changed the subject. 'How did you sleep last night?'

'Like a baby,' said Luke as the trio set off up the road. 'I was out as soon as my head hit the pillow. What about you?'

'I had loads of weird dreams,' Malc said, falling into a preoccupied state of mind. 'I had one where horrible robots were marching up from the mill and from that lift we came out of. They were, like, coming from both ends of the lodge and circling the houses. They all had blank faces and machine guns built into their hands. One of them shot that bloke who's always fishing, for no reason, and he fell in the pond.'

The children turned on to the main road. Luke was fascinated by Malcolm's nightmarish visions. 'What else happened?' he enthused. 'You said you had loads of dreams.'

'Well, I also dreamt that I was an android, but I didn't know I was an android,' continued Malcolm, absorbed in his tale. 'That is until I gashed my hand walking through those prickles over there.' He pointed to the place across the lodge where they had escaped the complex. 'When I looked at it, there were all, like, wires and circuits sticking out of my skin. Then I was in my bedroom and I pulled at my skin from the top of my head down to my chin, and it stretched and ripped like rubber, and there were all wires underneath. And I had massive, sort of, ping-pong ball eyes and a radio speaker where my voice came out.'

Luke punched the air with excitement and his blue eyes dazzled with fascination. 'Wow, freaky!' he grinned, his teeth all clean and white. They reached the part of the road that had once been a bridge and turned on to the disused railway embankment. The gravel path stretched down until it had banks of sloping grass on either side. After a short walk the embankment levelled out to what must have been at one time a level crossing, and forked off into two separate paths. The children took the second one meandering to their right.

A rather low and threatening heavy railway bridge stretched over the walkway further up. Meeting it on the left were a row of terraced houses, their back gardens cordoned off by a range of different fences.

Malcolm was still talking about his dreams. 'Then I had one where I was trapped in one of those air-duct tunnels, and no matter what I did or how far I crawled, I couldn't find a way out. It was horrible. Then I had one where we were in a corridor and it was, like, filling up with water. And we had to keep our heads up to the ceiling to breathe and there were, like, all these dead bodies floating about with their faces down in the water.'

'Yes, all right,' said Gezz, her tummy heaving as the two lads revelled in their morbid fantasies. They arrived at the little trench housing the den and glanced about, careful not to be seen. *Thank goodness it's not a school day,* thought Gezz, *otherwise we would have had to have someone on lookout.*

Each child jumped into the ditch and crouched down by the door of the half-buried air-raid shelter. Immediately the door flung open and Anne came out. It was as though she could not wait to meet them. The Professor followed and sealed the shelter behind him. He crouched on his haunches, his scientist's white coat abandoned for one of Anne's pullovers. It looked ridiculous on him, barely covering his tummy and his arms stretching out beyond the sleeves.

'So, my friends,' said Wolfgang Droyd, tapping his bottom lip with his forefinger and grinning mischievously. 'How did you go on explaining yourselves away last night?'

Luke was the first to speak. 'Oh, it was easy,' he said. 'I just said we'd been mucking about on the banking.'

'Only after you had got cleaned up at my house,' added Gezz, somewhat aggravated by her friend's careful editing of the truth. 'And you borrowed a pair of my jeans so your mum wouldn't go off her head.'

'Well,' scoffed Luke in retaliation. 'You told your mum that you fell in the lodge! If that's not telling lies I don't know what is.'

Gezz went very quiet and fumed to herself. It was true she had told her parents that both she and Luke had fallen into the lodge, but since the water that had flooded out the old war base was from the lodge, it didn't really seem like lying.

Malcolm said nothing and just looked at the ground. Gezz supposed his parents had not even been at home when he got back.

'My dad did say he'd read about the police coming to take the guards and scientist people away,' Luke offered, trying to better his version of events. 'It was all over the front page of the *Bolton Evening News*. I had to bin it when he wasn't looking.'

'Very good,' said the Professor.

'Oh,' began Gezz, as an afterthought, slipping the old woolly pump bag off her shoulder. She handed it to the old man. 'We clubbed together and brought you some food and stuff, just in case you need to run away again.' She dragged the coat from its plastic wrapping and handed it to him. 'And this coat will keep you warm when winter comes.'

The man's eyes turned glassy as he became overwhelmed by their gesture of compassion. He took the bag and opened it. 'Sandwiches and crisps and a bottle of *Coca Cola*,' he said with a smile. 'Excellent.'

Wolfgang pulled at the cord and the bag's floppy opening tightened itself into a little hole.

Malcolm reached out and touched the old man's arm. 'You won't be running away, though, will you?'

'Malcolm,' said Wolfgang gently. 'I have to get away from here. What if they investigate the Foundation and discover my involvement with them?'

Malcolm removed his spectacles and dabbed his eyes. 'But I don't want you to go.'

'You will cope,' said the Professor softly. He sat with his back against the den and faced his adopted grandchildren. 'You all will, because you are good people. You are kind and thoughtful and brave, and I don't know what I would have done should I never have met you that day in the wilderness.'

Gezz fought back the tears, and she had a job trying to stop her bottom lip from quivering. 'Where will you go?'

'I am not sure,' said the Professor. 'First of all, I shall retrieve the van that I hid on our first meeting. Then I may go to a hostel for the homeless, get myself some work and save up enough money to go back to Germany. I might be in my eighties, but I am a scientist, and a bionic one at that. When people see the things I can do they will employ me.'

'Germany?' said the three children in unison.

Droyd shrugged and smiled. 'I need to get out of Britain,' he said. 'My daughter will have fled there. I must find her and try to get her some help.'

Luke finally gave in to his emotions and burst into tears. In turn, Gezz and Malcolm began to sob as well. The Professor looked upset and glanced about, making sure people were not in earshot. 'Come now. Let's not get upset.'

Luke turned to face his robot love, her blonde ponytail swishing gently in the autumn morning breeze, and hugged her. 'Goodbye, Anne,' he snivelled. 'I will miss you.'

The others each in turn touched the automaton's hands and patted her shoulders. 'Goodbye, Anne,' they said. Gezz watched the two cheeks touch one another as Luke held the android in his arms. He cried and wiped his eyes, while Anne just looked straight ahead across his shoulder into the bank of grass opposite, her eyes glistening their zombie crystal blue. Even now she seemed unmoved, not aware of the pain her friends endured.

'You are mistaken,' said the Professor. 'Anne will not be coming with me.'

Luke pulled back and released his metal-boned friend. He dabbed his eyes. 'She won't?'

'No.'

Malcolm leaned forward, gesturing with his hand. 'But what will happen to her? You're not going to deactivate her, are you? Because if you are, I think it's very cruel.'

The Professor chuckled again, clearly touched by the loyalty the children were displaying for their companion. 'No, I am not going to deactivate her, for it would, as you say, be very cruel to do that.' He paused and smiled at the three of them. 'Especially as she has learned so much in the few weeks she has spent with you.'

The children listened with rapt attention as the Professor continued his proud delivery. 'When we first met and talked things over in this den, you were just three very frightened children, and Anne was just a sophisticated machine. She spoke only when I addressed her, and when she did it was just to clarify an instruction. But now.' His voice trembled with pride. 'Now she talks all the time. She offers observations and, on some issues, appears to have formed opinions. It is remarkable!'

Malcolm nodded in agreement. 'So you can't shut her down, can you?'

'No,' said the Professor. 'That would be as good as murder. Anne is no longer just a computer accepting instructions, she is a thinking, reasoning machine.' He gave a smile of fatherly love at his blank-faced creation. 'In fact, she has become a *person*.'

Gezz was a little worried by the way the conversation was going. 'So, if you're not taking her with you, and you are not shutting her down, what are you going to do with her? I mean, I hope you're not going to turn her over to a bunch of scientists or something.'

The Professor chuckled again, all the while shaking his head. 'Oh dear, oh dear, child,' he laughed. Then he went very serious. 'No. I cannot be seen travelling with a young girl, this is true. It would attract too much attention. I think she would be better off staying with her friends and learning to live like real children.'

Luke shot him a hard stare, unable to believe his ears. Gezz, too, dared not ask what he meant, just in case she had misunderstood. It was Malcolm who finally said, 'Do you mean you're leaving her with us?'

'Yes,' said the Professor simply.

'But why?'

'Because you have shown yourselves more than capable of looking after her.'

The children were stunned. It was true they'd had the most exciting time since the little automaton arrived in their lives, and they had grown to love her as their sister and best friend.

Not to mention their adventure under the lodge. Who would ever have thought that a secret abandoned military bunker had been beneath their feet all the while?

The Professor flexed his arms, getting ready to stand up. 'So,' he breathed. 'Will you accept the task? Will you continue as you have been doing? Do you promise to take good care of my little Anne until I return?'

Gezz, Malcolm and Luke each placed their right hand on the Professor's open palm, making a pact they knew deep down in their hearts they would have no problem keeping. 'Yes!' they said together, and then clambered to their feet.

The Professor brushed himself down, tossed his food pouch across his shoulder and took his rolled-up anorak under his arm. Then he checked for onlookers, and when the coast was clear, jumped on to ground level. The children followed with Malcolm taking up the rear as usual, and Anne leapt from the ditch on to the grass in one jump, as was her custom.

The old man stood smiling, his wild grey-white hair blowing gently in the breeze. He extended his free hand. 'Until we meet again,' he said. Luke and Malcolm took it in turns to shake it. Gezz, overwhelmed, gave him a big hug. 'We'll miss you,' she cried.

The Professor released her and smiled with great affection. 'And I will miss you too. All of you.' He approached his creation and patted her gently on her blonde head. He stared deep into the robot's blue eyes. 'Anne,' he said softly. 'I am leaving you again, and I don't know when I will be coming back.' He gestured to the children. 'You must stay in the company of your friends and continue to assimilate yourself into their culture. Remember, they are your guardians and your friends.' He broke off and considered one final instruction. 'Under no circumstances must you try to find me. I am leaving of my own free will. I shall not need rescuing this time. Do you understand the instruction?'

'Yes, Father,' replied Anne. 'I understand. I shall stay in the company of my friends and have the den as my home.'

The Professor stroked her face one last time with the back of his fingers, smiled at the children briefly, then turned and began walking down the track towards the low railway bridge in the distance. Gezz could take no more and broke down again. Luke instinctively took her in his arms and she cried on to his shoulder. 'Come on,' he said, his voice gentle and soothing. 'Let's go home.'

35

Four Go Home

The children were very subdued indeed as they walked up the road. Luke had his arm round Gezz's shoulders, while Anne walked at the back of the couple with Malcolm at her side. It was Malc who broke the tension. 'Hey,' he said quietly. 'Just think, we're going to have Anne as a pal for as long as we like.'

Gezz looked over and grinned, her tears drying up as she dabbed her eyes. 'Yes,' she said, blowing her nose on a paper hanky she had plucked from her jeans. 'She'll be coming to school with us and everything.'

'Not forgetting Bonfire Night,' Luke joined in. 'And Christmas.'

Gezz nodded, feeling much better all of a sudden. 'Yes. It's going to be great.'

Anne turned her head slightly as the group walked along. 'What is Bonfire Night?' she asked in the flat tone to which they had become accustomed.

'Well,' Gezz began. 'A few hundred years ago this bloke called Guy Fawkes decided he wanted to get rid of King James the First and his Parliament.'

'It was an extremist Catholic plot,' Luke chipped in. Then he smiled as he recalled something. 'Remember, remember,' he began, and the other two joined him with joyful enthusiasm, 'the fifth of November. Gunpowder, treason and plot.'

'So he got all this gunpowder in the basement of the Houses of Parliament,' Gezz resumed her explanation, 'in order to blow the King and his ministers to kingdom come.'

'Where is kingdom come?' asked Anne innocently.

Malcolm turned. 'It's just an expression. It means they were going to kill them, that's all.'

'Actually,' Gezz interjected. 'It comes from the Lord's Prayer: "Thy kingdom come".'

'Yeah, yeah,' said Luke cynically. 'Don't start preaching to us.'

Gezz was hurt by the remark, though she could see that Luke was regretting that he had made it. *That is his dad's attitude coming out in him*, she thought. 'Anyway,' she continued. 'Guy Fawkes was found out before he had the chance to do his dirty work. They condemned him to death, hanged him, and then cut his body up into four pieces.'

Luke nodded and confirmed, 'Hung, drawn and quartered.'

'Yuk,' said Malcolm, grimacing at the thought.

'So how does this link to Bonfire Night?' asked Anne.

'Well,' Luke chipped in again. 'We make a pretend Guy Fawkes out of paper and rubbish and old clothes, and then we build a massive fire and put him on the top.' He was getting rather excited now. 'Then on November the fifth, at night, we light the fire and burn Guy Fawkes.' His eyes bulged with zeal. 'And we have fireworks too.'

'Yeah,' grinned Malcolm, caught up in the mood. 'And potato hash and treacle toffee.' He rubbed his tummy, imagining the thrills of that cold winter night.

Anne came to an abrupt halt on the pavement. 'So you do this to celebrate the anniversary of Guy Fawkes being put to death?'

'Well,' offered Malcolm a little apprehensive, 'yes.'

The automaton nearly managed to frown, doubtless finding it hard to process the information she had been given. 'The original event occurred several hundred years ago,' she stated. 'And you still bear the grudge? This is not conducive to good mental health. Our dealings with Angela Droylsden have taught me that humans are better off not harbouring bad feelings for events which have occurred in the past.'

'No,' Luke shook his head disdainfully. 'We are not celebrating Guy Fawkes dying. We are celebrating the king being saved.' Gezz remained silent, almost embarrassed, in fact. It sounded like her friend was trying to convince himself rather than the android.

Malcolm attempted to change the subject. 'Well, I'm glad I didn't have to go through all that stuff myself. Imagine all that sneaking around in the cellar.' The children turned on to Century Lodge and stopped again, the partly drained lake and the crescent of houses stretching up to the old mill. In a way their adventure had been more terrifying than anything Guy Fawkes had got mixed up with. But they had got away with it.

To break the sombre mood, Malcolm began to whistle a tune and walk ahead at a jovial pace, his long tangled fringe bouncing over his glasses. The others followed, Luke taking the lead and Gezz pausing to adjust her hairband. Suddenly the three children fell to their knees, writhing on the pavement in agony as an ear-splitting high-pitched sound crippled their brains. It was Anne. She had decided to join in with the whistling.

The windscreens of parked cars and the windows of at least half the houses in the road cracked and smashed, fragments of glass falling on the seats of vehicles and great shards harpooning themselves into neatly cut lawns. Screwing her eyes tight, Gezz waved with one hand for the android to stop, hoping Anne would understand the gesture. Thankfully, she did. The whistle ceased, leaving the noise of whining burglar alarms and dogs barking in the distance.

Front doors were flung open and angry adults stormed out of their houses looking for someone to blame. Thankfully the children were not near enough to the first house to be considered the culprits. They got up from the pavement and sampled the destruction their friend had so innocently caused.

Luke was the first to go. He held his nose and went blood red, his shoulders shaking uncontrollably. 'I know I shouldn't laugh,' he said, stifling a giggle. Then Malcolm started, and Gezz had to concede that despite her principles, it was actually quite hilarious. The three children held their bellies in near-despair and laughed until they could laugh no more.

Then Malcolm pointed, gasping for breath. 'Look,' he said. 'Look at Anne. She's smiling.'

Gezz stared at the android girl. Except now she did not seem like an android. Luke could not take his eyes off her, for her usual deadpan emotionless face had indeed broken into a smile. The girl was suddenly very pretty. Her eyes twinkled and for the first time she seemed truly alive.

With a good feeling that swelled each of their hearts, the children led their special friend across the broken glass for lunch at Gezz's place, the warmth of the midday sun caressing their young faces.